Sangama

A Story of the Amazon Jungle

Other books by

Arturo D. Hernández

Selva Trágica: Captive in the Jungle

Bubinzana: The Magic Song of the Amazon

Tangarana and Other Tales

Sangama

A Story of the Amazon Jungle

Arturo D. Hernández

Translated by Raymond A. Enstam

Quaestor Press, Ltd

Sangama: A Story of the Amazon Jungle

Published by

Quaestor Press, Ltd
Dallas, Texas

Originally published in Spanish in Peru in 1942.

ISBN 9780978691400
Library of Congress Control Number: 2014947892

jacket concept: Liz Conrad Graphic Design

cover photograph by Pablo Hidalgo/Shutterstock.com

PUBLISHER'S NOTE

This is a work of fiction. Names, characters, places, and incidents either are the product of the author's imagination or are used fictitiously, and any resemblance to actual persons, living or dead, business establishments, events, or locales is entirely coincidental.

ACKNOWLEDGEMENT

I want to thank my wife, Elizabeth York Enstam, for her enthusiasm and encouragement, and my daughter, Gwendolyn Enstam, for her help and good advice with this project.

I also want to especially acknowledge and thank Ricardo Arturo Hernández San Martín, son of Arturo D. Hernández, for his extraordinary help and patience, and for his enduring faith in this project over many years.

Foreword

Arturo D. Hernández was a voice of the Amazon jungle. A writer from within the region, he spoke as a native son, not an outside observer like a naturalist, anthropologist, adventurer or missionary. Born in Peru on December 22, 1903, he grew up on the edges of the Alto (Upper) Ucayali River, a tributary of the Amazon. He died in 1970. During Hernández' childhood, his father worked as a rubber harvester, or *cauchero*, during the era of the great rubber boom in the Amazon. Hernández learned the trade of *cauchero* by working with his father to cut a *trocha* (a jungle path) through the wilderness in search of the trees that produced the "black gold" of the Amazon. At some time during his youth one of the many violent shifts in the course of Alto Ucayali swept away his native village, and he came to think of himself as a man without a birthplace. The early death of his father left him to his own resources.

He joined the Peruvian army, only to find himself a member of a unit that participated in an uprising in 1922 that advocated secession of the Amazon region from Peru. When the uprising failed Hernández and the other prisoners were taken to Lima. After his release, he eked out a living from a series of jobs, including time as a laborer on the roads, a construction worker, and a boat crewman. Ambitious for a better life, Hernández enrolled in San Marcos University and paid his own way with his scarce earnings. When that school closed, he transferred to the Catholic University of Lima where he graduated with a degree in law and became an attorney. He later took up a career as a magistrate of military justice, and eventually rose to the rank of General.

Hernández loved the jungle - harsh and dangerous as it was – and considered it to be his native land. He wanted to interpret the jungle region of the Ucayali to the outside world. To this end he wrote a series of short tales of the jungle, which he later tied together and which became the heart of this novel, *Sangama*. In the Prologue to his second novel, *Selva Trájica*, Hernández is quoted as saying: "*Sangama* was born by chance....and in reality what I wanted to create were small tales of the jungle, but then I realized that all was written except the beginning and, upon tying it all together, *Sangama* was the result."

For ten years Hernández held onto his unpublished manuscript, finally publishing it in 1942 in Peru. Ten years later, in 1952, *Sangama* was published in French in Paris under the title *Sangama: Roman de la Forêt Amazonienne*, and published in German in Zurich in 1955 under the title *Sangama: Der Erbe Der Inkas*. The novel became a best seller in Europe, which established the author's reputation at home in Peru. Peruvians still know Hernández's work, which is often read by students as an introduction to their nation's past and culture.

In writing about the Amazon region that he knew so well from personal experience, a world now lost forever, Hernández serves as an intermediary, a man educated in western culture who can interpret for us the lives and world of the local people. As Hernández tells it, their reality is sometimes like paradise, sometimes harsh to the point of demonic. *Sangama* blends reality, fable, and myth in a world where strange events may be perceived as supernatural or as natural phenomena poorly understood.

Sangama is set the vast Amazon region of the era before airplanes, telephones or radio. The only access was by boat or on foot through almost impassible jungle and mountains. The novel takes us into the isolated and remote Amazon jungle as it existed in the nineteenth and early twentieth century and as it had existed from time immemorial. It is a tale of a world dating back to the beginning of the earth, with life itself still evolving in its most primitive form. This might have been Eden as it actually existed, and the human beings as they first inhabited it.

The tale of *Sangama* has relevancy for today, too. Hernández understood the jungle as at times a dangerous enemy and at other times a paradise, but always more powerful than the humans who had to adapt to its laws. Today, the tables have turned. The jungle is in retreat before the relentless advance of civilization, a threat just beginning at the time of this novel. The stories of the indigenous peoples relentlessly pushed back or forced to adapt to modern and often destructive ways are precursors of the trend that continues today. As we struggle to preserve the rainforest, Hernández shows us the marvelous world we have almost lost.

The plot of *Sangama* is intertwined with the industry of harvesting natural rubber, a product with a long history in the Americas. The Mayas and other ancient peoples appreciated its elastic qualities and used it to make balls for their games. Rubber was merely a curiosity to the Spaniards upon their arrival in South and Central America, but its real commercial use was not developed until the 1820s. Around that time the Scottish industrialist Charles Macintosh developed a technique for using rubber to waterproof cloth, an invention that has lent his name to the eponymous raincoat. More important for rubber's future – and that of the Amazon people – was a discovery by the American Charles Goodyear. In the 1840s Charles Goodyear discovered the method of vulcanizing, a process that kept the rubber from becoming soft in the heat and brittle in the cold. Only then did rubber become important in evolving nineteenth century industries and fuel a major economic boom in the Amazon basin spanning Peru and Brazil. This was the native growing area of the *Hevea Brasiliensis,* the source tree of natural rubber. Great wealth and prosperity flowed into such cities as Iquitos, Peru, and Manaus, Brazil, where the newly rich built great houses and lived in an opulent style. Sudden and largely uncontrolled, the rubber boom also led to many abuses against the indigenous population. Hernández tells us some of this story in *Sangama*.

The Amazonian rubber industry was very labor intensive. The raw rubber had to be harvested from wild *Hevea* trees that did not grow in groves but were scattered in the jungle and distant from each other. Plantations were not feasible. A blight could spread easily among the monoculture of concentrated trees while their dispersal among different species in the jungle protected them from the disease. The decline of the Amazonian industry began with the planting of rubber trees in the East Indies, where great plantations were not only feasible but also much more efficient. With this competition the Amazonian rubber industry declined and, with the introduction of synthetic rubber during the Second World War, it effectively ended.

Hernández often uses many local words belonging to the jungle and its dwellers, and in many cases he defines them in his footnotes. To preserve the authentic sense of his work, I have kept these words and the author's notes. All of the footnotes are part of the original text and are the work of the author. Above all, I have tried to preserve the spirit in which Hernández wrote.

Raymond A. Enstam
Dallas, Texas
October 1, 2014

Chapter 1

I was full of hope as the riverboat carried me up the Bajo Ucayali, the river that bathes a great part of the Peruvian jungle. On the banks of the swollen river there stood lush and compact vegetation, high and uniform, that accentuated the monotony of the countryside, composed of the ocher of the water, the green of the jungle, and the indigo of an immaculate tropical sky.

We traveled on the first-class deck, where we were enjoying the refreshing gusts of the breeze. One of the passengers, who was leaning on the rail and attentively watching the changing riverbank, shouted with surprise:

"I can't be mistaken! When I passed in this very spot four years ago, there was a small prosperous village. Nearby, cattle grazed under the shade of some breadfruit trees."

"Sir," replied another passenger, "the place that the village occupied is now located at least three kilometers inland. The river deposited an immense shoreline in front of it that has been covered by lush vegetation . . . until it became what you see: jungle, nothing more than jungle."

The passenger who had replied was slender, with a pale face. Noting our interest in what he had just said, he continued:

"The river that crosses this region of floodplains changes course incessantly. Each turn is formed by a curve that retreats as it is worn away through erosion, and a point that advances as sediment is deposited from the erosion that the river causes upstream. When a curve becomes very tight, the river charges against the bank with the enormous power of its current, undermines the land, and swallows entire forests, developing a new course. At first the land enclosed by both arms constitutes an island; but the enormous quantity of sand

and organic materials carried by the current rapidly close the entrance to the abandoned river course, forming a new riverbank on which grows lush brush that is quickly converted into majestic jungle. Behind this, the old river course becomes a lake. It is because of this feature that the Bajo Ucayali region has been designated by some geographers as 'Region of the Lakes.'"

The first speaker quickly asked:

"Am I mistaken? I believe that I remember seeing years ago in this very spot something that I don't see: a line of small houses with a small church in the middle."

The small man with the pale face intervened again:

"You are referring to San Nicolás, where the missionary attempted to form a community. One night, after the villagers had quietly gone to bed, they woke up swimming. The river had taken a whim to pass by there . . . and it did! Let me explain." Then, resting against the railing, he continued:

"The peculiarity of this jungle zone has resulted in a paradoxical reality: the nomad village. As one of the banks of the river advances and the other recedes, the settlements are unstable. Someone who sees his house threatened by the proximity of the riverbank quickly takes it apart and reassembles it farther inland, and one by one by his neighbors follow him, and year after year they continue moving behind him. And if the waters take a new course, the river dwellers emigrate en masse, searching on the new edges of the river for the most appropriate place to situate themselves. The river is, therefore, everything in this region. It is the pantry that supplies abundant fish; it is the only route of travel; it is the element of defense against the hostility of the jungle; it is, in the end, the decisive factor in the establishment of the civilized man."

"What is that object near the riverbank where the river is 'eating'?" asked a young woman, squinting her eyelids with symptoms of myopia.

"Can't you see that it's a Saint Anthony?" several answered her in a chorus, smiling. "They have put it there to perform the miracle of stopping the river. It won't take long to wash away the saint and his faithful."

The traveler who started the conversation approached cautiously and said to me:

"Actually, I don't even know where I was born."

"What!" I replied, startled. "How can that be possible?"

"It's that I have my doubts. Let me explain. I was born twenty-five years ago, on the eastern edge of this river. Since then the waters have not stopped 'eating' on the opposite side, so that the place that I refer to has been moved kilometers and kilometers back from the river."

As the darkness fell that night, I found myself leaning on the rail at the bow of the boat, looking at the first houses of a small village that were lined up along the shore as if pushed there by the jungle. The pale man who had shown himself knowledgeable of the region by his prior explanations moved to my side, with an obvious desire to continue educating me:

"We find ourselves really in one of the strangest and rarest geographic zones of the world. It has been settled in great part by the courage of the inhabitants of the department of San Martín, seat of the most ancient settlements in eastern Peru. Intrepid explorers crossing the jungle in search of rubber tree groves came upon this imposing river that the old ones called Ucayali. Its source was lost in unknown forests, and its current, pouring into the Amazon, disappeared into the heart of Brazil. Although I don't yet consider myself an old man, I was one of those explorers who came down from the mountains and established themselves on this great course of water that appeared then to have neither beginning nor end. When someone asked their destination upon seeing rafts and canoes following the current, he received the reply 'Going down!' This 'down' could refer to the recently founded port of Iquitos or the end of the world. If one asked the same question of those staying close to the shore and going against the current—that is to say, were 'plowing,' in the sense that the word is used in the jungle—the response was 'Going up!' This 'up' could be any one of the small stopping places dispersed at various distances from each other, or could also refer to the inaccessible jungles that extended beyond, in the birthplace of the Ucayali or its tributaries. But there were very few who made such inquiries, if it were not for wanting to hear the voices of strangers in these solitary places. All knew that those who went with the current were 'going down', and those who went against the current 'plowed.' The Bajo Ucayali has a wild idiosyncrasy. It is a capricious monster that, according to the seasons, is a river at some times and at other times a sea. In winter it overflows and covers a great expanse of this zone; in summer it runs peacefully between white beaches. One would say that it sleeps sensually in its murmuring bed of sand, below the tropical sun."

My informant fell silent. The lights of the last houses of the small village were falling behind the luminous wake of the boat. I had immersed myself in the serious thoughts related to my journey, when suddenly I heard again that same voice speaking to me:

"The rogue who lives there, in the great house of zinc that can hardly be seen between the shadows, there in the distance, is one of the richest *shiringueros* in the entire area. He lives by exploiting the people, thanks to his position of authority. All the large *shiringales* of the surrounding area belong to him."

"And would there be empty land to work in this area?" I asked him.

"The jungle on the edges of this river and its tributaries has been explored, and there the intensive extraction of fine rubber is carried out. Everything is the property of the Governor . . ."

"Who is the Governor?" I interrupted him.

"The rogue of whom I spoke a moment ago. He lives in Santa Inés, the village we left behind . . . But, as I was going to tell you, the interior of these shores is unknown and evidently constitutes land that offers magnificent opportunities to the audacious man. To make *shiringales* is very simple. You don't know about this? Good. One goes to explore a piece of jungle in which one finds *shiringa* trees. From a set tree, he opens a path that connects with another and then another. He continues this way until he encloses more or less a hundred trees. We have an *estrada*. A group of *estradas* forms a *shiringal*. And the fortune is made. A *shiringal* gives a river of rubber that is, as we say, a flood of gold. And this lower part of the jungle is precisely where they produce the finest rubber in the

World. The tree from which it is extracted, like the most beautiful flowers of the jungle, grows in the swamps. I would have liked to work here . . . ; but nobody wants to deal with the Governor."

The explanation was sufficient. A merchant house in Iquitos had promised to open a line of credit for me if the region I was going to explore offered satisfactory conditions. Consequently, I resolved to get off at the first point at which we would dock and go from there to Santa Inés, where I hoped to find facilities for my undertaking. I was willing, if it proved necessary, to interest the Governor himself and, to inspire confidence, why not start as an employee?

Don Manuel Salazar, owner of the little inn where I disembarked the next day, received me with the open hospitality of the mountain people. I asked him to sell me a canoe to go downriver.

"Surely you are going to Santa Inés," he said, looking at me a little concerned.

"Yes, sir," I affirmed. "Will I find people there disposed to explore the jungle with me?"

"There everyone obeys the Governor. This area is occupied completely by his *shiringales*. One cannot pass near them without suffering some unpleasantness. What you are attempting seems to me very difficult."

"Would the Governor, at least, give me employment?"

"That, yes," he answered instantly, "but it would be better for you not to work for him. His employees never receive a good accounting. As soon as any of them has anything due to him for long months of work, the Governor invites him to gamble. You should understand that it is not possible to snub the Governor . . . particularly when the invitation is accompanied by special attentions . . . In one night the poor man loses the earnings of a year. There was one who refused to play, and . . . well, they will tell you there!"

Having acquired a canoe, I started downriver early the next morning before the burning sun of midday. I was about to be, without thinking about it, or even imagining it, the protagonist of one of the most intense dramas of the jungle.

Chapter 2

Brann! . . . A snake fell from the roof, landing at my feet and rapidly rising up in a menacing stance. I saw its flashing little evil eyes and its thin tongue moving in all directions. It could have been hunting rats in the roof of the little abandoned house on whose *emponado*[1] I was relaxing carelessly, trying to rest my sore limbs and shelter myself from the burning rays of the sun.

A shudder of terror ran through my body. I expected a deadly sting at any moment if the serpent noticed the slightest movement on my part. Instinct made me stay absolutely still. That little diamond-shaped head, rising up with insolent fierceness, fixed its eyes—like two drops of blood—on me with marked distrust; but at the end of a moment that to me seemed interminable, it rested on the ground and remained apparently still. I felt a great relief, since I thought that it would be leaving, but my anguish became deathly when I perceived its cold contact on one of my ankles. The worst was that, confusing the lower opening of my pant leg for a hole in which it could shelter itself, it began to slither up my leg. It quickly reached my thigh and continued advancing . . . ; it forced its way to my waist and then, uncomfortable because of the pressure of the fabric, retreated to an area that it found suitable, where it turned around, now calmly, now with frenzy, trying to make some space for itself.

Possibly a very few times some man has seen himself in such a desperate situation. That day, surely, I aged ten years. I do not know

---

[1] *Emponado:* a platform constructed with stalks split from a type of palm tree called *pona*.

how long this terrible anguish lasted, facing the certainty that nothing and nobody could help me.

From time to time, I heard a distant sound of oars passing in the river, but who would stop to visit that abandoned shack?

And the viper that had entered my pant leg, confusing it with a hollow log, was not settling down! If I were to make the slightest move, it would stab me with its fangs, injecting me with its venom. Its restlessness told me very clearly that the discomfort was irritating it more and more. My entire body trembled inside from the sensations of the vibrating movements of the reptile.

"Young man, your canoe was badly tied and was floating downstream with the current."

That call, which by some strange design of fate came to my aid so opportunely, was shouted from the bank of the river. As I did not answer, he approached, raising his voice:

"Young man!. . . . Have you fallen asleep?"

I heard the sound of his steps as he entered the shack. Before me appeared a man who stopped and looked at me, astonished. My eyes must have impressed him with the indescribable expression of terror and hope that they reflected. Fortunately, the movement in my pant leg revealed to him my tragedy.

"Be still!" he told me with an imperious tone.

Immediately he lit an enormous cigar and began to surround me in dense puffs of smoke. The viper relaxed and, little by little, stretched out until it remained almost lifeless.

And the man continued the fumigation with more force, speaking in the intervals in which his mouth remained empty of the smoke he was expelling:

"It will not take long to die. This is the rarest and most inexplicable thing that can happen in the jungle. Without a doubt, it is a question of a serpent gone crazy. No, it must be very old and blind because of age. To confuse the pants of a man with a hollow log . . . ! Inexplicable! One more moment and you will be free. The tail is still palpitating."

All at once, he gave a strong pull. The viper, suddenly pulled out, was twisting around at a distance, with its whitish mouth stabbing at the emptiness.

It was just in time! When I rose up, soaked with cold sweat, my head hurt terribly, and everything, dancing frenetically before me, had a pronounced reddish shade. There was the snake, twisting on the *emponado*. Using a stick, the man killed it with a precise blow to the head, while he said sorrowfully:

"It would have been easier to conquer it with music, since there is nothing that these pests like better. Nothing would have been simpler than get it out of there by calling it with the notes of a *quena*."

"You arrived just in time to save my life," I told him gratefully.

"The viper has the grayish color of age, and you can be quite sure that it was nearsighted," he continued calmly, as if he had not heard my words. "Miraculously, it has lived this long without being caught by a sparrow hawk. It's a jergón. Truly you have just been reborn."

"My name is Barcas . . . Abel Barcas," I interrupted him again. At that moment he realized that I was talking to him.

"With great pleasure, young man," he answered me. "My name is . . . The people around here call me Sangama. But, and keep this in mind, in the jungle a name is worth nothing."

Tall and muscular, the man revealed Herculean virility. His sharp-featured face, with large dark eyes, and his speech, succinct and persuasive, gave him the appearance of a prophet or sage.

Chapter 3

When someone became sick in Santa Inés, Dahua, the *curandero,* would shout, pointing in the direction of the house in the jungle where Sangama lived:

"There's the cause . . . The witch!"

And, saying this, he set himself to healing the patient. If he succeeded in curing him, he exclaimed, bragging and in a loud voice so that all could hear:

"I won! I won! If it were not for me, the witch would soon finish off all of you."

When the illness went from bad to worse, the family of the victim, tired of the *curandero*'s exorcisms and spells, resorted to the poultices, elixirs, washings, and fumigations of the so-called witch, which had the virtue of actually curing.

Then Dahua would say, winking significantly with one eye:

"Of course he was able to cure him! He himself placed the illness on him!"

Moreover, if the patient died in spite of the intervention of Sangama, the *curandero* went on with his curses:

"He was not willing to cure him, and he let him die! He himself made the man sick with the worst of curses! I saw in the night how the *virotes*[2] came from the house of the witch to lodge in the body of the dying person . . . I saw it! And the evil one acted as if he was curing him!"

---

[2] *Virotes:* small darts from a dart gun, which are supposed to be invisible in the case of curses.

At every opportunity when a group of the people had congregated, the enigmatic figure of the *curandero* appeared to come forth with his censuring:

"If we did not have the witch nearby . . . I always said it: we have to get rid of him. And the best thing in this case is to give him a potion of diluted excrement to drink until he bursts. Only in that way will the illnesses cease!"

One day he succeeded in arousing the people. Someone had just died suddenly, and the *curandero* took advantage of the opportunity to exacerbate the feelings.

"We have to get rid of him!" he shouted. "It's not possible for us to endure any longer the cause of all these afflictions! We should go right now and bring him back here tied up and make him drink the potion!"

Many approved the attack on Sangama's house, which was located on the edge of an inland lake, and the *curandero* offered to lead the people who, stirred up by his lies, had taken up all sorts of arms.

When they had come together and were ready for the march, the old Panduro appeared, holding himself up on thick canes, and said:

"I don't know how Sangama could be a witch. He heals everyone without asking that anyone pay him. He does all the good that he can without anyone giving him anything in return, and he is always satisfied with this. He is not like Dahua, who charges for his cures. I am an old man and I have lived here since before there were witches and *curanderos,* and the people died all the same."

"The witch has bought him," assured the *curandero*.

But the words poured forth by the old man had succeeded in placating, for the moment, their spirits.

Dahua, upon noting that his words were not producing the desired effect, resorted to a measure of proven efficacy: he began to distribute brandy.

By nightfall the drunkenness had become generalized, and the house in which these events were taking place became a beehive. Everyone was gesticulating and shouting, and speaking at the same time. Nobody was understood. The old Panduro, with his crude canes, was relegated to a corner, murmuring between his teeth:

"They're crazy . . . ! And all because of that rogue Dahua! Asking for the head of a man who has done us so much good? Horrors!"

But when Shupinghua also began to demand the head of Sangama, he couldn't control himself any longer, and he confronted him, saying:

"Old ingrate! It's thanks to the poultices that he put on you that you are still walking, and now you want them to kill him!"

"He himself made me sick! Dahua has said it! You, what are you talking about? You've sold out . . . ! You call me old, as if you weren't. You are the oldest of all . . . and also the dirtiest!"

A noisy chorus of coarse laughs and mocking followed the last words of Shupinghua. The old Panduro reacted:

"Yes, I am old! For this, all of you respect me when you are not drunk, and you give me consideration because I am honorable. You are as old as I am, but ungrateful. Remember that Sangama cured you and also your son. You're an old ingrate!"

The crippled old Panduro was found dead the next morning, flung below the floor of *ponas,* with his two canes on top of him. Those canes served first to beat him and afterward to make a cross for him.

The rioting mob was already determined to wade across the river, with the goal of attacking Sangama, when it appeared prudent to the Governor to intervene. He ordered that they bring the agitator before him. Panting furiously, he reprimanded him:

"You will stop this breach of the public order against me, eh? I won't stand for idiocies from you."

"Sir," Dahua hurried to respond, "it's because he bewitches the people . . ."

"Shut up!" interrupted the Governor. "That one doesn't bewitch anyone. The only idiot here is you!"

"He has dealings with serpents; he speaks with *bufeos*[3] and with

---

[3] *Bufeo:* a fish that, according to superstition among the natives, has extraordinary supernatural powers.

the *yacurunas;*[4] he does not drown underwater, and at night he watches over . . ."

"Enough lies!" roared the Governor, beside himself.

"He also makes gold . . ."

"Eh?"

"I have seen it myself, with these eyes, the *patacones*[5] with which he buys merchandise . . . They're pure gold! Shitu says he takes them from a large chest."

"Shut up . . .!"

The Governor remained thoughtful for a long time; then he asked suggestively:

"You say you have seen the *patacones*?"

"With these eyes!"

"And that he takes them from a large chest?"

"This is what Shitu saw. And it must be so, because he buys everything with gold and he never runs out."

"Hurnn!" And the little eyes of the Governor grew smaller, flashing with greed.

The uproar of the people had calmed down. The *curandero* looked attentively at the Governor, who paced around his Office with long strides. He was not alone: a huge figure observed from the darkest corner of the adjoining room and, through a small hidden door, a deformed and repugnant creature watched.

---

4 *Yacurunas:* demons that inhabit water.

5 *Patacones:* ancient coins.

Chapter 4

Portunduaga started out his career as Governor. Nobody remembered exactly when he arrived. The truth is—and he himself talked about it between laughs and bragging words when he was loaded with brandy—that one day he disembarked in the settlement, chose the best house, and entered it without giving even a good-morning greeting. Once comfortably seated inside, he said to the owner, who looked at him perplexed:

"Hello, Juan . . . !"

"Manuel, Sir. Manuel Barboza."

"Good, Manuel. I am the Governor. The authorities in Iquitos sent me to take care of this village for them. Hurnn! And accentuating his words with a fierce puffing, he showed him a paper full of seals and scribbling.

As the timid man tried to get close to see the contents of the document, Portunduaga puffed even more fiercely and, hitting the table with his fist, grabbed the paper and put it away.

"Well! Well . . . ! Hurnn . . . ! I now name you Lieutenant of the Police . . . Ink, pen, and paper, to make the appointment official!"

The good Barboza, respectful of the authority who honored his house, hurried to bring what was asked of him, but first he ordered his wife to kill the best chicken in the yard.

With a firm hand and large letters, the Governor formalized the so-called appointment, to which he affixed his signature with a huge flourish. And then he ceremoniously prepared to give the oath of office to the favored one.

"Do you swear before God . . . Stand up, Lieutenant—you are in the presence of the authority! Hurnn . . . ! Raise your right hand with the palm forward . . . ! But I just remembered that these acts should be carried out with your hand being placed on the Constitution and in the presence of witnesses. Go and bring me the leaders of the community! Hurnn . . . !"

And that night, in the presence of several neighbors, the honorable Governor administered the oath to the improvised Lieutenant, having him put his hand upon a book to which the Governor gave the pompous title of Constitution.

"Do you swear . . . I say, do you swear before God to blindly obey the Governor? Hurnn! Say: 'Yes, I swear!'"

"Yes, I swear, honorable Governor."

"If you don't do it, I will punish you."

Someone protested:

"But we don't need any governors here."

"Silence!" ordered the new police lieutenant.

Then the Governor named all of those present as policemen and ordered that all of those in the village and its surrounding areas were in "a state of service" and should appear to ask for their respective appointments. The next day he ordered a Government House to be built on the best site in the village. It was built, without any pay whatsoever, by all those who found themselves in "a state of service." Then he had some stocks constructed. Thus installed in his own house, he began his "government."

The truth is that with that daring nose, of extraordinarily resonant sound and so disproportionate and ruddy, Portunduaga could have equally made his way into any part of the world. Curved, wide at the base and in the nostrils, it was something like a powerful bow of a ship, capable of opening to its possessor, without being stopped, all the routes of the Earth. Behind it marched the chubby face of the Governor, animated by eyes full of astuteness, against which the modest and simple dwellers of Santa Inés were not able to present any obstacle whatsoever.

After the foregoing events, everyone became accustomed to seeing the honorable Governor as he spent the nights, giving resonant puffs and pants, in his zealous efforts, as someone said, to watch over the public order.

The authority of Portunduaga, however, did not at first have the omnipotence that he desired. To consolidate it, he proposed to take advantage of the first favorable opportunity that presented itself. The people there were accustomed to living without anyone governing them, and Portunduaga gave many puffs and pants without obtaining any effective benefit.

He did not have to wait long for the opportunity.

In a country house, one turn of the river distant, lived the terror of the region: a so-called Don Misael, who was nicknamed the Bull.

His house stood in the center of a clearing, where he passed his life wasting on liquor a fortune that, according to him, he had acquired in the rubber business, although there was no lack of those who would say that he had stolen it in the Alto Ucayali from several *caucheros* who had left the growing areas after a good harvest of rubber. From those reports, everyone was aware that one night the Bull had killed the *caucheros* and, after throwing their bodies in the river, seized their loaded rafts.

When repeated shots were heard coming from the outpost of Don Misael—and this occurred for at least eight months each year—they said that the latter was *"en bomba."* And no one dared pass by there, because it was known that he shot without hesitation and was a good marksman. People said that he refined his marksmanship by shooting down Indians in the river. This thing of shooting down Indians deserves an explanation.

In the quiet months, the natives climb the branches of the trees that project out over the water in which the *cupisos* and *taricayas,* those huge river turtles, amuse themselves by floating with their heads above the surface of the water. From their positions in the trees, in which they stay for hours, they can easily hunt the turtles with arrows. Don Misael was in the custom of going a good distance upriver and then turning around and coasting down in the center of the current. Upon spotting one of these Indians, he would grab his rifle and shoot. The Indians fell in the river like wounded birds. And Don Misael never missed a shot!

But what most irritated the simple settlers of Santa Inés and its surroundings was that Don Misael broke into their feasts drunk and terrorized all the people with gunshots. He would start to dance and shamelessly chase the girls that caught his fancy. One day several of the residents confronted him with the intention of putting an end to his outrages, but when Don Misael bent the barrel of a shotgun on the back of the first attacker, the rest lost heart completely.

Whenever there was a party, it was certain that Don Misael would attend drunk, eat more than anyone, drink like a sponge, dance like a spinning top, and chase the girls at will. When he had enough, he left, firing shots left and right. The truth is that Don Misael was equal in weight to four men, and his strength was such that he could knock down a bull with one punch, as people commonly said, to which ability he owed his nickname.

With the appearance of the Governor, the honest inhabitants of the small village had a brilliant idea: confront the brand-new authority with the bandit.

"He has to be good for something for us!" said some.

"Let the Governor take him prisoner and put him in the jail!" affirmed others.

Portunduaga immediately approved the request of his "governed." He armed various men and headed in a canoe to the Bull's outpost. Arriving at the riverbank, Don Portu—a contraction for "Portunduaga" that he was called behind his back—faced his men and said:

"Good . . . ! Hurnn . . . ! Now climb up. Just take him and bring him to me tied up."

The men looked at each other stupefied, but the Governor roused them from their astonishment by repeating the order:

"Governors are for giving orders. Go on and bring me that individual tied up!"

"But sir," one of them dared to object, "as soon as we stick our heads up from the riverbank, he is going to sweep us with shots."

"That means . . . Hurnn . . . ! that things can't be done when one wants . . . Hurnn . . . ! but when one can . . ."

"It's possible to circle the house and attack from behind," observed another who still retained a bit of enthusiasm. The others indicated approval.

"Forward!" ordered the Governor.

They loosed the boat and moved a little bit upstream, in order to climb the bank under shelter of the forest. They made a circle and stuck their heads through the trees in the backyard of Don Misael's house. Several fierce dogs rushed out to meet them, and a rain of bullets ended up dispersing them. The Governor, who had prudently stayed behind, embarked with complete tranquility and waited in the canoe for the return of the men, who were reappearing one by one. When all were there, he said to them:

"That's what I told you . . . ! Hrunn . . . ! Things are done in their due time. You have to seize the occasion by the hair! And the occasion only has one hair, understand . . . ? Hrunn . . . ! Hrunn . . . !" And the Governor swaggered, taking on airs of great importance.

One indiscreet person reported that very night in the village that the Governor himself had sent a warning to Don Misael to watch out.

"That can't be tolerated!" several shouted, indignant. "The Governor has betrayed us. Perhaps the Bull has already bought him. Let's go to his place!"

The Governor listened to them in silence; but when they finished, he put on the face of a wild animal and, coughing and panting almost to the point of bursting his nose, he told them:

"Hrunn . . . ! Hrunn . . . ! You don't know what you are talking about! The occasion only has one hair . . . Eh . . . ? And I am going to pull it. I alone, understand? Without need of anyone! Hrunn . . . ! And after I have locked up that criminal, I will finish off the gossips and those who speak without respect for the authority . . . Hrunn . . . !"

Intimidated, the protestors withdrew, giving signs of great respect and obedience to the honorable Governor.

And in due time, he kept his word.

It was one night during the Christmas season. Don Portu, guest of honor at the feast, did not dance. Seated in one corner, next to a rustic little altar on which the Baby Jesus lay, he was in the best humor in the world, playing cards for small change with a happy group of boys. This was the first time he had done this. Certainly that night, in a rare democratic openness, he appeared to have cast off the preeminence that he insisted upon with so much zeal. All were amazed by such a rare miracle. However, a close observer would have noticed Portunduaga was hiding some concern, since from time to time he would glance at the door and a sinister lightning flash shown in his eyes. The Governor was waiting . . .

Suddenly the Bull arrived, preceded by the characteristic detonations. A wave of unease and deep dislike swept through the room.

"Don Portu . . . The Bull is coming!"

"Just let him come. Keep playing, lads! Does anyone lack money? There's some . . . Hrunn . . . !" And he distributed a handful of small coins. The smaller boys were betting enthusiastically.

"Where is the owner?" shouted the giant who filled the door frame. "I am here dying of hunger and thirst. Pin . . . ! Pun . . . ! Pan . . . ! Where is the owner?"

And Don Misael, who was the intruder, firing his revolvers and knocking over furniture, advanced with the stride of a bully and a defiant look.

"Keep playing, boys, I'm winning . . . ! Bet . . . ! Hrunn . . . !" And the Governor's panting hardly sounded this time.

The criminal, already close to the players, stopped short. There was the Governor, not even looking at him. He stood motionless. Finally he reacted, approaching resolutely. When he was next to the table, the Governor, without raising a glance, said to him:

"If you want to play, just sit down."

"Bah! Centavos!" objected Don Misael contemptuously. "I play for pounds . . . pounds sterling!"

"I also play for them, but . . . bad luck has always followed me. Now it is just a matter of some fun on Christmas Eve . . . Hrunn . . . ! Just sit down!"

"I haven't brought any money," warned the bandit, half undecided.

"I will lend you some," answered the Governor in a friendly tone. "Here, I have some pounds. We will divide them . . . Hrunn . . . ! There are more in the house. . . Fifty . . . ! A hundred . . . ! Whatever you like." And, saying that, he pulled from his pocket a fistful of gold coins that he threw on the table.

The rubber harvest in the Montaña region brought, among other things, as an immediate consequence of the boom, the passion for gambling. There were many rubber workers who dedicated themselves to working eleven months of the year only to have something to lose in the one month of rest. And they wagered in the jungle, as in other parts of the world, entire fortunes in a single night. Those who lived in that period—many of whom are not yet old men—recount how in one stop a merchant lost his riverboat, loaded with merchandise. The criminal that Portunduaga had facing him was an amateur gambler, like all those of the Montaña, ignorant of the tricks and strategies of the game. He was a player who was in reality both boorish and presumptuous, which the Governor did not take long to discover.

"Gold is not wagered with cards . . . but with dice!" pronounced Don Misael.

"Like these?" replied Don Portu, pulling out a pair of dice.

The Bull could not hide his astonishment. Truly this Governor was a clever and cautious man. The Bull sat down, taking the coins that his opponent had left him. The chair and table creaked under the enormous weight of his body and the pressure of his huge hands, which would have been able to split the head of an elephant with one punch. The Bull won continuously until he left his opponent cleaned out.

The dancing had ceased. Everyone gathered around the table, over which the two players remained face-to-face. Don Misael laughed raucously each time he won. He had returned the loan to the Governor, and they continued playing.

"Ha . . . ha . . . ha . . . haa . . . ! This Governor is a marvel for me! *Cuadras!* What bad luck!"

"It's my specialty. I don't have any luck in gambling," murmured Portunduaga remorsefully. "Not even with women."

"I have luck in everything . . . especially with the women! Right, Pituco? Eh, you! Right?"

"Yes, Mister Don Misael . . . Yes, it's the truth," affirmed the target of the question, trembling.

"One time in Manaus . . . , I went into a café with music. There were beautiful women and good liquor . . . By the way, bring a bottle of brandy; I'm thirsty."

"Bring two!" ordered the Governor.

They brought two bottles and glasses. The Bull poured himself a little and began to drink.

"That's nothing!" interrupted Portunduaga. "This is how they drink who can really drink, like me!" And he drank, without blinking, all the contents of the glass he had previously filled up.

"You're challenging me with that, no? Now you will see!" replied the Bull, upset. And after filling and emptying his glass two times in a row, he set it face down on the table. "How about that? Ha . . . ha . . . ha . . . haa . . . ! You don't know whom you're dealing with, little Governor. Come at me with challenges! I could drink a whole jug nonstop. Ha . . . ha . . . ha . . . haa . . . ! Bring me more bottles!"

And the criminal laughed, opening his huge jaws and pounding the table with his fists as if about to destroy it. Then he started to talk, praising his good luck.

"I was the admiration and pride of the women there in Manaus. My ability in drinking dazzled the men. The women adored me . . . ! I gambled and won fortunes for them. By the way, shall we continue playing? Why not wager one hundred pounds at a time, little Governor! Eh?"

"Accepted!" responded the Governor, with eyes half-closed, "but first we have to get warmed up . . . If you have taken two, I will take three in a row!" Parsimoniously, he filled the glass three times, and as many times he drank it, without leaving a drop in the bottom. The Bull gave him a contemptuous and boastful look.

"With three in a row, no? Well, I will take four . . . five . . . six . . . ten!" And he went on drinking glass after glass until he was gorged and out of breath.

"For two hundred pounds . . . ! Hrunn . . . !" proposed Portunduaga with the voice of a drunk.

"Three hundred!" replied Don Misael.

"Four hundred!"

"Five hundred!"

"Six hundred!"

"One thousand!"

"Good, for the thousand . . . !"

All those present held their breath.

"Poor Governor!" commented someone compassionately.

"The Devil helps the Bull!" replied another, with his eyes bulging wide open. The dice flew.

"The Bull lost!" arose the general exclamation.

"Yes, I lost. What is happening . . . ? My revenge!"

"It turns out that you have no more money, Bull," replied the Governor.

"What don't I have? In my trunk there are two thousand pounds in hard cash."

"So be it . . . ! I believe you, Misael . . . ! There is no need to get upset." And the Governor half-closed his little eyes, to all appearances completely drunk.

The dice rolled again before the mute expectation of all. Quickly, the eyes of the Bull opened wide.

"The Bull lost again!"

"This time I wager my house and everything in it, my farm . . . except . . ."

"Except what?" inquired the Governor, coming to life with visible greed.

"Except my women . . . ! My women!"

"How many women do you have?"

"Four."

"*Caray!* With good reason you say you are lucky in love . . . ! Good! So be it! The house with all that it has, the farm . . . except the women, against the two thousand pounds that you owe me."

"You kidnapped them," someone shouted, dodging away.

"Shhh . . . ! Silence!"

The dice rolled again. The anxiety that gripped the bystanders was intense.

And again the Governor won.

"Curses!" screamed the Bull, pale and sweating gushers. He

drank another glass. Then he proposed: "The four women go."

"I don't want your women," said Portunduaga, hunched over, between grumbles and hiccups.

"What, you don't want them?"

"No! I don't want your women!"

"Swindler! Thief! Well, collect what you won if you're man enough!"

The Bull tried to get up with the clear intention of strangling the Governor, who, next to him, seemed a chubby dwarf. The Bull's legs did not obey him, and he stayed there with his fists clenched, trembling as he leaned against the table.

"Calm down, Bull!" roared the Governor, sitting up with a revolver in his hand. "Hrunn . . . ! You're a prisoner!"

The bystanders fell back, stunned. Portunduaga was on his feet—swaying, yes, but very far from losing his balance. His arm with the weapon scarcely moved, and his nose resonated as if explosives were bursting inside it. The Bull was paralyzed, with his mouth open, like an idiot . . . Once more the dwarf had defeated the giant; astuteness had defeated strength!

Don Misael woke up in the stocks, bound by his hands, feet, and head and being bled by the mosquitoes. He roared and shook himself with such force that the chains that held him screeched, threatening to yield to the desperate strength of the titan.

It was almost sunset when the Governor woke up. Immediately he went to visit his prisoner.

"Damn thief!" the latter shouted upon seeing him. "I'm going to skin you with my knife as soon as I break out of these cursed stocks. I'm going to bury you alive, you bastard."

Portunduaga didn't say a word. He carefully examined the stocks and silently disappeared.

The Bull passed from threats to pleading. Portunduaga had become deaf. He did not hear or understand anything. He consented to open the padlocks only when he was told that the Bull, to all appearances, showed no signs of life. Meanwhile, he had already gone to the Bull's farm, leaving it completely cleaned out. According to him, he had won it all fair and square.

"And even if it were not so," he added, "the goods of criminals pass to the administration of the authority. Hrunn . . . ! Hrunn . . . ! And especially," he pointed out in a triumphant tone, "when among them are many things that belonged to *caucheros* who mysteriously disappeared. I should keep it all until the source of all this is clarified. Hrunn . . . ! That's what the Constitution says!"

Later on, it was learned that the so-called Constitution, which the Governor invoked and consulted frequently, was nothing other than a pornographic novel.

Chapter 5

Since that time, the authority of the Governor had strengthened definitively and, with the passage of the years, he went on changing himself into a true little king. All the *shiringales* of the surrounding area belonged to him, as well as the warehouses for merchandise and products. There was no one who was not indebted to him, and consequently everyone worked for him. The prices of his merchandise were very arbitrary, set at his all-encompassing capriciousness; the products that his debtors extracted and submissively delivered to him were credited to their accounts at a laughable price. When the Bull appeared in public, completely rehabilitated thanks to the care received on his deathbed from Portunduaga himself, he did so transformed into the shadow of the latter, whom he accompanied with incredible servility. It was an inexplicable miracle for the people of the place. The Bull was his bodyguard, his unconditional instrument of extortion, his tamed fierce beast that the tamer unleashed to the attack at his will.

"In strength you will beat me," he was in the custom of saying, "but in astuteness and intelligence . . ." And threatening him, he added: "The day that you try to turn against me there will be no mercy for you, you lazy lout . . . Hurnn!"

The Bull opened his huge mouth and laughed fawningly:

"It's the truth, boss. That's how it will be, but . . . give me a little drink, only a little drink, boss."

"If you weren't the most contemptible of drunks, you would be worth something. Here, take it!" And he gave him a bottle of brandy.

The Governor did not hesitate in striking him frequently with a stick in public.

"Take this, dog, so that you learn to obey your master!"

The Bull, bending under the blows, ground his teeth his teeth with repressed fury.

At that time, the Governor made frequent trips to Iquitos, and on one of his return trips he brought with him not only a brand-new designation as Governor of the District, which he placed in the most visible part of his Office, but also a deformed being, of reduced stature, who walked limping on both legs. The locals took the opportunity to nickname him the "Piquicho,"[6] a nickname that was pleasing to all. Several months after his arrival in Santa Inés, this unique character completely lost his name of Blas Gómez, and transformed himself definitively into the "Piquicho."

In the first days after his arrival, no one would be able to say if the Piquicho lived constantly laughing or if that was his natural appearance. A formidable set of feline teeth, which stuck out of his mouth, did not permit his fleshy lips to close. The people ended up believing that the Piquicho enjoyed a good humor. On seeing him pass, the boys would say:

"Ah, there goes the Piquicho, laughing."

And they saw him everywhere at every hour in the company of the Bull. The two were in the habit of sitting under the mangrove by the port, on an old canoe pulled onshore that lay upside down. Nobody could say for sure what they were doing; but upon observing them carefully, it was easily discovered that the Bull was complaining of his fate, while the Piquicho cheered him up. They thus became inseparable friends.

When the "honorable" Governor had visits of importance and was drinking as usual, if anyone showed surprise at seeing those individuals so disproportionate, he had no qualms in informing them shamelessly:

"They are the most evil beings that I have ever known. I keep them because they are useful to me in a certain way. It is the using of evil to do good that is supreme wisdom of the ruler. Yes, gentlemen, I use them for the practice of good. If it were not for

---

[6] *Piquicho:* lame due to illness of the feet.

Saint Raphael, of whom I am a devote follower, vicious people would have already spread unfavorable tales about my personality, for the sole reason of having those subjects near me. Hurnn!"

"And is the giant submissive?" they inquired.

"Like a dog. Now you will see! Hey . . . ! You, *sachavaca,*[7] come running!"

The Bull came quickly, exaggerating the clumsiness of movements of his enormous body. When he arrived in front of the Governor, he bowed in a servile manner. The Governor took a large stick and pounded on his back with formidable determination, after which he patted the man on the shoulder, giving him a bottle of brandy.

"Take it. Go and sleep!"

"But why this undeserved punishment?" asked the scandalized bystanders.

"Because the day that this man finds me weak, he will attack me. Yes, he will attack me. He is the worst enemy that I have!"

Often the two of them, the Bull and the Piquicho, would leave on a secret mission.

What were those secret missions? Simply those that brought greater income to the authority.

The *caucheros* came down the Alto Ucayali in large rafts packed with rubber; the *shiringueros* came out of the growing areas with canoes overflowing with pellets of rubber. The first were met, at several turns of the river above Santa Inés, by the commissioners of the Governor with orders from him that they dock in the port to assure themselves that all went well. The raft people had to spend the night there.

In the front part of the raft, which was in contact with the edge of the river, they usually found a murdered man at sunrise. The authority would intervene immediately and imprison the *cauchero* who owned the raft as the person presumed responsible for the crime. Then he would escape, without anyone knowing how, but the next day was recaptured. He fled again, once again to fall prisoner

[7] *Sachavaca:* a tapir or large beast.

immediately. The Bull and the Piquicho, accompanied by several policemen, were the ones who distinguished themselves in those captures and recaptures.

"It seems that they proceed by instinct. They always come directly upon the fugitive," said the Governor, satisfied, so that all would hear him.

The sure thing about the case was that each flight diminished the contents of the rafts, while in equal proportion the Governor's storehouse was filling up. When the rafts were empty, then the owner succeeded in fleeing. Never before!

With the *shiringueros,* something similar happened. All of the Governor's competitors were eliminated one by one, losing to their *shiringales* and their products to him, always based on the mysterious murders and the usual flights.

I already found myself in the house of this rogue, as an employee to keep his books and serve him as a secretary, when a sensational incident took place involving Antenor García, a rich *shiringuero.* A terrible suspicion had grown in my mind since I first noticed such events. This time a dead and mutilated woman was discovered under the stairsteps that led into the house of García, who was arrested immediately. He was brought before the authority, and the latter ordered me to leave the office.

"Tomorrow we will draw up the official report," he told me. "Now you can go rest."

At sunrise, it turned out that that Don Antenor was not in the jail, and the guards received orders to bring him in dead or alive. Nobody explained how he was able to open the doors of his cell.

Only if he had had a key, I told myself. And my suspicion grew quickly.

García was recaptured in the afternoon of the following day.

Upon seeing him, the Governor began to bellow. I left the office before I was invited to do so. But under the shelter of the darkness, I slipped toward the back of the office. From there I heard all that they said:

"You put me at risk, you idiot! Why didn't you hide in Pintucocha, as I ordered you?"

"What! You told me to hide in Pintucaño. That's where they caught me . . ."

"Pintucocha! Pintucocha! You screwed yourself up by not listening well. Hurnn . . . !"

"Sir, give me another chance . . . I am innocent!"

"So that you can compromise me again? No!"

"For my children, sir, I beg you, if the friendship that we had isn't worth something!"

"That is already past. Now you are a prisoner . . . ! It could be that I would soften if you are reasonable."

"I already gave you what I had available."

"Nothing . . . ! Hurnn! I know that you still have a good quantity of rubber in the house. You have scarcely brought me a few miserable little pellets."

"And if I give you ten times more, will you let me escape?"

"Hurnn . . . ! Hurnn . . . ! You are bribing me again. This is very serious . . . ! Take a double drink and rethink . . . ! Hurnn . . . ! Perhaps for twenty I will risk myself again."

"I'll sign the delivery order for you."

In response, the Governor gave him some paper, and while García wrote, he went on transmitting instructions:

"This time go to Lagartococha. There you must stay a week; then leave and don't stop until you reach Brazil. I am not responsible if you don't follow my instructions to the letter. Now take the key to the door of the jail. I will have the police drink a good ration of brandy with something in it so that they will sleep."

At dark I entered the wilderness in order to circle around behind the so-called jail, hidden by the bushes. With my mouth placed against a crack of the back wall, I called him very quietly:

"Garcíaaa . . ."

I noted that he came close, and I heard his voice as a whisper:

"Who is it?"

"It's me, Abel Barcas, the accounting employee. Do exactly the opposite of what the Governor told you. Do not go to Lagartococha for any reason. Go down to Iquitos and denounce him without fear. Wait there for my letter with instructions and reports that will interest the authorities.

That said, I turned to hide myself in the brush.

The following day, the Governor roared with false anger. He dispatched the commissioners of law for the recapture, commissioners who returned after two days. The Bull, pushed by the Piquicho, was the first in presenting himself.

"We didn't find him," he announced with a gesture of fear.

"What?" voiced the Governor without paying any attention to me. "You have looked for him in Lagartococha?"

"We searched it entirely. There was nobody."

"Out of here, imbeciles! Idiots! Hurnn . . . !"

The two bandits disappeared as if by magic.

Chapter 6

Some days after the return of Portunduaga from his last trip to Iquitos, it was discovered that he had brought back something more than his important person. Passing through the corridors of the Government House, it appeared one morning. The curious passed by the area again and again, looking at the new arrival and making all sorts of comments:

"The Governor now has another woman!"

"She's beautiful . . . and smokes hard."

"She's a *gringa* . . . and doesn't look at anyone."

"She's different from the others. She looks like a doll!"

"She's plump . . . How wonderful!"

Accustomed to seeing her stroll alone behind the railing and through the yard, the inhabitants of Santa Inés, for lack of a name to call her, gave her the title of "Governess."

Almost simultaneously with her appearance, the Governor started to languish. He appeared in public less frequently. He was always indisposed. He was seen fussing about sporadically in his Office, with a wool tie wrapped around his neck and a white sash attached in front. He attended only to the most urgent of his duties, accompanied by noisy puffing. Afterwards, he closed the door and lost himself in the interior of the house. Apparently, the intimate things did not go well with the authority!

One day, the disturbing enigma cleared up almost completely. The news circulated through the village swiftly, like fire on a trail of gunpowder. The Governor, drunk, in the company of various individuals whom he had invited to drink, let loose his tongue. The

Bull and the Piquicho had received orders to zealously guard the door.

"As soon as anyone comes close, tell me without delay," he had said to them. And, sure that he would not be caught unaware in his confidences, he began:

"It was the last time I was in Iquitos . . . ! Hurnn . . . ! In the Café Cantante. I decided to let my hair down. And in this game I ended up with *cuadras*. Yes, I threw *cuadras*! Hurnn!"

"You would lose a great sum for sure," one of the listeners dared to interrupt.

"No, indeed, man! It seems you have your brains in the feet. Hurnn . . . ! I fell in love . . . ! I fell in love . . . ! Is that clear...? Hurnn . . . ! I fell in love with this woman . . . the one whom I have inside there . . . I invited her to my table, and we drank champagne. I talked to her about my loneliness and my wealth . . . Because I am rich, eh? I carelessly showed her some gold, enough gold . . . And we left together . . . ! Eh, you, idiot . . . ? Hurnn . . . ! "

These last words were directed at the one who had interrupted him shortly before. The latter, feeling himself the target of the comment, hunched down in his seat. The Governor could not abide interruptions when he spoke, least of all when he recounted one of his evil deeds. Satisfied with the effect produced, he declared:

"And I got ahold of her . . . ! Hurnn . . . ! Or, to put it romantically, she got ahold of me. Me, the most clever man in the business of love; expert, like no other, in every sort of trick and trap . . . ! Hurnn!"

He kept a moment of silence, while his chest inflated, whether from boastful satisfaction or stifled by sudden indignation, we do not know.

"Hurnn! Hurnn . . . !" He puffed deeply and continued: "The result is what you are seeing now. In the jungle a beautiful woman consumes, above all if she possesses the refined art of consuming! I'm undone, undone! There are things that in certain stages of life are poisons, no matter how much energy one has . . . ! And certainly I'm strong . . . ! But she has come with the intention of consuming me in order to take possession of my money! She wants to take from me the money that I have in the strongbox! The bandit . . . ! Hurnn! But the strongbox, sturdy and loyal, doesn't give away the secret of opening it . . ."

"Bastard! Drunkard! Swine! Liar! Thief!"

The door had suddenly opened, showing in its frame the beautiful and mysterious inhabitant of the Government House, who, with the unfailing cigarette in her mouth, stood looking with contempt and anger at the Governor. The latter remained mute, as if stupefied, with his eyes and mouth wide open. Little by little he was choking up as if he were about to explode. From the depth of his throat, hoarse from the excess of alcohol and anger, came some suffocated shouts.

"Shut up, you big bitch! Tomorrow I'll put you in the middle of the river, on a raft, so that the current can take you to Hell . . . and you'll never return!"

"I'll go when I want, when the whim strikes me," replied the woman with cynical aplomb. "But first I have to bury you, braggart, slob!"

And she disappeared tranquilly, closing the door behind her. The Governor became furious, yelling and shouting at the Bull and the Piquicho, who were nowhere to be found. He found them finally, stretched out behind the false door, in a deep sleep, and not even the fierce blows and kicks that he delivered succeeding in awakening them.

"They're as if dead from pure drunkenness! Hurnn!"

Next to them lay the jar that the Piquicho, slipping in while the Governor told the same old tale, filled several times from the carafe that the latter had at his feet alongside the table.

The next day everyone expected that the Governor would fulfill his terrible threat. But nothing happened, nor did he make the slightest appearance. The already well-known indisposition, aggravated without a doubt by the copious libation of the prior night, kept him in his quarters.

The attention of the people, meanwhile, was distracted with the happening of an extraordinary event: the arrival of the Missionary. Pale, with his beard grown over his angular face, bent over and badly covered in his shabby habit of sackcloth, he came up to the village surrounded by his faithful. He proceeded to the rustic little church, whose bells rang out happily. All saluted him as he passed by:

"Finally you have arrived, Father Gaspar!"

"Shitu already had her child. We were waiting for you so that you could marry her and for the baptism."

"Conce and Damian moved in together, tired of waiting for you."

The priest answered all the greetings and, with the soft voice of one accustomed to cleansing souls and returning peace to those who had lost it, he went on saying to them:

"Good . . . ! Good . . . ! We will take care of things . . . ! We will fix the bonds . . . ! "

That night the bells called out again. The women arrived hurriedly at the church, dressed up in their best clothing and their heads covered with beautiful kerchiefs. And they started the services that were always celebrated upon the arrival of the Missionary. The flickering candles lit up the altar and the compact group of kneeling women. The dull sound that the prayers produced droned on outside the church, where the moon spread its intense light, magically illuminating the countryside. The Governess appeared, dressed in wispy fabrics and pacing slowly from one end of the yard of the Government House to the other. She seemed to be lost in deep meditation. Possibly her thoughts flew uncontrolled, crossing fantastic distances. Not even the numerous mosquitoes that were flying about voraciously, following tenaciously upon her steps, attracted her attention.

Suddenly, looking toward the church, she stopped to listen to the sharp tenor voice that penetrated the thickness like a dagger stab and that, in the solitude of the night, translated the heroic emotions of the Missionary, bewitching the jungle with its strange and suggestive modulations. The Governess listened, absorbed, and hardly had the song ended when she resumed her pacing, visibly nervous. She left the yard and slowly approached the little church, and sheltered by the reigning darkness, without distracting the faithful, she entered by the front door. At that moment men and women were singing in a chorus. When the voice of the priest was heard again, she continued advancing as if drawn by some mysterious force. The light at the end of the aisle left her figure fully outlined, standing out distinct from all the rest. Her hallucinating eyes, fascinated, fixed on the priest, who, all spirituality at that moment, held his imploring gaze turned upward, in a great effort so that his prayers should arrive in Heaven and win infinite mercy. Upon ending his chant, as the chorus of women was again beginning, he lowered his gaze and met the eyes of the Governess, fixed on him; catlike eyes that, by their sharp firmness, appeared to be strangers to blinking. Their glances crossed: his, severe because this woman was not humbly kneeling as the others; hers, indefinable, hypnotizing like that of a reptile that has found its prey. One could be sure at first sight that they were they looks of defiance that good and evil direct at each other, the saint and the sinner.

That night the Missionary announced that on the following morning, after the mass, the marriages should take place. He recommended that all those cohabiting should hurry to receive the holy sacrament. The last to leave the church was the Governess.

Before full daylight of the following day, the people were already bustling about in an uproar, preparing for the marriages. The church was full when the mass began, after which the priest delivered an impressive sermon. He passed a glance over his faithful, his gaze falling suddenly upon the eyes of the Governess, who at one end of the nave, next to the rustic platform, was kneeling with eyes full of ecstasy and fixed on him. The priest became upset in spite of himself, a word forming a knot in his throat, and then, full of anger, he gave a start, raising the tone of his voice. He changed the theme to execrate, overwhelmingly, certain women whom he described as "aberrations of the law of life, agents of the Devil, monsters from whom the eye of God turns aside."

"Woe to you," he continued, "if you don't seek the guidance of confession and redeem yourselves with repentance in time! For you, the Kingdom of the Lord will be closed; for you there will be eternal damnation, the terrible pain of the pits of Hell."

This flagellating, anathematizing speech spread through the place, making the humble people, who did not understand the final part of his sermon, tremble. The speaker turned his challenging eyes toward the disconcerting woman, who at that moment had lost her arrogance, appearing humble and defeated. Her gaze, fixed on him, did not have the accustomed shine and was veiled by tears that did not falter in rolling down her cheeks. And he noticed the expression of repentance that placed upon her face a seal of sweetness. He felt himself strongly moved. In his spirit, tender and compassionate, the apotheosis of a grand triumph was celebrated. He had succeeded in moving that sinner who a moment before struck him as the symbol of the most depraved instincts and whom he now saw converted, unexpectedly, into a Magdalene, purified by pain and faith. He held a contemplative silence for a few minutes. Afterwards, as serene and peaceful as a saint, he softly blessed the faithful.

The hour of the marriages arrived. Everyone, full of enthusiasm, showed signs of wanting to get married. The couples formed a circle to receive the nuptial blessing. A voice said softly to Sajami:

"Hey . . . it was only a year ago that you got married!"

"Shut up! What does it matter to you?" replied the woman indignantly. "The more times we are married the better! You meddler!"

An Indian entered the church looking for his wife, and seeing her in the circle ready to marry another, he dragged her out.

Various people gathered at the foot of the altar, forming a circle, and the Missionary, who was praying while kneeling, stood up attentively and then arranged them by couples. The most enthusiastic appeared to be the boy Licuda. He kept turning around, first in one direction and then the other. Suddenly, without clearly realizing what he was doing, he grabbed the arm of the old woman Tiburcia and dragged her to the circle with gestures of triumph. The priest blessed the unions. The scenes that had just taken place unsettled him, even though he was accustomed to the strangest extravagances!

After receiving the sacrament, Licuda tried to leave; but the woman seized him by the shirt.

"But . . . the wedding has already ended!" exclaimed the boy, without understanding. "I'm leaving."

"The wedding has just started for us, sonny. Now you are my husband and we have to leave together."

Licuda opened his eyes, stupefied, before the face of the shrew who held him.

Father Gaspar appeared indifferent to the shouting that followed. He went out to look surreptitiously at the full-figured woman, with palpitating flesh, who was leaving in the direction of the Governor's house.

Licuda's parents intervened energetically, trying to free their son from the claws of that fright of a woman. The ruckus reached the house of the Governor, who came out of his Office, grumbling. When the facts were laid before him, he remained thoughtful and vacillating. But when it became obvious that he had the obligation to resolve the case, he reacted:

"Hurnn . . . ! Console yourself, sonny," he said to Licuda, "since you are not the first unfortunate to whom this has happened . . . Hurnn . . . ! As soon as you can, flee or kill yourself. Marriage cannot be dissolved! Hurnn!"

The priest, in effect, had said that. He also ordered that the woman should always follow the husband. But in this case it was poor Licuda who had to follow the woman, who dragged him off.

Chapter 7

That evening was muggy. The inhabitants of Santa Inés had gone to their small farms, leaving the village silent, as if it were uninhabited. The Governess slowly descended the steps of the house and headed toward the small church. She wavered a moment before entering. The priest was there alone, dozing in a lazy state. The sound of footsteps pulled him from his drowsiness. He opened his eyes and found himself face-to-face with the fascinating woman who was occupying his thoughts at that precise moment. They looked at each other in silence, but this time the looks did not express defiance. Hers was as a supplicant; his, welcoming.

The hours passed. The sun was about to disappear behind the dense foliage, and the shadows of the houses were growing longer, almost touching the river. Suddenly the sinner was seen leaving the church almost in flight. She fled swiftly, with her hair in disorder, choked by a hysterical laugh.

The next day, the faithful attended at the church early in the morning, without finding the priest. The Governess was not seen either. Portunduaga, in a somber attitude, was hardly puffing. For quite a while he had been standing silently before my worktable.

"It appears that they took flight," I ventured with foreboding.

He moved his head with a thoughtful air.

"From what I know at this time," he said, "I am a very fortunate man. If this had lasted a few more days, they would have ended up burying me! She was corrupt from the hair of her head to her toenails . . . ! Hurnn!"

What could have happened during the night or at sunrise?

The first news circulated two days afterward. Someone had seen the Missionary and the Governess in the abandoned house that once belonged to the individual who had been known as Don Misael and was now simply the Bull.

The devout Rosaura, who took care of the little church, was pulling out her hair and beating her chest. The Governor, having recovered his aggressive pomposity, appeared puffing noisily and smiling, apparently with perverse satisfaction. I felt plunged into the depths. The news had the effect on me of a sorrowful immersion in a sea, cold and bottomless. How could I explain to myself such strange events? He was a saint and she a pervert. "What happened? What happened?" I kept asking myself. The wind seized my question and carried it off, without giving me even the vaguest murmur that could seem to be a response.

Chapter 8

Superstitions spread rapidly among the inhabitants of Santa Inés. One night Don Bruno, the one who prepared and sold the *pusanga,* the magic potion that drove a person crazy with love, was surrounded by a group of people who listened to him attentively. With a cavernous and prophetic voice, as if he were in the presence of an oracle and revealing Destiny, he pronounced:

"This village is going to disappear. The *yacumama,*[8] immense mother of the waters, has crossed upstream on the riverbed. She will not delay in ordering the current in this direction. The riverbank will eat up in a single night all the land on which we live . . ."

"Horrors!" answered the people.

"And none of us will see again the light of Heaven nor the shadows of the jungle . . ."

"But why such a calamity?"

"There has walked on this land a diabolical mule, the concubine of the friar . . . !"

"Ah . . . !"

"The pure truth!" agreed Dahua, the *curandero.*

"We all know," continued Don Bruno, "how those women who deliver themselves to the friars are transformed, in the nights of the moon, into mules that gallop crazily, casting sparks from their nostrils, ridden by the Devil himself."

"The old ones have always assured us of this," confirmed one man whose hair stood on end with superstitious terror. "May God deliver us!"

---

[8] *Yacumama:* a demon in the form of a serpent that inhabits the waters that it is supposed to have created.

"It's the Mule . . . the concubine of Father Gaspar," continued Don Bruno. "Last night she passed in front of my house, galloping. And her hooves did not touch the ground. I took aim at her with my shotgun and shot at her, but the cursed one kept on galloping. I also saw the Devil who was riding her. He was a black and hairy monster whose eyes burned like hot coals."

"And what can we do?" asked several, full of terror.

"In this case, only the copal resin can save us," answered Bruno. "When she sleeps, she is harmless. We will grab her and cover her in a coating of copal resin melted in the fire, and we will burn her . . . ! That way not even any ashes will remain!"

"Perhaps the Mule is already in a covenant with the witch," said Dahua insidiously, trying to mix his hated enemy into the affair.

The people didn't need much to decide to carry out the act that would avoid such a calamity, freeing them from the curse that already weighed on Santa Inés. The peaceful and simple residents suffered a radical transformation: they painted their faces strangely with *achiote,* the paint that keeps away evil spirits; and from docile lambs, they converted themselves into apocalyptic beasts.

The Governor woke me up, shaking me. I sat up, rubbing my eyes and protesting against the abuse of his seeking my services at such an awful hour.

"The public order is in danger . . . ! Hrunn . . . ! Go and find out the cause of this tumult. A while ago I sent the Piquicho, and the idiot still has not returned. I need to know what is happening . . . ! Hrunn!"

I went, and mixing with the mob, I was very quickly able to ascertain that they intended to commit this horrible crime. Without bothering to inform the Governor, I took a light canoe and launched myself upriver. My oars did not stop until I reached the point where my craft hit the moist soil of the shore that I was seeking. I found myself at the abandoned farm. With difficulty I climbed the riverbank in the dark, because there were not any stairsteps anywhere. After great effort I managed to arrive at the abandoned dwelling area. The clearing that at one time surrounded the house had become an overgrown, pathless labyrinth. The old house had to be somewhere nearby. Taking advantage of the weak light of the scattered stars, I started to search for it feverishly. The outlines of the trees covered with climbing vines, and the thick brush that was struggling to reach up, had in the night a ghostly and disorienting appearance. A certain unease took possession of me. Would the Governess be nearby, converted into a mule, galloping and ridden by the Devil? Of course, when I heard the superstitions of the conjurer Bruno and the *curandero* Dahua, I felt the greatest of contempt for them; but in that moment, surrounded by fierce, gloomy wilderness, in which the sounds gained an impressive intensity, I was capable of believing, not only in such silly things but in anything that the most hallucinating and wicked fantasy could conceive. I looked back. It would have been better not to have done so: in that lamentable state of mind, alone, in the middle of the mysterious jungle, to look back is deadly. I thought I saw a hundred goblins trying to surround me, stalking me cautiously. To my ears came the mutterings of those that I perceived as being the closest. I turned around and started to run forward. A black shadow blocked my way . . .

"Father Gaspar . . . ! Father Gaspar . . . !" I shouted.

One end of the shadow lit up, making the outline of the house stand out before my eyes. There was still time! I leapt up the stairs of insect-eaten planks. My steps echoed hauntingly.

"Father Gaspar . . . ! Father Gaspar . . . !"

"Who is there?" asked a feminine voice from inside the house.

"Barcas!" I answered with great relief. "Open the door, *señora*. Don't be afraid! I have come for both of you!"

Immediately the door opened. On the threshold appeared the Governess with a lit candle and pointing a revolver at me. On seeing my face, her expression took on a strange look.

"What's happening to you? Why are you coming here like this?"

"I got lost before getting here. Where is Father Gaspar?"

"He left yesterday!"

"To where?"

The Governess shrugged her shoulders, looking at me fixedly.

"He abandoned you perhaps?" I asked, wavering.

"He will return soon for me!" she asserted. "But you, what are you looking for? What do you want?" she asked, distrustful.

"We don't have time to lose! At sunrise they will burn you alive covered in a coating of resin . . . !"

"Is it possible? What have I done to them?" and her expression of distrust changed into one of fear. "Won't Portunduaga stop them?" she asked, confronting me.

"In these regions when the Indians and even the non-Indians among them get stirred up, driven by one of their deeply rooted superstitions, there is no force or authority that can contain them. Moreover," I added, trying to make my sentences convincing, "I don't believe he is disposed to take your side and defend you, after what has happened. Hurry . . . ! Hurry! They are coming!"

Confused echoes were now heard from the direction of the river. Only then did the Governess realize her imminent danger. Without offering a single word, she headed toward the bedrooms. Hiding behind one of the pillars of the house, I had my view fixed on the darkness. There I was able to perceive the cautious approach of several forms. I ran inside and flung myself on the light that the Governess still held in her hand.

"They are already surrounding the house . . . We must flee instantly!"

We left quickly. Crawling on the floor, we managed to keep ourselves low, and we slid out through the rear door. What followed was a crazy flight through the darkness. At every moment we crashed into something and stopped fearfully to look about and orient ourselves.

"If you could just light a match . . . I can't see anything!" she murmured pleadingly.

As she clung tightly to my arm, I felt her tremble.

"I can't see either," I answered in her ear. "But that's impossible. The light would betray us instantly."

After an exhausting search, we found the riverbank.

"You'll have to wait for me here. The canoe is farther downriver," I told her, pulling myself free of the hand that held my arm prisoner.

I thought she was going to plead with me not to leave her alone, but mutely she let me depart. I walked a long stretch along the edge of the riverbank, plunging down among the fallen tree trunks, lit slightly by a weak phosphorescence that glimmered on the waters, weaving complex patterns with subtle white fibers. The canoe could not be seen anywhere. Would it be farther on down? The call of a rooster fixed in my mind that it was three in the morning.

Like a tree trunk stuck on the bank, I saw a craft floating. I went down hurriedly, sliding on the fragile soil, and came upon a canoe that was definitely not mine. In the bottom, several wet oars shone like metal sheets. It undoubtedly was one of those used by the attackers. I untied it, setting off upriver without the slightest noise.

"Who goes there?" a voice lashed out from above.

I kept absolute silence. I considered it dangerous to identify myself. Sliding down the riverbank, several forms fell into the river near the canoe. One of them grabbed the bow, while the other advanced threateningly toward me, brandishing a machete overhead.

"You're caught in the act, bastard!" I shouted, raising the oar in a resolute manner.

"It's the young employee," announced the one who held the canoe. He hesitated a moment; then, recognizing the canoe, he shouted:

"This canoe is not yours! Where are you taking it? Answer me!"

Instinctively I realized that the slightest sign of fear would have been fatal for me with those people dominated by superstition. I rose up, shouting even louder:

"You're going to ask that of your grandfather . . . ! Get way!" And as he hesitated in letting loose, I knocked him into the water with a well-aimed oar. The other let loose of the bow to help his companion, a circumstance that I took advantage of to push away from the shore, while exclaiming:

"You still haven't felt my club on your back, but I have you marked!"

I managed to hear his voice muttering some ill-tempered words.

How was I going to find the Governess in such a bad situation? If I had not had the prior encounter, I would have been able to continue ahead, calling her until I discovered her whereabouts; but surely the two men would be following me on top of the riverbank and would not be long in bumping into the woman who was waiting for me. I continued rowing while my eyes scrutinized the upper edge of the riverbank in the effort to find her in time. For a few moments I feared I had already gone too far upriver. That idea stopped me, and while I dried the sweat from my forehead, from a recess in the riverbank and almost at water level appeared the clear form of the Governess, speaking to me. She had slid down the riverbank and was standing in the water. I breathed with relief. Upon taking her aboard, I had her lie flat in the bottom of the canoe, concealed by the sides, to prevent her being seen from the shore. In that very instant I realized that she carried with her a large bag and a rifle. Immediately I rowed to the center of the river to go downstream. In a few moments we passed in front of the village of Santa Inés, which was sleeping amid the last shadows of the night, lulled by the murmur of the flowing current.

Before the first rays of sunrise, we could see an enormous flame in the depths of the wilderness that we had left behind. The house that once had been Don Misael's had been converted into a gigantic bonfire. The jungle would soon cover the ashes, erasing forever every trace.

Chapter 9

The sun was already high when the Governess and I sat down on the sand under the shade of some bushes, at the beginning of a beach that extended for several river bends below the village of Santa Inés. Her clothing was wet and torn in shreds by the flight that we had just carried out. And despite the gauntness of her cheeks, her face had acquired its original characteristics, which I contemplated, absorbed. Reclining with apparent indolence on a log, she was looking at the river in whose waters came and went the changing and mysterious life of the jungle. Her face, which still retained traces of youth, expressed unfathomable concerns.

"What are you thinking about?" I inquired, breaking the silence.

"About my life!" she responded, without taking her gaze off the restless surface of the water.

"Ah! Your history . . . ?"

"Who does not have a history? Our history goes on weaving itself without our realizing it. Our paths have comings and goings, and through them we can go forward or backward. But life is not a path, since we wander everywhere, often not knowing if we advance or retreat, if we go up or we go down. And, in the moment least expected, we find ourselves very low, with an overwhelming burden of misery on our back . . . That is what has happened to me. Many feel pride in their history; others appear to do so, hiding remorse and shame. They go through life inventing stories, depending on who is listening to them. We do not need to pretend . . . we simply lie. And when the occasion presents itself, when the pain finally wakes us and crushes our soul, we tell it all, absolutely all, to release the pent up suffering . . . We remember the first disappointment that appeared unbearable to us; then, tired of crying uselessly and understanding that the doors of honor will never open again once they close behind us, we continue through life like flowers pulled from the plant, to be hung in the nearest straw hut. And as time passes relentlessly, leaving us greater disappointments and disillusions, we learn to believe that we don't feel, to be indifferent to all."

I sat up, anxious to not miss a word. The Governess let out a sigh that seemed to enclose all of her life of adventure. She contracted her lips, simulating a smile that degenerated into a trembling grimace, and continued:

"The first thing that happens to a woman is to run into the man. Then she follows the man. And the man invariably happens."

"The man . . . !"

"The man, who is as infinite as Heaven and as variable as it. The women who presume to know much assure that there are two classes: he who destroys and he who redeems . . . if perhaps there is redemption."

"Don't you believe you have found him . . . ?"

"How do you know it? They all present themselves as redeemers. The last one . . . you have already seen it. He also left. If he returns, he will possibly find me with another. The worse curse that can befall a woman is be born beautiful . . ."

Upon saying this, she fixed on me her luminous eyes, opened wide.

"And why have you saved me? Why are you with me?"

"You don't have to fear anything," I said, somewhat disturbed.

"That's strange! That's strange! Do you believe in the sorcery of the trees?"

"All the trees, from the origin of the world, fulfill the identical mission: they incite sin. Perhaps from them emanates the impulse that governs life. I have heard that said many times, *señora*."

"*Señora . . . ! Señora . . . !* I had to come to the jungle and undergo such frightful ordeals, so that someone would again call me *señora* when, without it meaning anything to them, I might not be married."

"In the jungle everyone is transformed," I replied philosophically. "Our innate nature, that which is the essential part of our being, surges forth suddenly and imposes itself on us when we have hardly had our first contact with the jungle. Here the civilized person tears away the mask with which he deceives that world; he does not fear the repression or the social censure of those around him. Thus, those who are thrown away like trash by the city are regenerated here, if there still remains any goodness within their soul."

"You are well spoken . . . I would like to be like that so I could tell you my story."

"I would be interested in hearing it."

"I want to unburden myself . . . !"

After that exclamation, the Governess first fell silent, only to then overflow in a heroic climax, as the river does when it carries too much water.

"They gave me the name of Tula when I was born. It doesn't matter where, because it was far away, beyond the sea in a large city. I was very poor and grew up between two bad counselors: misery and work. I was still very young when I ran into the 'Madame.' She taught me to value the beauty of my face and the luxuriance of my body. She made me disdain the percale and love the silk. She dressed me in luxury. And I even dazzled myself upon discovering in myself unsuspected charms. I found myself coveted by admirers who offered me infinite good fortune. Thus I fell into the arms of the man to whom my corruptor sold me."

"The old story," I interrupted.

"The old story, the oldest of all the stories and, of course, always the newest . . ."

And what she then told me was so complicated and intense that it would be worthwhile narrating it fully if it did not take us away from the jungle, from that gigantic crucible in which life boils in this savage and mysterious scenario, in which the stories woven by men in the cities do not deserve any mention. But there were passages of brutal reality, of such strong coloring, whose multiple details, expressed by the heroine herself, contained unimaginable nuances on the palette of pleasure and of life. In one of the most exciting passages, I had to beg her, before she ended:

"One moment!" and I ran toward the river, into whose waters I plunged headfirst without even undressing. I was submerged a long time. When I began to feel cold, I left the water.

"What happened to you?" she asked with curiosity and irony.

"Nothing," I answered, embarrassed.

The Governess shrugged her shoulders, possessed of the fatalism of life. Then she renewed her narrative, often becoming excited with the memory of certain episodes. Suddenly she noticed that her clothes and shoes were wet. Without stopping talking, she took off her shoes and, apparently unconscious of what she was doing, started to undress. Her shoulders appeared, then the beginning of her breasts. I looked away, pretending interest in the countryside that extended on the other side of the river.

"I am not going to completely undress," she told me with a certain reproach, upon being surprised by my attitude; and covering again her shoulders, she brusquely changed the topic.

"That old Portunduaga brought me here offering me a lot, and he gave me nothing."

"He said that you intended to kill him."

"It depends on how one sees things. He induced me to see the Missionary so that, according to him, I would return to the good path. God knows what plans that old toad was cherishing! But, in the end, Gaspar saved him . . ."

"Gaspar . . . !"

"What an interesting man! I don't know precisely what I experienced upon seeing and hearing him the first time. I felt myself attracted, strongly magnetized by his look. The tone of his voice and the things he said. I who laughed so much at all the preaching and counsel with which the puritanical people attempted to guide me. I don't know if it was his chanting, his preaching, his appearance of one martyred, or simply the jungle. I believed docilely in his words . . . ; but in them, as in those of all men, there was nothing but deception . . ."

I held my breath. With a vague look, as if she were speaking alone, she continued:

"Yes, he deceived me. Better said, we deceived each other. He spoke so much about virtue and recommended so much the confession that, resolving to be a good Christian, I asked him to hear my confession. I thought I should tell him all. And it had been so long that I had been wanting to let it out, pouring out my flood of adventures . . . that I found myself kneeling at his feet, and I was telling him all . . ."

"All? Did you tell him your story as you have just told it to me?"

"Isn't that what confession is? I didn't want to hold back anything. I was sincerely moved."

"Horrors!" I exclaimed, scandalized.

"What's happening to you?"

"I see a river of temptation drowning a saint. He was too good and pure to resist a shock of that intensity in the jungle. He was born for the holiness of the convent cloisters, and he lacked the strong character of his heroic predecessors in these missions."

The poor woman looked at me, stupefied, without understanding the significance of my words. Little by little the expression on her face was changing, until it reflected fear.

"What a fool I have been!" she exclaimed, covering her face with her hands. "Now I understand. I only wanted to be a good Christian . . . ! This is atrocious!"

"Don't distress yourself so. In this case you weren't guilty. It is the unconquerable influence of the jungle!"

"How horrible that scene was!" she continued, with a horrified expression. "I had not finished the confession when he rose up with his eyes wild."

And the Governess, agitated by nervous convulsions, fell eloquently silent. Then she wiped away a tear and, with a broken voice, continued:

"I spent all night awake with the ringing of his last words. Then I understood that I loved him, and I decided to save him. The next day, very early, I found him haggard, with his eyes sunken from lack of sleep. We agreed to flee immediately. We filled the canoe with sacks of supplies that the pious people had brought for the Father.

We went to stay in the abandoned house. Without stopping to measure the abyss into which we had fallen, we made plans for the future. He had to hang up the habits, and I to renounce my life of adventures. We knew that we faced a future charged with worries, dark and uncertain. We needed to go very far away. 'To carry out our plans, we need money,' I ended up telling him. 'Money?' he repeated, opening his eyes. And after a short meditation, he exclaimed: 'Quiet! I know where there is some gold. I will bring you lots of it.' And he left, promising to send for me quickly. Father Gaspar, known the whole length of the river, could not go about accompanied by a woman . . . I would have liked to have waited for him as he left me . . ."

"He went for gold?" I interrupted her, curious.

Without answering, she asked in turn:

"Where do you think he could find it?"

"In the sources of the tributary streams, up there in the Alto Ucayali, where the savages claim that the stars have been scattered in the sandy beds that are washed by the waters."

"Perhaps I came upon the forbidden man?"

I remained silent. That terrible question distressed me.

"Answer!" the woman shouted, frightened.

"The jungle does not allow for prohibitions of that nature," I responded thoughtfully.

Chapter 10

Without a doubt, the long confession that she had just finished telling me had drained her strength, already fully weakened by the shocks experienced in the precipitous flight. Making herself comfortable in the shelter of the welcoming shade that a thick branch cast across the sand and overcome by tiredness, she gave herself over to a heavy sleep. I took advantage of that time to gather wild fruits in the nearby area in order to attend to our nourishment with them. And we certainly needed it! Having gathered a generous supply of melons and other fruit on the beach, I returned to her side and I dedicated the remaining time to looking at her leisurely, with the ample detail that her deep sleep and the solitude of the place permitted me.

In that moment she appeared beautiful to me. How long was I in that mute and delightful contemplation? In the jungle, time is not measured by what the clocks mark or what the calendars fix. The seconds, the minutes, the hours, lose their importance and cede place to events. Thus, no one makes an appointment at this or that hour, for this or that date, but at the cry of the rooster, the rising or setting of the sun, at the lunch hour, or for the Feast of San Juan or Christmas; and they count from when the river rose, from the last harvest, since so-and-so arrived, or since the death of such-and-such person.

Today when I evoke that scene with a dispassionate spirit, I cannot distinguish nor put in order the series of swift and tangled ideas that crossed my mind on that occasion. From the time that I first discovered the criminal intentions held by the superstitious mob that attributed diabolical and ill-fated properties to the seductive woman who had conquered the chastity of the Missionary, until the moment in which I heard her confession beset by insuperable temptations, very few hours had passed. Notwithstanding, I seemed to have lived a long time.

Little by little my strength was abandoning me. Things were imperceptibly distancing themselves from me, blurring into the background, wrapped in an ever-thicker fog. The river murmured monotonously in its eternal passage, and the branches of the foliage were speaking soothing counsel. Finally I sank into the depths of sleep.

The night was well along when Tula—as we will call her from here forward—woke me up softly, asking:

"How long are we going to be here?"

Returning suddenly from the fantastic world of my dreams, I said to her:

"We will see! Now we have to rest."

"But we have already rested, and we can't stay here on this shore forever, like some shipwrecks. I'm very weak; I haven't eaten anything since yesterday!"

"Ah, yes. I have something here. Go ahead and eat."

Like a ravenous child, she devoured the fruits that I offered her. Then, comforted and satisfied, she insisted:

"And now, what are we going to do?"

"Take to the river in the canoe and let the current take us at its whim. We will arrive somewhere soon."

"It would be better to pass the night where we are. I am afraid of the dark. I don't know how to swim."

"There is no danger, but if you wish, we will wait until the morning light to depart."

God took pity on us. The night was serene and clear. A fire fed with branches and dry leaves chased off the danger of wild beasts and the voracious annoyance of the insects. During that night we didn't stop talking, taking very little concern for ourselves. The conversation flowed principally about the jungle, its characteristics and its mysteries, about which she knew nothing and desired to learn in great detail. I informed her, up to the point that my knowledge permitted, of the plants and their properties; of the animals and their habits; of men and the idiosyncrasies that the jungle imposed on them; and above all, about the river, king and master, that nourishes the jungle below, transforms it, and even moves it about capriciously.

"One could spend a long time listening to you," she said with enthusiasm, taking advantage of a moment of silence. "A man like you would have made my life very different. Nobody has ever talked to me like this, or tried to teach me anything good or useful. I heard only unending flattery, vulgarities, and lies. Promises that were never fulfilled. Lies and more lies that defeated my faith and killed my illusions and my hopes. And to think that today, after a life of shame, a new horizon is revealed before my eyes, a new vision of a life, one that I would have wanted to live, as good as I was born. It is very sad, really! But would I still be able to redeem myself?"

I did not know what to say in response to those expressions overflowing with bitterness in which I perceived, nevertheless, a ray of hope. Her large blue eyes, which were fixed on me, filled with tears, displayed an intention that made me shudder.

"You have nothing to say to me?" she asked.

"Truly, I don't know what to answer you. We are living moments of uncertainty. We will see tomorrow . . ."

"Tomorrow!" she repeated, fixing her gaze on the farthest stars. "Tomorrow . . . ! In all the promises of men there was always a tomorrow."

And the morning arrived promising and jubilant, greeting us with that prodigious hymn that the wild nature raises to its creator. Listening to it we remained in ecstasy, like two savages upon hearing the marvelous rendition of a musical poem executed by the most complicated orchestra.

"This is beautiful, isn't it? . . . And you, what's your name? I know you are Barcas, but you must have another name. Maybe your name is Salvador! It would fit you well!"

"No, my name is Abel."

"Abel? Abel? Now, that name reminds me of something vague, very far away."

"Yes, the first Abel was murdered by his brother Cain."

"Now I get it! It was in childhood. I heard it from the lips of my darling mother when I was good . . . and knew how to pray." And turning her gaze toward the turbulent river, she suddenly exclaimed: "Look, there's a riverboat coming! I have to get on . . . !"

In truth, one the boats that made up the commercial traffic in the Ucayali was approaching, heading upriver. It was going to pass in front of us, staying close to the opposite shore. I fired three shots and it stopped. The merchant in charge put on a very unfriendly face upon seeing that what he was going to pick up was not pellets of raw rubber but a badly dressed woman; but upon observing her up close and finding her beautiful in spite of the deplorable condition of her clothing, he abruptly changed his expression and welcomed her with pretentious expressions of crude sailor gallantry. As he was examining her arms, neckline, and waist with insolent brazenness that she appeared not to notice, his face became marked with the traces of faunlike obscenity.

He promised to take her upriver to wherever she wanted. The farewell made a deep impression on me, not so much for the feeling produced in me by the separation from that woman, whose memory would surely follow me forever, but rather because she appeared so indifferent to everything. That left me unsettled. Thus we separated without making any promises to each other, except the cold promise that one day I would hear news from her.

"I am going. I will try to remedy the evil that I have done in spite of my best wishes," she told me, with her gaze lost in the ocher surface of the waters.

Upon returning to the shore, I saw her for the last time, upright at the rail, holding the rifle in her right hand as if she were standing guard, ready for the defense. She didn't even follow me with her gaze. "Poor thing," I thought, feeling something akin to a remorse for having abandoned her in the power of a dangerous satyr. And I stood watching the wake that the riverboat left behind as it became longer and longer, and the plume of smoke from the smokestack that was dispersing, thinning out into the blue and crystalline sky.

Almost without effort I arrived hours later at Santa Inés, where nobody seemed to expect me. My arrival produced an unexpected uproar. The first ones to see me appear over the riverbank rubbed their eyes and, far from greeting me, fled from me as if I had the plague.

"Here's Barcas!" shouted one, and he took off running as if he had seen the Devil.

The Governor, without doubt notified instantly, could not hide his surprise. However, he then affected an air of great indifference and started to look distractedly at the yard. I greeted him as if we had never stopped seeing each other and put myself immediately to my work. His nervous panting, which took place at short intervals, revealed the impatience that was devouring him. I opted to remain silent.

He did not delay in requiring my presence in his Office, and as soon as he had me in front of him, he raised his eyes to meet mine and said:

"Hurnn! Well, little gentleman, where are we? I send you to find out about a tumult a hundred steps from here . . . and you return two days later. As if nothing had happened! What coolness!"

"They were going to burn her alive . . . and she was alone," I answered.

"That I already know," he affirmed, without trying to hide his anger. "But I didn't send you to save her . . . Hurnn! Tell me the truth. You found out the other had abandoned her, and it occurred to you to take advantage . . . Hurnn! She paid you well for the rescue, eh?"

"It would have been a shameful cowardice not to aid her. I felt obligated, without more reason than doing a good deed."

"Good grief! You preach better than the friar. Hurnn! But with me that won't wash . . . bad! bad . . . ! From here on I will have to be alert against your good deeds. For whom you feel compassionate, no?"

I wanted to be explain myself:

"The poor thing had a soul full of anguish . . ." I started without being able to avoid a sigh.

"And what about it?"

I pretended I had not heard the interruption, and continued:

"She poured out to me all her pain; she trusted herself to my aid. And so I took her to safety, and I accompanied her until we separated."

"Hurnn . . . ! Hurnn . . . ! I despair of people who don't speak clearly. I like few words. I prefer crude speech for its expressiveness. Only when I insult and people tremble do I realize that I have power, that they understand me and respect me. Leave off, then, with the trifles, and get to the point . . . ! Hurnn! What have you done with her?"

I had to explain to him, omitting details, how I had managed to help her escape from the infuriated mob and how I had sent her aboard the little riverboat.

"She went upriver? Are you sure?"

I affirmed with repeated nodding of the head.

"Just as well!" he agreed. "That way she won't set foot in these parts again."

But in spite of the apparent tranquillity of Portunduaga, it was easy for me to notice that he lived as prey to constant conflict. Even to the point of my being sure that he was the victim of poorly contained jealousy and spite. Tula, even if she had not been able to steal away the money that he had in the strongbox, had left empty the treasure box of his heart.

"Do you know if she had any money?" he asked me one day, without warning.

"I don't know. She took only a large bag and a rifle. That was all she carried."

"The treasury and the defense! A woman on guard and calculating! Hurnn!"

The Governor had recovered, to all appearances, all of his arrogant Caesarism. But the deep distress that weighed him down did not pass unnoticed by me. He spoke less than usual, and he was permanently drunk. In his lucid intervals, when he directed a word at me so as not to explode with impatience, it was always to refer to the absent woman with a sadness that he couldn't hide.

Chapter 11

In those days a certain type of traffic intensified that constituted one of the most abominable crimes perpetrated in the jungle. From the headwaters of the river, rafts came down, loaded with Indian children for sale. Little taciturn Indians, exhausted by torture and deprivation, were bought by the dwellers along the riverbanks who usually dedicated them to domestic service. The adolescent girls brought the highest prices among the *shiringueros,* who fought for them in frenetic bidding. On the occasion related in this account, the dealers in such strange merchandise were very upset.

"Those stupid creatures have been taken by the *'rabia.'* They refuse to eat, and they are dying. Yesterday alone we lost two of the eight that remained," announced the pilot of one of the rafts. "This business is not as good as is believed . . . and with the risks that one takes!"

What those criminals called *rabia* was nothing more than the tragic exhaustion that their evil deeds brought on in the captive children.

"We have *correrías* from the Alto Ucayali," commented the Governor, upon seeing them arrive.

The merchants held a long conference with the authority. As they were completely enclosed in the Office, under guard by the Bull and the Piquicho, one could sense them talking in a low voice, without being able to infer the subject involved. But some transaction must have been effectuated, because without even trying to do so, I could hear the characteristic sound of the gold coins that they were counting, and the raised voice of the Governor who ended the interview by saying with satisfaction:

"With so much pleading, I accept, although, in truth, if this becomes known in Iquitos . . . Hurnn . . . ! The displeasure is going to be great."

And how did they carry out the *"correrías"*?

Various failed *caucheros*, in a shady plot, armed themselves to the teeth and, taking advantage of the knowledge that they had of the jungle and the customs of the savages, surprised a village by night, killed the adult males, and captured the young women and all the children.

If the savages were not among the *bravos,*[9] the criminals would cunningly present themselves as being friends. They solicited the hospitality that the natives always are quick to offer to the white men who come in a peaceful manner. Then one night they would attack them treacherously. In those cases only the young children remained alive, constituting the coveted prize. The adults, if they were not killed and managed to escape, became dangerous, since they would thereafter be hostile and fierce.

A few days after the events just described, a new party of captives arrived. It consisted of a half dozen skeleton-like children, for whom no one was willing to give a centavo, because they appeared about to die at any moment. The dealers, like those who had come before, had the same old secret conference with Portunduaga.

I had prepared for such a case and arranged things in such a way that I could place my ear to the wall and find out everything happening, although the role of spy is repugnant to me. Thus I learned that the roguish Governor was extorting the bandits, demanding that they give him a large share in the business, in exchange for not exercising against them the power that he had to impede their criminal activity by taking them prisoners, dead or alive.

Since the business did not turn out this time to be as profitable as they expected, and Portunduaga did not show signs of yielding in his demands, the leader proposed to make a deal in exchange for some rings.

---

[9] *Bravos:* savages hostile to civilized persons.

"I will look at them," Portunduaga said, feigning disinterest. "Nothing is lost. They could be worth something."

When he had them in his hand, he couldn't contain his shock:

"These are the ones I gave to Tula in Iquitos! Where did you see her? Where did you leave her . . . ? Hurnn . . . ! Hurnn . . . !"

The respondent started to reply:

"She told us she was going in search of Father Gaspar. After we assured her that we had not seen him pass, she disembarked from the canoe in which she was traveling, accompanied by two natives."

Feeling sure that it would be possible for me to stop the criminals and obtain full information from them, without the discomfort that the presence of the Governor imposed on them, I decided to stop listening, even though I was being devoured by anxiety to find out at once all I could about what had happened to the unfortunate Tula. I imagined her completely unsheltered, exposed to all kinds of deprivations and outrages in those areas where adventurers and savage *bravos* abounded. As much because I held a pleasant memory of the poor fugitive as because I felt responsible for what could happen to her, I connived to talk that very night with the traffickers of children, in spite of the disgust that they inspired in me.

Subsequently, the tales of other traffickers of the same type, as well as reports from the merchant who took her upriver in the riverboat and from the two rowers who had accompanied her, completed the information that I needed to write in detail of the tragic outcome of the pilgrimage of our heroine.

Already in the Alto Ucayali, Tula went ashore at all the posts at which the ship stopped to ask for news of Father Gaspar. As everyone knew the Missionary, they answered her:

"He passed by several days ago. He was going upriver."

Until one day they told her:

"He has not passed by. Without doubt he stayed below."

She disembarked immediately. She acquired a canoe, and accompanied by two rowers, she went from place to place, checking out the ravines, the numerous islands, and the tributaries. In the mouth of one the latter she came upon some rafts that were tied up.

Near them, on a flat piece of the land, burned several bonfires at which individuals with sinister faces and expressions busied themselves, cooking their meal.

"Hey you, pretty one!" one of them shouted at her upon seeing her. "If your merchandise is for sale, don't come any farther . . ."

The canoe drew closer. Tula couldn't continue on without checking for the man whom she was seeking with so much diligence. The leader of the band, the same one who had directed the prior words to her, came forward, brash and insinuating:

"A trinket, the best that you choose . . . Go on, pretty one. It's a good price . . ."

"I am looking for Father Gaspar," the woman explained, without appearing to notice the words that had just been spoken to her, and she added, almost with shyness: "Have the goodness to tell me where he is . . . if you have seen him."

"I am a father . . . of my children, and my name is Gaspar. Come, little dove, for as a father and a Gaspar, I will know how to please you."

A chorus of raucous laughter followed, and various voices called out festively:

"This one has enough for all!"

She opened her large eyes, sweeping the entire crew with a contemptuous glance. All of them were devouring her with eyes sparking with lust.

From one of the rafts, someone shouted:

"Here is one with the *rabia*! She hasn't eaten any of the yucca that we gave her!"

He was referring to a little creature about six years of age, extremely pale and contorted, whose gaze was fixed forward as if she were seeing something beloved that had stayed in the jungle.

"Force her to eat!" ordered the lead bandit, who, in his manner, continued his gallantry with Tula.

Then, accentuated by gross curses, his imperious voice thundered: "Eat!"

"It's no use. We are losing her!" muttered the voice from the raft, irritated.

The little Indian girl did not obey the order. Her little open eyes remained fixed in the distance.

"Eat!" insisted the one in the raft, and as the little Indian girl did not change her attitude, he raised a whip that he had in his hand, roaring: "Die once and for all!"

A boy of about twelve years of age, who was watching the scene in anguish, flung himself forward, protecting the girl with his body. The blow fell on his naked shoulders. The boy could not avoid a sharp cry of pain and a violent contortion. Grabbing him cruelly by one arm, the bandit raised the whip again, this time landing it on the scrawny little body of the girl, who fell facedown on the log floor of the craft, lifeless. With the resilience of a jaguar, the boy leapt on the executioner and sunk his teeth into the hand that held the whip.

"Another with *rabia*!" the bandit exclaimed while pulling himself from the boy and grabbing a machete to defend himself.

"Stop!" intervened the leader from the shore. "That boy is worth at least twenty pounds sterling."

He held the weapon high, but he did not carry out its threat.

Tula, giving a shout of fear, descended to the craft in aid of the girl, from whose mouth escaped a thread of blood. She found the girl already lifeless.

"They were brother and sister," announced a woman who belonged to the same tribe as the victims and who, domesticated years earlier, lived with one of the bandits. "They are the children of the High Chief."

Tula, horrified by such cruelty, did not know what to do. Suddenly the boy, who was twisting with pain in the raft, rose up like a living metal statue and started to gesticulate in a strange way, while offering, between strange shouts, incomprehensible words. Perhaps he was formulating curses or beseeching mercy. His arms reached up desperately to the sky, to the river, to the jungle, to the men . . . So angry and fierce was his attitude that on all their faces was painted a sudden expression of respect. The bandits exchanged grim looks questioningly. A reddish cloud began to spread slowly in the sky, the purple of the waters became dark, and a strong gust of wind made the surrounding trees shudder.

Tula, who had gotten up with the little dead girl in her arms, cried in silence. Impelled by a sudden determination, she deposited the girl on the leaf-covered ground and returned to the raft, where the little Indian boy continued with his angry posture. She came close to him and tried to take him by the hand to lead him to the shore. The timid boy watched her approach with open distrust, preparing to reject her; but because he remembered seeing her compassionately pick up his little sister, he dropped his defensive attitude and let himself be led off docilely.

The leader, who along with his companions had watched the scene with astonishment, reacted:

"If you don't pay what he is worth, you don't take him away!"

Tula, indignant, looked at him with disgust. From one of her fine fingers she pulled a ring and threw it at the feet of the villain, saying:

"Take it! That's worth much more!"

"It's not bad," replied the smiling slave trader, examining the jewel. "It has some little diamonds. Perhaps my partner can exchange it below for a little rubber."

An agonized moan that escaped from the other raft announced the dying state of another little Indian. Around him the smallest ones were crying.

Tula quickly approached the slave trader and, removing the earrings that adorned her ears, said to him:

"They are of gold, emeralds, and large diamonds! In exchange give me all the children who are in danger of dying!"

The bandit looked at her, stupefied and indecisive. He appeared to be thinking about the convenience of the unexpected proposal. Then, like one who decides to accept a good trade, he shrugged his shoulders and started to examine the jewels.

"No!" she stopped him. "When you bring them to me. They are worth more than a hundred pounds sterling. Do you understand?"

The slave trader headed to the rafts and soon returned with four little creatures, weakened beyond belief, transparent from paleness. Their little heads were bowed on their chests, emaciated and defeated, as if they weighed more than their scrawny bodies could hold up.

"Go on, miser!" reproached Tula. "You are going to lose those in any event. You are only giving them to me so I can bury them. Bring me more if you want to keep the earrings!"

The scoundrel went again to the raft, picked out two more children and brought them to the woman.

"I won't give you one more," he said angrily, at the same time that he was delivering the creatures. "We are not here to exchange children for petty jewels, when farther on they will pay us for them in gold and without bargaining."

"Look at that little one who is turning to the others, crying!" replied Tula in almost a pleading tone, trying to get as much advantage as possible from the jewel.

The slave trader looked at the speaker from head to foot, pausing his lustful gaze on her curves. He turned around and moved away to return with the child and deposit him in the arms of Tula, who started to carry her new acquisition to the place where the other children were.

"One more. Pick the one you want . . . !" proposed the swine, insinuating and brash.

Tula didn't let him finish. Turning on him in a flash, she gave him a loud slap on the face. And when the bandit attempted to control her, she confronted him resolutely, after putting down the child she had been grasping against her breast.

"Criminals! Murderers! Monsters!"

There was such desperate courage in her gestures that the villain stopped short. What he had in front of him was not a woman but a wild animal. With her eyes flashing, her hands converted into claws, Tula started to move back without removing her sharp gaze from her enemy, as jaguars do before jumping on their victims. She picked up the rifle that she had left next to a tree, and she again confronted the bandit, who prudently hurried to put land and trees between them. He did it just in time, since several shots followed him, causing him to speed up his flight.

Meanwhile the other criminals were untying the rafts. The leader hurriedly embarked on one of them, and the tragic flotilla, dragging its tie ropes, slowly departed in the center of the current until it disappeared behind a distant bend.

Tula had fallen on her knees with her face turned toward the sky, which was outlined between the lush and gently moving foliage.

"My God!" she implored, "I want to be good, simply good! Is it possible that I don't deserve your mercy?"

The moans of the children, who were moving on the dried leaves on the forest floor, made her lower her head. She found herself surrounded by little Indian children, exhausted, sick, and dying. She understood that she did not have any means to cure them. Moreover, any resources would have proved useless because the poor thing did not know what action would have been appropriate in such circumstances.

In such a precarious state, Tula took charge of her own situation. She no longer had anything with which to continue paying the rowers. After consulting with them, they were unwilling to continue upriver. The provisions were short, and there was no way to replenish them in that direction. How could they continue like that?

Plunging into the bottom of her purse and collecting all the coins that she had, she said to the rowers in a persuasive tone:

"I only have this money and the canoe. Go look for help. We will wait for you here."

The men exchanged some words between them. One of them reverently delivered his machete to the little Chieftain. They embarked and departed downriver. On turning the bend in the river, they saw for the last time the group that stood around a smoking fire on the distant shore.

It is said by all those who have spoken to the inhabitants of a small river village that several days later those who were interested in the fate of the white woman went to her aid in several canoes. But upon arriving at the same small clearing, led by the same rowers, they found only cold ashes of a fire and some tracks that vanished into the mystery of the impenetrable wilderness.

Tula had been swallowed by the jungle.

Chapter 12

Sometime after the flight of Tula, Sangama was put in prison. Someone had undertaken to denounce him for homicide, and Dahua brought evidence to support the accusation. Portunduaga set about to convoke what he called the summary. The chief of the commission who was sent to take him prisoner, a worthy successor to Barboza, announced that he had found Sangama near the edge of the lake where he had built his house, examining the trail of a paca.

The Governor dismissed the others in order to question Sangama alone. Fortunately the night was already advanced, and I was able to slip out of my room, where I had pretended to be sleeping when Portunduaga cautiously opened the door to find out if I could hear him. As soon as he withdrew, satisfied with his inspection, I jumped from the bed and, as I had done on earlier occasions, placed my ear against the wall.

"Hurnn . . . ! I am sorry, Sangama," he said. "The people accuse you!"

"Not the people, sir; it's the *curandero*."

"But the people have risen up . . . Hurnn . . . ! Hurnn . . . !"

"The people here are good, sir, but unfortunately very suggestible. The bad thing is that among them lives a man who knows how to exploit this weakness to his own advantage."

"Hurnn . . . ! Huayta, whom you raised from his bed of a cripple, claims that you have killed his brother . . . He is an ingrate, isn't he?"

"I do good and, I must confess, I feel fortunate if someone thanks me. I suffer when they pay me with evil, but it is not for me, sir, but for them. They are like children and don't know what they are doing. The day will come in which a supreme authority will rise up in this land, with the mission to perfect men by means of complying with the great commandment, which includes the wisdom of the ancients: 'Don't be a thief, nor lazy, nor a liar.'"

"It's the truth, isn't it? Hurnn . . . ! Perhaps with the new triumph of Piérola . . ."

"All of them will fall. All the governments of today, inspired only by ambition, selfishness, and convenience . . ."

"Hurnn . . . ! It's a conspiracy . . . ? You're a prisoner! Confess it all!"

Sangama remained silent. The Governor blew his nose as hard as he could. He stood up and began to pace the room with long strides. A moment passed, and I heard again his voice in a suggestive tone:

"Listen, Sangama: I remember when you stopped my gangrene. I am going to give you the opportunity to escape; but since this is very serious, I too will have to flee when they chase me. Do you understand? Hurnn . . . ! And for this I need gold . . . How much do you have?"

"I have gold, sir; but I do not want to escape. Moreover, the gold is for the Great Cause . . ."

"Tell me about this!"

"I can't. I don't have anything to say."

"I am going to deliver you to Dahua!"

Sangama did not answer the threat. The Governor continued:

"Look, he has a certain potion ready for you . . . Hurnn . . . ! You already know . . . Hurnn . . . !"

"Very well, sir. I will flee."

"How much will you give me?"

"Is one hundred grams of gold enough?"

"Hurnn . . . ! Don't be such a miser with this poor old man. You have so much . . . !"

"Half a kilo, then?"

"And why not a little old kilo once and for all?"

"Very well!"

"You'll bring me the gold this very night?"

"Impossible, sir. You know that my house is far away."

"This very day you can depart and return tomorrow well after nightfall so that no one finds out you have left. But well weighed down with gold, eh? I will say that you are still inside. The day after tomorrow you will escape."

"That's how it will be, sir."

"As the people will search for you everywhere, it is necessary that you hide where I am going to tell you: in Pintucaño. There you will stay a week. I'll make sure that the commissioners don't go in that place. Then you will go downriver undisturbed, and you will go as far as you can."

"Very far, sir!"

"I will announce that you haven't . . ."

"That's the way it will be, sir."

"I'll let you out tonight. Pity on you if you deceive me! Fortunately for me, and for you also, you are honorable."

"I will return!"

Sangama departed. And while the Governor drank several glasses of liquor, very satisfied with his luck, I slipped away stealthily after Sangama. I overtook him in the port and warned him:

"It's a trick of Portunduaga's. Pintucaño is exactly where he will send the people to capture you. That's his trick."

"Thanks!" he answered me, gripping my hand, "I had already imagined this."

"If you want to save yourself, you must do exactly the opposite of what he advises."

Smiling, he took leave of me with an embrace. He boarded a canoe and left. I did not notice that a shadow had followed my steps, and hidden behind a tree, he had heard all my words. It was the Piquicho!

Chapter 13

For the previous several days, before falling asleep I had given myself over to pondering the random nature of the life that I was leading without any possible compensation. I became more and more strongly convinced that nothing good was going to develop for me in Santa Inés. As much as I searched my brain, I could not discover any possibility of achieving the fortune that had brought me to such a strange region. I was at the point of falling asleep that night, when the Governor violently opened the door to my bedroom and entered, stomping his feet forcefully. The Bull and the Piquicho followed him. He could hardly keep standing for his drunkenness. He talked like a madman:

"Hurnn! What else are you up to, little traitor, eh? Now I am going to teach you what I do with loudmouths." And without giving me time to recover from the shock and explain myself, he ordered: "To the jail! If Sangama doesn't show up with the gold, I will finish off this insect on the gallows. Hurnn! Now you are going to pay me for everything. Let's see if Tula comes to save you, whippersnapper!"

I was speechless. The Bull pulled me from the bed and lifted me into the air. Shoving me, he and the Pichicho forced me down the stairs and locked me in the jail, mocking my protests. The Piquicho, as he was locking the door, said with disappointment:

"It would have been better to take him directly to the gallows. It has been several days since we've seen someone die."

Several hours later I heard the sound of the bustle and shouts of people who were preparing to leave the village. I was able to determine that the drunken population, with Dahua at the head, was going to undertake the hunt for Sangama, undoubtedly with the pleased consent of the honorable Governor. It was not hard for me to realize the magnitude of the danger that all this signified for me, reduced to the most absolute helplessness. I tried to put my ideas in order. Two weeks had already passed since the flight of García. If he had proceeded in accordance with the instructions that I had fortunately sent to him by letter, attaching proven accusations against Portunduaga, it was possible, almost certain, that the superior authorities would take the proper measures. In that event the commission would show up at any moment in Santa Inés, charged with taking the criminal prisoner and returning peace to the region. Only this way could the detestable satrap who unjustly exploited the region be prevented from continuing to perpetrate atrocities.

The noisy hullabaloo became more and more intense. The people were excited by freely distributed alcohol and were predisposed to crimes.

Fortunately, my name couldn't be heard at all. I was able to discern, however, that the Bull and the Piquicho were not taking part in the event. It appeared that the rioters were not aware that I was in the jail. Some of them, leaning back on the planks that formed my jail, were making sinister plans, blaming poor Sangama for all the evils that happened in Santa Inés, even those that took place before he settled in the area. Farther away, angry voices led me to deduce that they were fighting among themselves and that Dahua, also drunk, could not impose any order.

Finally, the commotion starting moving farther and farther away, until the village was submerged in absolute silence. The roosters were just starting to call from time to time and from yard to yard, tearing the air with their sharp trumpet calls, and one dog or another howled, lonely and gloomily prophetic.

The first rays of daybreak were greeted by a voice that approached the jail, shouting:

"Rogues! Miserable bastards! I don't know when this will end! I return from the rubber growing areas and the first thing they tell me is that Barcas is imprisoned and will be taken to the gallows by order of Portunduaga! I cannot permit one more crime to be committed!"

I thought I was the victim of a hallucination.

The door began to shake and creak under a strong and slow pressure. Finally it opened as the padlocks yielded. In the hazy light of the morning, a man entered, brandishing the bar with which he had just finished breaking the locks. Immediately I recognized Purificación Luna, who, by reason of his job as Matero[10] was almost always absent from the village, exploring the virgin jungle.

I expressed my gratitude with a strong embrace. We were already in the yard when he informed me:

"They're all drunk and going over there to take Sangama prisoner. The worst is that Dahua is in love with his daughter. Two years ago he went to ask for her in marriage, and the father threw him out. That is the cause of the intense hatred he holds. Now he is going to get his revenge. What barbarity! The rest don't know what they are doing. They say that the Governor has given the order."

I almost didn't hear him. I was sharpening my imagination, searching for a way to escape, but at the same time I wanted to find the means to cause some damage to Portunduaga before leaving. The Matero continued talking: "They all say that the daughter is very pretty, but few have managed to see her, among them the *curandero,* who spent many days prowling in the nearby wilderness with the goal of learning something about Sangama's life. What possible good could await the poor girl with this *achuni* [11] Dahua and the hoard of drunks that he commands!"

At that moment we heard some frightful, hate-filled shouts, like those of trapped wild beasts that roar their powerlessness. They were mixed with deep cracking sounds of a whip, coming from the Governor's rooms.

The curious Matero left me and went to investigate. I followed

---

[10] *Matero:* an expert in the exploration of the jungle and a technician in the opening of *estradas.*

[11] *Achuni:* an animal similar to an anteater, with a small bone to which aphrodisiac properties are attributed.

him so as not to remain alone. We climbed up to the wall of scrapped planks, and through the gaps between the boards we saw the Bull writhing under the fierce lashes that the chubby Governor was unleashing on him with a whip made of manatee leather, while he brandished a revolver threateningly in the other hand.

"Did you believe, you imbecile, that I was not on guard . . . ! Hurnn . . . and you planned to attack me! Yes, they're all gone, but I need only myself to kill you like a dog . . . ! Hurnn!"

And the lashes fell, leaving long and bloody wounds on the half-naked flesh of the Bull.

"He is crazy with rage," the Matero told me in a low voice. "Could it be delirium tremens? They say he lives constantly drunk."

"Yes, from punishment."

"From punishment?"

"Let's go," I urged him, without answering his question.

Once again in the yard of the jail, I observed that the Matero was pale and that, notwithstanding the cold of the morning, his face was covered with sweat.

"I'm going to lose myself in my wilderness," he said. "If I fall into the clutches of that criminal, I know what awaits me for having set you free. If you want, follow me. As bad as it could be there, it will not be worse than what awaits us here."

"We're wasting precious time," I told him, realizing that the minutes were flying by. "Let's go help Sangama. With him beside us, our luck will change!"

"It's not possible," he replied. "It was a large number of people who went. How can we stop them?"

"Coward! I will go alone!" I censured him without being able to contain myself, and I started to leave.

The Matero looked at me with alarm, but seeing that my decision was made, he agreed:

"All right, I'll follow you, whatever the outcome may be! Let's go, even if they finish us both off! But first we need to arm ourselves."

In an instant he brought rifles, a supply of bullets, and two sharp machetes. We took a light canoe and crossed the river. My companion knew a shortcut. We rowed vigorously, and upon arriving at a bend in the narrow lake we were following, we stopped.

The silence that surrounded us was evidence that this was not the route followed by the mob. We tied up the canoe, and cautiously we cut a path through the forest in the direction of the house, which could be made out through the foliage.

Suddenly, repeated shots rang out. We quickened our pace, hiding ourselves among the brush. From the edge of the clearing we made out the mob, which was hurling itself into the attack without any order.

"Let's burn the sorcerer! Let's burn the house!" was the animated cry of the assault.

"No! No!" someone shouted while trying to intervene.

"It's Dahua, who's making an effort to save the girl," the Matero told me, kneeling on the leafy ground and hidden behind a bush.

From the house, two rifle mouths spit bullets. Several of the mob fell. The *curandero,* well sheltered, shouted orders for the people to attack. Captivated by a strong sense of excitement, we observed the scene. Suddenly the Matero said:

"This one is ours! What a beautiful *cotomono*![12] I'll shoot it!"

And raising his rifle, he took aim and shot. The *curandero,* whose back offered us an excellent target, fell, cursing. An enormous dog, with the hair raised on its back, leaped from the *emponado* of the house and, by inexplicable instinct, went as swift as lightning and finished him off.

This resulted in a complete rout. Everyone fled in different directions toward the forest. We came out of our hiding place and approached the house. As we walked, the Matero commented with satisfaction:

"I wouldn't have believed it!"

I added:

"You see now how we arrived on time and how easy it was?"

"I wouldn't have believed it . . . ! I wouldn't have believed it . . . ! I assure you that when I set to blast him away, I saw him as if

---

[12] *Cotomono:* the largest of the apes of the region.

he were a *cotomono,* with his colorful *cushma.*[13]

Leaving the corpse of the *curandero,* the furious dog flung itself toward us. But a whistle stopped him. We lifted our eyes and saw Sangama in the doorway of the house.

With a show of gratitude, he invited us in. Next to him, a young woman dressed in white welcomed us. With her fine hands she caressed a rifle.

"My daughter Chuya . . . ," he introduced her to us.

"Rosa María," she corrected gracefully, with a trembling angel-like voice. "I thank you so much! Do us the favor of coming in."

"Where are we, Chuya or Rosa María?" I had the intention of asking, but the words knotted in my throat.

As she still was not recovered from the impact the attack had on her, it was easy to detect her nervousness. I was fascinated by the dark green color of her eyes and seduced by the sweetness of her voice. As for the Matero, he was left speechless.

Neither Chuya nor her father seemed to realize what was happening to the Matero and me.

After they had calmed down from the excitement caused by the attack, we discussed the recent events. We all agreed in blaming Portunduaga, who had supplied the alcohol that Dahua distributed among those men, whom Sangama described as good but ignorant and, as such, suggestible.

I was the most determined that some punishment should take place for the Governor as soon as possible. Therefore, accompanying my words with action, I got up in a gesture of leaving and observed:

"It would be a good idea to go quickly to get there before the defeated men arrive. They must still be wandering in the wilderness, fearful of presenting themselves before Portunduaga without having carried out his orders."

Sangama insisted in accompanying us, in spite of our efforts to dissuade him.

---

[13] *Cushma:* a type of garment woven from cotton and worn by the local tribes.

As we were leaving, Chuya told us with great concern:

"Be careful, for God's sake, that I don't end up without a father!"

From the yard I answered her:

"If I am allowed to return, I will bring him back safe and sound."

The most welcoming and friendly smile formed on her adorable lips, and opening her arms affectionately, she said to me:

"I will be waiting for all of you here."

"She seems like an image of the Virgin," observed Luna in a low voice as we went down to get the canoe.

"She's an angel come down from Heaven," I opined, without being able to avoid a romantic sigh.

We still did not know what the punishment would be, but we were in agreement that it should be something radical that would finish the power of the Governor.

I explained to my companions what fell to me to work out with Antenor García and the confidence that I held in his actions. Based on this, I conceived the plan to appear before Portunduaga well armed, notifying him that he had been discharged from office and that the orders would soon arrive to take him prisoner. We would invite him to flee immediately, but if he did not wish to go, we would then lock him up to protect our own lives. I warned my companions that some dangers could present themselves, however, since it was possible that some of those whom he had invested with authority would defend him.

"If we work with decisiveness and caution, all will turn out well. What do you think?" I asked optimistically.

"First class!" exclaimed the Matero. "But it must be understood we are risking everything. If we don't remove him from there, he will remove us, as surely as three and two are five."

Before embarking, we proceeded to quickly bury the body of the *curandero*. We tried to make up for lost time during the trip, and as soon as we arrived at Santa Inés, we resolutely went up to the Office.

"Prepare your rifle, Matero, just in case," I warned him before putting a foot on the stairsteps leading to the Government House. "If it's necessary, act as if he were another *cotomono*."

"Don't worry. I'm on guard," he hurried to respond while he caressed his weapon with delight.

Without a doubt, the Governor thought we were some of the attackers and were bringing him good news. He appeared in the doorway of his Office with his accustomed puffing. Upon seeing me, he was shocked and turned red with anger. He tried to speak, but I went first:

"You're discharged from office. Antenor García has denounced you in Iquitos. A commission is already coming to arrest you. If you want to save yourself, flee immediately."

An intense pallor covered his face. We entered the Office, forcing him to back up. But he reacted insolently:

"A lie! Antenor García knows nothing." And speaking in this way, he went toward his desk with the obvious purpose of opening a drawer.

The Matero pointed his rifle at him, and having discerned his intentions, I shouted:

"Halt! If you take one more step, you'll be cut down by a shot!"

He stopped as if petrified. His arms fell limp at his sides. He breathed tiredly.

"He's a coward, like every criminal," observed Sangama with contempt, but he quickly corrected himself. "Look out! He is cunning and is faking!"

Confirming these words, the eyes of the Governor sparked for an instant and then, with a murky and impenetrable look, started to observe us. Suddenly he appeared to make a decision:

"Listen, Sangama," he said: "you have always been good; remember when I saved you from Dahua. Protect me. Don't let anyone know this. I will flee!"

I had the feeling that the monster was trying to gain time.

A crashing of wood planks being violently destroyed shook the room. We all turned to look in the direction from which the loud noise came. Half naked, the enormity of the Bull advanced with ragged pants stained with recently spilled blood. His face was deformed by multiple wounds and bruises. He was truly a terrifying figure. With his eyes bulging and his mouth drooling, he went for Portunduaga.

"You are no longer Governor . . . you are nothing now!" resounded the words of the giant, who would have seemed contemptible without his resolute and aggressive attitude. "I have killed people because you ordered me . . . but you are no longer Governor, you can no longer grab your revolver and whip . . ."

And he continued approaching Portunduaga. His hairy arms were extended like powerful hooks, ready to seize their prey. Enormous and monstrous, he was advancing slowly, surely. The Governor backed away until he hit the wall that blocked escape behind him. There he fell, attacked by terror.

"Don't kill me! I will return your money, your women, all. You will be the master, but don't kill me."

The Bull, blind with vengeance, implacable, repeated:

"Now you can't get your revolver . . . nor your whip . . . !"

And his hands landed fatally. He joined his body with that of his victim, and a desperate groan of dying was mixed with the macabre sound of breaking bones.

"Save me . . . !" Portunduaga managed to say. Then, only a nasal death rattle came out of his half-open mouth.

The Bull lifted him up as if he were a light package and, hoisting him on his back, left the office and went down the stairs.

Mute and motionless, we had witnessed the playing out of a tremendous drama. Screeching creaks from the steps returned us to reality. We went out hurriedly. The Bull, with his macabre charge, was going swiftly toward the river. The dying man moved his impotent arms and, almost without a moan, hung like a doll over the back of the giant.

"Stop, Bull! What are you going to do?" Sangama shouted at him, running to overtake him.

When we arrived at the port, the Bull had already reached the shore and was holding the Governor under the muddy water. A stream of bubbles was stirring the surface. When these stopped rising to the surface, the executioner raised his arms and let himself fall on the humid soil, with his thick legs sunk in the mud. The water continued slipping past the shore, as if nothing had happened.

In that moment the prophetic words of the Governor resounded in my memory: “The day that this man sees me as weak, he will attack me.”

Chapter 14

The news of the murder of Portunduaga spread like the rain in the wilderness. Nobody knew the precise reason for the act. A few hours after the event, Santa Inés found itself silent and deserted, as if the plague had decimated the population. The Bull, who in addition to his old crimes carried the enormous burden of having killed the Governor, had also fled, followed by the Piquicho, without anyone knowing where.

For my part, I know enough to say that the series of events that occurred after my jailing up to this moment produced such an effect on my spirit that I felt stunned. I wandered through the village, answering, machinelike, the questions that some directed at me. I don't know how I arrived at my room, nor how long I remained sunk in a profound sleep.

Sangama woke me up, shaking me. When I opened my eyes, I had the sensation of just coming out of a nightmare. Suddenly my thoughts became clear, all the scenes parading by, one by one, with bitter clarity. "But is it possible," I wondered, "that the events happened so rapidly and brutally?"

Sangama, who appeared to have the gift of reading my mind, said to me:

"It is the jungle, my little friend. Nobody can extricate himself from the inexorable law of the jungle!" And grabbing me by the arm, he demanded of me: "Let's go! There is still a lot to do."

"I can't! I want to keep resting. I'm worn out!"

"What! Is that how you keep your promises?"

I was struck dumb by shock, because in truth I didn't know what promises he was referring to. The smile that preceded the clarification was almost compassionate:

"Didn't you promise Chuya that you would return me safe and sound . . . ?"

"Ah!" I exclaimed, remembering it instantly. "That's true. Let's go!"

"And let's go quickly. Today is her birthday, and it isn't fair that we give her more grief as a gift. Let's take her at least the happiness of our return."

I quickly regained control of myself. It was enough that Sangama only mention her name for the face of that beautiful maiden who had so impressed me to appear in my mind. Leaping to my feet, I demanded:

"Let's go, quickly! Let's not lose any more time!"

Sangama, smiling maliciously upon noting my sudden impatience, stopped me:

"Not such a hurry! We have to wait for Luna. He won't be long in getting here."

"But . . . where is he? What is he doing?"

"He's securing the doors of the Government House to avoid robberies."

My impatience was very brief, since our friend soon showed up.

"Everything is taken care of now," he said. "What a scattering! There is not a soul in the village!" And while he spoke with Sangama, informing him of his work, I headed for a small nearby garden and prepared a bouquet with the roses that struggled to survive among the asphyxiating thicket.

"It's not very good," I said on showing it to them, "but it's the best that could be found."

We departed and rowed tirelessly, like someone fleeing. We were soon approaching at great speed the small beach from which we had embarked the prior evening under such different conditions.

The appearance of the house brought to my memory the bloody events of the day before. There, at the foot of a tree, still remained the coagulated blood in which the *curandero* had died, writhing.

Here and there remained other, equally informative stains, showing that many of the attackers had paid a high price for their rash action. I did not see a single corpse. If there had been any, the others would have collected them, since in the jungle, when someone falls defeated, relatives, friends or even strangers rush to bury him, impelled by superstitious prejudices. They believe that the souls of the unburied wander through the places that they frequented in life, to frighten those who have the misfortune to find themselves there.

Sultan, who patrolled the surrounding area vigilantly, came to welcome us happily, wagging his tail. At almost the same moment, on the top step, appeared the graceful figure of Chuya.

She awaited us, anxious to know the results of our trip. We informed her of the Governor's death, denying that it had any importance. Apparently, she was satisfied.

Guided by her and Sangama, we toured the entire house, which contrasted with the majority of the local houses by its structure and the convenient placing of the furniture and bedrooms. That there was sufficient comfort and good taste in the arrangement could be discerned everywhere. There was a study for work, agreeable and thought provoking, with an abundance of books. Our attention was drawn to a large room, with the roof of palm leaves skillfully interwoven and the floor covered with the jaguar skins, in one of whose corners could be seen rustic but comfortable furniture.

The uncertainty that had weighed on the young woman since our departure the day before did not permit her to make preparations. For the house to be put into motion, it was only necessary that we remind her of her birthday with our congratulations. Hours later, she presented us with a true banquet to which, overcoming the state of our spirits, we made the due honors demonstrating happiness and good humor. Chuya, who appeared very happy, showered us with attention and, commenting on our aid, placed us on the level of heroes.

Demonstrating agility unusual for her age, the old woman Ana, whom Chuya affectionately called "mama," was everywhere in providing services, aided by Ahuanari, an energetic young Indian man.

"Heaven has remembered us by bringing friendly faces and voices to celebrate with my girl," the "mama" repeated frequently.

Having finished the meal, which we praised effusively, we went to the hospitable corner that I had observed on our arrival. Sangama lit his pipe, and Chuya, overflowing with youth and spirit, spoke of her memories of Lima. She told us of the convent school, of her studies directed by gentle nuns, of religious festivals, of her fellow students. Her language was so clear and her knowledge so wide that I could not avoid a comment:

"You are a very cultured person, young lady."

"No, just a jungle girl who went to civilization and took something from it."

I looked attentively at a guitar that was on a piece of furniture. After a moment of hesitation, I stood up, repressing my excessive shyness. I blushed upon tripping on the animal furs that covered the floor, and making an effort to show courage and detachment, I turned to Chuya, begging her to sing something. Pleased, she acceded and smiled as she picked up the instrument, while the Matero fixed his eyes on me, admiring my audacity and the success obtained. Her hands strummed the guitar like two agile playful doves, and after a brief introduction, the melody of a beautiful jungle song poured forth like a torrent of the purest crystalline water. I gazed through the window that faced outside, where the moon bathed the countryside with burnished silver. A light wind rippled the surface of the lake, upon which a mixture of mercury and crystals seemed to boil up. The thick trees of the shore trembled lightly in a magic luminous flowering. Lulled by that soft voice and the influence of the vision of that prodigious night, I felt myself transported to an enchanted region. And when from the lips of Chuya surged the notes that interpreted the lament of the passionate lover, I believed that the mysterious soul of the jungle had taken possession of me, flowing into my very being. My memory fled from the recent events. I felt myself bathed in a transparent sweetness, owner of a diaphanous and sensitive spirit, romantically possessed by the moon, by the breeze, and, above all, by the melody that came forth enchantingly from the throat of Chuya.

In the bosom of the jungle, music, like all things, acquires special tonalities. There, by some inexplicable paradox, the sounds that delight and give ecstasy in civilized centers torture those who listen to them. Thus the song of Chuya, as it spread across the surrounding area, saturated it with irresistible sadness. It seemed as if infinite invisible hands were rejoicing in tearing apart the most intimate fibers of my soul.

Even the rustic Matero could not escape the spell. Deeply excited, he translated the emotion that possessed him:

"It seems as if a child lost in the jungle were calling to its mother . . ."

Chuya became quiet. An absolute silence fell over the house, during which all thoughts remained suspended. The voice of the Matero pulled us from the contemplation, warning:

"It's already late! We should return . . ."

A little later, he had to leave alone. Sangama, guessing my desires, held me back:

"What are you going to do in Santa Inés? Stay with us a few days while things are arranged there. Sometimes our roof should shelter a friend." And turning toward his daughter, he consulted her: "Isn't that right, Chuya?"

Blushing, she agreed, nodding her pretty head in affirmation.

They also invited the Matero, but he couldn't stay. He had a family in the village who no doubt were waiting for him anxiously in these times of disorder.

Chapter 15

The few days I stayed in the house of Sangama I felt like a member of the family. Perhaps, from the time that we met, Chuya and I loved each other. However, we had not exchanged a single word that would express such a sentiment.

I simply noted, with the consequent surprise, that we spoke to each other in familiar terms. The community of the trees engenders among humans the community of souls. There it is impossible to live closely for several days without the relationship becoming heart-to-heart.

One morning Chuya approached me, happy and playful, with a proposal:

"They tell me a Missionary has arrived. Would you like to take me to hear mass?
Papa has no reason to oppose it. I am going check it out with him."

And, sure of my affirmative response, she left, running to the room where Sangama was working at taking notes, buried in his numerous books.

"A Missionary?" I thought. "Perhaps he comes in search of Father Gaspar and his presence would wake the memory of Tula and the role that the circumstances obliged me to undertake in those absurd events. And if Chuya found out, how could I explain the events to her? Would she understand me? What new caprice of the jungle was threatening to complicate my life in these moments in which such a peaceful and bountiful path stretched out before me?"

The voice of Sangama, who led Chula by the arm, put an end to my ponderings.

"One day not too long ago, you took the father from here, promising to return him safe and sound. You kept your word. I am sure that now, on taking away the daughter without any promise whatsoever, not only will you return her safe and sound but also happy."

At the break of the following day, we left. In front of me in the bow of the fragile boat she was smiling with the simple satisfaction of the pure souls. It was then that I noticed in all its intensity the light of her green eyes, with variable nuances like the jungle itself and, like the jungle, hypnotizing. They were a mirror of the jungle itself. An involuntary shudder shook me upon thinking that I discovered in those eyes, large and beautiful, not the crystalline and promising green of hope but something else, enigmatic, indefinable, full of terrible omens. At that moment Chuya was talking to me of happy and trivial things, as if she wished to mix them into the happiness that overflowed her soul. Admiring her and listening to her, I was happily distracted, and the worries that were attacking me were fading away as if by enchantment. She spoke with the soft intonation of the chirping and cooing of the birds and the breeze, with the everlasting courtship of the branches and flowers. Every man carries within himself the potential and the inspiration of the poets. I felt that all of Nature—flowers, scents, stars, and melodies—had blended together to create this bounty of harmony that made me, by a certain pride, suitable to act as one of the knights in shining armor of fairy tales. I felt the pulse of the powerful oar strokes, expanding my chest as I breathed in the aroma that emanated from her hair and came toward me, intoxicating, on the wings of the wind.

My distraction had been such during the trip that I did not think for a single instant about Santa Inés nor of what could have occurred there since my departure. It was the first view of the village that suddenly opened before me a series of abrupt inquiries.

"What could have happened there?" I asked out loud. Chuya explained to me:

"Papa has been up-to-date on everything. It appears that there is absolute tranquillity."

But that information was not very satisfactory. In that instant the mystery that the new Missionary constituted again presented itself to me, after the ill-fated visit of Father Gaspar. Surely in the village there were comments about the adventure in which I had to undertake such an important role.

Surprised, the villagers opened a way to let us pass in the direction of the little altar where a Missionary was explaining a Christian parable in simple terms.

We sat together; then we knelt, and together we raised our souls to God. She prayed. I would have liked to have done so with equal devotion. The words that vibrated on my lips certainly did not express the throng of ideas that stirred feverishly in my brain.

When we left the small church after the service finished, it did not take long to encounter a disagreeable occurrence. In the yard a very ordinary man approached me saying, almost in my ear, something related to Chuya's beauty that seemed to me a profanity. The sentence did not contain anything offensive, but in such circumstances my sensitivity was extreme. I felt obliged to rebuff to it, which provoked the just censorship of Chuya. She could not conceive that one would take such an attitude over words that lacked significance.

This motivated me to start the return trip immediately. After crossing the river and finding ourselves in the middle of the lake, I finally felt free of threats and in the mood to savor the good fortune that the trip offered me. The burning sun reverberated on the waters, shimmering like gold. Whenever we found a bit of shade projected by the branches from the shore, I stopped the canoe to relax. Night had almost fallen when we arrived at the house. Sangama appeared, smiling, to welcome us.

"There have been a lot of masses, apparently," he said alluding to the advanced hour.

"No," I replied instantly. "I have just been learning to pray during the trip."

Chuya blushed.

"I hope the journey has been pleasant and that my girl feels happy," he concluded, embracing her.

***

One day the good fortune that I was enjoying in that hospitable house was interrupted. It occurred to me to invite Chuya to fish with rods, an invitation that she accepted enthusiastically. In the nearby lake we passed delightful hours under the *inciral* trees loaded with fruits that constantly disturbed the waters as they fell by the thousands from the branches shaken by the wind. Around the canoe the *lisas* and *gamitanas* devoured the fruits instantly. The fishing was abundant, and before the afternoon had advanced very far, we had returned.

It was then that the event occurred without forethought. Having had time to think, I would never have done it. I declare by my honor that, even now, I feel ashamed and sorry. It was the rain. That torrential and sudden rain soaked us in a second. The thin dress of Chuya was pressed against her, outlining her delicate and statuesque figure. Confused, I flung myself on her like a wild hungry beast that had discovered the much-sought prey. The violent rejection made me rethink, and she took advantage of the situation to leap to the shore and disappear, running among the trees, headed toward her house.

Upon seeing her flee in fright, I fully realized my misfortune, desiring with all my soul that the earth would open at my feet and bury me forever. What shame I felt! But I insist in maintaining that I was not to blame, and I cannot explain to myself how this could happen to me. These impulses happen frequently to the jungle dweller. There is nothing that opposes the free man in the jungle, who takes from it all that he desires, all that he instinctively needs. And in that moment, Chuya was a jungle flower!

Disheartened, I wandered until very late in the surrounding area without daring to enter the house. It even occurred to me to flee, but whether it was because I felt tied to Chuya or because I understood that my attitude would end up arousing Sangama's distrust, I opted to present myself. They were waiting for me to eat. The tranquillity with which Sangama welcomed me, friendly and affectionate, churned my soul within my body. Chuya conducted herself with the courtesy and delicateness that was always her custom.

The following day it was not possible for me to find her, and at nightfall I had to appear alone at the front steps on which we had talked at length about love, exchanging hopes and promises. And during the following days when, as was his custom, Sangama came down to the yard draped in moonlight to pour out his discussions so full of original teachings, she alleged slight indispositions and did not appear as before, hanging onto the strong arm of her father.

The world ended for me. I tried every way to talk to her alone, but my efforts were useless despite my tenacity. I could see her only in the presence of her father. In those instances she took her solicitousness to extremes, producing in me, by that very thing, a terrible distress. I would have preferred her censure. I felt that in her attitude there was a great deal of contempt, and it was humiliating in the extreme. I thought that my misfortune had no remedy and that consequently I should return to Santa Inés to undertake from there my wandering pilgrimage through the world, if it were not better to hang myself in the branches of whatever tree to finish once and for all the martyrdom that made my life intolerable. What thoughts has the passionate and inexpert youth! Desperate, I resolved to make a final effort and visited the kitchen in which the old woman "mama" was poking the embers of the fire.

"Mama," I said to her, affectionately and pleading, "tell Chuya that I am very unhappy, that I can no longer live this way, that if she doesn't pardon me I will understand that I have no hopes and I will leave tomorrow."

"Mama" repeated the charge several times, and by her compassionate look more than by the sentences that she spoke to me, I understood that she would deliver the message.

That night I waited in vain. Sangama came down to the yard, and I accompanied him, pretending to listen to his interesting dissertations, but being as upset as I found myself, I did not understand anything about what the good man was saying.

As one condemned to death en route to the gallows, I went the following morning to prepare the canoe in which I would leave. I was already going to say my farewell, swallowing the knot of anguish that blocked my throat, when "mama" came to meet me and, on behalf of Chuya, told me that I should wait until nightfall. What could this message mean? Was it the much-sought pardon? Ceaselessly I watched the sun, and it always seemed in the same spot, as if some new perverse Joshua had ordered it to stop in its path. How long those hours were during which I could see Chuya from time to time, indifferent, attending to her daily chores! I tried to discover a gesture, an expression that would foretell the sentence that waited for me. But expressionless, mute as the sphinx, she was escaping from my scrutinizing look without letting me perceive the slightest detail. The first shadows of the night were finally starting to dress the horizon in mourning, while in my soul, already tired from waiting, the desolate darkness began appearing.

To see if the night, taking pity on me, was accelerating its pace, I undertook to go down to the yard; but a white and perfumed shadow blocked my passage, and I felt the arms of the beloved encircling my neck delicately and her lips joining with mine. When Chuya pulled free of my arms, which were squeezing her almost to the point of injury, I remained stunned, paralyzed in body and spirit by such ineffable good fortune. As quickly as she appeared, she left and faded rapidly into the shadows of the enormous old house.

A little later, having recovered my serenity, I was walking with Sangama in the yard, effusing with such loquaciousness and joy that it motivated his admiration and applause. He also appeared very satisfied, happier than usual.

I can affirm that the following days were the happiest of my life. Our daily excursions to the small farms and the lakes resumed. Like a child with such agility and courage that I frequently surprised myself, I climbed the trees each time that she discovered a ripe fruit or an orchid to adorn her silky hair.

Chapter 16

"**Some maintain** that the jungle is a green prison. Others claim that is the true Hell. Others describe it as an environment fit only for the life of the trees, but not for the dwelling of men."

When Sangama discoursed in a certain tone and about topics related to science and history, one had to be quiet and listen. That day he spoke with unexpected enthusiasm. The foregoing being said, he meditated some seconds and proceeded:

"Everyone writes the history of civilization by criticizing it from his personal point of view, that is to say, from the environment that formed his standards, his particular manner of feeling things and appreciating them. The historian, the geographer, and the anthropologist, when referring to the jungle, have never shed this restrictive influence. They have studied it, considering it as an awesome reality opposed in every way to their concept of civilization. The jungle is, above all, according to them, the physical medium of the savage. The savage is the primitive state of the human species, a benighted state where man lives within a small range of mystical, magical, and totemic existence. The civilized man comes to the jungle and wants to impose his customs, his habits, and his laws on the environment. And, as is logical, he has to fail: from a civilized man, he is converted into a barbarian, and from his collision with the jungle he produces the intense drama that is formed from errors and is always resolved in failures.

"Why not adapt to the dictates of the jungle and create in it a new type of civilization? Because—it is necessary to confess it according to our experience—the true man is free here, but it is only a question of the man being adapted to the surroundings. What would be the criticism of the civilized world according to the criteria of the jungle?"

And, upon asking me this question, Sangama smiled with irony. He puffed on his enormous cigar several times and proceeded again:

"Here we have the key to the welfare of future humanity. Here exist inspiration, stimulation, and mystery. How many secrets to be taken from the prodigious nature and put in the service of mankind! How many mysteries that appear undecipherable! Observing it and taking inspiration from it, so old and also so new, we would be able to write here the true history of Humanity! The customs of civilization, distilled through the filters of traditions, of morality, and of religion, have been humorously criticized many times from the points of view from which one supposes other natural species contemplate them. Let us be specific: What is the jungle? It is a duplication of the life of the civilized societies, represented by the trees and the animals that populate it. Here, a formidable tree has risen up over the expanse of vegetation that surrounds it, crowning itself with a leafy peak and maintaining itself erect in spite of the battering of the storms. It has stood upright as protector and tyrant of the lower-level life beneath it. Near it no young tree succeeds in rising up to reach the kingdom of the clouds and the birds without its first allowing a suitable path between its own branches. Those that do not merit its favors will try in vain to develop themselves; their life will pass miserably, beaten down by the gigantic branches that block their progress. The vine that, like the reptile, was born to crawl, sinuous and adaptable, slithers up the powerful trunk, attaches itself in the branches, and, finally, crowns the heights, making the strong tree the supporting frame of its ambitions. But if the colossus falls, struck down by lightning or because old age and decrepitude waste its roots, it drags down and crushes in its fall the multitude that surround it, as happens with magnates and politicians. And thus, thanks to that fall, others find the field free to prosper, but not without the most inexorable competition being undertaken among them to advance and gain the advantage, to occupy the greater space, and finally to impose their dominion."

And Sangama, enthused with his exposition and after giving several puffs on his cigar, continued:

"Next to quiet crystalline lagoons in which the magnificence of the jungle and the splendors of the sky are reflected, weak rushes and timid palm trees sway to the caresses of the wind as modest maidens, proud nonetheless of the slenderness of their graceful stalks, while in the immediate area, the cunning and low-lying *renaco,* in the manner of born criminals, stalks its victims to strangle them. In the swampy land and between the rotten trunks, the most delicate and beautiful flowers are born. Fair competition, unrestrained ambition, struggle, betrayal, madness, virtue, vice . . . all is found here, before our eyes, which are not fit to appreciate the complex and marvelous process that has occurred in the jungle since the world began. The crawling and poisonous reptile; the lithe feline, quick in hunger and with its claw; the inoffensive deer with its gentle eyes; the hawk with its sharp eye, alert and swift; the wood pigeon, cooing; the deceptive *cotomono;* the slow sloth; the old turtle; the lavish toucan; each and every one represents appropriately its corresponding type in the civilized collective. The jungle has places of unbreathable air that poison and intoxicate the soul, as the city has its taverns and brothels. Inhospitable regions from which the animals flee, because in them life is impossible. Zones in which the trees, instead of bearing fruit, grow spines, because they fear being attacked without warning and must be ready for the defense—just as in certain districts all the men are aggressive and miserly, and the doors are closed to the passage of needy travelers. In some bounteous and paradisiacal regions, in which the land is the loving mother of man, the serpent kills, the bird of prey robs, the falcon carries its booty, and the vampire sucks, as much as it can, the blood of men and beasts."

"What surprising analogies!" I exclaimed, astonished.

"The trees, among themselves, are also friends and enemies, as are men," continued Sangama with growing enthusiasm. "They offer their placid and comforting shade, or they oppress villainously to the point of killing. The animals are sometimes accompanying and sustaining, other times attacking and devouring, the same as with men. But in referring to civilization—and we should say 'our civilization,' because it is not only that of men who live outside the jungle—we need to consider ourselves a flowering of it, an exotic flowering that rises under the foliage, amidst the jungle, on the edge of the swamp. Civilization is a perfection of the past as it relates to the domination of man over nature. But in the cultural aspect the man of the city has retreated. The sanctuary lamp of faith has been consumed almost to the point of being extinguished, because religion has been made into a custom without transcendence. The human education process has been reversed. It goes from bottom to top, from the material to the spiritual. Before lifting himself in search of the ideal, man satisfies all his material aspirations, satiates all his appetites, surrounds himself with riches, power, and selfishness. Such is the attitude of the wild beasts: after filling themselves, they look at the moon. The past has forgotten paths over which the human vision, with its feverish contemporary restlessness, passes indifferently. Morality and Religion, which sustain a powerful Empire of happy peoples, of the true civilization, have been set aside! Morality and Religion, supreme columns over which a better humanity could arise, and without which the collapse of the current one will become inevitable. The restoration of that great Empire is within the orbit of my projects. It will have as a geographic frame the jungle in which we live and a great part of that which was encompassed in the Tahuantinsuyo. The Idol . . . !"

Sangama's last words were completely incomprehensible for me. His annoyed gesture gave me the impression that he believed he had spoken too much. This was the second time that he had referred to such projects, whose reach I was far from imagining. Observing the concern that my face undoubtedly revealed, he brusquely changed the subject, saying:

"That poor Luna is very distressed. A year ago his father left to explore the *renacal,* and he still has not returned. Luna wants to leave to search for him . . . I think I will go with him."

"You're a wise man, Sangama," I dared to interrupt him.

"Wise! Bah . . . ! I will not say I am ignorant . . . but that erudite Italian who lives at two days' distance of sailing upriver never stops causing me a little envy. The tale of his voyages, his explorations and adventures, is fascinating! An eminent polyglot, when he is not studying the properties of certain plants he has discovered or collecting insects for a great museum, he translates from Sanskrit some documents unknown to me and sends his work to scientific reviews in his country. He arrived in this jungle while passing through to Brazil, crossing the continent. The river seduced him, and he stays on its edges. Just as wise as he is the German who, inoculating himself with vaccines to immunize himself against the tropical diseases, and working in infected swamps, dives into his small improvised laboratory, struggling to decipher the origin of life by making cultures of swamp substances in which animal and vegetable life swarm in their primordial links. And what can be said about the ancient French naturalist, a true encyclopedia of anecdotes, who comes and goes along the edges of the river, studying the life of the beetles and the phylogeny of the animals. I am a good friend of the three of them. Periodically I visit them because their science constantly gives me very valuable information and because their activities are pleasant and instructive. They know how to find distinctions that pass unperceived to the rest of men, and natural laws that seem absurd. The three are great humorists and indefatigable conversationalists. Who would imagine, on passing along this river, that its margins would shelter outstanding scholars, whose work is felt in the best scientific centers by the contributions that these men bring to their progress!"

The personality of Sangama had taken on prestige before my eyes. I realized very well that his staying in the jungle was due to powerful reasons related to some undertaking of major portent. Therefore, from that day I dedicated myself to observing his life. Frequently he went into different parts of the jungle, returning very late in the night.

One time, on seeing him depart, Chuya informed me:

"When Papa enters the forest, we do not get upset, because we have the assurance that nothing bad will happen to him. When crossing dangerous places, he whistles with the intonation proper to the situation. The serpents, upon hearing him, coil themselves up and, with their heads resting on their coils, watch him pass peacefully because he has communicated messages of peace to them; and even the treacherous jaguars, which hide in the low branches of trees in wait for prey to pass within their reach, come down submissively and follow the man who gives them part of his hunt, offering them words of friendship. Therefore he can dedicate himself tranquilly to the examination of the strange climbing vines that purify the blood, to the roots that enrich it, to the aquatic plants that prolong life and renew energy, to those that give instant death, to the mushroom that cures the evil eye, the tuber that heals injuries, and the leaves that they say predispose one to love . . . Only when some man calls him, sounding his horn from the opposite bank of the lake to signal that some dying person is asking for his presence, do we wait anxiously for his return."

At times Sangama would be fishing in the lake.

"What is he doing there on the shore, as still as a fallen tree, with that little net suitable for catching butterflies?" I asked one time.

"He's fishing . . . The fish come close, attracted by a whistle, and come to the surface of the water. Thus it is very easy to capture them with the net."

"A whistle? Do the fish like music?"

"It's not a matter of music such as we know and perform it. It's an imitation of the language of the fish. On many occasions Papa has told me that it is enough to bring the ear to the surface of the water, or to submerge oneself in it, to perceive this language and learn to imitate it. Look, you can see how he returns with a full basket! And it's hardly a moment since he left."

Every day a new aspect of Sangama revealed itself to me. Undoubtedly, this man knew all the secrets of the jungle and the characteristics of its varied fauna and infinite flora. I even came to attribute to him, as did many of the simple dwellers of Santa Inés, the supernatural talents that made them take him for a sorcerer.

One day, not without overcoming a certain hesitation, I asked Chuya:

"And is it true that he flies and stays submerged in the water as if it were his element . . . ?"

“Fly? No! In the lake he does accomplish great feats. He is a great swimmer . . . The only thing mysterious and strange that I note in him are the periodic long excursions he makes to the wilderness. I believe that the long stay is due to the *ayahuasca*. Each year he disappears in the season, after begging us not to be alarmed by his long absence. One time he confessed to me that he was going to take that potion. From his reports I managed to find out the technique of its administration. One should find a plant that has never been disturbed by human eyes, and after making the potion and drinking it, the patient needs to remain in a lethargic state an extended time. For that, one constructs a small hut. Once one is awake, it is obligatory to observe a rigorous diet that contributes to the entire organism, saturating oneself with the essence of the vines. Only in this way, according to him, does one experience the prodigious effects. He returns thin, worn out, with a vague look, as if he were seeing something fascinating beyond the reach of his vision.”

“And, on those occasions, have you heard him talk of the Great Cause, of the Restoration of the Empire, of the Idol?”

“Exactly. It appears that he is dreaming awake. Perhaps he leaves some of his sanity in the jungle . . . It even frightens me!”

Chapter 17

On one occasion I had the opportunity to accompany Sangama, who was making an effort to reveal to me the secrets of the jungle, on a visit he made to a Chama village.

"For nothing in the world would they pardon me if I were to miss their annual festival," he told me in a low voice the evening before our departure. "They are very sensitive and would take it as an insult on my part. On the other hand, it is a question of some very interesting and entertaining things. I assure you that it is going to be to your liking."

"And Chuya isn't coming?"

"No. She knows nothing about such a festival, and besides, it is inappropriate for young ladies. You will soon realize this . . ."

My curiosity piqued, I accepted the invitation. Chuya, who saw us make the preparations, was burning with desire to know where her father was taking me, but despite my constant effort to please her in all that was within my power, I believed myself correct in being silent. Nor did she venture to ask, hiding her curiosity as much as she could, and she appeared to be in agreement when we left.

Sangama knew the route perfectly. We entered a narrow channel that exited from one end of the lake near the house. We then entered another, larger lake covered almost entirely by aquatic plants that were completely intertwined. With substantial difficulty we succeeded in crossing it, opening a passage for the canoe on the dense surface, and we then entered the clear waters under the shadow of the waterside trees. Navigating with ease, we skirted the extensive shoreline and came upon a wide channel, which most resembled a flooded road, by which we continued directly to the village we proposed to visit.

The monotonous sound of drums, which became more intense as we advanced, brought us to the place where the Chamas had gathered.

The arrival of Sangama was the cause of great joy. With special attention, we were led to the main house, in which the men, seated on the ground and forming a circle, drank continuous *mocahuas*[14] of tasty fermented *chicha*.

They directed us to a place at the side of the Cacique Uque, who informed us that the festivities had already begun. Sangama spoke with naturalness and ease, showing that his relations with the members of the tribe were cordial and that he spoke their language fluently.

Two young Indian girls approached us solicitously and offered us *mocahuas* of *chicha* that we drank with sufficient pleasure. The ceramic vessels being used attracted my attention because of the originality of the designs that adorned them, which, for the most part, were composed of straight lines with varied and vivid colors. Since then, I have remembered many of those designs for their similarity to the ornamental stylizations that the Egyptians used in ancient times.

"Now we are going to witness the competition," Sangama informed me, translating what Uque told him. "Ampu, the prettiest and most sought-after girl of the tribe, is going to be given as a prize to whichever of her suitors comes out as the winner. We'll see who will win her."

The competition consisted of a tournament of skill in the handling of weapons in hunting or in fishing. In this way the suitors demonstrated their ability to satisfy the basic needs of the home.

This time hunting constituted the proof. The aspirants gathered at a determined distance from the site where the prey had to pass by, with each one's arrows painted a distinct color in order to identify them once launched. At the agreed signal, they drew the bows, adorned with colorful fringes of feathers, and prepared for the

---

[14] *Mocahua:* a terra-cotta container with a wide mouth, from which the Chamas poured the chicha.

action. Quickly a javelina appeared, turned loose and fleeing toward the wilderness. The arrows crossed through the air, whistling, and several lodged in the body of the animal, which fell dead almost immediately. The elders examined the victim and, after detailed comparisons, calculations, and wise disputations, agreed that the deadly arrow had been shot by Muri, a handsome young man who was proclaimed the winner.

But the victory had to be confirmed by a test of courage and stoicism. Muri was surrounded immediately by all his rivals, who, as if they were infuriated and determined to victimize him, pulled out and displayed their curved, sharp *ushates*[15] and lunged at him, dealing him many cuts in the scalp without his showing the least sign of protest or pain, thus demonstrating his physical strength and iron will in full view of all those gathered there. As the cuts became more numerous, the blood burst forth profusely, running all over his red-stained body, which acquired a savage beauty. His defiant gaze was becoming glazed little by little, and his face, until then expressionless, contracted finally in a grimace of pain. His strength exhausted by the hemorrhaging, his knees gave way and he collapsed to the earth, rolling in his own blood. He made an extreme effort to rise but ended up falling in a dead faint. Placated, his adversaries, separated, shouting:

"Let Ampu heal you! Let Ampu heal you!"

"Why this torture?" I asked Sangama.

Shrugging his shoulders, he answered:

"They say that it's very healthy. The young men of this tribe temper their character in this manner."

The bride, apparently proud to have been won in this manner, approached Muri and undertook, lovingly and diligently, to stanch the wounds incurred for her love.

The principal objective of the annual fiesta of the Chamas, as far as I could tell, is to carry out marriages of young people who had reached a suitable age. All those who arrive at that age must contract

---

[15] *Ushate:* a short curved knife, sharpened on the interior edge of the curve.

marriage on this occasion.

Upon waking up the following day, we witnessed how justice is carried out among the Chamas. All the old men of the tribe sat in the yard, forming a great circle around the offender and the aggrieved, who had to apply the punishment. The order being given by the oldest of them, the accuser attacked the offender, cutting him with an *ushate* all over his body except in the vital parts, which had to be respected. When the accuser had him exhausted on the ground, almost dying, the old men consulted, showing themselves to be satisfied. Then the Cacique Uque ordered the punishment to stop. After the barbarous punishment, the accuser had to forget the offense, because once the fiestas had ended, all offenses were pardoned.

One day later, having finished a banquet that was served in our honor, and at which fresh game meat, fish, yucca, and, above all, *chicha* abounded, we undertook our return, being sent off with an effusive display by the tribe en masse, to the harmonies of fifes and drums.

In the jungle, the spirit is toughened. For that reason, the tests that I had witnessed did not impress me much. I knew that the tribes that were spread among the swamps and forests had a series of unique customs more or less as strange as those of the Chamas. As soon as we said our farewells, a meditative relaxation hit me. To distract me, Sangama kept talking to me during the trip about the tribes that he knew.

"The Chamas are not the most original in their customs. We have the Huitotos, for example, whose women give birth in water like fish. A woman comes out of the river with her infant in her arms, and she heads to the little hut where, upon seeing her arrive, the husband pretends pains, grabs his head, and goes to bed with the infant. He then receives the congratulations of the neighbors while the woman undertakes carrying out the domestic chores, apparently with the recent birth having had no effect on her. The most remarkable thing is that she makes a great effort to prepare special food for the loafer, which he gulps down, appearing to suffer the exhaustion of the birth."

“That custom is ridiculous, but not as savage as that which we have just witnessed . . .”

“The most bloody and fierce are the Jibaros,” he interrupted me. “As a form of personal decoration, they display, hung from the neck, the heads of their decapitated enemies, reduced to the size of a clenched fist by a method that they keep in absolute secrecy. There are tribes that deform the head of their children so that when the become adults, they exhibit an upward prolongation in the form of a cone. Others sharpen their teeth by filing them with stone to the point of converting their teeth to a saw blade. Evidently, their aesthetic sense is very different from ours, which, on the other hand, should not surprise us much, since going through the world, we would also find a sufficient number of strange customs among civilized people. Without going very far, there are people who, as a sign of mourning, dress in white, there are others who dress in red, and those who prefer black are very common.”

In spite of the state of my spirits, predisposed only to meditation, I could not avoid a smile. Sangama also smiled and, to promote even more the good humor that he believed he had provoked in me, added:

“Among the civilized people it is indispensable to cinch up the pants well when one goes to carry out a violent act or to enter combat, believing that having them well tightened will increase agility and courage. In Asia, however, there exists a people whose men, to attack their enemies, lower their pants and, in the fiercest combat, remove them completely. If we undertake to search for strange things in the world, we will come upon trees that don’t give shade, mammals that live in water like fish, and birds without wings to fly.”

Chapter 18

My stay in Sangama's house was extended, to my great delight, as much for the generosity with which I was treated as for the good fortune to be with Chuya. But, as content as I was, I understood that this situation could not be prolonged indefinitely. I made frequent trips to Santa Inés to keep myself current as to what was occurring there. I was informed that the life in the village had returned to being as tranquil and happy as they said it was before the evil Portunduaga appeared to unleash the series of events that we have just narrated. The Bull and the Piquicho had reappeared and constituted the only reason for apprehension. Trustworthy news coming from Iquitos gave hope for the prompt arrival of the authorities and of a capitalist who, they assured, had acquired the ownership of the Governor's *shiringales* and who proposed to undertake large-scale exploitation of the raw rubber.

Taking advantage of the free hours left to me by Chuya, in whose loving company I passed the most time possible working out plans, I undertook some minor chores that Sangama entrusted to me at my request. Thus passed the days and the months.

One morning I had remained alone after Sangama's departure to one of his mysterious and frequent excursions. I was waiting impatiently for Chuya to appear at the rail to renew our dialogue of love and continue weaving the fine fabric of our dreams, when I heard the penetrating sound of a horn that came from the opposite edge of the lake, where a canoe was departing, rowing at top speed.

It didn't us take long to recognize the likable and happy Matero

Luna, whom I received with affection and curiosity. Sangama also made his appearance, attracted by the call, which he heard when he had not yet gone far from the house.

"I didn't want to break the custom of calling before coming here," he told us while he received our enthusiastic embraces, after having greeted Chuya courteously. Immediately turning to me, he added:

"I have come with the mission to bring you back. Señor Rojas is impatient to speak with you."

"Who is this Señor Rojas?" I inquired, perplexed.

"Well, he's the successor to Portunduaga!"

"In the Government House?"

"No way! He is the new owner the *shiringales* and the warehouses. The personal effects of Portunduaga and the strongbox have been taken to Iquitos. Señor Rojas has been in Santa Inés six days now. He wants to see you!"

I agreed to leave immediately. Something told me that the hour so long awaited was now tolling in the clock of my life. Promising Chuya to return very soon, I bid her farewell without paying attention to the side conversation going on between Sangama and the Matero, who were speaking together in low voices.

Luna gave me little advance information during the brief trip. It appeared that Rojas was a sufficiently cultured person. During the days that he had been in Santa Inés, he had not arranged or ordered anything, limiting himself to asking for information and taking notes.

He gave me a warm welcome. His fine manners revealed a man of the world who was familiar with business. In very few words he explained to me that he had acquired those interests upon his return from Europe, and he had just come to take possession of them and engage someone who would represent him in their administration.

"You have been highly recommended to me in Iquitos," he told me. "I have come with the assurance of finding in you the man that I need. Everyone here has confirmed those references, especially this congenial Luna. I don't exactly need an employee . . . I wish to offer you something better: a partnership in my businesses on this river.

We are in the midst of a vast jungle, unexplored and rich in rubber, it appears. We should undertake its exploitation on the grandest scale . . . I know that Luna's father has left to search in the *renacal,* where he hoped to find large areas of *shiringas*. They tell me that this is at a point somewhere between this river and the Huallaga River. And since Luna's father has not returned, notwithstanding the passage of a year, we can start by going to his aid. I will cover all the costs. As for you, who will be my absolute representative in this place, you will have one-half of the *shiringales* that you are able to put together, starting from today. Do you agree?"

Certainly I agreed! I seemed to be dreaming. I delayed very little in expressing my enthusiastic acceptance. All the problems of my life seemed resolved. Soon, very soon, I would be able to marry Chuya and consider myself the happiest man in the world.

The contract having been executed, I dedicated myself to preparing the expedition. When all was ready and we awaited only the order of Don Ramón Rojas to depart, a request by him suddenly snatched the happiness away from me.

"Everyone has a bad opinion of those poor devils, the Bull and the Piquicho, who have come to me humbly asking for work. They ask that we have concern for them and protect them because they are dying of hunger and are involved in the inquiry that is proceeding concerning the crimes of the famous Governor and his death. I know that they won't do as *shiringueros,* but it seems to me that they can be useful in this expedition. They appear to be very submissive men . . ."

Stunned, I rejected the proposal outright. But Don Ramón was able to overcome my reservations. On the other hand, it was proverbial that the virgin jungle tamed even the most unruly. "What harm could that pair of human rags do, defeated by hunger and vice?" he asked.

The Matero, who was to be the soul of the work of exploration, received the news with a groan of displeasure.

"This is becoming very ugly," he said to me in open disagreement. "And the worst is that Sangama is not going to agree."

"What does Sangama have to do with this matter?" I asked intrigued.

"He is going with us! And also the Señorita Rosa . . . or Chuya, as you call her. All is arranged with the approval of Don Ramón."

The news left me perplexed. Incredulous, I replied:

"Don't joke, man. Sangama hasn't told me anything."

"We were going to tell you right now. Here he is. Ask him."

Sangama, appearing satisfied, confirmed the plan to me as if it were a matter of the most natural thing in the world.

"It's true," he responded to my question. "For some time now I have been waiting for an good opportunity to cross the jungle in the direction of the Huallaga."

"And I . . . ? Didn't you know about it, Sangama . . . ?"

"Yes, I know something . . . And I am happy with the affection that you two have for each other. I believe that you are the man that she needs . . . but I think there is something much more important than drawing sap from tree trunks by torturing them with slashes. Something that has historic transcendence . . ."

For a moment I believed that Sangama was crazy. Why was he relating the great undertaking that he was proposing with this simple exploration of the *renacal*?

"Please explain. I don't understand what you are trying to tell me."

"You will know all in due time. Then, I am sure, you will leave all of this and you will follow our destiny."

Sangama pronounced the last words with a certain fascinating and prophetic expression, which left me baffled.

" I don't know what is involved, nor will I insist in knowing it, but I will go with you two to the end of the world," I affirmed energetically.

"That is what I expected of you!" he replied, full of satisfaction. "Chuya, with whom I have already spoken about the journey, will be very happy to know it. I'm going to tell her that . . . But first, what is the problem in bringing those two men? We have already seen how to make them useful. Señor Rojas has just finished talking to me about it, and it seems to me that he is right. They are our fellow human beings, and if we abandon them, they will be lost, since there are many people here who are prepared to take vengeance against them."

I was overwhelmed. With Chuya along, the question of the Bull and the Piquicho became even more complicated.

"The company of those two does not please me at all," I communicated to the Matero when we were alone. "Their stares make Chuya blush."

But Luna, already in agreement, replied:

"They don't know the wilderness. There they will be like two tame dogs."

For the departure, we had to await the arrival of the steamboat that would tow us to Puca-Curo, the closest point to the mouth of a narrow navigable river. From there we would then proceed by another route that was apparently wise to follow by rowing against the current up the Pacaya, the navigation of which would be long and painful.

The riverboat arrived, and we boarded. Our happiness was such that we spent the evening dancing and singing with the other passengers to the chords of a guitar masterfully strummed by one of the engine crew.

Chuya was the object of much special attention that, even though it flattered me at first, ended up making me feel the stabs of jealousy for the first time.

At dawn the steamboat stopped, and on the near shore appeared the mouth of the channel, opening like a gigantic jaw. Through it, shortly thereafter, the jungle swallowed us.

Chapter 19

After a day of struggle with the treacherous current and the steep riverbanks that, from place to place, seemed to oppose our navigation, night caught us at a point called El Varadero. This was a path of some width that crossed an isthmus between two lakes, covered for its entire area by small logs that served, like rollers, to help move any cargo. The following day we transported the canoe and the cargo by this path.

From that point I began to lament the presence of the Bull and the Piquicho, that pair of individuals in whom one could not place any confidence whatsoever. They lazily carried the smallest burdens, and they resisted orders or carried them out incorrectly. It appeared that they were motivated by the goal of being an obstacle for everything. The porters, their companions, viewed them with suspicious contempt.

As soon as we were able to establish ourselves on the edge of the other lake, we fell into the improvised beds, worn down by fatigue. All remained soundly asleep while I stayed vigilant, fearful that the Bull and the Piquicho would play some trick on us. I don't know if I succeeded in sleeping a few moments, but what is certain is that each time they changed position, my eyes, open and attentive, were fixed on their deformed bodies asleep under the mosquito netting, following their every movement.

Very early in the morning, we started the navigation, crossing the lake and entering a wide channel of deep water, whose irregular shores appeared to have suffered a violent geological transformation. Both banks were covered with low-lying vegetation of multicolored plants, from which protruded bushes with short trunks, and decaying grasses and ferns. Above that compact brush, one could distinguish scattered trunks of dead trees, which protruded like deformed blackened amputated arms, pointing ghostlike to the heights.

Lacking living trees, the channel passed through a land without shade, which, in this infernally hot tropical zone wrapped in soporific vapors, made the navigation unbearable and very slow. There were no signs of birds or other species of large animals, only very small lizards and a wide variety of pesky insects swarming about the interminable sinkholes, in which the mud seemed to boil without leaving even the slightest piece of firm ground visible. The slow and rhythmic beating of our oars interrupted the overwhelming silence of nature. The rowers, knowledgeable of the place and confident of the famous expertise of the Matero, were not disturbed, and only the Bull bellowed in a tiresome manner and the Piquicho screeched. A small frame covered by palm leaves in the center of the canoe protected Chuya and the old woman Ana, sleepy from the mugginess. It was as if the silence of the countryside had infiltrated our souls, rendering them mute.

The curves of the channel stretched forth, hardly definable. The continuous current had to be overcome by force of the oars, without stopping for an instant. The distances grew longer. It was as if we were navigating over a dense liquid that the canoe cut through with great effort.

"In this channel we won't find a place to tie up and prepare food!" I shouted from the stern, upon seeing that midday was approaching and that hunger and fatigue were overcoming us.

"We will arrive soon at 'Padre Micunan' (Where the Padre Had Lunch)," the Matero announced. "There are only a pair of turns left farther upriver. Let's go on!"

In the rivers of the jungle, the river dwellers measure the distances by curves that the waters pass by in their journey. This manner of determining the distance results in a disconcerting arbitrariness, since some long turns can equal several short ones. But there is no other way to refer to the distance already covered or yet to advance.

"We have a while," I grumbled, distrustful because of previous experiences.

But, as all comes to an end in this world, after a period of time that seemed to me longer than it really was, the point man, Fababa, extended his arm, pointing:

"There it is . . . !"

There was a little tree with knotty branches that grew, surrounded by mud, on a small piece of solid land on which not more than four persons would fit. We had to take turns to stretch our legs and remove the numbness. The porters hurried to prepare the cooking pot in the canoe. The dog Sultan, prevented from wandering, limited himself to rolling and shaking, and then sniffing about the surrounding mud distrustfully. So that there would be sufficient space to make a fire, all of us except one had to return to the canoe.

At the Matero's urging, we restarted the painful trip as soon as the frugal lunch was finished, because, as he explained, the distance to advance each day was great and we should not take the chance of passing the night in the channel.

"From here we go to 'Padre Samacunan' (Where the Padre Rested) and from there to 'Padre Ishpanan' (Where the Padre Made Waters)," he had informed us, "basic points at which the canoe can stop on these riverbanks made up of quagmires."

Surely in times already long past, some Missionary, on a trip of exploration, was going ashore at those places his companions baptized in accordance with what he did in each of those places.

The first of the places mentioned by the Matero turned out to be a narrow flooded place, which the canoe was able to penetrate and where it could receive a bit of shade; the second, a tree whose strong roots extended over the mud, offering a conventional point of support. As one of the rowers showed great urgency to disembark, Luna hurried to warn him:

"Here one can't . . . it is very obvious. Further on, at 'Padre Ismanan' (Where the Padre Did It . . .)."

This last site turned out to be a thick log, almost fossilized, with one end submerged in the channel and the other end lost, sunken among the brush. The rower had to carry out a huge battle with pests and mosquitoes.

We passed the night at "Padre Puñunan" (Where the Padre Slept), a piece of sufficiently clean solid land among a mass of trees. We prepared the beds, and after eating lightly, we got together to exchange impressions at the edge of the shore, since the weariness, far from producing sleep, kept us up awake.

As Sangama and the Matero smoked while discussing topics related to the nature that surrounded us, Chuya and I, seated closely together, watched in silence the waters of the channel, which reflected the majesty of the tropical sky, sparkling with stars. The vegetation of both shores, covered with silvery and brilliant projections, gave the sensation that we had camped in an extraterrestrial place. The voice of Sangama, who was explaining to the Matero, drew me out of that contemplative mood:

"You know, friend," he was saying to him, "we are on lands in the process of formation. Millions of years ago—and this is not a fantasy, since in geology the more one speaks of millions, the closer one will be to the truth—the earth on which now flourishes the most advanced civilization must have had this same appearance. The tropical jungle is becoming conditioned little by little for the dwelling of mankind, but that is not the labor of decades nor of centuries. Geological evolution is not measured in time, which is related to astronomy. What changes will the jungle undergo in space and time? Nobody knows. What is beyond doubt is that in the past this zone constituted the deepest part of a sea locked in the heart of South America, which the muddy flow of the Ucayali and the Huallaga and their multiple tributaries have been filling with material transported, in fabulous quantities, from the mountain ranges and their foothills. The muddy summer waters with their sediments and the jungle itself with its branches and trunks hurried the geological action. If we were to dig here, we would find vestiges of marine fauna, those fossils that are found in lands in the process of formation and that belong to species evidently nonexistent in the rivers these days . . . The inhabitants of the heights and the intermountain meadows are moving toward the river basin as new lands are formed, and the proof of that is that, apart from the ocelot, that fierce wildcat predator of hens and piglets, none of the animal species that form an integral part of the jungle fauna has yet arrived here, such as the jaguar, the largest of the cats and one of the early inhabitants of the mountain area, to judge by its presence in Andean ceramics. The fantastic exuberance of the jungle that we have just left, and that very soon we will see again, is in the process of formation and appears to have the disorder of madness before the collective harmony of nature. Farther on we will encounter, if I am not mistaken, surface zones more ancient, but still relatively recent if one compares them with the other parts of the continent. The one hundred and some inches of water that fall here each year and the enormous quantity of flood materials that the rivers leave are enough to make the peculiar appearance of the jungle change constantly . . . ! Look! What can you say, my friend Luna, of the places through which we have just passed? Have you seen the thick low brush over deep sinkholes, across whose closely woven diverse vegetation not even a snake could open a passage? And those worm-eaten trunks that rise up over it like tragic mutilated crosses?"

Sangama's voice, waxing eloquent, had attracted everyone's attention. Only the Bull and the Piquicho showed no interest and, turning over in their beds of leaves, were murmuring a display of their distaste. Sangama spoke of things so strange that, even if they were not understood in their totality, were interesting to hear.

As if catching his breath to continue, or perhaps searching for some new idea to develop or concept to expound, Sangama made a prolonged pause, at the end of which I searched his face, and in his expression I noted great discouragement. He was looking pained at the Matero, who, to judge by his deep and noisy breathing, had fallen asleep. Sangama shook him to the point that he believed he had woken him and, as he appeared to have taken on one of his accustomed excesses of loquacity, again started to question the Matero insinuatingly:

"What do you think, little Matero, about the migrations? Or, speaking in other terms, did men come out of the jungle or did they move into it?"

"Upriver . . . ? Downriver . . . ?" asked Luna, half asleep.

"This poor man has no concept of life other than that which the Ucayali River imposes on him," Sangama observed in a commiserating tone. But not wishing to consider himself defeated, he insisted in shaking the Matero. "Come on! Pay attention a moment! What explanation do you give for these dead trees in this extraordinary jungle?"

"Yes, yes," answered Luna, trying to open his eyes. "The dead ones in the strange tree . . . Now I remember! You taught me, telling me that the trunk had been decapitated . . . and, moreover, there were others who were decapitated as patriots and heretics . . ."

The shout that Sangama let out completely shocked his companion. It was the protest of the disappointed man of wisdom. And, regretting his attitude, he responded by asking paternally:

"Keep sleeping, my friend Luna. I wasn't exactly referring to my genealogical tree. Sleep . . . You don't understand these things!"

The Matero attempted to make amends:

"It's just that here we can't know what you are talking about. Beyond our grandparents, we don't know who existed and what they did . . . Perhaps they have done nothing good, and for that they were decapitated. Perhaps our grandchildren would do something . . . God spare them . . . !"

"Sleep, friend, sleep . . . ," insisted Sangama. "You don't have the slightest idea of what lineage, heritage, and nobility mean. You don't know, poor friend, the relationship of causes and effects that govern life, according to which the powerful lion and the elemental leech cannot have the same origin, nor the gigantic oak and the vile *renaco*."

The truth was that in front of Sangama I felt more and more in the presence of an enigmatic and unusual being. Extraordinary woodsman, he hunted and fished with exceptional skill. The dense wilderness was his medium; he climbed the trees with the agility of the most skilled bushman and was a master at imitating the calls of all the animals. By observing him up close, it was possible to notice that during his periods of silence a deep spiritual unease frequently possessed him, as if storms were being unleashed in his soul. On the other hand, at times he became very talkative, affable, and communicative, especially under the moonlit nights. Analytical by temperament, he created for himself a type of science that explained in simple terms the natural phenomena that in the jungle constituted obscure mysteries for others. Sometimes he appeared almost naive; at other times, clever and sullen. He was, paradoxically, absent-minded and perfectionistic, religious and heretical, skeptic and believer—a true enigma and contradiction! Even his true name was unknown, but, on the other hand, nobody was interested in finding it out.

He had remained silent, smoking nervously while the Matero slept with his head supported on a tree. As I looked at his face, which the playing of lights and shadows filled with changing lines, his expression seemed to me to reveal a profound distress.

I started to feel sleepy. Chuya, leaning back on my shoulder, had closed her eyes. By her breathing, tranquil and rhythmic, I knew that she was asleep.

The shouts of the Piquicho and the Bull, who sat up alarmed, caused us to look toward the place that they indicated. A brilliant stain was advancing toward us, covering the entire width of the channel. We all jumped to our feet, startled. As it approached, we could distinguish that it was formed by an infinity of luminous points endowed with great mobility.

"Don't be afraid! Don't be afraid!" shouted Sangama: "It is the *mijanada*!"

In effect it was a great mass of fish that was moving in a compact formation. Using oars, machetes, and even simple sticks, we set ourselves to fishing. After a successful catch, we fell into a restorative sleep.

Chapter 20

The countryside we passed through the following day was almost all the same. The Bull and the Piquicho amounted to a useless dead weight that we dragged along, much to our sorrow. But they appeared to be docile, because they understood, without a doubt, their small value in such circumstances. Unarmed and afflicted by the lack of alcohol, they moved with great effort, exchanging painful glances between them. They understood very well that, in spite of the painful nature of the journey, they were at least free of the dangers that staying in Santa Inés would have meant for them. Even their voracious hunger had diminished, and frequently it was necessary to require them to take rations. With good reason the Matero had said: "In the jungle they will become as tame as two dogs."

Without noteworthy incidents, we arrived at the Pacaya River, whose clear and rapid waters were starting to ebb due to the end of the rainy season at that time.

When the night arrived, we had already made camp in a *shiringuero* post. The next day, we left two of the rowers there so that they could proceed with the rubber extraction, which appeared easy in that place. At the break of dawn we were again in the canoe, but this time we went with the current, and almost all the effort was reduced to taking care that our craft stayed in the center of the river. In the evening we entered the mouth of a tributary that would lead us to the very heart of the unknown jungle. The entrance looked like a gigantic tunnel drilled through a dense green mass. I confess that when we passed through that large opening, I felt the fear of the unknown. To increase the unease that came over me, the *chicua* made its appearance, that bird of ill omen so detested by the jungle dwellers and whose raucous laugh is considered an ill-fated portent. The dog increased my discomfort by responding to the *chicua* with long, mournful howls.

"A bad sign! A bad sign!" said the superstitious Matero.

Sangama himself adopted a pensive air. Fortunately, the caresses of Chuya and the old woman Ana quickly placated the terrorized Sultan, and the various sounds of the forest and waters made us forget the noisy raucous laugh of the worthless creature.

The canoe, relieved of the weight of the two rowers we had left behind, overcame the current with sufficient agility. To the errors made by the Bull and the Piquicho we owed continuous stops to avoid being caught in the low-lying branches woven above us. If it had not been for the opposition of Sangama, I would have abandoned them to their fate anywhere. What irritated me most were the frequent stares, full of savage appetite, that they cast at Chuya.

It was many years ago, as a very young man, that I carried out that ill-fated trip. And even if I remember it today with the clarity of the unforgettable, I declare that many of the details cannot be narrated with exhaustive accuracy. I have noted that some of the distances were unmeasured and that there were events whose preciseness lacks clarity. One or another deficiency should be forgiven in acknowledgment of the fact that the awesome drama that I lived is disclosed with total fidelity.

The next day, the difficulties grew. At each step, we encountered trees fallen across our path from one side to the other. According to the circumstances, we would either totally empty the canoe with the most painful effort, depositing the baggage on the shore, and then submerge the canoe and pass it under the obstacle, or we would drag the canoe over the log, using the bark of the *cetico.* When moistened, that bark produces a viscous substance on its internal surface that makes it extremely slippery. Without employing this aid, discovered by the Indians, many times we would not have been able to overcome the barriers that confronted us.

At night we would camp on some riverbank where we set up

beds on layers of dead leaves and palm branches, under the indispensable mosquito nets. We always had to secure the canoe firmly with long vines as a precaution against its being dragged away by the current or being left on dry land if the water flow dropped during the night.

One time we spent the night on a narrow strip of land that extended between the creek and a swampy lagoon. At midnight I woke up, startled. An enormous body, cold and slimy and moving slowly behind the mosquito netting, was pressing my head. Without realizing what it was, I jumped up in alarm, calling to Sangama and the Matero. The latter quickly lit a lamp in whose light we saw that it was a huge anaconda, which, having come out of the swamp, was slowly submerging itself in the river.

Sangama took up his machete and headed resolutely toward the serpent, glancing over the entire visible part of it as if he were calculating its dimensions.

"Careful! It could catch you!" I shouted.

"The larger these animals are, the slower," he answered me calmly. "Moreover, it already has its head in the water, which makes it harmless."

And to our astonishment, he almost divided the enormous mass of muscles with a fierce machete chop. Three or four more slashes finished the task by cutting it apart completely.

"There's no more danger," assured Sangama, while he cleaned the machete that had been employed with such efficiency.

The Matero diligently proceeded to move my bed to another location.

This hair-raising scene had unfolded in silence, but everyone had shown up to witness it. Chuya and her old caretaker appeared terrified, but thanks to Sangama's serenity, an apparent calm returned. However, a certain wariness continued to show on all the faces.

From that moment, very few were able to sleep. In the darkness I heard all the sounds and movements, and I could clearly distinguish the sighs of the women and the panting of the Bull and the Piquicho.

The next day we found something unexpected. Passing near a

mountain of fallen, piled-up tree trunks that formed a fenced enclosure, we heard weak howls. Sultan, his hair standing on end from neck to tail, leapt from the canoe, sniffed a scent, and proceeded cautiously in the direction from which it came. The Matero followed him anxiously. Fearful, we saw them move away from us. A choked exclamation, a mixture of happiness, pain, and surprise, left us paralyzed. Sultan reinforced that exclamation with a strong, prolonged barking. We set out, intent on rescuing the Matero, who had disappeared among the trees, when we saw him reappear, carrying a starving dog in his arms.

"Litero!" exclaimed Luna upon recognizing him. "Where's my father?"

We surrounded the animal instantly. One of the porters brought some small pieces of fish, which the dog devoured avidly while showing his happiness by wagging his tail. The Matero caressed him, without ceasing to ask him:

"Where's my father? Where has the old man gone?"

As if he understood, the dog left the food and went to scratch on a piece of wood, almost hidden in the enclosed area, which it was not hard to recognize as the remains of a canoe.

"The old man's canoe!" affirmed Luna, stunned.

"The elder Luna's dog!" added Sangama. "Faithful to the end."

"What would he tell us if he could speak?" I asked thoughtfully.

The dog regained his spirits, apparently more from the satisfaction of finding himself with the Matero than from the food consumed, and was whimpering with happiness. Frequently he raised his head, looking upriver.

Brought aboard, Litero voluntarily occupied the bow of the craft, always looking ahead and with the clear intention of leaping to shore as soon as he would come upon the place he was seeking. At every stop, Litero was the first to disembark and would sniff about the area with obvious unease, always finding some track or mark left behind. Sangama examined in detail the places indicated by the dog, and he found evidence of the old explorer whom we sought. It could be said that Litero was the guide we obeyed in those hours.

Thus we arrived at narrow spot where the trees had been cut, a clear sign that men lived nearby. Entering by a narrow pathway that climbed up the ravine, we came upon a piece of cleared wilderness in which the brush was fighting to take root. In the center stood an abandoned shack. Litero barked furiously. Sultan followed him from one place to another, growling and with his fur standing on end.

"The shack is my old man's!" exclaimed Luna, pierced with anxiety and fear.

We merely followed Luna. Bunches of colorful feathers were hanging on the walls, dry provisions wrapped in leaves, and, in one corner, an empty and unkempt bed that the Matero recognized as that of his father. Here and there, scattered in disarray across the floor, were some garments and assorted utensils. On one side of the shack, under a small cover made of branches, was a fireplace, over which a small pot hung from a wooden hook. The quantity of ashes revealed that firewood had been burnt there over a long period.

There was very little that we could say. Surely we were on the trail of the missing man, but the surprise that awaited us could well be pleasant or unpleasant.

Outside of the shack, several bunches of sugarcane had been seeded, and some withered papaya trees were dying, choked by the underbrush. On a tree stump there was a sharpening stone, worn by use. Silently we examined the surrounding area. One of the rowers discovered a narrow path that, like a sign, pointed to the mysterious heart of the jungle.

"Old man! Where are you?" shouted Luna with all his strength.

Sangama, compassionate, put his hand on the man's shoulder, telling him:

"Don't yell. Nobody will answer you. It has been eight months at least since this site was abandoned. Let's follow that path."

We spent all that day clearing the brush around the small hut to leave an open area cleared and clean. The stove was soon smoking, and the food that we served ourselves under the covered area seemed tastier than ever.

Plans were drawn up. At my suggestion, Sangama took charge of directing the exploration.

In spite of his unease, Luna spotted the tops of several *shiringa* trees at a distance, which filled me with enthusiasm, but Sangama ended my plans to begin to set up *estradas* when he told me that Chuya, the old "mama," and Ahuanari should stay in the shack while the rest proceeded with the search for the elder Luna.

"Sultan will also stay with them. We will return very soon," he added.

The truth was that I still did not understand why Chuya had been brought this far, and I was expecting the decision that she not continue to suffer the pains of this trip, which was dangerous even for the most determined men. Several times I had said this to Chuya, but she always replied that when going with her father, she did not have the slightest fear and could endure it all. Her faith in Sangama was unlimited. The arrangement appeared reasonable to me when Sangama explained to us that night why he had adopted it.

"It would have been dangerous to leave her on the Ucayali. Here things are different. She will be safe and sheltered from risks. Our return will be a matter of a few days. Upon our return, we'll follow the current of this river, which by then will already be overflowing because of the winter rains. We'll take the *sacarita*[16] that we should find nearby, and we'll transfer to the first watercourse that leads to the Huallaga. The jungle always fondly shelters my girl."

And as I was showing sadness about the separation, he approached me paternally and added:

"Upon our return. Upon our return, we will have important matters to deal with."

During that night, which I spent wide-awake, trying to coordinate ideas and plans, the laments of the Matero and the howls of the dogs sounded in the very depths of my soul.

The tops of the trees were already golden from the sun when I went in search of Chuya, whom I found near a small creek, deeply saddened. She had just placed her head against a tree trunk and appeared to be asking something of Heaven.

"Do you know that we're departing and that we're leaving you

---

[16] *Sacarita:* a narrow channel that connects rivers and lakes and that also cuts across the base of river peninsulas.

behind?" I asked her with an uncertain voice.

"I know it!" and, sighing deeply, she continued, "I have strongly charged my father with taking care of you. Have confidence in him. He has promised to return you as you returned him one time: safe and sound."

"Are you not afraid to stay, my love?" I managed to ask.

"Doesn't this happen often in the jungle? When my father has left me before, he has always found me without anything bad having happened."

"I'll try to return quickly. How sad this trip is going to be for me!"

"I'll await you here, praying to God that all goes well with you."

"Your love will be my best guide. I will see your smile in all the flowers of the thicket, your eyes will always be watching me from the green forest, and your voice will flatter me in the soft chirping of the birds. Let me kiss you!"

"Upon your return!" she answered me, upset. She broke lose from my arms and fled, covering her beautiful face with her hands, assuredly so that I would not see her cry.

Chapter 21

The separation was very painful for me. I could not deny that it was necessary, but a sadness mixed with foreboding was taking possession of me. Upon starting the journey, I hung back and watched all of our companions pass by, one by one. When my turn arrived, I turned my gaze toward the shack, at whose doorway Chuya, motionless and serene, was watching us depart. I confess that after waving good-bye to her apprehensively, I had to close my eyes, as those who commit suicide must do when they make the fatal decision, and I advanced gropingly, plunging into the jungle. I felt the powerful desire to return to her and embrace her once again, to kiss her hands and repeat to her with emotion how much I loved her. My first steps were clumsy and unsure. I gathered my strength and hurried my step to join the others who had already gone on ahead.

The Matero had the lead on this occasion. With an accurate eye, he closely examined each tree, and his machete, brandished with expert determination, cleared the narrow path of the new branches that struggled to erase it. Hours later the path was lost at the edges of a swampy and impenetrable forest. We had to decide between crossing that expanse of jungle, which the Matero judged not to be very extensive, or circling around it. We decided on the first option, and we threw ourselves into the crossing, in a struggle with the luxuriant natural growth that had twisted together in that area to form the densest tangle of branches and roots that could be imagined. This section of the jungle had been formed with three factors that gave it peculiar characteristics: the sun, which radiated with scorching fierceness; the very frequent torrential rains; and the low terrain, completely flat, in which great quantities of organic material are deposited to ferment and decay. On top of that decomposing mass, which direct sunlight does not reach, life germinates, flourishes, and perishes. There seeds germinate among lichens, mushrooms, spores, and endophytes. In this hotbed, rare transformations occur, and new growth appears in an inexorable struggle to survive or perish. The atmosphere is dense and asphyxiating because of the continuous emanation from the waters and decomposed juices. The new tree struggles intensely, trying to open a passageway between the formidable treetops, searching for the vital space that would give it air and light; the climbing vine wraps around the trunks and branches; the lower animals employ claws, tentacles, teeth, needles, and suction cups with which they cling to life, while they secrete poisons and toxins to defend themselves. In this environment, where such unknown forces and elements struggle, one can see the most beautiful flowers in a paradoxical promiscuity, growing in the mud or clinging to the decomposing trunks that offer them sustenance. The epiphytes, such as the begonias and orchids, of countless varieties, flourish in marvelous profusion. On the surface of the swamp, ferns alternate with bamboos and reeds, in dangerous proximity to the *renacos,* whose trunks and roots extend in every direction. One notices the total lack of birds and mammals; only certain lower species of bats and an occasional hawk, a predator of snakes, venture into these places in search of food. The anaconda, wrapped around the low trunks and forming a gruesome knot, digests the prey that it obtained in the higher zones that border those swamps. In such places, where the flora and fauna of the future are formed, man can live only by passing through.

With the mud almost to our knees, we followed the Matero, who directed the march, passing closely by sinkholes and at times making us climb up on the roots that extended over the quaking bog.

In these places it is almost impossible to look out for the others. All one’s strength and attention have to work together in selfish attention to oneself. Therefore, the curses of the Bull and the howls of the Piquicho were hardly noticed. In spite of all, I realized that for them the thing was much worse than for the rest of us. I would not have been surprised to hear their laments suddenly stop and know that some sinkhole had swallowed them, which would have caused me a certain malign satisfaction. We all proceeded, using long canes of bamboo. Close to me, the Matero slipped and sank up to his thighs in the thick mud. Upon pulling him out, we noticed that his legs were totally covered with leeches that were voraciously sucking his blood. The task of freeing him was difficult. Once again Sangama showed his deep knowledge of the jungle's secrets. From the brush, he picked out some sharp-pointed leaves whose juice made all the bloodsuckers detach themselves. After rubbing his legs with those shredded leaves, Luna was able to continue the journey, following Sangama.

Suddenly the jungle became dark, and a heavy rain began to fall on us. The lack of an appropriate place to open the baggage prevented us getting our raincoats out. We continued forward, soaked and almost groping our way amid the dull sounds that the downpour made in the branches. We had to proceed onward without rest. Sangama's long cane casually touched a branch, and a nest of ants fell on Luna, breaking apart over his shoulders, and instantly his entire body was covered with very small reddish insects. The Matero, who was unlucky that day, quickly removed his baggage and clothing, a task in which we all aided him. However, in spite of our diligence, Luna's neck and ears and part of his back were covered with welts.

"It's the *puca-curo,*" said Sangama

Luna bellowed as if hot irons were touching him. I lamented that that this accident had not happened to the Bull, who revealed his evil indolence, or to the Piquicho, who limited himself to unleashing one of his loud, ratlike laughs.

These are ants that do not sting; simple contact with them burns the skin and fills it with sores. Feverish with pain, the poor Matero followed the procession, grinding his teeth.

The rain did not stop, and the woods truly became a lagoon, through which we advanced with the water up to our waists. The slimy mud boiled up around us. At times I thought I detected in the swamp the movements of the *yacumama,* stalking us.

I extended my arm to brace myself on a branch, but I noticed just in time that it was no such thing, but rather a snake that was hanging down, lying in wait for a passing victim. Fortunately it fled before I touched it. At almost the same time, Sangama killed a poisonous snake that, on sensing our approach, wound itself into a spiral, prepared to attack.

"Keep a sharp eye," counseled Sangama, "because here snakes the color of the branches abound. Look out for the *chicharra-machácuy* that are attached to the bark of the trees with their needle ready to stab.

The jungle was becoming darker and darker, and we were unable to find a suitable place to rest. Sangama, who advanced in the lead, and the Bull, who brought up the rear, lit torches, and with the aid of this flickering light we continued several hours more. If the swampy jungle was discouraging by day, in the night and in the rain, it became maddening. A moment arrived in which, losing all good judgment, I shouted at Sangama to stop.

"I can't stand any more! We are all going to die here! This will never end!"

"It's the jungle sickness that is trying to take him," Sangama said, turning to Luna. "We will stop a while until it passes."

I felt as if my head were about to explode. All the jungle filled with a reddish light, and the trees stirred in disorder, extending their branches to take me prisoner. Suddenly it became dark, and I lost consciousness.

When I returned to reality, we were on a kind of island. The Bull and the Piquicho held me by the arms on a bed of palm leaves.

"Now it's passing," commented the Matero, who did not seem to be concerned about his very swollen neck and ears.

"We'll spend the night here," Sangama decided. "We will continue at the first light of dawn."

Things finally took their natural forms and proportions after that infernal night, and I felt very relieved. With the light of the new day, the rain ceased. A little hot coffee ended up comforting me, putting me in condition to resume the march. With great happiness we finally set foot on firm land a short time later. We selected the piece of land on which we would camp. There we changed clothes and prepared breakfast.

"We committed a great blunder in crossing here," said Luna, after carefully examining the stopping place. "We have not advanced very far. It would have been better to go around on solid ground."

The rest was not very long. Starting on the expedition again, we came upon a place in which several palm trees had been cut down. Sangama examined the marks on the bark of several trees.

"The elder Luna has been here," he commented.

Standing close to him, the Matero showed great concern.

Sangama made a pathway by dint of machete blows, following the clues he found. From time to time, he brought to his lips his old *antara,* on which he played short and sad melodies of the melancholy flavor that characterizes the native playing. After each musical phrase, he coughed strongly, as if to push away the depressing influence of the notes. The chords resounded weakly in the distance, producing a sensation of anguish. Sangama listened attentively to those echoes, which acquired diverse tonalities, as if he were deducing something. He then took a decidedly new direction, cutting at an even height the branches that blocked his way. We followed him in silence, completely given over to his leadership. We passed under an imposing and very high canopy of steep treetops and over a crunching carpet of dry leaves. Sangama stopped, threw his gear on the ground, and, turning to us, said out loud:

"Now it's time to rest. The night will arrive soon."

We cleared away a patch of the thicket, collected firewood, and set up our beds. Moments later, we gathered around the crackling fire. Worn down by exhaustion, we went to bed. Only Sangama remained beside the fire. Until I fell asleep, I could contemplate his shadow, which grew and shrank at the caprice of the flames, and was able to make out the red point of his cigar in the half-light.

The next morning the Indian Fababa did not get up. Under his fallen mosquito netting we found him lifeless, his mouth overflowing with white foam. It took us a great effort to try to revive him. The Bull said he had heard him complain during the night, but he did not become alarmed because he always talked aloud between snores as he slept.

"This Fababa will give us a lot to do," commented Sangama. "He is very susceptible to suffering the jungle's influence. And because he snores, it is possible that, when least expected, some jaguar might catch him at night while he is sleeping."

It is a deeply rooted belief in the jungle that those who snore are invariably victims of jaguars. It is of no avail that they sleep in the center of the camp to protect themselves from the attacks of those astute felines. Oriented by the snores, the jaguar slips in, reaches its enormous sharp claws under the mosquito netting, and cuts the throat of its victim, whom it drags at once into the thicket.

When Fababa was able to speak, he told us that a demon had approached him during the night, tortured him with horrible gestures, and finally tore down the mosquito netting.

"It's the *chulla-chaqui,*[17] which has also been wanting to play with me," assured the Matero, without giving great importance to the event. "One of these nights we will see the tracks of his feet in the ashes."

Then he explained to us that the *chulla-chaqui* are little playful devils of the jungle; they do no harm and are distinguished by having one foot large and the other small, a deformation to which they owe their name.

The Bull and the Piquicho, whose hair was standing on end because they believed that some ghost had wanted to kill Fababa, showed great satisfaction on hearing this report. We dedicated that morning to exploring the surrounding area, searching for Luna's father.

Leaving the Bull and the Piquicho in charge of food preparations, we followed Sangama, who continued discovering marks on the tree trunks, as well as numerous branches broken uniformly. At first the accuracy with which he came upon clues

---

[17] *Chulla-chaqui:* a jungle demon with unequal feet.

seemed almost supernatural to me, but with a little effort to do so, I also could distinguish them. Following these marks, we penetrated farther and farther into this thick tangle of brush. The greatest difficulty we encountered was the existence of many signs that the Matero and Sangama interpreted as indications of bifurcations in the *trochas.*[18] Guided by instinct, we chose the route that appeared most convenient, and we continued the advance, frequently coming across creeks and little rivers that we crossed by means of bridges improvised out of weak stalks that swayed upon our passage. In those cases we had to make a prodigious effort of balancing, so as not to fall into the muddy currents.

As the tracks continued interminably and we did not encounter any evidence indicating that we were making progress, we decided to return. It surprised the Matero that his father would direct himself toward the most impenetrable part of the jungle, and the multiplicity of his tracks was not justified by the presence of any *shiringa* trees.

"Only when one proposes the formation of *estradas* does one proceed in this manner," he commented, frustrated. "This appears to go nowhere! Many times I have passed through these same places and others nearby as if I have been going in circles. We have to leave this thing for today. These marks, it turns out, were made a long time ago. The old man is no longer around here."

"It is my opinion," said Sangama, "that we should continue in the direction that we took when we left the shack. If we don't find him there, nothing will prevent us from returning to this place. Taking a shortcut, we can arrive at the old man's shack in a little less than a day."

When I heard the mention of the shack, the face of Chuya burst into my mind. Remembering her, my strength redoubled. It would be necessary to return to her side like the ancient heroes after a campaign, full of scars but upright, haughty, and proud, to put at the feet of the beloved the newly won trophies.

Engrossed in such pleasing thoughts, I could not pay attention to the conversation in which Sangama and the Matero were engaged.

---

[18] *Trocha:* a path opened by men through the jungle.

Only when they agreed on the return did I became aware again of the place where I was and the wilderness that surrounded us.

The return path was shorter. When we arrived at the place from which we had departed, the sun was already descending. We entered at the precise moment in which the Piquicho was dying of laughter. We stopped, surprised. The Bull, who was going in search of water in a nearby riverbed, turned his head, shouting:

"If you don't shut up, deformed rat, I will squash you with a stomp of my foot."

But the Piquicho continued laughing, unable to contain himself, with his peculiar raucous laugh of a deformed person.

"Ha, ha, ha, ha!"

Suddenly the Matero leaped, shouting at the Bull, who stopped. The warning was late. A snake that was at his feet rose up quickly, and we heard the loud crack of a lash that left the Bull swaying from fright and pain. The reptile disappeared quickly, vanishing into the brush along the shore.

"An *afaninga*!" exclaimed Sangama. "Fortunately, it is not a poisonous snake."

The Bull, roaring with indignation, headed toward the Piquicho, picking up his machete on the way, but the latter, as agile as a deer, ran to the wilderness and disappeared, crawling into it. But after a moment he reappeared, poking out among the branches. He approached cautiously while, with a poorly concealed smile, he was expressing himself wickedly:

"I was watching it. The Bull was going to step on it. Ha, ha, ha! The fool was looking upward. Ha, ha, ha!"

The Bull, becoming like a madman, lunged forward in a gesture as if to strangle him, but the Piquicho was much nimbler and again slipped away like a mouse in the brush.

This time he waited longer before returning. Because the Bull did not hide his anger, I believed that the friendship between the two villains had ended, which gave me no end of satisfaction, since from now on each would have to spend a great effort in watching the other. Great was my disappointment when I later saw them talking like brothers, as if nothing had happened. Even in this the jungle imposes its uniqueness. Within it the evil ones, those banished by civilization, forget their grudges and seek each other out, while in any other place they would take vengeance for the offenses that they feel.

We took advantage of the remaining hours of the afternoon to move ourselves to a stand of trees free of underbrush. It was already getting dark when we made camp among thick trees and over a soft leafy floor that invited repose.

"Here it certainly invites sleep," said the Bull, as he prepared his bed. "What a tranquil night I am going to have, finally."

How mistaken he was!

Chapter 22

We lit the fire to prepare supper, during which a discussion ensued about the incidents of the day that had just ended, and some plans were made for the following day. On the advice of the Matero, to keep away the jaguars that came following our steps, we made the bonfire larger, piling a great quantity of firewood near it so as to keep it lit all night. Sangama offered to watch the fire so that the rest of us would be able to rest without worries.

During the night I was awakened, startled by a terrifying explosion similar to a cannon shot that echoed, shaking the trees. The strong detonation was repeated with decreasing intensity in the distance.

"What's happening, Sangama?" I asked fearfully.

"It's the Sachamaman, which comes out of the *lupuna*. It will not be long before it passes here."

The quiet and serene tone with which Sangama answered me from inside his mosquito net, where he was awake, smoking, gave me a quite strange feeling but had the virtue of returning tranquillity to me. He would not seem so confident, I thought, if the impressive phenomenon constituted a danger.

But moments later, when the heavy beating of gigantic wings passing over us shook the leaves with violent gusts of air, I had the feeling that something supernatural was occurring. Silence returned to reign around us, but it was no longer possible for me to sleep. With eyes wide open, I searched among the shadows for an explanation of the phenomenon. And as I saw that Sangama had remained awake, smoking cigar after cigar, I called to him, complaining about the intensity of the heat. He suggested that we go out and sit together at the fire. There we were joined by the Matero, who also had remained awake and heard the detonation as well as the sound of the mysterious wings.

It was then that I observed the sight of the jungle in all its grandeur. Darkness did not reign there as might be supposed. Thousands of insects, which scattered a weak light, illuminated the space in a really marvelous manner. The forest appeared to be something like the interior of a fabulous palace, of immeasurable proportions and adorned with precious stonework, on whose edges infinite beams of light and brilliant colors were broken. The tall, thick tree trunks seemed liked colossal columns, the supports of domes that in the vague half-light dominating the scene seemed to reach the height of the heavens. The leaves and branches that carpeted the ground also gave off effervescent points of flickering phosphorescent light. The silence was not absolute. Shortly after this observation, I could perceive soft sounds. There, at a distance that struck me as infinite, the fireflies wove a clear gauze, as if they were trying to surround the circle of trees that enclosed us with a curtain of diffuse light.

Almost removed from reality, I remained absorbed in contemplating nature, like a child through whose imagination a fairy tale-like panorama passed. My senses continued to be paralyzed, intoxicated by a strange drowsiness that distorted and slowly erased things. Suddenly a distant scream could be heard. It was an anguished voice that seemed to ask for help. My hair stood on end, and I had the sensation that my body was growing to attain the magnitude of the jungle.

"Someone is shouting!" I exclaimed, looking for the faces of Sangama and the Matero.

"To bed . . . ! Quickly!" ordered Sangama. "And cover your ears well! It is the call of the *supay*![19]

And without giving better explanations, he ran to his bed. The Matero and I quickly followed. Wrapped up under the blankets, I

---

[19] *Supay:* Devil.

covered my ears so as not to hear anything; but sharpening my senses in spite of my wishes, I could hear the sound of swift steps near my bed. It was not possible for me to resist the mixture of fear and curiosity that took possession of me. Because the noise of the steps was followed by stomping that seemed to be from a struggle, I believed that one of my companions was in danger, and lifting the mosquito netting, I sat up, ready to leap from my bed. Then I saw how Fababa, breaking loose from Sangama's grip, was fleeing desperately toward the thicket, into whose depths he disappeared.

Sangama tried to pursue him in vain. His disappearance was instantaneous. In vain our voices called to him vigorously:

"Stop, Fababa! Don't go!"

Notwithstanding my nervousness, I had managed to see that Fababa looked back before losing himself among the trees. Pure horror! Contracted by a diabolical grimace and with his eyes completely wild, his face had a terrified expression. It was something that I will never be able to forget.

I covered myself up again, wishing to erase the frightful vision of Fababa and remove myself from its influence. But with my head completely wrapped up, I still managed to hear repeated raucous laughs that struck me as being those of the poor fugitive, who had surely lost his mind. Shaking me vigorously, Sangama had me leave the mosquito netting and approach the large bonfire, which threw forth living tongues of flame in whose yellowish glow the jungle acquired a ghostlike appearance. The logs sparked and crackled as they burned, giving off dense columns of smoke. Close to the fire, huddled together, were the Matero, the Bull, and the Piquicho, who were frequently looking to each side and behind, as if they feared discovering the presence of some monster. I sat close to the Matero, without daring to say a word. Sangama threw more and more firewood on the fire, and waving his enormous hat vigorously, he directed the smoke toward us, trying to surround us in it.

"The fire purifies everything. The fire removes curses," he said pithily.

"What are you trying to do?" I ventured to ask, since the smoke was asphyxiating me.

As if he had not heard my question, he continued speaking:

"The enemy is not there," and he pointed his finger toward the place where Fababa had disappeared. "Nor has it left . . . ! It's here!"

"Eh?" we all chorused with a tone of fear.

"It is here among us, surrounding us everywhere . . . !"

"Eh . . . ?"

"Yes! Even within ourselves . . . ! The air . . . ! The deadly shadow!"

With strange expressions in our faces, we looked at each other. Without a doubt, each one of us wanted to discover in the others the signs of demonic possession.

"Let's flee!" the Bull proposed.

"It will be worse! Beyond the circle of light is madness. Be calm!" ordered Sangama.

"God save us!" murmured the Piquicho.

The Bull crossed himself grotesquely.

"Touch me, Luna," I begged him. "This is a horrible nightmare, isn't it?"

"Yes," he replied. "A nightmare . . . But the truth is that we are wide awake. The *supay* called us, and it carried off Fababa!"

We all fell silent. We passed the rest of the night terribly frightened, without daring to make the slightest movement. Only the crackling of the wood that the fire was devouring and the whimpering howls of Litero disturbed the silence of the scene.

As soon as the light of dawn started to dissipate the shadows, showing the profiles of the trees, we hurriedly packed the beds and departed, following Sangama, who directed the flight.

We had not covered a great distance—at least so it seemed, such was our eagerness to leave that place in which we had passed that unforgettable vigil—when Sangama stopped, minutely examined the place, and told us:

"Here we are out of danger!"

"But we haven't gotten away from the *supay*!" argued Luna, ready to continue farther.

"When someone has his soul saturated with superstitions, every phenomenon of this nature is always explained by relating it to the

Devil," said Sangama, looking at the Matero with pity. "It was necessary to agree with you that it was the Devil. It would have been impossible to convince you of the contrary." And turning toward me, he proposed:

"Will you come with me to examine the terrain and find an explanation as to what happened to us last night? Don't be afraid!"

Apparently Sangama had undergone his accustomed transformation. From jungle dweller, with all his primitive beliefs, he was converting himself suddenly into a scientist who analyzes everything and explains it in accordance with natural laws.

I had to follow him. When we entered the place in which we had spent the night, the rays of the sun were already filtering to the ground through the foliage. Among the highest golden treetops, we made out the splendors of a beautiful summer day. Millions of trembling golden disks splashed the leafy floor. Furtive gusts of fragrant summer breezes slid among the trunks, happily moving the branches and leaves of the bushes. No one would have imagined that such a maddening night would have occurred in this almost enchanting place. Before us, trees of great size rose up, toward which Sangama directed his steps. He plunged the point of his machete into one of the trunks, making a deep incision, from which a dense latex spilled forth.

"It is an old *catahua,*" he informed me. "Although I know that it is one of the poisonous trees of the jungle, I never believed that its shadow would be deadly."

Immediately we went on to examine the next tree, whose stalk, because of its capriciously placed white and dark stains, bore a strange resemblance to the body of a snake. Before attacking it with his machete, my companion stood several long minutes, contemplating it.

"What sort of tree will this be? Perhaps it is harmless, like so many others that the jungle contains, and has nothing in particular except these curious stains," he said finally.

Since the point of his tool could not penetrate the bark, he attacked it with furious machete strokes, causing several chips to fly out, one of which he examined in detail. We established that it had no odor, but we prudently abstained from tasting it, a frequent practice in this region. We continued examining the other trees without discovering anything that caught our attention. We breathed in the air, filling our lungs, but no revelation came to us. Then Sangama proceeded to dig into the leaf-covered ground and found various animal skeletons. He stood up quickly, and after remaining pensive a moment as if to put his ideas in order and make deductions, he continued:

"This amply confirms my hypothesis, about which I still had some doubts. It was the air . . . the shadow. And if it wasn't this, what else could it be? Because, after all, that call we heard does exist among the jungle myths. They say it has the capacity to drive people crazy immediately, drawing in those who listen to it."

I shrugged my shoulders. My brain rejected all reasoning, something that was not unusual for me, since my brain was fleeing from the problems that were torturing it with logical inductions and deductions and tiresome comparisons.

Before my indolent indifference, Sangama continued his investigation of the surrounding area.

"If I could remain here even a week, I would end up solving the mystery," he lamented. "Perhaps at certain hours of the day or the night, or only certain days of the week, perhaps the month, if it is not only—which appears to me most probable—in a certain phase of the moon, these trees project a deadly shadow. Possibly each one of them, growing isolated, would be harmless, but joined together they form an association of villains. And this hypothesis explains to me the reason that, during all of my time in the jungle, I have not heard of any tree whose shadow had the properties of the *manzanillo*. The uneducated people relate everything to the Devil; with wandering spirits of the dead; with the witch, who unleashes illnesses among his fellow beings; or with the *curandero,* who neutralizes the curses of the witch and the malign influences of the Devil by means of magic arts. The Devil, who has no lack of people who would want to placate him by means of ridiculous exorcisms and invocations; the Devil, universal concept of evil, who in the jungle surely had his origin in the impossibility of explaining the causes of death and the phenomena of the jungle. Well, as I see that you are putting on the face of a martyr upon hearing this reasoning, it would be better if we return. They will already be worried by our lateness."

Indeed, they were anxiously awaiting us, fearing for our fate. Upon seeing us arrive, calm and lacking absolutely nothing, they couldn't hide their satisfaction. The Bull didn't stop circling me to assure himself that I had not brought something supernatural and monstrous attached to my back.

"What did you see?" the Matero asked in my ear.

"Nothing, absolutely nothing," I responded with exaggerated indifference, and to remove all importance from the subject, I asked: "And how did things go here?"

Sangama, the only one to remain serene after the experiences of the night before, told us that on the following morning we should undertake a search for Fababa.

"We will depart after breakfast, having recovered our strength," a direction that we all accepted as if it were an order.

The summer climate showed extraordinary ferocity. It had rained very little during the previous days, and the jungle was very dry in the zone where we found ourselves. The beds of the rivers had almost no water, and we were unpleasantly surprised when the Matero and the Bull, who had gone for water, returned with the pot empty, for we never imagined that the shortage would get to this extreme. They had to leave in the opposite direction and did not take long in returning with the container filled to the top.

We were trying to put the water over the fire, using a hook of wood to hang the pot, when Sangama, who had disappeared moments before among the trees, appeared in a hurry and asked:

"Where did you collect that water?"

And when the Matero described the place, he grabbed the pot and emptied its contents.

"It's infected. Come and see," he told us.

Following him, we arrived at the place from which they had taken it. It was a little pool of stagnant water that had remained in the dry riverbed of a small creek. There he showed us a *catahua* tree whose roots were submerged in the water, and he pointed out to us some branches broken off and sunken from the same tree and from others nearby, many of which were fully putrefied.

"The animals, by instinct, keep away from this well, which contains virulent germs of one of the worst tropical diseases. We have to flee quickly before a mosquito or fly inoculates us with the bacillus.

"Fortunately, we didn't drink," said the Matero.

"And with the thirst that I had . . . !" answered the Piquicho.

We packed up the small campsite to transfer it to the place that Sangama judged to be sufficiently removed from the deadly well. We made camp alongside the thicket and next to a dry and deep creek.

"It's a question of digging in a such way as to encourage the filtration of the water; but the important thing is to hit upon a place where it will flow immediately in order to prepare the food," Sangama carried on his monologue, while he passed over the creek bed, searching for an appropriate place for the excavation.

Futilely, we traveled along the creek bed for a considerable distance. The Matero, who had left without our having noticed, suddenly called us with shouts and whistles. When we were nearby, he pointed out to us, with a triumphal air, a thick vine that hung down to the ground from the high branches of a tree. After conveniently placing the pot, he cut the vine with one slash. Instantly a gusher of crystalline water burst forth. Once the pot was full, all of us managed to drink.

"It's the purest water that is found in the jungle," the Matero assured us proudly.

As we had agreed, we were quickly ready to undertake the search for Fababa.

"We won't gain anything going forward," said the Bull, in a haughty tone and with rifle in hand. "We demand of you that we return, Sangama."

"And you too, snotty brat," added the Piquicho, taking on some courage and looking at me insolently, while caressing his machete.

"Good," answered Sangama with the greatest tranquillity in the world. "You two stay. We'll go for Fababa. We can't continue without doing everything possible to find him. When we get back, we'll start the return trip."

The bandits' threatening attitude calmed down when we entrusted the care of our equipment to them, a sign that we would return soon. We departed, and the three of us walked on, visibly concerned. It was necessary to agree immediately on a plan of action to counter the open rebellion of the criminals.

"It's just a matter of leaving them somewhere from which they can't return to the shack," I proposed.

"But they can't walk alone four blocks in the wilderness," observed Luna.

And as all of us agreed with this observation, we resolved to abandon them where they were.

In view of the unforeseen circumstances, it appeared useless for us to continue searching for Fababa, an undertaking that would require time and patience, since finding him in the jungle would be like finding a needle in the bottom of a swampy lake. Since it suited us that the Bull and the Piquicho should believe that our search had been extensive, we passed some time stretched out on the leafy ground.

Later in the day we returned, carrying an agouti that the little dog Litero had seized in the interior of the worm-eaten trunk of a palm tree.

We found the criminals with sullen faces and their rifles in hand, stretched out close together on the ground, as they had been on our departure. Apparently, they were determined to have their way. They said nothing to us, but their attitude was disturbing, which gave us reason not to lose sight of them, staying on guard against any kind of surprise.

As the afternoon passed without anyone attending to the agouti or to other food, the Bull became impatient and, confronting the Matero, told him:

"Well, what are we waiting for?"

"For what?"

"We're hungry, idiot!"

"And why are you telling me this?"

"Filthy rat! I am going to shred you!"

"Don't fight. I'll cook," intervened Sangama, at the precise instant in which the villain was about to smash Luna's head with the butt of his rifle.

I hurried to assist Sangama in the preparation of the food. While one of us revived the fire, the other undertook to cut up the agouti. The famished Bull frequently examined the pieces of meat, which moved about in the boiling water. His displeasure was enormous because the meat did not become tender as quickly as he would have liked. The animal was very old. As the evening progressed, it became necessary to take down the pot as it was. We formed a circle as usual around the wide leaves spread on the ground. Sangama divided up the portion of soup, and then he distributed the pieces of meat. The Matero bit his and vigorously tugged on it in his eagerness to pull it apart, but the elastic skin stretched time and again, resisting his effort. Finally it broke, but with some bad luck for the Piquicho, who was eating at his right, and the hand of the gallant Luna smashed against his face in a loud slap. The deformed one started to spurt blood from his mouth and nose. He quickly reacted and seized a lit firebrand, which he tried to shove in the face of the surprised Luna, who hardly was able to ward off the attack. We had to intervene because the two criminals moved to confront Luna, brandishing their machetes.

After emotions calmed down and the meal had been ended with a serving of farina, we proceeded to bed down for the night. The criminals kept talking in a low voice for a long time. Grumbling loudly, the Piquicho took no precautions to avoid being heard expressing that the blow had been intentional. They agreed on some revenge and then apparently remained calm. Several times I woke up and was able to confirm that all were sleeping confidently, as if no danger were threatening us.

Chapter 23

The stillness was pleasant. A loving sensation of peace surrounded us, as if we had received in full the compensation we deserved for all the incidents of the prior days. From time to time I opened my eyes, overwhelmed by the tranquillity that reigned about us. Only the flames of the fires were stirring, twisting as if they wished to separate from the firewood that was producing them and fly away to extinguish themselves, weakened, in the dome of shadows that denied us a view of the sky. It was in that period of wakefulness that precedes sleep, in which things are slowly erased from the imagination and from reality, when I felt that something was crawling close to my bed. I stealthily raised the mosquito netting and could make out a form that was moving in the direction of the Matero's bed, where his long and strong breathing revealed a deep slumber. I noticed that the form carried a machete. I cried out the alarm in time. The Piquicho—since it was none other than he who was sneaking up in an attempt on the Matero's life—leaped quickly to the side of the Bull, who sat up with a rifle in his hands, pointing it at the three of us in turn.

"Hands up!" he ordered. "None of you three move, if you don't want to die! Move to the front!"

In complying with the order, we grouped together in the indicated place. The attack had taken us by surprise, and we were at the mercy of those cold-blooded individuals for whom we had done only good deeds and granted undeserved protection.

"Now, if you don't want to die shot down like dogs," the Bull ordered, still pointing the weapon at us, "as soon as it is light, we start on the return trip."

The Piquicho eagerly fed the fire so that they would not lack sufficient light to ensure the effectiveness of their treacherous attack.

Sangama, to our general shock and contradicting our warnings, confronted the giant, speaking with overwhelming serenity:

"We continue going forward. Pity on you, Bull, if you try to touch even a hair on our heads!"

The Bull, furious but inhibited by Sangama's disconcerting attitude, continued to threaten without deciding to shoot.

"You will not continue," he said, filling with rage. "The three of you will stay here, riddled with bullets!"

"We'll see if you dare!" answered Sangama in a mocking tone. "Soon we'll have you tied up like a wild animal, and the same for that viper that accompanies you."

"Kill them, Bull, and show some courage for once. All you have to do is shoot. Just one of them will be enough to enable our return . . . ," could be heard the screeching, hardly perceptible, voice of the Piquicho.

Without paying attention to the Bull's insults or the words of his accomplice, Sangama leaned back on a nearby tree trunk and, without taking his gaze from the irritated giant, intoned a strange succession of notes, nasal and deep, strident and sharp, which Litero, lying humble and trembling at his feet, accentuated with haunting howls, producing a sleep-inducing duet that overcame the free will.

"Shut up, damn you!" I managed to hear Bull's voice saying.

"This is pure witchcraft, Bull," screeched the deformed one. "Squeeze the trigger, while there's still time . . ."

The intonation continued, some times violent, sometimes calm. It was like a colossal, savage organ played by demons. A detonation and a bullet that pierced the ground at our feet were the last manifestations of our attacker's fury. Then I saw him collapse, out of control, struggling to get up. His friend, who could hardly stay on his feet, snatched the rifle from him and attempted to shoot at Sangama, but the Matero, armed with a log and taking advantage of the fact that the furiously barking little dog was biting the Piquicho's legs, delivered a blow to the head that sent him rolling.

My legs had buckled under the influence of this soporific and terrible music. I felt that around me everything was being distorted, and it seemed to me that some arms of imprecise dimensions were reducing me to helplessness. The Matero, stretched out on the ground next to me, was also half asleep. Suddenly our friend interrupted his melody to drag us out of the place. Immediately he returned to the side of the criminals to repeat the song, which I heard in the distance, recovering my senses little by little.

I sat up, rubbing my eyes as if to chase away a hallucination. In vain I tried to explain to myself what had happened. Luna gripped one of my arms tightly in fear. We looked at each other, stunned and not knowing what to say.

Sangama came over to us and shook us violently. Then he ordered:

"Help me tie them up! They're still asleep!"

We quickly had them firmly tied by their hands and feet. It was then that Sangama, whose face already showed great serenity, explained to us:

"I put little pieces of *ayahuasca* in the soup, but because it was slow in having its effect, I had to chant the Song of Sleep."

"What a song, yet not a song!" I exclaimed, reacting. "It had something of the sighs of the wind when it crosses the forest, of the roar of the jaguar, of the scream of the anaconda. What a strange thing!"

"In effect, the Song of Sleep is produced by the wind, which collects all sounds. Mixed within it are the notes that the wild beasts emit to put their victims to sleep. It is the Song of the Full Moon, which is heard when the vast tender grass fields spread out, covering the land, made humid and fertile by the winter floods, with pastures. The full moon! Abundance, solace, and relaxation for the herbivores that appear, coming out of the jungle's darkness to spread out through the fields, full of light, where no shadow is projected over the silvery grasses, which sway in rhythmic undulations like the waters of a tranquil sea, caressed by the soft gusts of a subtle wind.

There the animals eat their fill, devouring the stalks, juicy with sap and dew. It is the season in which they become fat with sumptuous feasts, after which they mate without fear of attack by treacherous carnivores. Their powerful instincts and sharp senses shelter them against such stalking. One has to see the largest, like great beasts, raise their heads over the grass that covers them, to look in every direction, to smell the air that comes to them unhindered, and to return, satisfied from the inspection, to fill their jaws with tasty bunches of vegetation, which they chew avidly. Their perception would easily determine whether the movement of the leaves is produced by the wind or by some stalking wild beast, crawling at the level of the ground. Afterward, before the hours of sleepiness and relaxation arrive, the cautious ones quickly enter the thicket to give themselves over to sleep in their customary secure places, while the unwary and confident ones hold back lazily. It is then that the moan of the winds acquires sudden sleep-inducing modulations, the song of the water lulls with mysterious accents, and dull enervating sounds arise from the swamp and from among the brush: they are the guttural sounds and roars, barely perceptible, that the throats of the anacondas and jaguars produce, trying to hypnotize their victims. All these diverse elements combined constitute the Song of Sleep that I learned in my long walks along the banks of the rivers and the edges of the lakes. The omnipotent anaconda and the cunning jaguar, astute and open to every advantage, steal smoothly to the places that the cautious herbivores occupy and, closing in on the stragglers, make an end to their feast. The poor animals wake up to a deadly clawing or the pressure of crushing coils."

Sangama made himself comfortable on the ground and, giving off white puffs of smoke from his cigar, continued:

"It often happens that the jaguar, king of the thicket, and the anaconda, queen of the waters, find themselves attacking the same prey at the same moment. And as they have been the most irreconcilable enemies since the beginning of the jungle, since the draining of the ancient sea that existed in the center of this continent, the titanic struggle, always renewed, is produced again. They never attack without forethought. They set aside the dead prey and look at each other with ancestral hatred. They measure each other in every sense, each irritating the other fiercely. The jaguar crouches, stretching out on the ground in such a manner that it appears part of it, and all that stand out are the naked claws and the enormous head, in which the eyes of the feline shine, lighting up its opponent like two intense bulbs. The anaconda draws itself up like a corkscrew, drives its tail into the ground, and flings part of its body forward, like a lance destined to damage an enemy. The jaguar avoids the blow and in turn attacks when the anaconda, disappointed by its failure or prudently desiring to avoid a fight with such a formidable contender, turns its head in the direction of the waters where it rules. Swift as lightning, it strikes the anaconda with teeth and claws and then moves away to evade the response, roaring furiously. Its powerful voice makes the jungle shudder far into the distance. All the animals that hear it flee, terrified. The armadillo and the paca scurry into their holes. The birds, trembling, hide their head under their wings, and the mothers squeeze the chicks into the nest. They all know, in such circumstances, that the sovereign of the jungle is angry because the intruder has come out of the waters to compete with him over supremacy of the land. The anaconda remains indecisive for a moment from the suddenness of the attack; then, feeling itself injured, turns to wind itself up and attacks, moving forward and sideways, so dizzying that the human vision cannot follow the path of the pointed head as it searches for the jaguar with an open mouth, quick to seize it. The old jaguars, cautious and skillful, know the trick of their enemy and know how to take advantage of the fraction of a second before the swift attack, especially the female jaguars grown old in the hunting, which, by their ferocity and astuteness, are the most feared of the jungle; but the cubs, bewildered and petulant, which prematurely search for adventures and quarrels before having learned to fight and before having learned the wise counsel of the grandmother, are seized and wrapped in the coils of the swift adversary. However, even in that situation the jaguar still is not defeated. It expands its body at the exact moment in which the anaconda squeezes; then that body, inflated like a balloon and consisting of muscles of steel, as soon as it feels the reptile yield to prepare the next squeeze, compresses itself, stretching unbelievably and almost taking the elongated form of the serpent itself, slides among from the coils, and with one leap puts itself outside the reach of its adversary. All of this only the jaguars can do. It is for good reason that they are the kings of the jungle. They know by instinct that, the first effort having failed, the anaconda needs a certain space of time to execute a second, which is of deadly effect since, concentrating its tremendous power upon that strike, it crushes the bones of its victim, leaving it, no matter how powerful it may be, converted into a formless mass ready to be swallowed."

Sangama remained silent, his gaze fixed on us to observe the effect that his explanations had on us and, after expelling large puffs of smoke, continued again:

"The second attack of the anaconda having failed, the jaguar faces it resolutely. No longer are there leaps or parries. The fight is continuous and ferocious. The serpent's head, with incredible speed, tries to fool the feline, which defends itself with tooth and claw, employing in its turn extraordinary nimbleness. The terrible fight, which shakes the earth and the waters, often turns out indecisive. When exhaustion obliges them to cease the combat, both remain unmoving, panting, each eyeing the other with hatred. The anaconda turns contemptuously to enter the waters, and the jaguar, proud though battered, roars defiantly and enters the thicket. These two monarchs of the jungle have justifiable reasons to hate each other and to be irreconcilable adversaries, when one or the other invades the opponent's sphere of influence. The jaguar at times becomes a fisherman. It disguises its body by crouching on some trunk that floats or grows at the level of the water, and from there it uses its claws to hunt the fish that arrive, attracted by the whiskers that it submerges and moves in the manner of insects. When the anaconda learns of this, it becomes furious to the point of despair. It would very much like to surprise the jaguar there on the riverbank, where the anaconda could defeat it easily; but the jaguar knows this very well and takes precautions to avoid coming close to the muddy waters, to the very deep pools, and to the water's edges, full of trees that could hide its implacable enemy. It is not that the jaguar is afraid—its great valor, almost always rash, is fully proven—so much so that it frequently looks for the opportunity to seize the jaw of the manatee, submerge itself with the animal, and remain in the water long enough to kill it, in order to give itself a feast among the trees on the shore afterward. Another of its risky achievements is that of slipping into the brush at the edge of the same river to send forth its powerful roar. There is no alligator that dares to move after hearing it, no matter how awake it might be. The jaguar strolls among them, selects the fattest ones, and eats their tails. I cannot explain why this mutilation, which must be very painful, is born by the victims without the slightest protest. They allow the amputation, apparently with tranquillity, of however many morsels the beast desires, and they remain immobilized until their aggressor leaves, satisfied. They then fling themselves in the river, screaming in pain."

A prolonged groan from the Bull obliged Sangama to cut off the interesting exposition that had distracted us for a while. The sunrise had found us listening to him as if the scene might have unfolded in a comfortable district of the city.

When it was light enough, we noticed that the Bull and the Piquicho were looking at each other dumbfounded, without clearly realizing what had happened. Shortly thereafter the cowardly giant was sobbing about his misfortune in the most ridiculous way. As for his companion in misfortune, it was difficult to make out whether he was crying or laughing, so strange were the sounds he emitted. But abundant tears rolled down his deformed face.

Without giving the two of them any importance or taking any care to prevent them from hearing us, we started to discuss what we should do next.

Sangama argued for the continuation of the expedition without more loss of time, since what had occurred since our departure had already prolonged the journey beyond all calculations. The Matero insinuated the convenience of doing away with the two villains. I also was of this opinion, but I refrained from stating it, sure that Sangama would reject it. Sangama limited himself to saying:

"We will leave them here until our return. There are many vines from which they can get water. As a last resort, they can dig a well in the riverbed."

While I pointed a rifle at them, the Matero untied them, and after moving away from them, he warned them:

"Do you see that oak tree on the right? Go over to it in a couple of hours. I am going to leave you a rifle."

The villains renewed their lamenting and imploring, but once they were convinced that we would not allow them in our company, they burst out with gross threats.

"We'll see about this, Sangama, if I'm still alive when you return! Witch of the Devil!" bellowed the Bull.

"I'll bite you, damn you!" added the Piquicho. "I'll bite you . . . I have venom in my teeth!"

Mocking those vile creatures as we departed, I pointed out the opposite bank of the creek, where the jungle was thickest, and told them:

"The way back is in that direction . . ."

Chapter 24

As in the days before, Sangama took the lead and, with strokes of his machete, opened a way through the thick brush, taking care to mark the trees so that they would serve as a reference for us on our return trip.

At nightfall our progress became very slow in our eagerness to hunt something, because our provisions were growing short since we had left the greater part of them with the Bull and the Piquicho and had consumed some during the delay.

The diligent Litero soon gave us a great surprise. Following the direction in which he almost forced us with howling and running about, nips on the legs, and leaps forward, we came across a *trocha* that had been recently opened, judging by visible tracks and marks.

"This indicates that we are closely following the steps of the elder Luna," said Sangama, after a brief investigation.

Contrary to what we had hoped, we had not been able to hunt a single game animal nor to find water during the entire trek. The shadows of the night surrounded us, and we had to camp, contenting ourselves with a scant ration and a few swallows of water that Sangama had in his canteen.

Nothing worthy of relating happened that night. It seemed that the spirits of the jungle protected us, seeing us free of the ill-fated company of the criminals who had caused us so many tribulations in the days before.

Very early in the morning we resumed our journey, always following Sangama, who advanced confidently through the *trocha* we had discovered. The environment was extremely suffocating.

The vegetation was taking on a pronounced gray color due to the fierceness of the merciless summer sun. Thirst was devouring us. Fortunately, in a clearing that doubtless had been a swamp, we found some thick reeds from whose insides we extracted abundant liquid with which we placated our thirst, and we prepared some food by mixing water with flour of banana and manioc. Our strength recovered, we continued the journey through a completely uninhabited jungle.

When it does not rain for several consecutive days, the drying leaves become discolored and detach from the branches, falling to form a thick layer of dead leaves that crunch under one's feet. The animals, driven by the drought, search the edges of the lakes and the banks of the rivers. It is in those areas where nature then acquires an unexpected display of life.

The jungle is roiled with an indescribable hullabaloo resonant with voices and noises, adorning itself with shifting and varied colors. The parrots and macaws shout in a scandalous competition. The trumpeter bellows, in a serious tone, with the bluster of a great civilized gentleman, but skittish and quick. The hammer blows of the woodpecker sound as it drills the dried trunks with its sharpened peak. The *yungururo* partridge, notable for being the largest of the partridges, takes flight, producing a pronounced whistle as it tears through the air. The *unchala* sings happily, searching for snails with the agility afforded by the long legs on which its small cinnamon body swaggers. The *tuqui-tuqui* hurries across the aquatic plants, emitting strident cries. The enormous *camunguy,* with spurs at the ends of its wings and inhabiting areas where vegetation growing over the water is strong enough to support its weight, announces its existence in a voice so loud that it can be heard at great distances. The voluminous curassow, with its reddish bulky beak; the toucan, with lively colors, that takes flight with a beak out of proportion to its size; the romantic wood pigeon and so many other birds that form part of that deafening orchestra that performs an infernal anthem or a placid melody. On the humid earth or at the surface of the water, myriads of butterflies flutter about, making the mud and bushes of the shore flower with capricious and dazzling bouquets.

Higher up, on firm ground, the deer graze, watching cautiously over their delicate young; the squirrels leap playfully from branch to branch, shaking their thick tails, with which they cover themselves, cuddling up as soon as they feel the first drops of rain. In the brush the rodents hide: the highly prized agouti, and the nocturnal paca, expert tracer of trails from its den to the lake, where it is accustomed to drink, and whose meat is the most sought after in the jungle.

But what the animals seek with the most interest, especially the birds, are the almost dry beds of the creeks and lakes, in whose deepest parts a profusion of little ponds have remained, where the scaly fish form almost compact masses. The fish without scales dig along the edges, under the fallen trees, to make their summer homes, consisting of caves of differing depths in which the water remains fresh until the first rains return. There the *shitari* rides out the drought, that digger who likes the mud and drills a network of caves in the hard lands washed by torrential waters; the *shirue,* of interwoven scales; the treacherous electric eel, which kills with its electrical discharges; and the *shuyos*. The latter have the very audacity to cross the jungle when it is still humid, migrating to larger lakes, which many times permits hunters to fish in the middle of the forest and on dry land.

The sparrow hawks flee, attacked by tiny birds that have the advantage over them in speed of flight. And even the jaguars prowl in the distance so as not to be corralled by the *huangana,*[20] which enjoys its *collpa.*[21] This is the time of the year in which the small animals get fat while the wild predators languish in hunger. It is the phenomenon that is opposite to what occurs in winter, when, numb from cold under the incessant rain and seeking fruits to nourish themselves, all the jungle fauna take refuge on the mud banks, long little islands that the rising waters do not manage to cover; it is a period in which the predators hunt freely.

That explained why the area we were passing through was

---

[20] *Huangana:* javelina or peccary.

[21] *Collpa:* a very muddy area where the huangana herd rests and sleeps.

uninhabited. It was necessary to hurry if we did not want to die of hunger and thirst.

"This will soon end," said Sangama, understanding that our silence was the result of the fear that dominated us. "Within a short time we'll arrive at the edge of some river or lake, where we'll be able to reward ourselves."

Our journey following the *trocha* had almost turned into a flight. It was at early dusk the next day, when we already doubted that the encouraging prediction would ever come true, that we perceived in the distance the peculiar noise of the inhabited jungle. And opening up before us was an extensive clearing covered with low vegetation, whose confines could hardly be perceived in the hazy distance. Great masses of yellowish steam were floating over that green pampa, whose undulating surface appeared before our eyes, like a sea with remote shores that the sun wished to incinerate.

"We have arrived at the *renacal,*" Sangama said with a sigh. "The elder Luna could not have gone beyond this, no matter how knowledgeable he is of the jungle."

We descended the small depression of land to its very edge, where we halted.

Captivated, I remained a long time contemplating the strange marshy jungle that stretched out at our feet.

Chapter 25

Only some of the most daring explorers had ever arrived at the *renacal,* a region that extends between the great Huallaga and Ucayali rivers and borders on the lower jungle that characterizes the area across which the *renacal* spreads.

This strange vegetation has grown above an enormous sea of muddy water. The *renacal* is made up exclusively of the *renaco,* a plant that thrives especially in very wet places or in swamps, where it forms compact clusters. When it takes root in isolation, it spreads rapidly. From its first branches random roots spring forth, which grow downward in search of the soil; but if a tree of another species stands nearby, the *renaco* spreads out until it contacts that tree, twists itself around its stalk one or more times, and then continues its path into the earth, deeply penetrating it. From then on, the *renaco,* twisted like a giant snake, keeps adjusting its coils in an implacable process of strangulation that ends up splitting the tree and bringing it down. Since it carries out this operation with all the trees that are near it, it ends up alone. From each of the root systems that served for the strangulation shoots will sprout that in time become independent of the mother stalk. It often happens that when they do not find another species to attach to, they grow together into a cluster so strange that one would call it a single tree of multiple deformed stalks and with treetops that do not match the trunks. Little by little, carrying out its own nature as assassin, the *renaco* proceeds, forming forests where it does not permit the existence of any other species of tree.

Often the wind carries the minuscule seed of the *renaco* over a distance and deposits it on the bark of another tree. There it germinates among the wrinkles and develops as a parasite, growing at the expense of the sap that it sucks out, while it wraps the tree with the tentacles of its roots until it covers the tree completely. Asphyxiated, the tree finally dies, and the strangler plant continues to live on its decomposing remains until it in turn dies from lack of sustenance.

In very swampy places where conditions do not exist for it to prosper by sinking down its roots, the *renaco* adapts itself and succeeds in developing admirably. Its branches and roots weave together and cover the muddy surface with a thick, strong tangle, under which live anacondas of extraordinary size.

The *renacal,* on whose edges we found ourselves, was formed in this manner. From a large lake of mud grew a tangled forest of strange configuration, in which some branches wrapped around others, as the impalpable fibers of anguish must intertwine themselves in the minds of the insane. The surface of this tangled net was not continuous. At intervals dark openings were seen, at the bottom of which and in the stagnant black waters dwelled huge reptiles.

Sangama looked thoughtfully at that fantastic expanse. What swirl of ideas was turning over in his mind? He contemplated the *renacal* with a fixedness, as if he would like to tear from it some very important secret. Without guessing the cause of his being so deeply self-engrossed, we remained at his side, keeping a respectful silence. As if he had returned from a long trip, he made clear to us in a very quiet voice that we should prepare to pass the night there and attend to feeding ourselves.

At a short distance, on the edge of the dry land, we noticed a large group of *chambira* palms, whose tender leaves produce the fiber the Indians used for weaving their hammocks and whose fruits, a type of small coconut, contain a tasty and nutritious pulp. To furnish ourselves with water other than the black muddy water pooled between the roots of the *renacos,* we enthusiastically dug a hole in the sands in the bed of a dried-up creek, which promptly started to fill with the sought-after liquid. Next to this little well we set up a small campsite. Luna cut down several palm trees, permitting us to use its fruits to satiate the hunger that was devouring us. The night arrived, finding us well situated, ready to hunt the animals that came to drink. The expert Luna hung a small ball of the *huimba*[22] on each rifle to assure marksmanship in the dark. We didn't have to wait very long; before midnight we had already taken a deer and several pacas.

The morning light found us already up, striving to construct a campsite from the trunks and leaves of palm trees that would shelter us comfortably in case of rain, while the pot boiled with succulent pieces of fresh meat and some aromatic chops turned golden over the hot coals.

We rested all that day, a rest certainly well deserved after the arduous trek we had just completed.

It was then that I could take my ease, as I had not done since we had set out on the expedition, turning to the memory of my beloved, whose stay in the distant shack concerned me very much. I ran over in my imagination all the moments in my life since I had the good fortune to meet her. How serenely, how sweetly, how softly passed the hours in that pleasant remembrance! While the scenes of the love poem in which we were the protagonists paraded through my brain, I kept myself distant from the others.

I would have continued unraveling the fabric of such ineffable fantasizing if the Matero had not interrupted. He was supremely bored, since Sangama continued to be immersed in his meditations, mute and stretched out on the ground with his elbows supported on the earth and his head held by both hands, his vision fixed in the monotonous distance of the immense *renacal*.

We remembered the Bull and the Piquicho, who we imagined dying of terror, begging to all the saints that we would return to pick them up.

In the evening I noted that Sangama appeared worried. Speaking out loud, Luna formulated our hunting plans for that night and the

---

[22] *Huimba:* a large tree whose flower is a valuable vegetable silk.

next day, apparently determined to remain in this location and continue resting.

Sangama's attitude disturbed me, but I didn't dare to question him, despite the interest that I had in knowing the peculiarities of the place that lay before us. I hoped that he would come out of his ponderings at any moment and that he would start with the same old dissertation. This time he undoubtedly would discourse about the *renacal* and its mysteries.

Late in the night I saw him get up, trying to avoid attracting our attention, and head toward the edge of the *renacal.* I looked at Luna's face, and as the latter did not immediately return my look, I approached him and proposed to him by signs that we follow Sangama to see what he was doing. We found him seated at the edge of a small ravine, from which he continued his persistent observation. Soon he stood up and directed his steps to a small gnarled tree, which he climbed in order to look about in all directions, with his right hand extended over his eyes like a visor.

"It seems that he is trying to see what is beyond the *renacal,*" the Matero whispered in my ear.

"Hush! He isn't going to like it that we are spying on him," I answered, as softly as I could.

"If he hasn't gone crazy, he's close to it. He's not even thinking about coming down."

In truth, Sangama did not tire of inspecting the distance with deep meticulousness, without the passage of time seeming to have any importance to him. When he descended, night had already fallen. He returned to sit wide awake in the same place that he had been before.

The meddlesome Matero, who was not a man to occupy himself in certain ponderings and who did not understand how one could dedicate so much time to the contemplation of something that for him lacked any particular interest, could not contain himself. Drawing close, he made a mocking inquiry that to me appeared inappropriate to be used with Sangama, whose meditations always infused me with respect.

"Have you lost something in the *renacal* . . . ?"

The object of the question did not respond. His expression upon turning his head and facing us was like that of someone waking from a deep sleep and being surprised by reality. First he looked attentively at the Matero, and then he fixed on me, half hidden behind a bush.

"Spying on me . . . eh?" he said to us with a tone of reproach.

"Man . . . ! Since you didn't return to the hut, we had to come looking for you," I intervened.

"I am trying to establish if this is the lake, absorbed by the jungle, that I have glimpsed in my hours of telepathy . . . ! But it is not the island of the legend . . ."

"Good grief . . . !" I replied. "What are you talking about . . . ? You are incomprehensible!"

"Sangama's journey to these parts already seemed inexplicable enough to me," Luna interjected, surprised.

"You both know that I have never been selfish. I have come to search for the elder Luna. But I have, at the same time, another fundamental motive, the driving goal of my life, one could say. The moment has arrived to take you into a great confidence and ask you to help me . . . If things are as I believe, transcendental historic events are approaching."

The Matero and I looked at each other, stunned. Evidently Sangama had gone crazy or, at the very least, was suffering from disorientation.

Upon returning to the camp—if our improvised little shack merited such a designation—in the reddish blaze of the fire, he told us the following story.

Chapter 26

"**I can only start by confessing,**" Sangama began, "that our great mission, that of my ancestors and of me, is sustained by a legend that was transmitted to my grandfather by the Huillac Umu, the High Priest who accompanied the martyr Amaru. Thus it has for me the most evocative and transcendental character. In my telepathic hours, I have seen indistinctly a lake absorbed by the jungle . . . this one, here in view. And lost in it is the island where the god of my elders lies buried, represented by a statute of pure gold, and next to it a skull. As of today I have not been able to find the island, a fact that continues to cause me a great deal of concern. Listen to the legend:

"The Inca Amaru found himself in difficulties. The last resistance against the Spanish conqueror had failed, and he was fleeing from the heights of Vilcabamba toward the jungle, pursued very closely by the battle-hardened troops of Captain Martín García de Loyola.

"After a long march, harassed unceasingly by the Spanish, the Inca stopped in the last Tampu, which marked the Empire's border with the land of the Antis.

"He was surrounded by a small group of followers, all from the imperial nobility, among whom the ancient Huillac Umu stood out. Prostrate before the statue of gold, the Huillac Umu beseeched for his Lord the protection of the gods of the Empire.

"'Have you not received any message from Huiracocha?' the sovereign asked him anxiously.

"'Huiracocha is angry with his children . . . he continues to be angry. He appears mute and deaf to the invocation.'

"The Inca inclined his head very sadly. The priest continued solemnly.

"'He has abandoned us to our fate since the fratricidal battles. In his temples, in place of the blood of sacrifices, ran human blood, the sinful blood. The covetous white men, conquerors of Atahualpa, satiated their appetites in the sacred places . . . Five generations will pass before the descendants of the Sons of the Sun will again have their blood purified by their sufferings. Then, and only then, will the divine word be for them.'

"An overwhelming tiredness quickly overcame the monarch, who fell asleep on the great stone that served as his throne. His servants surrounded him, watching solicitously over his sleep.

"Suddenly the Inca's chest stirred convulsively. Thick drops of sweat broke out on his forehead and rolled down his cheeks, leaving wet lines on them. Unintelligible words escaped from his half-opened mouth.

"Night fell, and thick torches were fixed on the walls of the Tampu, giving off sparks and pouring yellowish light through the outpost.

"Very late in the night, the fugitive sovereign woke up gasping, as if he had just endured a dreadful battle. He looked around and, wiping his forehead, called to the Huillac Umu and to Quispe, one of the young nobles who was most devoted to him.

"'I have seen Huiracocha,' he told them. 'His eyes looked at me in anger upon announcing to me my approaching death. He has ordered that we save his image so that, with the power that it holds, one of my descendants will one day expel the invader. I order you, Quispe, to depart without losing any time, together with the men you select, and go into the jungle. Open well your ears, and listen.

"'You will go, following the course of this river, until you find a bird of prey on a rock, devouring a serpent. As soon as you see it, it will take flight toward the North without releasing its prey, whose excessive weight will make it descend frequently, and in each one of those stops it will renew its feast, giving you time to catch up. Upon your presence, it will again take flight as many times as are necessary, and it will fly always in the same direction. Follow it without rest. Thus you must arrive at the edge of a large river, whose long course you will follow, without regard to how many days it takes. When you find a mountain of salt on the shore, stop as long as is necessary to fill your drinking cup, and continue following. Do not fear the roughness of the waters, from which Huiracocha will protect you. You will thus arrive at the unknown lands where the naked Antis dwell. You will leave the river only when you see flocks of white birds crossing the sky, headed toward the East in search of inland lakes. You will follow that direction without deviation, beloved Quispe. But before abandoning the river, sharpen your *champi* well, because trunks and branches will rise up to block your passage. Cut and cut much, Quispe; do not tire of cutting. The route you are opening will permit you to return to the mountain of salt in the times when the sky is not crossed by birds. The flocks of birds will show you the route that leads to the shore of a lake, in the middle of whose waters stands an island. There you will wait until one of our descendants goes in search of you. For provisions, be sure to take seeds, since only Huiracocha knows the day when you will have to return to your Lord the statue that I entrust to you. Go!'

"Quispe prostrated himself on his knees before the Inca. He stretched his arms forward in a sign of obedience and adoration, and he departed, followed by Auca, who carried the sacred image on his powerful shoulders.

"Immediately the monarch turned to the Huillac Umu, telling him, 'You must also depart before it is too late. Your mission in due time will be that of finding the most worthy of our descendants who have survived the annihilation of our lineage. Communicate to him the mandate of Huiracocha. He, his sons, and the sons of his sons will go in search of Quispe, receiving the statue and reconquering the Empire.'

"As soon as the Huillac Umu disappeared, the Spaniards fell upon the Tampu and took the Inca and all of his retinue as prisoners. None of the imperial family nor any of the nobility of the Tahuantinsuyo escaped alive the rage of the Viceroy Toledo.

History has gathered in its pages the horrible massacre that he ordered and that earned him, in the last years of his life, the reproach of the King of Spain, which made him die of grief.

"Long years had passed since then.

"One evening, while strolling arrogantly through the streets of Seville, a nobleman, a genuine descendant of the imperial race and a Captain of the Royal Forces of Spain, was stopped by a vagabond who seemed to come in search of him after a long pilgrimage across the seas and continents.

"'I have a message for you,' he told the Captain abruptly. 'Follow me!'

"Such words, the strange appearance of the subject, and his voice, which seemed to come from a tomb, impressed the Captain deeply. Without asking for explanations, he followed the mysterious person to an extremely impoverished dwelling whose window looked out on the river. Once inside, the strange individual closed the door, and sitting down in one of the corners of the room that was sheltered in a shadowy darkness, he went on relating, in a lugubrious and tired tone, everything that I have just told you, adding:

"'Here you have the description of the caves that enclose the wisdom of the Empire's sages and also the great hidden treasures that will serve you to direct the World in favor of the Great Cause of our race; but the first thing that you have to do, oh, Son of the Sun, is find the statue of Huiracocha that is hidden in the jungle. The five generations have now passed, and the anger of the great guardian god of the Empire has been placated. He will guide you in the search for his image, which you, who have abandoned the faith of our forefathers, disrespectfully call an idol.'

"'And who are you?' asked the Captain, suddenly believing himself to be the object of a prank.

"'I am the Huillac Umu, to whom the Inca entrusted the mission of transmitting to you his words.'

"'Liar! Impostor!' shouted the proud soldier angrily, convinced that it was a prank. 'You will pay for your insolence and your brashness . . . ! It has been two centuries since Amaru was executed, and you show up this way as an impostor!'

"And drawing his weapon, he ran a sword through the stranger, who did not make the slightest move to defend himself. The thrust produced a macabre sound of bones. The Captain flung himself upon the sinister character and, with one tug, pulled off the large hat and the scarf with which he hid his face. Before his stunned gaze a white skull was revealed, which rolled away and stopped in a corner, facing him. He suddenly had a deep impression that the skull was looking at him fixedly from eternity. He then heard a dull sound of bones scattering on the floor, and he saw the rags, stripped of their contents, piling up and folding upon themselves, diminishing until they disappeared completely.

"The Captain fell to the ground as if struck by lightning, saying, 'Yes, Lord, I will comply with your mandate,' and he fainted.

"At midnight, when he recovered his senses, he found himself stretched out on the cobblestones of the street, surrounded by several passersby.

"'What drunkenness!' exclaimed one as he walked away, an exclamation that was followed by a chorus of coarse laughs.

"Outraged by the supposed prank, he set out to find the house in which it had been perpetrated. He found a nearby staircase that he had noticed as he turned his eyes in the precise moment in which he entered the shadowy street, but the house that he sought did not exist, and he could not find the alleyway anywhere. He believed himself the victim of a hallucination; but as he undressed to go to bed in his elegant residence after the events just narrated, his eyes fixed upon some faded papers that protruded from one of his pockets. The papers that the phantom had left him!

"That nobleman was my grandfather," continued Sangama. "He failed in the search for the idol, as my father failed years later. Both died in the jungle. I was obsessed by that mission, which it was now up to me to carry out. I came very young to the edges of the Ucayali, and I learned, in addition to the vast knowledge that they strived so diligently to teach me, the secrets that the jungle contains. By drinking the magic juice, after many years I have succeeded in assimilating the powers that it gives. Thanks to the clairvoyant properties of the *ayahuasca,* I discovered this jungle filled with serpents . . . the jungle we see before us."

"Perhaps at one time it was a lake?" I managed to ask, wishing to shake off the bewilderment the tale had produced in me.

"The cursed plant covered it!" said Sangama. "Every *renaco* contains a malign spirit. Observe how some look like human beings with their deformed extremities extended toward us like claws to menace us. The *renaco* is always ready for the attack. With its branches and roots it assaults and murders the trees, and by means of the anacondas that it shelters beneath the net with which it covers the swamp, it attacks and kills all the animals that may approach it. The *renaco* would end up conquering all the jungle and absorbing it, if the other trees didn't defend themselves. There a strangled tree falls on hundreds of *renacos* that were invading its high terrain, destroying them in its fall. To avoid the deadly regrowth, varied bushes have rapidly covered the empty space. Over there is another that has the form of a corkscrew because the *renaco* that had tortured it died, crushed in the fall of one of its victims. It is the collective defense of the jungle against the evil element that threatens its very existence . . . !"

Chapter 27

When Sangama brought his tale to an end, I had the sensation that something indefinable was menacing us, and when I cast a glance behind me, it seemed to me that I perceived the outline of a strange form hidden in the thicket. However, taking control of myself, I said nothing to my companions. The Matero, without a doubt, was also nervous, since he was listening carefully while looking in every direction into the surrounding jungle, faintly lit by the reddish bonfire before which we found ourselves.

Since I couldn't go to sleep, I reviewed in my imagination the precise details of this story. I was able to find the logical relationship it had with the statements that Sangama had made on several occasions, to which I never attributed such transcendental importance. But because of the occasion on which the tale had been told, I did not dare to doubt its accuracy. It explained to me clearly the reason why Sangama, on the occasions when he was carried away with enthusiasm, always alluded to the "Great Cause" and to the "Idol."

My dream was very troubled, populated by all sorts of fantasies, in which the figure of Sangama acquired huge proportions, with sufficient power to destroy the *renacos*.

When I awoke, tired as if I had undergone a bitter struggle, I had to make a great effort to convince myself that I had not suffered any physical injury. The Matero, who was stretching himself, said to me:

"How does Sangama's story strike you? I think he's half crazy. Since he doesn't believe in demons or ghosts, how could he give credence to that story, in which characters from the otherworld take part?"

"I don't know," I hurried to respond. "But there must be some truth to it. Our companion is not a man who could be so easily deceived."

The appearance of Sangama, who was returning from an inspection of the *renacal,* prevented us from continuing.

After breakfast, Sangama, who until then had remained sunken in his meditations, turned to me, saying:

"You have the face of a living corpse. You need to rest. Surely you have slept badly. By day there is no danger in this place, and you can take advantage of this while we hunt."

The Matero assured me that they would not be long, since game abounded in the surrounding area. I wanted to accompany them, but they stubbornly refused to let me go with them. I finally had to accept their decision, which gave me very little satisfaction.

Following their advice and harassed by mosquitoes, I resolved to get under the mosquito netting, but after a few moments, I experienced an inexplicable fear. I was sure that some danger was closing in on me. I considered the ease of an attack and the difficulty of defending myself in the situation in which I found myself, inside that contraption without any view of the outside.

I got out of the shelter. Not without a certain nervousness, I piled up handfuls of dry leaves and set fire to them. The smoke quickly chased away the clouds of mosquitoes, and the miserable buzzing they produced ceased. I was looking with unease in every direction, trying to penetrate the depths of the thicket. From the place in which I found myself, I could see a long stretch of forest, since the ground was almost completely free of brush, and if there were bushes here and there, they were dry or mutilated.

There was a moment in which I saw the branches of a tree stir in a strange manner. I approached it, but no matter how much I tried to examine the branches, I could discover nothing noteworthy about them. Just as well that Sangama and the Matero would be back soon, I thought in order to give myself courage. But unfortunately midday passed without them making an appearance.

Solitude is a bad companion. I was sure that if there were danger, Sangama would not have left me in the little shelter, but it was impossible to avoid the feeling of helplessness that invaded me.

The progress of the sun was very slow. The hours were growing longer and longer. Some shots in the distance made me suppose that my friends were already returning. I could not conceive, with abundant game in the immediate area, that they were going to take so much time. I listened a long time without hearing any noise or seeing anything out of the ordinary. My discomfort grew as the minutes passed by and the curtains of the night were being drawn over the jungle. I paced uneasily, like a wild beast inside a cage, from one end of the narrow clearing to the other.

I had the persistent impression that two eyes were fixed on me from somewhere, waiting for an auspicious moment to attack. I threw a great quantity of dry leaves on the fire, and since I was exhausted from so much walking, I sat down next to the fire, in whose changing glow I seemed to find relief. Evidently it was not a question of the emotion that produces cowardice. More than once I had demonstrated in the course of my life that I know how to confront dangers decisively. But in this place, in these circumstances, as a consequence of the influence of the jungle, a new sense was developing: the sensation of stalking danger.

When the flames of the fire finally died for lack of fuel, I was half asleep. It was then that something I feared, whose nature was impossible for me to determine, fell upon me without warning. I didn't know if it fell from the branches tangled above my head, if it sprang from behind one of the tree trunks that surrounded me, or if it rose up from within the depths of the earth itself.

I fell violently to the ground as some claws grabbed hold of my throat and a sort of fetid beard swept my face. From a face almost totally covered with long, tangled hair, some murderous eyes, full of a strange brilliance, looked at me.

In the first moment, I thought myself lost, but as I was still breathing freely, I resolved, driven by instinct, to defend myself and sell dearly the life that the monster sought to snatch from me. I reached out my arms to seize my enemy, and I touched a hairless body, cold, bony, and moist with sweat. My hands fixed on two points that seemed to be human shoulders, and with great effort I separated myself from the gnarled vines that pressed against my throat. I tried desperately to get up, but its thighs, gripping my body, held me fast against the ground. I fought with fury, with all the violence and force that one employs in those supreme moments to defend one's life. Although the attack was determined and continuous, I quickly realized that it did not have the advantage over me in strength. Its agility was truly superhuman. It was always on top of me, fighting to seize me again by the throat or attack me with its teeth. I soon realized that its breathing was becoming more and more tired and its movements less nimble. To save myself, it was necessary to continue resisting until I exhausted it completely. Better still, to give it no rest, I had to take the initiative in the struggle. This I did. I searched for its neck and pressed with all my strength. As it yielded, gasping, I let it go in order to pick up my rifle or machete, which I thought to be close by. As I extended my hand, I felt a fierce bite on my arm; it was the bite of a wild beast and caused me a sharp pain. With one leap it was beyond my reach and disappeared in the thicket like a shadow, leaving me with an injured arm.

Instantly I grabbed the rifle and emptied it, pointing at the place to which the creature had fled. As if I had gone crazy, I continuously reloaded the weapon and shot randomly in every direction.

Exhausted by the effort, I stretched out on the ground. A great anxiety took possession of me, imagining that my companions had become lost in the immensity of the jungle and perhaps would never return. I remained alone, injured, surrounded by inconceivable dangers, at many leagues from inhabited places, to which it would be impossible to return without the help of a guide. I suddenly felt strong impulses run away and plunge into the jungle. An instant more . . . and madness.

An animal threw itself at my feet and, licking my hands, rubbed against my body . . . It was a dog! It was Litero, who had left Sangama and Luna and come looking for me!

Chapter 28

When an obsessed hunter, following a flock of wild turkeys or toucans, or running enthusiastically after a herd of javelinas, leaves the *trocha* and plunges confidently into the unknown jungle, it is because he is possessed by hunter fever. He overcomes obstacles, takes shortcuts, climbs, and descends; he runs and leaps, denying all fatigue, without measuring distances or sparing efforts. He advances rapidly, obsessed, following the prey that flees from him; he looks about, sharpening his view in a great effort to make out the slightest movement in the brush or branches that betrays the passage of the prey he pursues.

He has no time to meditate, fix on details, or note markers that determine his orientation and establish the direction that he follows at random in his confusion. He hardly looks at the ground that his feet are treading on, disdaining the thorns that tear at him and the branches that try to hold him back.

The hours fly in that dizzying chase that exhausts the man as well as the animal. Finally, the former manages to take aim, shoot, and wound, and he stops, panting and satisfied, next to the collected prey. He finishes it off triumphantly, ties it up, tosses it on his back, and starts the return trip. Now it is a matter of finding the proper direction. He looks around, surprised to find a large tree, which he approaches in order to give it a machete cut on the bark so that this bleeding mark fixes the point of departure. This instinctive action is the mark that the hunter leaves as a reference of his passing through the forest. He then believes he has oriented himself, and he departs in a determined direction, which he decides is the most direct return. He changes the direction before a ravine, a creek, a swamp, or any other barrier that is difficult to overcome. And he corrects it again and again. He stops, indecisive, and experiences a discouraging sensation that disturbs his intellect. However, he continues on and continues drawing energy from where there is none, in order to stop suddenly in front of a robust trunk that attracts his attention and revives a vague memory. He approaches and finds the fresh wound, flowing, as he himself left it. It is the tree from which he departed hours before, wanting to return. A mysterious, inexplicable force has brought him back to the side of the avenging tree. It is a phenomenon that happens almost invariably to those who get lost in the jungle. Only then does he realize the terrifying truth. He is lost!

They say that not even the authoritative "Every man for himself!" that carries over the roar of the storm and penetrates to the marrow of the bones, bringing panic to the crew and passengers, produces terror comparable to that experienced by the prisoner of the jungle when he perceives, trembling with terror, the cry of his consciousness: Lost . . . ! It seems that the tree trunks acquire mobility and, transformed into extraordinary beings, move closer to him, tightening more and more the circle that encloses him. The hunter undertakes the fatal flight. His senses vanish, and he sees only the threat of the trees that pursue him. He hears inaudible sounds and voices from beyond this earth. He runs and runs, destroying his flesh in the brambles, injuring his feet as he strikes the roots and trunks, suffering the implacable punishment of flagellating branches. Even the wild beasts and the reptiles flee at his passage!

Paradoxically, that deathwatch over his flight is slow and is sometimes prolonged days and nights until the wretch falls exhausted, never to rise again. Generally, those who get lost in the jungle end up rolling to the bottom of some ravine or sinking into some quicksand.

When a hunter does not return to his hut on the same day as his departure or during that night, the news spreads, and many who know him gather the next day to search for him. Divided into groups, they walk through the wilderness in different directions, firing frequent shots to give notice of their presence and to orient the lost hunter.

The circles described by a raven flying at a great height indicate that the hunter has died. Soon these birds, joining together in great numbers, descend in narrowing circles and finally come to rest on the branches near the cadaver.

On such occasions those who search for the lost hunter orient themselves by the flock of ravens that they discover by looking to the sky, and they go to rescue the cadaver before it is torn to pieces.

The natives withstand many days lost in the jungle, and it is not unusual that they manage to escape it, following their instinctive impulses of orientation; but when a civilized man ventures alone in the jungle and has the misfortune to get lost, his fate is sealed.

There are three things that cause a sudden reaction in the hunter who flees frenetically: the call of a rooster, the sound of a shot, and the barking of a dog. Upon hearing one of those unmistakable sounds that the strange acoustics of the jungle carry a great distance, the unfortunate man stops suddenly, his brain starts to function normally, the witchcraft of the jungle vanishes, and as if guided by providential hand, he returns to the distant campsite or he finds himself with those who have come to search for him.

The presence of Litero quickly returned my tranquillity. His happiness was indescribable. He appeared to realize, with pride, that he was helping me. Growling with joy, he was licking my hands to return the caresses I was lavishing on him. I shared with him my ration of food, which had remained intact, and while I was entertaining myself by watching him gnaw the bones, Sangama showed up, followed by the Matero, and, with forced aplomb, told me:

"Ah, the dog has gone on ahead . . . ! How are things?"

The Matero added, "We thought that an entire tribe had attacked you. So many shots . . ."

The irony froze on Luna's lips when he observed that I was hurt and discovered the marks of the struggle on my face. Sangama became pale. Both threw down their load of dead animals, and, in concerned silence, the former revived the fire the while latter treated my wounds.

"Tomorrow you'll be better," Sangama had told me while bandaging my arm. He quickly added with obvious surprise, "But this is the bite of an animal . . . !"

"Clearly not!" I answered him. "I was attacked by a type of human!"

As I described the event, Luna, who did not miss a word, exchanged frequent significant glances with Sangama.

"Possibly the one who attacked you is a madman who wanders around here," deduced Sangama.

Upon hearing that statement, the Matero exclaimed:

"We found his footprint at the edge of the water. We followed his trail in the wilderness a long distance, and we came upon the sites where he sleeps next to the creek. But we also determined that he hasn't been there for several days. That is why we went so far, delaying our return."

That night, while we stayed up on watch, the three of us talked spiritedly, covered by the mosquito nets, which were set up very close together below the small roof that sheltered us. We remembered the bandits and agreed to not worry about them, because if they ventured to return, leaving the well that we advised them to open in the dry channel of the ravine, they would go to a certain death. Moreover, they would not be able to discover the marks that Sangama had left to orient our return. For the moment the important thing was the attack of which I had been the victim. Sangama could not keep silent any longer about the suspicion he had formed.

"The elder Luna was prowling around here. His soul has been absorbed by the jungle, and his body wanders chained to the *renacal*."

"But do you believe in that, Sangama?" I asked with a trace of irony.

"Starting tomorrow we will watch for him in the *collpa* where he is accustomed to drink," the Matero interjected, avoiding a possible discourse by Sangama about the existence of the jungle myths.

Without a doubt the only thing that interested him was his father.

"He grabbed me by surprise," I explained. "If I had been able to take up my rifle in time, I would have shot at him, believing him a wild animal . . ." And I added, almost mournfully: "I must have injured him, since I fired so many shots in the direction he fled. I thought I heard a cry between the shots."

We agreed to search for him in the nearby area until we came upon him, watching over the place described by Luna. But when the latter called to wake us up the next day after he had made a morning excursion, the bright light of day already reigned in the forest.

"Come! Come!" he called us. "Here . . . !" And he pointed with his finger at a line of drops of blood that vanished into the thicket.

We followed the tracks, aided by Litero, who stopped from time to time to sniff them. Although the stains were far apart, the dog was always able to find them. Moreover, the shape of the thicket itself clearly indicated to us the places where a man had passed. Sangama, who took the lead, was describing the incidents of the flight in a slow voice, as if talking to himself.

"His passage was rapid through here. The drops are very far apart . . . Aha! He has the wound on the left side of the waist. This little branch stained with blood shows that. Hell! He crawled here! Not because he couldn't stand up, but because there was no other way to pass. The madman knew the path where he was escaping, since ten men with machetes would not have been able to clear this site," and raising his voice, in the tone of a command, he ordered us: "Crouch down too!"

He threw himself to the ground and started to crawl into a dark hole that cut through the tangle of the vines that seemed to fill the forest, and into which Litero had just disappeared with determination.

"Careful! I could be a nest of vipers!" I shouted.

Sangama replied confidently:

"A madman has passed through here. When a madman passes by a place in the jungle, it's because there is no danger. Only one who has complete control of his senses is capable of putting himself within the reach of jaguar claws or into a nest of vipers. And the dog seems to know the trail. We must follow him. Aren't you coming?"

He had already plunged completely inside the tunnel. His question came to us from its depths. The Matero threw himself to the ground and also entered. I slide in behind him without hesitating. Sangama's voice arrived muffled, as if we were speaking from very far.

"Don't be afraid. All the pests are gone now to where there is water and mud. They are stalking their prey there. The vipers have left in search of toads and birds. In this baked jungle there aren't even any scorpions."

After crossing through this dark tunnel, which had a series of turns and twists, with our stomachs scraping the ground and our backs against the roof of brush, vines, fallen trunks, and dry leaves, we exited into an open space. Litero had disappeared, but it was not difficult for us to find the trail of blood that continued ahead.

"The wound must be grave," commented Sangama. "Very soon we will come upon him."

There was a moment when we had to stop after we lost the tracks. Guided by Litero's barking, we were soon on the trail again. The drops of blood were marking some large side tunnels. We proceeded into them. Sangama stopped when he discovered a puddle of blood on the dry leaves, flattened by a body that had rested there for some time.

"He spent the night here," said the Matero, anxiously. "Surely he's not far."

The tracks continued under an overhang and led toward the *renacal.*

"He has gone to the lake," affirmed the Matero, hurrying his pace. "He's looking for water."

As we advanced, the stains were fresher and fresher. The little branches were no longer broken. It was evident that the injured one was losing his strength, since he rested against each tree and continued bleeding at each step.

At last we came upon him! He had fallen into a depression in the ground—a drainage ditch of the winter rains—and his head was raised up, resting on some roots. He was almost naked, extremely thin, with his hair and beard grown out, hairy and tangled. His chest rose up at each breath, showing his ribs under the weathered skin. We could hardly make out his features, especially his deeply sunken eyes, whose faded pupils could be seen within the rough, red eye sockets that surrounded them. The wound had in fact been on his left side and still oozed drops of blood. As soon as he had us in sight, he tried to get up, shouting:

"Get away, accursed demons! It's you who didn't let me return!"

"Old man! It's me, your boy, your Puricho! We have come to take you away!" the Matero exclaimed, while hurrying ahead to affectionately support his father.

The demented man got up with great effort, struggling to reject him.

"Demon! You have come to kill me! Leave me! Go away!"

But when the Matero held him in his arms, the old man started to tremble. He nodded his head, covered his eyes with a skeletal arm to avoid seeing what was in front of him, and started to talk in a tone both pitiful and pleading:

"Yes! I hear you. I can't escape because I have lost the way. No! It wasn't me who attacked you. Go away! Don't keep killing me . . . It wasn't me . . . ! Water . . . ! Water . . . !"

He collapsed in the arms of his son, vomiting frothy blood. We placed the poor old man, who was burning with fever, on an improvised bed of dead leaves.

Litero did not cease his howling, licking the hands and feet of the dying man. From the man's side, he kept leaping indiscriminately toward any one of us, as if he were trying to advise us that this was his master and he wanted to invoke our protection for him.

Sangama quickly brought his large hat filled of water. Leaning before the old man, he refreshed his forehead and chest, after having washed his mouth. The contact of the cold water produced a sudden reaction. The old man opened his eyes, which the fever made shine with a sinister glow. His son raised his head to give him water to drink. The agitation of his chest calmed visibly. Upon finding his gaze meeting that of the Matero, who was crying silently while carefully holding him up, he shook violently.

"My son! My Puricho! Is it you, my cub?" he said with anxiety, passing his hand along the Matero's forehead.

"Yes, it's me, father! We came searching for you."

Sangama and I looked at each other, moving our heads with that gesture that is imposed by the unavoidable.

"Lean me back, my son . . . It was a horrible nightmare . . . ! I am dying . . . ! The *supay* seized me . . . ! Give me water!"

We tried to continue giving him something to drink, but the dying man could no longer open his mouth. The pupils of his eyes, in which the gradual extinction of life could be seen, were fixed on the Matero's face. A grimace, a caricature of a proud smile, contracted his dry and trembling lips.

Perhaps in that supreme moment, upon abandoning life, he remembered the old trails, the little house in the cane field, in whose field frolicked his strong cub, his Puricho, who had followed him through all the paths of the jungle ever since his shoulder could withstand the weight of the rifle and his legs withstand the interminable daily marches; his Puricho, who had become a great *matero,* as he himself was, and who had come in search of him as a conqueror of the jungle.

Slowly the old man's eyes were extinguished in the loving arms of his son, those eyes in which we saw reflected the last instant of a heroic life.

My pain was infinite. Destiny had made use of my hands to put an end to the torment of that man driven insane by the jungle.

Chapter 29

The burial of the elder Luna took us the entire morning of the next day, since we wanted the tomb to be capable of resisting the coming floods. On a small piece of land we dug the grave, which we lined with palm leaves. Carefully carrying the body, we deposited it with the most respectful silence. The task concluded, there was nothing more for us to do in this place, which should have been the final point of our expedition. However, having resolved to support Sangama in his undertaking, even though we were unable to understand the transcendent importance that he attributed to it, we were ready to follow him wherever he went and at least attempt the recovery of the idol. It was clear that we had become infected with some of our guide's enthusiasm.

It's easy to imagine why we slept well that night. Very early on the following morning we were ready to continue the exploration. Without even asking where he was taking us, we began the journey, following Sangama. He headed for the edge of the *renacal,* which frequently formed inlets where the *tuqui-tuquis* and the *tangrillas* jumped gracefully between the aquatic plants, producing a deafening hullabaloo when they took note of our presence. Almost all the branches were loaded with wood pigeons, parrots, and thrushes, creating an uproar. Squirrels bustled in the trees, dragging their furry tails along, and in the high branches parrots chattered, breaking apart acorns and almonds. With its reddish coat shimmering in the sun, and shouting scandalously in its eagerness to attract the attention of all, the *cotomono* always seemed to me the most vain animal of the jungle.

The Matero, who brought up the rear on the journey, was bent over as if he were carrying an enormous burden on his back. We continued like this all day, without any incident worth mentioning. That night, while he ate his ration of food, Luna ventured his opinion:

"It would be better if we began the trip back. Our families are waiting for us . . . Any further and we might not be able to return."

Sangama, surprised, looked at him attentively. I would very much have liked to have added my opinion to Luna's, but Sangama's gesture stopped me. The Matero's words, spoken slowly, resounded as if charged with an omen: "Any further and we might not be able to return . . ." That was very possible, especially if we continued plunging into that hostile, unknown region. I thought of the old man recently buried. I thought about Chuya, abandoned in a shack in the heart of the jungle. But it was necessary to resign oneself. We were at the mercy of Sangama, and it was not possible to make him change his decision.

Later on, taking me aside, Sangama informed me:

"He has the *manchari,*" and as I looked at him without understanding, he added: "Well, it's the sickness from fright and pain. That's very dangerous in the jungle. It's necessary that we stop here to purge him with the *ojé*. There should be some over there on the shore, next to the *renacal*."

I confess that I also felt afflicted by the sickness. I was frightened and felt a deep pain. But at the bottom of all those torments, an enormous force gave me courage. It was my confidence in Sangama and the love that tied me to Chuya. She asked him to care for me, and he would certainly know how to carry out that charge.

When the first rays of the new dawn fell upon us, and we lifted our eyes to give thanks to Heaven, that instinctive movement that obliges all who wake up in the countryside to raise their soul upward to gaze at the heavens, we discovered an *ojé* tree, that bountiful tree that grows in the low places and, at the end of winter when the flooded jungle becomes suitable for fish to thrive, is filled with yellow fruit similar to figs. Then the water under the branches of the tree becomes a fishpond where dense masses of fish of different sizes swarm, attracted by the sound the fruits make when falling, and the fish devour them avidly.

Every minute that passes in the lower jungle is a drop of blood that one loses. The mosquitoes and horseflies suck it out ceaselessly. The multiple intestinal parasites produce an irritation and a disproportionate growth of the belly.

In both cases, the *chuchuhuasha,* that root whose bark renews the blood's red cells, and the *ojé,* whose juice acts as a germicidal purge, return health to the patients. The wisdom of nature has placed the remedy next to the illness.

When Sangama presented the Matero with the jar of *ojé,* diluted so that he could take it, the latter drank it in almost a single swallow.

"You have the *manchari,*" he had told him. And the opinion of Sangama, when he diagnosed an illness and administered the medicine, had the prestige of sacred things. It was necessary to obey him without an argument.

We expanded the campsite where we had spent the night, and we dug a well near the shore to filter clean water, since we had to remain there two long days, the amount of time that Sangama said was sufficient for Luna to recover completely.

The second night, Sangama communicated to us that we would continue the expedition the next day, very early.

As we had discussed, Sangama had the idea of reaching the higher land that could be seen in some places protruding from the edge of the *renacal* and that had a bluish appearance in the distance.

"From those heights we will be able make a better examination of the interior of the lake, which is covered with *renacos*," he told us, pointing them out to us as we were leaving our improvised campsite. "Perhaps from there we can see the island we are seeking, if it exists. Afterwards we will try to find a ford."

The hunting was very abundant. A rowdy flock of birds and monkeys constantly accompanied our path. Very near us, an enormous tapir stopped to look at us with stunned curiosity. All the fauna of the jungle appeared to have made an appointment along those shores where the water abounded.

We continued following the shore of the *renacal* as closely as we could, on occasion venturing into that aquatic jungle, walking over the net that the roots of the *renacos* had woven; but the unmistakable screams of the anacondas caused us to leave more than quickly. We then witnessed something so hair-raising that it left us without appetite for several days.

It happened in the mouth of a narrow river dried up by the intense drought. We were approaching it quickly after we heard loud, desperate cries apparently emitted by an animal that found itself in a difficult situation. The Matero went forward bravely and pushed aside the branches that blocked our passage, and to our astonishment, there appeared a quivering heap, a formless mass that struggled in spasmodic movements. It took us some effort to realize exactly what was happening there.

An anaconda of considerable size was making an effort to swallow, whole and alive, an enormous black alligator, whose hard skin could not be shredded by its powerful coils.

The ingestion was slow and laborious. Already the tail and a great part of the body of the reptile had disappeared between the jaws of the serpent, which contracted and expanded as it opened its huge mouth to swallow a few more inches of the difficult prey. Exhausted by the tremendous effort, it remained immobile a few moments, and then restarting the task, it continued absorbing a bit more of its victim.

The alligator, which had hardly more than its head outside of the mouth of its enemy, shrieked frightfully with its eyes bulging out of their sockets from terror.

"I can't stand any more!" shouted the Matero. And taking up his rifle, he fired several times into the anaconda's body, which was glowing in the sunlight.

Feeling itself wounded, the serpent shook violently, without letting go of its prey.

"I will only be able to kill it by hitting it in the head," Luna added. And approaching resolutely, without regard for the animal's threatening tail, he fired two shots at the flat-nosed head that protruded over the alligator's torso, displaying its beady little eyes.

With its brains blown out, after a few brief convulsions it fell still, stretched out to its full length. Little by little, it was expelling the gigantic body that it could not swallow. The emerging body was covered by a viscous substance formed by the anaconda's powerful intestinal acids, which had already started to produce their dissolving action.

Assuredly, the exhausting task of the serpent, which must have started many hours before, was preceded by a fierce combat, since for a great stretch the earth was dug up and numerous bushes were torn out by the roots.

With disgust I turned my gaze from the spectacle and moved away, followed by Litero, who shivered silently. A while later, the Matero told me that the alligator was not able to move from the spot, and he predicted that it would quickly be swallowed by another anaconda.

Chapter 30

Sangama's anxiety was growing in direct relationship to the advance of the sun. He was constantly climbing the trees nearest to the shore, whose tops surpassed in height the *renacos* that covered the ghostly lake. Then he would come down, clearly frustrated, and proceed to the next high tree to carry out the identical operation. The Matero and I awaited his descent with the hope the he would have discovered what he was looking for with so much interest, but in view of his frustrated expression, we refrained from questioning him, limiting ourselves to exchanging discreet glances.

Picking up his pack, which he always put at the foot of the tree he was climbing, he spoke to us before again undertaking a change of position:

"Possibly the *renacos* have exterminated all the trees on the island and, if so, at this distance only a small elevation would be noted."

As it was getting close to setting, the sun lit up the shore in an unusual manner, and Sangama invited me to climb a gnarled tree. He wanted someone else to observe a raised area. Having climbed to one of the highest branches, I looked toward the distant point that the finger of my friend indicated. Before my eyes appeared a great gray-green savanna, over which the final radiance of the sun was playing. At a certain distance, something like a fold could be guessed at more than seen in that expanse of vegetation.

"In reality, it looks like an island," I said with my gaze fixed on the far distance. "But I can't imagine how we would get there."

“That is precisely the problem that we need to resolve. Perhaps it will be necessary to venture among the *renacos,*” Sangama sighed, with a marked tone of sadness.

“We’ll go! We have to take the chance!” I hurried to tell him, with the intent of encouraging him.

I continued searching in every direction. In front of me, a dark strip of tall vegetation seemed to be the opposite shore of the lake. Farther ahead on the shore where we stood, the heights that were apparently Sangama’s objective appeared in profile. Thick foliage could be seen on them, and the plume of a palm tree, proudly dominating the mass of treetops, protruded here and there.

Clouds of raucous parrots crossed the sky, and a large flock of toucans, ignoring our presence, came to rest in the branches of the same tree that was serving as our observation post. The Matero shouted to us to come down, since he wished to shoot a few.

Thus ended that day. On the following day we continued along the shore, examining the forest of *renacos* at each step without being able to discover an auspicious fording place. We came to the edge of a small river of tranquil clear water that slowly lost itself under the *renacal.* In that spot the *renacos* were growing less densely, leaving spaces through which the course of the lazy current could be observed. Near the surface of the crystalline water, some beautiful shad appeared, which the Matero set himself to hunt with machete slashes from the shore, to proudly offer us a comforting *chilcano* as a trophy of his skill.

On the other side of this stream stood the hills we had been observing. Since it was necessary to construct a raft to cross the watercourse, the Matero and I set about to cut the necessary timber, but we soon had to delay that task. Sangama proposed that we first retrace our steps a bit because he had observed that we had earlier passed a place where the *renacal* was so thick that one could try to cross on top of it with great probability of success. The Matero, completely recovered from his recent illness, appeared more active and spirited than usual. He seemed to believe himself already in possession of the famous idol of the Incas.

We returned to the site Sangama indicated, which was not very far away. We stopped there to examine it. In truth, with sufficient balance, agility, and luck, we could attempt to ford the *renacal* at this site. We spent the night there, and on the following morning, supplied with long, strong poles, we set out over the tangle of roots that covered the muddy water. We did not realize that we were embarking on the most fantastic and dangerous of adventures.

Under our weight the entire *renacal* trembled. The advance was very difficult. Each step by one person endangered the others, under whose feet the roots moved, sinking in the mud. Sangama and the Matero carried provisions for several days on their backs, in addition to their personal clothing. Litero followed us with grave misgivings.

Attentive to the path and making great efforts at balancing, we plunged over that gigantic swaying net of roots, supporting ourselves on the poles and on tree trunks. From among the roots, innumerable heads of anacondas started to emerge, emitting hair-raising shrieks and shaking the net when we defended ourselves with the sharp points of our poles. Fearful that Litero would be seized, I had to carry him tied to my back, which even further encumbered my efforts to move beyond the trees by passing below or above their profuse upper roots. There was no time to weigh the danger. Lurching forward, without taking our eyes from the quivering mesh, we continued our rash advance with the slowness and caution of those who find themselves surrounded by dangers and have to choose the least immediate danger, without thinking that in the end they are delivering themselves to another, even greater one.

Suddenly Sangama, who was in the lead, shouted to us to stop. We looked up and saw that he was shooting at a huge anaconda that was coming toward us with its head in an attack posture.

The effect of the shot, although it suppressed the immediate threat, turned out counterproductive and frightful. Hundreds of serpents appeared everywhere, in an infernal flowering of jaws and throats that were emitting deafening, uncontrolled shrieks. Fortunately, all of them were a good distance from us. The three of us instinctively sharpened the points of our poles with our machetes, preparing to defend ourselves. Little by little the undulating bodies were approaching ominously, weaving a monstrous fence around us that narrowed from moment to moment. Some serpents formed into coils, lifting up their shifting heads and, after a few short seconds, continued advancing.

In the face of such a critical situation, all we could do was delay the end by climbing to the tops of the trees. Thus, the voice of Sangama telling us to climb higher surprised us halfway up the trees. When I had the chance to look down, I found that an anaconda was wrapping itself around the trunk of the tree that supported me. As soon as I had it within my reach, I gave it an energetic stab, which only stoked its aggressiveness. I multiplied my efforts and wounded it time and again, managing to penetrate deeply into its hard skin. Then it let loose, shaking itself in pain. Sangama kept encouraging us:

"I'm going there! Hoo! Go up higher! Go out on the branches! Hoo . . . ! Hoo . . . !"

Sangama's constant shouts made me believe that he had lost his senses. It seemed that we were doomed. But given that one redoubles all efforts in such situations, the Matero and I undertook the task of joining Sangama, moving from one branch to another. I don't know how we arrived at the old thick *renaco* in which Sangama awaited us and around which many reptiles had gathered, with their heads lifted up, struggling to coil around the tree and climb up to seize us.

"I never imagined that these animals could gather together like this. We have fallen into the greatest breeding ground of anacondas in the Amazon," he told us sorrowfully.

Suddenly we felt the tree sinking.

"Now we surely won't escape!" I shouted, full of terror.

The Matero, gripping a branch, lost all the color in his face. Realizing the disaster, he shouted:

"Most Holy Mary! We're sinking! We're going to fall straight into those mouths!"

Suddenly a fantastic tone came from Sangama's nose. How could he use his nose to emit such sounds? He was imitating the shrieks of the anacondas themselves and was adding spasmodic modulations that rattled the nerves. Falling silent to catch his breath, he advised us:

"Hold on tightly, and don't move."

We observed with astonishment that the reptiles slowly calmed down and those that were coming to the tree from different directions stopped their advance. The most daring, the one crawling up the trunk of the tree that sheltered us, let itself fall into one the numerous puddles that the roots left open. Others followed it through different openings between the roots, but most stopped where they were and stretched out or lazily coiled themselves up. The tree, free of the enormous weight of the serpent, regained its position, to our great relief.

"This one is the king of sorcerers. There is no room for doubt," the Matero whispered in my ear. "I believe we should help him with a few bullets."

And as he made a gesture to shoot, Sangama rushed to warn him:

"If you shoot, more will come and all the *renacal* will be in an uproar."

"Don't do it," I interceded. "They'll finish us quickly, without fail."

The sun was burning us from straight overhead. Not even the slightest breeze was moving. Thin clouds of yellowish steam rose off the *renacal,* wrapping us in a pronounced nauseating odor. The dog, which I placed on a branch so I could rest from carrying its weight, was suffocating, cowering without any energy to move.

"I am not going any farther even if you beat me with sticks," Luna communicated to me.

"We would all be very happy to get back to shore. We need calmness to think about the next step," I quickly answered him.

Sangama did not cease producing the infernal nasal symphony. But the situation could not have been any more desperate. My imagination was working feverishly to find some means of salvation. The idea of climbing from branch to branch to gain the nearest shore, which was the one from which we had departed, at first seemed to me to be feasible. Reconsidering, I had to discard that as impractical since only by an act of providence would the *renacos* have strong interwoven branches over that entire distance to facilitate our escape.

With the same anxiety with which a shipwrecked person without sails or oars would look at the lifesaving coastline, I could see, above the foliage, the nearby line of high trees that announced the existence of firm land. But how could we cross the distance that separated us? I looked questioningly at Sangama, who remained silent. I thought of his fertile imagination, which had always found a way to get us to safety in the most desperate circumstances. "Couldn't he save us one more time?" I wondered with a mix of hope and anxiety. "Wouldn't he end up finding a miraculous remedy to ward off the imminent danger that threatened us?" But the anacondas remained there quietly, sleeping without any indication of leaving.

The Matero, nudging me with his elbow, whispered to me softly:

"If they don't leave, we are still in the same situation."

I looked at him with pity, and turning to Sangama, I asked him:

"Can we escape?"

"I don't know if we can do it. Only a miracle . . . !"

And then the miracle happened. The shore from which we had embarked on the dangerous undertaking was suddenly filled with cries, as if it were being covered with swarms of furious pigs. The anacondas awoke, terrified, and fled. In a moment, not a single one remained in sight.

"The *huanganas*! The *huanganas*!" the Matero shouted, full of joy.

"That is what I needed to imitate," murmured Sangama, wiping away the sweat that bathed his face. "The cry of the *huangana*!"

Chapter 31

The ***huangana*** is the most gregarious mammal of the jungle, and also the most nomadic. In groups that reach many thousands they carry out their travels through the virgin jungle. They form herds of truly wild beasts, more aggressive and more voracious than the javelinas, which they resemble in all respects. Each herd follows a trio of guides, which are in command; it obeys the flankers, which prevent it from drifting apart, and it is defended by the rear guard, which fights with the jaguars that always follow behind it, anxious to seize young ones that straggle behind from fatigue. There are many felines that have been destroyed by the rear guard when, spurred on by hunger, they throw themselves upon some *huangana* not yet far enough behind. The principal guide, which determines the direction to be taken, is a small, tough specimen. Its notable difference from the general run of the herd makes one think that it is a genetically selected individual, since it orients itself with a peculiar skill, leading its army to one or another stand of palm trees whose rocklike fruits, which pile up year after year at the foot of the plant, contain delicious kernels that fatten the herd. There is nothing that opposes the passage of the herd when it undertakes a journey. With the greatest ease it crosses swift rivers, lakes, and impenetrable expanses of the jungle. There are stories of times when steamboats have had to stop navigating for hours because of the dense mass of *huanganas* that filled the river. Nothing pleases these animals as much as coming upon a swamp, into which the herd plunges like a flood. The mud stirred up from the bottom by the strong snouts becomes uniform in density and thus constitutes the soft bed in which the *huanganas* rest. The *collpa* should be extensive enough to shelter the entire herd; if not, they leave it for another, more ample one, in which submerged up to the snout, they sleep placidly, assured that nothing will disturb them.

The anacondas and the alligators, lords of the swamps, flee upon sensing the proximity of the horde that descends on them like an unstoppable *huaico.*[23] The gigantic anaconda that is trapped, whose strength is capable of converting the massive tapir or the fat bull into a sack of shredded bones and muscles, is torn to pieces by hundreds of jaws wounding it at the same time. In a few minutes, all that remains of this enormous animal, the largest and strongest of the jungle, is the shredded skin, floating above the bloodstained mud.

The instantaneous disappearance of the frightening ring of serpents that had fenced us in was, therefore, quite explainable.

Luna was the first to abandon the tree we were in. The terrible fright and the instinct of self-preservation appeared to give him wings. In one incredible leap he jumped from the branch that had supported him next to me, falling to the ground with loud impact.

"He killed himself!" I shouted in distress.

But, as if by some miracle, he stood up and began a dizzying run, jumping from root to root, urging us by shouts to follow him. But he had to stop abruptly when he heard Sangama's voice:

"Do you want the *huanganas* to catch you . . . ? They are in that direction."

The Matero had to return, disappointed, limping in pain and rubbing his hips. The nearest shore was completely covered by the herd. The only accessible point, without taking a great risk, was on the opposite side of the river's mouth and on which stood the highest of the hills already mentioned. After Luna had rejoined us, Sangama headed toward that point, inviting us to follow him.

"Hurry! Let's take shelter over there! These trees are not very strong. Against that mob nothing is secure in the jungle!"

We had not gone very far when the forest opened before us,

---

[23] *Huaico:* devastating flood of mud and rock brought on by the first winter floods on the coast.

divided by the river, whose course, covered by innumerable floating bridges of roots, we crossed with the water waist-high. Fortunately, those interlaced roots that sank under our weight held up well enough to prevent us from sinking completely. The water glided past us slowly, and Sangama confirmed that this part of the *renacal* was free of reptiles.

Having reached the other shore, we quickly continued our journey through that strange jungle until we arrived before a steep slope, totally clear of vegetation and rising almost vertically to a height of four meters.

As always, Sangama discovered the method to overcome the difficulty that blocked our path.

***

"You're going to go up first," our guide told me. And without giving me time to formulate a response about going first, he tied the end of his pole to my waist. Strongly propelled by the pole and catching hold with my hands and feet in the few cracks in the surface, I could overcome the obstacle and seize the strong roots that were hanging over the edge of the ravine, the beginning of the lush vegetation that covered the surface above. Afterwards, conveniently attached to the end of the same pole, Litero was lifted up. Luna came up in the same manner, hooked to the pole and aided from below by Sangama, while I in turn was pulling from above.

The ascension of the Matero having been accomplished, I suddenly felt an inexplicable foreboding and looked anxiously at the place where Sangama stood a few meters below, expecting that we would be able to provide him some aid. At his side was an opening surrounded with roots, like the mouth of a well, full of murky dark water. Since at that moment Luna had moved away to obtain a vine with which to lift up our companion, I called to him, shouting:

"The pole is enough! Come help me," and turning to Sangama, I yelled to him: "Attach yourself to the pole so we can pull you up!"

As I was waiting for Sangama to follow my urgings, a flat head arose from the opening next to one of his legs and, with lightning speed, lifted him into the air, let him fall violently, and then dragged him toward the well. The surprise did not permit me even to let out a shout. Stunned, I saw one of his hands grab a root whose end was submerged in the dense liquid as he was being pulled into it by the irresistible force. His hand slipped over the root with such pressure that it tore off the hard bark. A second must have gone by since that clenched hand tried to hold on to life, until it disappeared into the water, whose surface quickly recovered its stillness, leaving a quivering, bare root as its only trace.

"He's finished! He's finished . . . ! Good-bye, Sangama, and your idol!" offered Luna, who had arrived in time to witness the deadly scene.

"We have to save him, Luna! Do something! Don't look at me with that idiotic expression!" I shouted desperately.

The Matero grimaced, shrugging his shoulders and crossing his arms, by which he indicated eloquently that there was nothing, absolutely nothing, that could be done. Then, with irritating tranquillity, he invited me to climb up higher.

"I'm staying here!" I replied. "What difference can it make? In this cursed jungle everywhere is the same! I'm going to fire all my bullets against this hell."

"Everywhere is not the same," he replied in a low voice, as if talking to himself. And pointing to the *renacal,* he added philosophically: "There is certain death. Here is salvation. Up there—do you see?—that way is the way home."

Convinced that I would not move, he began the climb alone, but he did not delay in turning back and retracing his steps, doubtless repentant for his attitude.

"Let's go, man! You know that I can't leave you. Night is already closing in, and we can't stay here."

And seizing me by the arm, he almost dragged me on his back, opening a passage through the brush. The dog was following us, howling mournfully. A cold wind coming off the *renacal* was brushing our backs. I let myself be carried. Bewildered, I felt as if my soul, hanging on to the hole through which Sangama had disappeared, was farther away from me with each step.

Finally Luna stopped. We were on flat terrain, under a small overhang. He threw to the ground the bundle he was carrying on his back and, after relieving me of the one I was carrying, proceeded to clear a bit of the wilderness, where he made his bed, leaving a space for mine. Mute and very still, I watched him act without experiencing the slightest desire to help him. I saw him open the packet of leaves where he kept the cold meat. When he called me to eat, I responded:

"How can you think about eating, man?" I said to him, stunned, adding a series of obscenities.

"There is nothing else to do," he answered me, without changing his expression. "I am hungry . . . and I eat. Afterward, if you want to, we'll talk about what happened. Soon we'll have time to cry, if you also want to do that."

Many times I had admired the Matero's resignation and serenity, but his attitude on that day went beyond the limits of what is tolerable.

"It seems that it doesn't matter to you what happened to a man who was always the best of friends to us," I replied, looking at him intently.

"No! I am hurting very badly . . . Or don't you believe that I am capable of feeling sorrow? I suffered so much for my *taita* . . . ! But it's just that I don't believe . . ."

"What is it that you believe, you with no feelings?"

"I don't know . . . I don't want to accept it . . . I cannot believe that he is dead."

"Explain it to me, idiot. Didn't you see it yourself? You have doubts, perhaps? What do you base that on?" I insisted angrily.

"Fair enough. We'll talk tomorrow. Nothing is gained by raging," he responded, disappearing under the mosquito netting.

Moments later, the rhythmic sound of his breathing revealed that he slept tranquilly.

Seated facing this gloomy plain, wrapped in the hazy light of the moon that could be made out through the humid atmosphere, I was trying in vain to sharpen my senses in order to perceive something. A weak and remote hope made me also doubt Sangama's death.

Possibly, that remote doubt was determined by the difficulty with which one accepts the greatest misfortunes when they occur without warning. I could not accept that this marvelous man, capable of dominating and resolving everything, had ended his life in such a vulgar way, in the belly of a reptile, when it was so easy for him to subjugate the wild beasts and overcome all the dangers of the jungle. But I also considered that, as an animal tamer can at any moment die under the claws of his slaves, this tamer of all the elements had been exterminated by one of the reptiles that moments before he had at his feet, hypnotized. At the depth of these thoughts, which filled my brain, battering it, I seemed to hear a call that I supposed was coming from the other world.

"Hooo . . . !"

An intense shiver ran through my entire body. I sharpened my ears as much as I could. The silence that surrounded me was absolute. What was it that I heard? I cannot be precise about the amount of time that passed. Tired of waiting, I had to convince myself that I had suffered a hallucination. Imperceptibly I went from sensory activity to imagination. The old Sangama appeared to me in my mind, tall, muscular, with his bearing of an Inca Amauta who looked at me kindly when he saw me beside his daughter, that blushing girl with green eyes and musical throat who adored the flowers, the birds, and poetry. I remembered the talks I had with her and the lively scenes at her side in the distant house in the forest. And I was frightened by the idea of how much she would suffer when she saw us return to the shack in which we had left her, without bringing her father with us. Oh, Sangama, old friend, to whom I owed so much protection and affection! How much I had always felt his vigilant and paternal gaze around me during that entire unforgettable trip! And now he was being digested by his captor, which would have swallowed him after converting him into a mass of muscles and bones. Where would that anaconda be sleeping, as that species usually does when digesting, without knowing that its prey was the most marvelous man that had ever walked the jungle?

I found myself with a dry throat, gushing sweat, and feverish. My eyes clouded up, and I felt warm tears run down my cheeks.

Crying? In the jungle the men cry only when they are drunk. The women cry, yes, for whatever reason, as in all parts of the world. And that brute of the Matero was sleeping like a saint, as if the horrible misfortune did not matter to him in the least. Such stupid laziness made me angry.

"Get up!" I shouted, knocking down his mosquito netting. "You seem to be made of wood!"

"I can't sleep tonight, damn it!" he grumbled. "Go to sleep man, and let a Christian sleep in peace!"

He started to look diligently for something next to his bed. It was the stub of a candle, which he lit to look at me in its brightness, with stunned eyes.

"Are you crying . . . ? Hell, man! It's just as well that my *taita* said that men also cried from anger . . . But," he added thoughtfully, "I also cried from sorrow when we buried the old man . . . Yes, I cried! Although you two didn't see me."

He spoke slowly, with long pauses, as if through the sleep that was overtaking him. He bent forward slackly, supported his head on his knees, and fell asleep seated like an Inca mummy, while I went crazy with desperation.

Chapter 32

In the early morning of that ill-fated night I felt an intense cold. The Matero continued sleeping, wrapped up in his blankets. I had to curl up at the foot of a tree, with my head supported on the waterproof bag that held my few pieces of equipment. It was evident that we had entered a climate zone different from that which we left hours before and which, starting on the small hill on which we found ourselves, was confined to the drainage basin of the Huallaga River, whose topography is different from that of the Bajo Ucayali.

The next day greeted us with its profusion of light and the concert of the birds that were awakening and taking flight. Viewed from those heights, the expanse of the lower lands resembled the vast surface of a sea of foliage. Clouds of steam rose up from the *renacal,* as if from a gigantic kettle, as it was struck by the burning sun, whose rays would doubtless cross the sky without striking even the faintest cloud.

The Matero picked up his rifle, on hearing the shouts of a flock of macaws that were enjoying their share of acorns in the nearby branches.

"A pair of macaws on the grill will do us a lot of good," he said, plunging into the thicket. But as he entered the brush, the raucous flight of several startled partridges distracted him, and he set out up the hill after them.

At the same time I picked up my rifle and went in the opposite direction, traveling across the stretch of land we had come through the day before. I felt depressed. I set out without any intention of descending the hill, but a mysterious force subconsciously pulled me downward, in spite of the decision I made the night before to get away as soon as possible and forever from those lands, to all appearances forsaken by God. I went along, turning over in my mind the details of the events of the prior evening. I felt the need to walk along the shore at the very foot of the abrupt slope. I quickly took heart from the idea of surprising the filthy serpent that had seized our companion and tranquilly dedicated itself to the task of digesting its extraordinary catch.

Thus I soon arrived at the place where the incident took place. The pole remained near the shore, with its lower end caught among the roots that surrounded that deep hole filled to the top with black water. My gaze stopped immediately on the tragic root, almost torn apart, on which it seemed I could still see the powerful hand grasping with the superhuman energy with which it was trying to save its life. On this mesh of roots I saw something that I did not see the night before: the bag that Sangama had laid down to help us climb up the side of the ravine.

I cut a branch into a hook and put it on the lower part of the pole, on whose sharp point I noted, with disgust, the bloodstains of the anacondas that we had wounded in the *renacal*. It was not hard for me to lift the bag to put it in a more secure place. It seemed to me that in it would be hiding something of the spirit of that supernatural man who had so decidedly taken part in my life since that day I arrived, full of ambitious dreams, in the area of Santa Inés. Litero, who had followed me, suddenly gave strange signs of distress.

Unconscious of what I was doing, I wandered by the edge, tasting the bitter sadness of that area. I was retracing my steps on the pathway in order to pass over it again, as if some bond held me tight to the piece of jungle where Sangama had been lost, when suddenly I thought I heard a sort of moan that came from the direction of the mouth of the river. I stopped nervously, trying to hear the faintest sounds and notice the slightest movements. Litero had also stopped as if alerted for the same reason. I was sure the dog shared my own unease. After a prolonged wait, the voice came to us again, more clearly. It was a human moan, emitted by someone who could not shout. The dog took off, and I ran after him, shouting with all my strength. At the bottom of the ravine, at my feet, there came a voice, hoarse and muffled:

"Here . . ."

I don't know how I slid down to the shore, followed by the little dog, who was growling desperately.

How great was my surprise as I pushed apart a clump of branches and found Sangama, almost hidden in the brush along the shore, in a place where the ground sloped downward toward the bed of the river! He was there! There was no doubt! But in what a condition!

All his clothes were destroyed, and he was covered with that black stench-filled mud of the *renacal;* his hair and arms were also smeared with the same stinking mass, which swarmed with quantities of flies, as on a cadaver. I leaned over him, after chasing away the pests with a branch. I could hardly comprehend this gratifying reality. Like someone coming out of a hypnotic dream, he slowly opened his tired eyes, and with an expression of deep relief he muttered:

"I knew you would come to help me . . ."

Leaving him with the dog, who was gleefully demonstrating his joy, I went for the bag I had recently recovered and took out clothing and a washcloth. I undressed him delicately, and with the fresh, clear water of the river, I bathed him until he was clean. Then I dressed him and with great effort moved him up to a flat, clear place. His body, almost inert, weighed too much. I laid him over a bed of fresh leaves.

The bath, the dry clothing, the rest, and possibly my company slowly revived him. Pointing to a nearby tree, he asked me to take him there. He leaned back, and with his head and shoulders supported on the trunk and roots, he seemed to fall asleep. Only then could I measure the intensity of my happiness. With the resurrection of Sangama, I felt strong again, agile, capable of embarking on the most audacious adventures.

Next to Sangama, watching over his sleep, I tried to explain to myself the providential event. But how could this happen? It was a miracle whose explanation only he could give. As if he had heard my thoughts, Sangama opened his eyes and looked at me paternally, saying:

"It was something terrible, something that the imagination cannot conceive. A little sleep will make me much better."

When I wanted to go look for the Matero and some food, he stopped me:

"I don't need anything but rest for the moment; but I want to know that you are at my side. Don't leave."

I stayed there in silence, trying to boost his spirits. I was almost overcome by sleepiness, against my will, when I was jolted by some detonations that came from the heights. Shortly thereafter, I heard Luna's voice, calling me. I responded, shouting as loudly as I could. Litero went to meet him, barking scandalously.

From amid the trembling branches, the Matero appeared, guided by my shouts and the dog's barking. Seeing Sangama, the Matero just stood there overwhelmed by the shock. Finally he reacted and said, with apparent naturalness:

"Hello, Sangama!"

He did not think to say anything else. With his eyes enlivened by the surprise and with that penetrating look of persons accustomed to continuously scrutinizing the thicket, he examined Sangama in detail.

"Hello, Matero!" Sangama answered, making an effort to smile. "I'm with you two again!"

Chapter 33

The two long, tranquil days spent in the small flat area where we had set up our camp permitted Sangama to recover. He had convalesced with amazing rapidity and appeared anxious to continue the undertaking, about which he almost never ceased talking to us, praising its importance and waxing enthusiastic with the success that he expected to achieve. The Matero was very diligent and had regained my appreciation. I understood that his apathy was only in the face of events that had already occurred, for which, in his opinion, there was no remedy. Analyzing his conduct, I found it to be almost justified in that environment where events developed in surprising and dangerous ways, requiring the full use of all one's faculties in order to survive.

On the third day of our stay in the camp, the Matero set out enthusiastically to explore the surroundings, taking with him a good supply of cartridges for hunting. This was a truly happy day for me, since I saw the good Sangama able to walk, having recovered from his alarming episode.

"One surely needs a constitution of steel to recover so quickly," I told him admiringly, "and from that condition you were in when I found you down there . . . !"

Sangama stretched out to rest on a fresh mattress of palm leaves, watching the capricious flight of a splendid butterfly that was weaving delicate arabesques over the bushes, fluttering among a cloud of diaphanous dragonflies. Soon he turned his gaze to the distance, passing slowly over the horizon, as if he wished to discover a precise point lost in the jungle. Not knowing what he was trying to do, I also fixed my gaze in the depths of the jungle and thought about the little shack where I imagined waiting for me the girl who in my fantasy was the most adorable and beautiful one in creation. Perhaps in that same instant her thoughts also flew toward me across the thicket, like a white butterfly.

So far the expedition had succeeded in accomplishing its first objective, which was locating the elder Luna; the second, which now interested us all, appeared to be leading us lurching from one place to another, doomed to ultimate failure. What struck me as most important in that moment was to return as soon as possible to the shack where Chuya had stayed. She had to be uneasy due to our long absence. The unpleasant faces of the Bull and the Piquicho also appeared in my thoughts, with all their repugnance. We had left them prisoners of the wilderness, which they were not able to leave, because of their inability to orient themselves, unless they wished to march to a certain death.

From the distance, my gaze passed to the branches that extended over us, and from there it moved to settle on the ground, which was blanketed with dark fallen leaves and over which were moving flickering disks of luminous gold. A pair of mockingbirds sang happily, flying from treetop to treetop through the nearby bushes.

Up to that moment, in spite of my curiosity, I had avoided questioning Sangama about the miracle of his salvation, since I considered it ill-advised to remind him of such scenes and circumstances when they could affect his state of health. But he himself wanted to speak about the details that day, while he entertained himself by pushing together the dispersed embers to revive the fire and prepare lunch. I was opposed to his assuming any of these chores but he insisted, assuring me that he was already well and that the distraction would be good for him.

He didn't speak in a direct manner but as someone who related something experienced by another, touching on the facts from different points of view, as if it were a matter of hiding something in order to reveal it at the end in the most complete manner.

"I'm aware that you two are burning with curiosity to know how

I got free from the reptile, considered the strongest animal of the jungle," he commenced hesitatingly, measuring his words, as if at the same time that he was trying to satisfy my curiosity, he was undertaking to prolong it. "The alligators and the crocodiles are more fishers than hunters. The anacondas are more hunters than fishers. Both species have their own ways of behaving, but they never devour the prey underwater, but rather on the water's surface or on the land. In this they are alike. The alligators and crocodiles cannot fish underwater and are not even capable of pursuing fish when they swim at the surface. They situate themselves between two bodies of water, in the places where schools of fish are found, and they close the pharynx with a special contraction and open their mouth, staying completely motionless until the unwary prey, pursued by larger fish, enters the cavity, surely confusing it with the floating logs. Feeling the fish in its mouth cavity, the alligator lifts its head it out of the water and holds it almost vertical. The victim falls by its own weight through the length of the open esophagus. That operation cannot be effectuated underwater, because water would fill the alligator's stomach and the animal would drown. Have you ever seen anyone kill a black alligator . . . ? When it involves the most fearsome of them, the ones whose shell, moldy with age, cannot be perforated even by bullets, those who know the secret usually kill them with ease. They cover a piece of *topa*[24] with meat and throw it in the water, where it floats. The hungry animal flings itself upon the supposed prey with its jaws wide open and seizes it with its ferocious teeth. The *topa*—or what is the same thing, the stick of balsa—besides being buoyant, is very soft. Any sharp thing can penetrate it with great ease, but it doesn't come out in the same way. The alligator's teeth, upon biting it, penetrate the treacherous wood entirely and remain stuck in it, preventing the mouth from opening or closing completely. The water then flows through the open throat until it fills the stomach cavity. In a few minutes the alligator sinks. It's possible that it doesn't drown immediately and continues struggling futilely in the depths; but in the end it appears,

[24] *Topa:* a wood that is soft and very light.

floating belly up, a sign that it is dead. With the anacondas it happens the same way. They are very fond of the delicate flesh of the birds, and to hunt them, an anaconda only has to raise its head where it can be seen and emit its shriek, which sounds something like the whinnying of horses, and it immediately paralyzes the little birds with terror. Those that are in the nearest trees fall as if struck by a dart, and the anaconda then collects them in its immense stomach. The large mammals, like the heavy tapir, the grass-eating capaybara, or the swift hornless deer are hunted only when they carelessly come close to drink. The art of camouflage has reached perfection among the animals of the jungle. No deer or tapir would be able to realize that under what looks exactly like a rotting log—and there are many everywhere on the riverbanks—hardly centimeters from its view, there is an anaconda lying in wait that will attack with lightning speed as soon as the animal comes within its reach. It then tears its prey to shreds and swallows it. When the anaconda fishes in shallow waters, it lifts its head out of the water and then lets it fall on the chosen fish; if it catches the fish, the anaconda turns again to lift its head up to swallow it in the air. It would not be able to swallow it underwater because the water would fill its enormous stomach, which expands like a balloon and stretches and contracts like an accordion."

There was an extended silence, as if Sangama were struggling to overcome some difficulty, without my daring to interrupt him. He was opening and closing his eyes and giving the impression of making an effort to swallow something that had stuck in his throat. Finally he continued:

"When an anaconda succeeds in seizing an animal, it keeps it submerged only long enough to drown it, then takes it to the shore. The anacondas know that the animals of the jungle that walk on two or four paws, or simply crawl, drown easily in the water. It is enough to prevent them from lifting their heads out of the water, for which those reptiles don't need to use much effort. They hold the victim under by simply taking advantage of their enormous weight, and they kill it merely by waiting long enough. Therefore, the anacondas are proud of being able to act equally well in or out of the water. They are not built to kill a prey capable of lasting long enough under the water to be able to support itself on the bottom and attack in its turn. Have you seen the enormous bite that it gave me on the thigh? The bite of an anaconda not willing to let go until its victim is completely dead . . . But I assure you that that serpent will not hunt again while it lives, which will be for a very short time. I attacked it through its only vulnerable part, its eyes, which I succeeded in tearing out of their sockets. That head, so swift when attacking, could never realize how some fingers, apparently harmless but guided by the human intelligence, could succeed in defeating it by leaving it blind. That anaconda will never hunt again!"

Anyone hearing Sangama's detailed account would have believed that it involved a peaceful naturalist who was remembering his experiences in the jungle, and not someone who had miraculously escaped a monstrous embrace, from which no one had ever escaped until then, and the memory of which was enough to make one's nerves flinch. As if he were guessing my thoughts and knew that I could not completely accept it, he added:

"It all depends on systematic exercise. Remain underwater long enough? The fakirs and yogis have done more astonishing things!"

***

The extensive account had absorbed us for a substantial time, and when the Matero did not return, we had to resign ourselves to eat only a piece of grilled meat with manioc flour for lunch.

"Don't worry," Sangama advised me. "The nature of the terrain won't let him get lost. He'll return soon."

In fact, our ears picked up frequent detonations in the distance, produced by shots announcing that the harvest was going to be abundant. At nightfall Luna returned, very sweaty. He threw his heavy burden of partridges, agoutis, and curassows before us, which Litero patrolled as if charged with guarding them.

"I wasn't able to go very far, since the other river is very wide and I didn't find any way to cross it," he informed us.

"What river?" asked Sangama, with acute interest.

"Well, it's a river that empties into the other side of the *renacal*. This one near us, from which we take water, is only a branch of the other."

"Then we are on an island?" Sangama asked again.

"That's what I'm saying," answered the Matero, satisfied. "Neither more nor less. We are on an island."

This news appeared to disturb Sangama. He went to bed quite late that night, after the Matero had already spent many hours snoring as if blessed.

As the new day dawned, we climbed to the highest part of the hill. At the summit we discovered some very stout leafy trees, whose stalks showed some strange deformities.

"What a beautiful spot to camp!" exclaimed Sangama, ecstatic.

As the Matero and I were of the same opinion, we ran to get the few items that constituted our equipment. When we returned, we found our companion leaning against a tree trunk, looking attentively at the sturdy trees. The lower part of one of them, singularly deformed and gnarled, caught my attention when I fixed my eyes on it, following Sangama's gaze. The morning breeze blew pleasantly, the occasional gusts rocking the high treetops and communicating to us a sense of life and happiness that we had not felt for some time. The Matero, showing signs of contentment, sang picaresque jungle airs while he was cutting branches and leaves to improvise a new shelter, a task to which Sangama and I contributed enthusiastically.

"We can rest here a few days, and when Sangama recovers, we can start back," said the Matero, emphasizing the words and giving me a meaningful wink to let me know that, by this means, he wished to discover what plans were crossing the mind of the person in question. Then, since there was no reaction, looking toward the depths of the *renacal,* he added: "It's just that I won't go back there for anything . . . Or perhaps you two are thinking about twisting the Devil's tail a second time . . . ?"

After lunch, we stretched out on the leafy ground. Looking at the puffs of bluish smoke from Sangama's huge cigar, we silently enjoyed the peacefulness of the environment that surrounded us. Even the chirps of the thrushes seemed sweeter to us, as if they were taking care to welcome us. An irresistible sleepiness was coming over me, and I was about to fall asleep, when a noisy shout from the Matero brought me back, startled.

"What a beautiful squirrel, by Christ . . . !"

He stood up quickly and, with his rifle in his hands, turned toward the darkest and knottiest of the trees, on whose trunk the most beautiful of squirrels was climbing. The Matero took aim and killed it, but immediately the tree was filled with frightened squirrels that sprang forth, from where we did not know. Luna disappeared behind the tree trunk, following Litero, who had left in pursuit of the dead squirrel, but it wasn't long before Luna reappeared, pale and unable to speak.

"What is it? What is it?" I asked, intrigued. "An immense snake, surely!"

"No!" the Matero was able to say with great effort. "It's a skull!"

Hearing this, Sangama, who had been almost smiling while observing the scene, jumped up as if a scorpion had bitten him and headed for the Matero, asking him nervously:

"Where . . . ? Where is it?"

"There!" answered the Matero, without looking away. "There in the large tree . . . ! On the other side!"

We ran to the place he indicated, where Litero had remained, howling without taking his eyes off a large opening in the trunk, almost at ground level. In its depths rested a bleached white skull, staring at us with its empty eye sockets. I had the impression of the past reaching out to me through them, as if they were making some frightful revelation.

Sangama reached resolutely into the hollow tree trunk, seized the skull, and put it in my hands, which were unable to reject the macabre charge. Immediately he went about using his machete to reveal a complete human skeleton that was covered with a crust of dried earth. Then, in a fever pitch of activity, he continued the excavation until some multicolored fabrics appeared that fell apart on contact with his trembling hands. I had moved the skull and bones a short distance away. When I started to do the same with the rags, Sangama advised me:

"Very careful . . . !"

The Matero, mistrustful and superstitious like a good mountain man, kept his distance, and only when he was convinced that nothing supernatural was happening to us did him come close.

Sangama spent a long time on that task. When he came out of this cave of sorts, he was unrecognizable, his face covered with a layer of gray dust. He was breathing heavily. After breathing fresh air and cleaning his sweaty face, he exclaimed:

"We are on *the* island . . . ! The one who was waiting for me died centuries ago."

Sangama did not go to bed that entire night. My sleep was not continuous or peaceful either. Each time that I woke up, I made out his figure outlined by the glow of the bonfire, beside which he remained like a mummy, crouching with his head supported on one hand and the large cigar in his mouth.

I found him there at daybreak, engrossed as if he were exploring incredible distances, searching for a presumed key to the deepest mystery. I watched him closely for some time without his even being aware of my presence. I finally spoke to him, and he appeared to return from the distant journey. Rubbing his eyes, he said:

"We are on the island! I seem to feel the closeness of the Idol that has brought me here! At last we are going to have the answer to the mystery that it holds! At last . . . !"

Chapter 34

The Matero used the last portion of flour that we had when he prepared lunch that morning. After that, roasted meat and palm shoots were all we had left for feeding ourselves.

"If only I had a pot . . . ," sighed the Matero. "I'm really tired of roasted meat."

"Over there, inside the tree, is one in good condition that I dug up yesterday," Sangama told him.

"No, for God's sake!" the Matero protested superstitiously. "Eat from the pot of a dead man . . . ! Not even if they kill me!"

The sun had scarcely appeared when Sangama was already digging feverishly. From the dry earth, his nervous hands extracted shabby robes and cotton fabrics, which we admired for their symmetrical designs embroidered in multicolored threads. From one end he removed some utensils of baked clay and wood and some stone instruments. Finally he emerged from the hollow of the tree, carrying in his arms, as ceremoniously as a priest performing sacred rituals, a crude box, which he carried to the campsite while in a low voice his lips emitted something that had to be a prayer. Full of curiosity and ever more encouraged, I attentively followed Sangama's movements, strangely slow and meticulous, such as those that legends attribute to prophets and high priests. Without getting too close, for fear of disturbing him, I could see how he carefully opened the box and extracted from it a ball of ropes of different colors, which he unraveled and submitted to a detailed examination. He then proceeded to spread them out in order over the dried leaves that covered the ground. As he carried out this painstaking task, his face acquired a pathetic expression in which all the cruel elements of disappointment and despair, strangely mixed together, could be detected.

He spent all the rest of the day lost in thought, bent over the ancient discovery. The Matero and I watched him, intrigued, without daring to distract his attention, since, without a doubt, he was deciphering the meaning contained in those *quipus*.

When he finished the task, the evening was already languishing, fading into the first shadows of the night. The jungle held a dense feeling of desolation and was covered in an asphyxiating odor. The trees that formed that tall leafy forest were displaying their fantastic silhouettes against the tormented dying sky of the evening.

That night, with the three of us seated close together as the pale light of the moon filtered through the thick foliage, splashing the interior of the forest with silver streaks, Sangama read to us, with deliberately chosen words, the message contained in the *quipus*. We listened to him, stunned as if on the very threshold of life he was revealing to us the mysteries from beyond the tomb.

I still remember those words, which were engraved in my memory with indelible precision. They read as follows:

"To you, who carries in your veins the blood of our race and who comes across time to this wilderness in search of the Sacred Image that your elders guarded in secret, this message is directed, which, if our gods permit, arrives in your hands and is understood by your mind. Quispe the Noble respectfully salutes you, who are perhaps the last Son of the Sun.

"Obedient to the order that our lord, the Inca, found me worthy to receive, I have come here, after finding the bird of prey that was devouring a serpent, following the course of the great river, on whose shores stands the mountain of salt, and defying the turbulence of the torrential waters that I left only when the white birds directed me toward the East, my efforts to carry out the mission being blocked by an impenetrable thicket. I arrived, weary of foot, in this remote and unknown place, which has welcomed me with hospitality for so many years . . . This is the island that I had to reach as my long journey ended, and this is the summit that most closely approaches the sun and is where I buried, as I was entrusted, the image that the strong back of Auca, my faithful companion, brought here.

"In this area I cleared the wilderness and sowed the seeds I brought, which gave to me, year after year, abundant harvests. I have returned many times to the mountain of salt, to supply myself with the pink rock that seasons meats and grains. I could see, farther up the river, our lands desolated and our brothers driven, under the lash of the conquistador, to perish by the thousands in the dark depths of the mines.

"Here I have waited for you, moon after moon, countless winters and summers, with the hope that you would come to collect the inheritance of power and wisdom that the Golden Statue holds, protective guide of your ancestors, with which you would lead us to the reconquest. Night after night I have dreamed that under the spell of your voice all the peoples quickly gathered, that the innumerable warriors, aroused by your words full of inspiration and wisdom, followed you bravely into combat and won battle after battle, and that the Great Empire was resurrected as moral and religious as before, but stronger and more united. You have not yet arrived. Leaving this World to continue my life in the region where Huiracocha dwells, I depart with the sorrow of not having heard your shout of liberation, nor your fiery words in combat.

"When your feet finally tread upon this remote island, do not worry that you do not find me to welcome you. My soul, hanging from the branches, will see you. And although you do not hear my speech or see my human form, I will be looking for you here in order to recognize you if you are the foreordained Son of the Sun."

At this point Luna felt ill.

"You know, Sangama," he said uneasily, scrutinizing the branches that wove their long arms over our heads, "perhaps it would be better if you continue reading to us from the little ropes tomorrow, when there is sunlight . . . ?"

"Go on, go on, Sangama. Don't stop! I would die of anxiety if I had to wait until tomorrow!" I begged.

"So be it!" answered the latter, looking compassionately at the

Matero, who appeared to resign himself. And he continued reading:

"I will look at you across the years . . . perhaps across the centuries. Because I will always be here, until the day of your arrival. The snow of old age has fallen upon my head; my hands, made weak by time, can no longer clear the wilderness nor dig the furrows; my step is slow. And I am completely alone, abandoned. Auca, the faithful servant and companion, has fallen years ago from old age and sadness. I buried him close by, with his eyes looking up, so that he can see your arrival from the earth that covers him."

The Matero could not stand any more.

"I am going to sleep . . . I am very sleepy!" came his stifled voice, as he moved away to get under the mosquito netting. From there came his last words, muffled by the covers:

"I don't like anything to do with those of the other World!"

Sangama lowered his voice and continued reading:

"How much all has changed since we arrived! Then we were young and strong, and many hopes encouraged us. Now all I see is gray, withered like the leaves that fall in winter and are scattered by the cold breath of unending sunsets. The wide lake, once clean, which reflected the moon and the rainbow, has started to become murky, and unknown plants invade the surface. It seems condemned to disappear. The mother of the waters, the giant serpent, has appeared, hunting the gentle deer that come to drink at its shores.

"I feel that the infinite night is arriving for me, that in which one sleeps and does not awake. There is the Image, under the tree, where we buried it upon arriving. I want to see it for the last time. In its inner hollow is the key of wisdom: the word of God, which the Huillac Umu interpreted at the time of the great historic events. The future of the Empire that your elders founded, what will it be?

"Pardon, Lord! I have profaned the statue of Huiracocha! Astounded, I looked inside! Incredulous, I searched inside it for that which my eyes did not see . . . ! There was nothing, Lord . . . ! It was empty! The mystery of humanity, a shadow wounded by the light, faded away before my profaning eyes that wanted to see the Truth before closing forever . . . ! The Empire has fallen forever!

"If someday you decipher this message, don't stop to meditate on it, nor try to understand more than its words say. As quickly as possible, turn on your steps and leave this place. Do not search for the statue of Huiracocha. It is deeply buried so that it will do no harm to men. Of it only the gold remains, pure gold, that metal that sets the soul afire with greed and leads to crime. Therefore do not search for it: it is death. You will die at the hands of criminals if you try to remove it, and those that take possession of it will also perish. Much blood will be spilled before the jungle returns the treasure held in its eager bosom.

"Do you want gold, sir? You will find it there in the heights, following the wild ravine. Hidden in a grotto under the torrent exists the greatest treasure on Earth, that which your elders brought together and hid in the days before their temples were profaned and the Virgins of the Sun violated.

"But be aware, sir, that gold in the treasure chests of nations is ambition, war, extermination, and in those of men, it is vice, degeneracy, madness. Stifle your cry, Son of the Sun, and continue through the World! Your arm is powerful, and your intelligence clear. They will open the way for you . . ."

No sooner had Sangama finished than we heard the loud cracking sound of the *lupuna* tree, which resounded through the jungle. The foliage above us shook violently, as if from the passage of a hurricane. And two black clouds opened up like two immense waves, darkening the jungle. The fire crackled, sputtering as if something were impeding its burning. And the dog awoke, emitting a sinister howl.

"When will I be free of all this, my God!" exclaimed the Matero, turning over in fear.

***

That night we remained awake on watch. Sangama dedicated himself to keeping the fire, removing the ashes and throwing on more dry logs and branches. In the shifting reddish light that the fire projected, things acquired an unreal, ghostly aspect. Overcoming my natural nervousness, I helped him in the efforts that he undertook.

We gathered up the human skeleton and reburied it next to the chest that contained the mysterious *quipus*.

When the box had disappeared under the soil that we threw over it, I was surprised to find that Sangama did not show any anguish whatsoever and that his face had become expressionless.

Now that I know the importance of the *quipus,* the universal importance that the interpretation and publication of the valuable secrets they contained would have had, I can only experience a painful regret for not having even asked Sangama to instruct me in the art of the *quipucamayos,* since he surely was the last of those who had mastered it. With him the heritage of the marvelous Inca culture remains forever sunken in mystery.

The task completed, we prepared for the return that the Matero and I so fervently desired and that, from that moment, also seemed to be Sangama's wish. We rapidly descended the slope toward the river, on whose shore the morning light found us improvising a log bridge to cross it. Having reached the other side, the Matero went ahead in search of the hut where we had spent the night before our attempt to cross the *renacal.* Luckily, in it he found the scant supplies and objects that we had left, and they were intact, miraculously respected by the hoard of *huanganas*. Sangama followed him, disconsolate. Litero, recognizing the tracks of our previous passage through those places, went back and forth, sniffing.

Expert in following any route, the Matero walked without hesitation, never missing a turn. Thus, to my great surprise, we arrived at the tomb of the elder Luna, which I had supposed to be still far away.

Without stopping, the Matero, hat in hand and making the sign of the Cross, said, as if swearing an oath:

"Someday I'll return to see you, old man!"

Provisioned with fresh water and torches, we then left the *renacal* and entered the dry zone. Sometime after nightfall we stopped to sleep several hours and resume the journey before daybreak. The hard labors of the previous day and, above all, the lack of rest at night exhausted me to such an extent that I was making enormous efforts to move forward with the same speed as my companions, who frequently had to stop to wait for me, fearful that I would get lost.

In the days that followed, we stopped only to eat some food and sleep a few hours. In the middle of the night, we crossed the majesty of the jungle like phantoms, in the uncertain light of the torches. Soaked with sweat, we approached with surprising rapidity the site where we had left the Bull and the Piquicho.

Making a stop, the Matero examined the surroundings, and after calculating distances and orientations, he said to Sangama:

"We have passed all the places where we slept on the trip out. I have them counted. Now we should meet those outlaws. I'm sure that it won't be long before we meet them. You, what do you think, Sangama?"

Sangama nodded his head in agreement.

The Matero, satisfied, asked again:

"Listen, Sangama, how would it have gone for them with the anacondas in the *renacal* . . . ? Eh?"

In spite of the state of my spirits and the exhaustion I felt, I could not avoid this observation:

"And what would have awaited us with such criminals if we were bringing the golden idol!"

My feet hurt terribly. My shoes, unable to last any longer, had given out several hours before, and the remnants were tied together with strips that broke constantly, making it clear to me that very soon it would be necessary to continue the journey barefoot.

We didn't stay there for long. The Matero, in a bad humor because his words did not receive any attention, wanted to continue the journey after a short time. Sangama, who seemed to have accepted his leadership after the tremendous failure that he himself suffered, stood up, ready to follow him. I had to do the same, despite feeling that it would be difficult to stay on my feet. Tripping at each step and in sharp pain, I continued that accelerated journey, in the course of which I paid not only for all the sins I had ever committed but for all those I could commit for the rest of my life.

Finally we arrived at the shore of the dry riverbed, in whose immediate area the villains had remained. Great was our surprise at not finding them. Sangama was dumbstruck. And since they could not be found anywhere and the shack showed unequivocal signs of abandonment, I also became upset.

Luna, incredulous, called them with powerful shouts.

Sangama warned him:

"It's useless. They've left."

"But how . . . ?

"That is what I would like to know," replied Sangama, dropping as if he had sustained a terrible blow.

Chapter 35

The awful surprise quickly swept away our exhaustion. We immediately undertook an examination of the surrounding area to discover the direction they had taken. Convinced of the hopelessness of our efforts, the Matero and I quickly returned to the starting point. We were looking at each other, indecisive and silent, when Sangama appeared and extended his arm to point to the opposite side:

"They went in that direction . . ."

It was exactly the direction that we had not inspected, because there was only impenetrable jungle that extended from the very shore of the riverbed. Proceeding in that direction, the Matero examined the stand of trees and quickly let out his characteristic shout of admiration upon seeing the pinkish bark on the thick trunk of a *shiringa*. Acting as if by habit, he advanced resolutely toward it. It was the first one that we had seen since we left the elder Luna's shed, and the Matero would not fail to take advantage of the opportunity to slice into the glassy bark with the blade of his machete to find out if it were rich in latex. He knew from experience that some of these trees, generally those of modest appearance, produced like overflowing udders while others, which by their appearance could be compared to the most beautiful of the jungle, very often gave only a few drops. The former produce the finest rubber, used in the best articles of the most important contemporary industries; the latter, whose juice did not merit being collected daily and manipulated into pellets, gave the ordinary rubber allowed to mix with the rust in the tin cans.

The Matero could not cross the creek immediately, because

sections of it hid a dangerous mudflat, so he followed it until he came upon a small bridge. We saw him disappear to the other side behind the heavy thicket, soon to surprise us with the shout that we least expected:

"A *trochaaa . . .* !"

And in fact it was, as we established as soon as we arrived at the foot of the *shiringa* tree. At this point the *trocha,* which came in from one direction and took a turn, made an angle both of whose sides moved away from the zone we had explored.

"It is an *estrada,*" the Matero said happily. "An *estrada* opened by my *taita,* before going crazy."

Sangama dedicated himself to searching carefully for tracks in the soil. Litero helped him with the tracking. They quickly came upon the evidence.

"There can't be the slightest doubt," he told us. "They left in this direction. They found this *trocha,* and they were confident they wouldn't get lost."

"But they must have taken many turns in this labyrinth. It's possible that they are still in the *estrada* and not able to get out. If we don't waste time, it's very possible that by following the route that brought us, we'll arrive at the supply shack before them," the Matero suggested.

"Exactly," Sangama quickly agreed. "We have to make the effort. I beg you, let's set out immediately."

Since my shoes were destroyed, I had to contrive a way, taking advantage of some vines, to tie them to my feet like sandals. As soon as I was ready, we set out, determined.

We resolutely moved into the thicket after the intrepid Matero, who led the expedition with a great show of skill. Our advance was so rapid that it could have been judged a flight, an appearance increased by the frequent stops of the Matero, who often turned to look back. Confident in his expertise as explorer, we followed him silently across the multicolored swamp, which extended in every direction, populated only by indefinable sounds and the monotonous, tireless screech of the cicadas in raucous mating under the leaves.

Several hours after our departure, the jungle filled with a yellowish luminosity that turned opaque and gray a little later, blocking the view of the entire surrounding area. The Matero lit his torch and, holding it high, continued the advance, opening the path with his machete. An unbreathable fiery atmosphere surrounded us, and the heat from the dense steam was melting us, making us sweat profusely.

"Awful! Awful!" said Sangama. "It's almost a torture. Fortunately we're about to finish going around the edge of the swamp that afflicted us so on the trip out."

The Matero redoubled the enormous impetus of the march. He no longer stopped to cut the branches that blocked our advance. The movements of the torch were a precise indication for us of the twists and turns that we had to make to follow him.

"We're doing well. We're doing well," Sangama said approvingly when Luna stopped to orient himself.

Suddenly the jungle trembled. The Matero stopped. In the reddish glow of the torch, I saw that he was cupping his ear with his right hand, trying to perceive the intensity of the sound. The echo having stopped, a distant noise was produced that was coming closer by the second as it increased in volume. A strong gust of wind extinguished the torch, plunging us into absolute darkness at the same time that an enormous quantity of leaves came loose from the trees and fell on us.

"The hurricane has overtaken us!" we heard the alarmed voice of Sangama say. "It's the arrival of winter! If we don't find a place to seek shelter very soon, we won't see the sun again. What a frightful night!"

Loud noises, flashes of blinding light, trees breaking apart and making the earth tremble as they fell, broken branches flying across the sky, whistling as if they were darts. It seemed that the jungle wanted to disintegrate in apocalyptic throes of death.

The forest thundered with the passing of the savage runaway wind. The high treetops, battered furiously, opened up, giving us a view of pieces of ashen sky, which was producing a sickish half-light that allowed us to see the tree trunks twisting in epileptic contortions. Tons of leaves and branches fell on us, threatening to bury us. The sudden flashes of lightning permitted me to contemplate the awesome spectacle of the jungle gone crazy.

"It's a *shihuahuaco*!" the Matero shouted. "Quickly, quickly!"

His cries reached me, barely perceptible. I almost had to guess at his words. I advanced with my eyes closed, carrying Litero, who was trembling with fear, in my arms. Luna's words reached me at intervals, unconnected and without meaning, but they were sufficient to orient me toward him and allow me to go forward, groping. Several times I fell, dazed—I don't know whether it was because my feet got tangled in the branches or if the branches dragged me down as they fell. I felt an enormous tree trunk fall behind me. It produced such noise and commotion that it flung me against a branch, leaving me stunned by the blow.

The Matero and Sangama backtracked, calling to me, distressed. I answered them with all my strength, but they certainly did not hear me, since they continued shouting my name. I had the sensation that a hopeless distance separated us. However, they soon stumbled upon me, pulled me from a heap of branches and leaves that held me prisoner, and dragged me a short distance. Finally we came upon the rough trunk of the *shihuahuaco,* considered, apart from the *huacapú,* the strongest tree of the jungle. There I could stand up, content to find myself with my companions. The jungle continued thundering, shaking in every direction as if all the forces of Creation had been unleashed upon it.

This must be the end of the World, I thought, clinging tightly to the strong trunk, which I felt creaking in spite of its formidable diameter. The rain of leaves was ever more intense, and it required constant work to keep from being buried completely.

It was impossible to see anything in that darkness except the pale flashes of the lightning that ran through the thicket, followed by severe shaking. When I felt the trees shaking, it seemed to me as if they were trying to pull themselves out by their very roots and flee. Our survival depended solely on the strength of the tree where we had sought asylum, which, in my opinion, was a little doubtful. Sangama and the Matero spoke in a loud voice, and despite being very close to them, I could not understand what was going on. Their voices were mixed with the powerful noises and were reaching me sporadically, lacking any sense.

When the hurricane's fury subsided, a heavy rain started to fall, often becoming a torrent, as if a swift river were falling from the sky.

"Thanks be to God!" I could hear Sangama saying. "The wind is no longer blowing so furiously!"

Sangama was so close to me that his warm breath arrived with his words. Otherwise I would not have been able to hear him, such was the infernal roar that resounded in the jungle.

Suddenly I saw points of light everywhere that seemed to come from many lanterns carried by a large crowd that was actively searching for something in the brush. Startled, I asked Sangama about the cause of that phenomenon.

"They are . . . Well, it's the water that comes in contact with decomposing materials under the layer of dried leaves . . . the ones that become phosphorescent." And he added, dismissively: "It's nothing!"

Thus we passed the hours that still separated us from daylight. Infinite hours! Unmoving, as if lifeless, I felt the water flowing in torrents over my body as an inanimate object.

"Onward, Matero!" Sangama's voice sounded. "I can already make out something! If we delay, we won't be able to walk, because of the flooding of the jungle!"

As much as I tried, I couldn't see anything, which made me think it rash to start out in the jungle, as disoriented as we were by the storm. In that darkness it was just about impossible to establish a point of reference. But they set out without fear, and I had to follow them. In those moments I realized that, to my misfortune, I was completely shoeless. I said nothing and continued enduring the stabs and scrapes of the branches that covered the ground. My feet constantly became more irritated, and the pain became sharper, increasing the clumsiness of my steps. It seemed to me that we were repeatedly passing the same place. The Matero stopped before a palm tree and cut some leaves, under which he managed to light the wet torch, thanks to his tenacity and using up the matches that he found in the bottom of his travel bag.

The light being protected by the canopy of leaves that the Matero had put together, Sangama dedicated himself to examining the bark of a small tree that he selected from among those that surrounded us. The result did not seem to satisfy him, since, with a gesture of doubt, he scraped more bark from other trees around us to continue his protracted analysis of the splinters that he obtained from those diverse places, at times using his fingernails. After some moments I could see that an expression of triumph replaced the sign of impatience that showed on his face. Then, raising an arm, he signaled the direction that we should follow, precisely along the way that we had just passed to reach that small tree.

"This man knows incredible things," the Matero whispered in my ear, looking at Sangama with admiration. Then he proceeded to take the lead, holding aloft his torch, which was soon extinguished again, soaked by the rain.

We followed him. Often we had to detour around some impenetrable zones and then correct the direction. It was an orientation done blindly, based on the Matero's extraordinary instinct. It was good that the silhouettes of the nearest tree trunks were now beginning to appear before my eyes. My poor feet, which I was imagining destroyed, were more and more painful, and it was necessary for me to grit my teeth tighter to keep from breaking out in shouts of pain when some small branch jabbed into the sole of my foot.

We crossed small ravines where there were running torrents of muddy water, and losing precious time, we had to go around numerous places where the storm had formed mountains of branches and trunks. The task of preserving the correct orientation was thus extremely arduous.

After hitting my foot on a root, it was impossible to contain a moan. I had to sit down on the ground to squeeze the injured part, and I was surprised to see that my feet were swollen and bleeding. Sangama and the Matero stopped when they heard me.

"My feet are destroyed!" I shouted, twisting in pain. "Go on!

Don't stop!"

The two looked at each other with something between displeasure and compassion. I kept insisting that they continue, that they leave me because it was impossible for me to keep up with them.

"I'll stay here, Sangama. Tell Chuya that I couldn't continue. You two go on. Don't lose any time. There's no way that I'll be able to get there. It's all the same whether I stop here or farther on!"

"Man!" Luna hurried to say to me. "Even if the path becomes more arduous, we can't abandon you. We'll carry you if necessary."

"It's useless!" I shouted. "I beg you to leave me."

And as I saw that they did not move, I finished by telling them the reason for my insistence, what worried me horribly and what I had never wanted to say for fear that my words would be prophetic.

"Go on! Go on! Chuya is in danger . . . You have to save her!"

Commiserating, Sangama contemplated me, while I persisted in pleading with them to proceed with the journey in order to arrive as soon as possible. Suddenly he took off the wide, long sash that served to hold up his pants and hold in his stomach, replacing it with a vine, and proceeded to bandage my feet with it in a manner that would substitute for shoes. The operation over, he helped me stand up, asking me:

"Can you hold yourself up and walk?"

Not only could I hold myself up perfectly, but feeling great relief, I could also walk with confidence and ease.

"Forward!" I said spiritedly. "With this I can endure several more hours!"

"The exact number!" added the Matero. "We won't be long now in arriving at the supply shack."

And the Matero went on happily, as if the solution of my situation would mean something in itself in regard to the grave problem that worried us so. The rain had already calmed down, and through its monotonous drumming one could hear, sharp and fresh, the tune that the Matero was whistling.

His whistle, which was becoming more and more skilled, reverberated in my eager heart with strange resonance. The Matero's spirit evidently was becoming happier, a sad happiness as if in a humorous paradox. Tired of whistling, he cast a song into the air:

When I left my land
I said good-bye to no one;
Only the stones saw me
And they cried for me.

This Matero, I thought, has such a nature that, instead of a final dying cry, there will come from his throat, with his last breath, a jungle song.

Chapter 36

Sangama quickly recognized some marks we had left in the trees when we started the ill-fated exploration. Then he hastened his step, taking the lead. We were already close to the shack. Anxiety kept us from speaking, but on the other hand, it redoubled our energy, making us walk vigorously.

Finally we arrived! From the edge of the forest, we spotted the roof of the shack and, shortly thereafter, smoke coming from the kitchen. Sultan came out to greet us, bounding toward Sangama.

I had my eyes fastened on the supply shack, from which I expected to see the enchanting figure of Chuya appear, happy and affectionate. I was greatly disturbed when the only one to come out upon hearing our voices was the old servant woman, who remained mute and petrified before Sangama. He flung the pack he was carrying to the ground and resolutely entered into the shack, from which we then heard sporadic moans.

Attracted by the barking of the dogs, Ahuanari came hurrying from the riverbank.

"You have finally arrived!" he exclaimed, giving a strong sigh of relief.

And as he met our questioning looks, provoked by the sobs that continued inside the shack, he informed us starkly:

"They raped her . . . !"

I grasped my head with both hands in desperation because I felt it about to explode. A large knot squeezed my throat, choking me, and my vision became blurred. A black abyss opened up suddenly at my feet, into which I felt myself falling. Overcoming the pain, I ran toward Sangama, who was coming out of the shack, staggering.

"We'll take revenge! We'll take revenge!" I repeated several times, swelling up with fury.

"We'll catch him," added the Matero, who had just learned that only the Bull was still alive. "Ahuanari said that at night he cries out in the nearby wilderness . . . ! He will have to be hunted down! What else can be done? He's worse than a jaguar!"

"Tomorrow," pleaded Sangama. "Today I can't go with you . . ."

Stunned by the terrible reality, almost unconsciously I headed step by step toward the edge of the river. It is true that the greatest pains dull the senses. Exhausted by the blow that I had just received, I sat down on the riverbank to contemplate the restless waters that swirled by, dragging in their unending flow the trunks and branches pulled out by the hurricane. As if I were witnessing something outside of me that was emerging in the distance, all the scenes of the past night were repeated in my imagination. It seemed to me that the terrible storm was the protest of the elements against the crime that was committed. My attention lingered on each of the things that surrounded me: on the canoe pulled ashore on the small beach, which signified the return home, life for all of us; on the thick mat of aquatic plants that the river was dragging, transported peacefully by the current from some unknown lagoon where they had formed; on the plants on the shore, soaked by the rain, fragile but tough, like the human soul, which is oppressed and beaten down until it feels itself dying and which resists all the tempests; on the high treetops, which were swaying noisily under the rain as if they had not suffered, shortly before, the torture of the hurricane.

Through the clear spaces that the treetops left between them, I saw flocks of storks cross by as they moved away into the distance, fleeing the winter for other, more welcoming regions. I envied those birds because they could leave this stifling green prison; they could find new horizons with the thrust of their wings until they reached a spot where one could forget.

I continued thinking randomly, allowing some ideas to follow others, without any desire to arrive at any conclusion, without any interest other than to continue thinking and thinking.

The friendly voice of the Matero put an end to my aimless

pondering. He sat at my side and wanted to convince me of the necessity of returning to the shack to change our clothing, have some food, and rest. Then, putting an arm affectionately around my shoulders, he added "Do you know how it happened? The bandits arrived yesterday, claiming that Sangama had sent them ahead to prepare for his return, and consequently it was necessary to send the young man hunting to increase the inventory of provisions. Chuya, believing them, welcomed them and set about carrying out her father's directions. Ahuanari left immediately, accompanied by Sultan. On his return, Ahuanari found the two women locked inside, rifle in hand, weeping and with their hair disheveled. The old "mama" then led him to a corner of the shack and informed him that, a few minutes after his departure, the villains grabbed them by surprise and tied them hand and foot. A few moments later, just long enough for them to put all they wanted to take with them into the canoe, they heard the Piquicho inciting the Bull to abuse the poor girl before embarking and fleeing."

"Be quiet, brother," I pleaded, covering his mouth. "Be quiet, for God's sake."

"If you want, I'll be quiet," the Matero answered me, falling silent. But then I heard his voice again, as if it had not suffered any interruption: "The Bull took the girl, who had passed out, to the canoe and, believing her dead, removed her bonds and left her, while the Piquicho protested because his companion did not permit him to rape her too. Then several shots rang out. The Piquicho fell, pierced by a bullet, and the Bull felt a wound. Seeing that Chuya, who had regained consciousness, had seized a rifle from the canoe and was advancing, shooting at him, he fled to the wilderness. Later that night Ahuanari threw the Piquicho's body in the river."

While I was listening to this tale that the Matero told, without adding any of my own commentary, I was seeing in my imagination the particular scenes, and I took on the sufferings of that fragile creature, whose courage would have drawn a shout of admiration and applause from me if my throat had not been choked up. I remained mute, drying the sweat that sprung from my forehead.

"Tomorrow we'll catch him. You'll see what is waiting for Don

Misael!" the Matero concluded, with a tone both indignant and mocking.

"Tomorrow we'll catch him!" I roared, thirsty for revenge.

The landscape was already totally erased, wrapped in the shadows of the somber evening. The sky began again to cry inconsolably with that savage weeping that the land could not wipe away. The noise had become extraordinary. It seemed that the jungle complained in pain under the black mantle with which the night was covering it. Almost dragging me, the Matero took me to the shack.

A weak wick of oil struggled to light the corner of the shack where we found Sangama, sunken into the most painful of meditations, with his face buried in the space that was formed by his two joined hands.

Careful not to disturb his thoughts, I contemplated him in the reddish glow of the lamp, thinking with great sympathy of the double tragedy that weighed down on that brave and strong man so heavily. The two great ideals of his life, brought together in duty and in love, had collapsed simultaneously. It was as if Destiny was perversely playing with him, putting that soul, so restrained in the face of danger, to the highest test of strength.

Later in that infinitely sad night, the force of the rain stopped again, and the jungle remained enveloped in the sobbing whisper of the trees. The dogs barked at the edge of the forest in the direction where the Bull's laments could be heard. Even the Matero, who had been sleeping curled up near me, opened his eyes from time to time when he heard the sounds of the criminal. Then he stared at me and, winking with implication, gave me to understand that it was necessary only to have a little bit of patience for our desires to be fulfilled. To distract my thoughts, I would very much have liked to discuss with the Matero the details of the hunt for the wild beast, which I was sure we were going to undertake as soon as the morning light appeared, but I did not dare even to move. From the neighboring room, where the women were shut away, frequent sighs could be heard that contributed to intensifying even more the pain I was suffering, if that were possible.

Early in the morning, Sangama invited us outside. He wanted to agree on the details of the hunt for the human beast.

"We'll come upon him easily. He's prowling in this direction," he told us, pointing to the area where the groans had resounded during the night. "But it's necessary to proceed with great caution. That wild beast will try to defend himself."

Armed with rifles, we started the hunt, accompanied by the dogs, which were running around us.

On entering the thicket, with our rifles ready, we separated a little without ever losing sight of each other, so that we could come to each other's aid in case it was necessary. We advanced slowly, cautiously examining the places that could be hiding the beast, from whom we feared a surprise attack. The dogs were barking more frequently, sniffing the tracks and stopping often, which indicated that the criminal had been wandering in these parts. We sharpened our attention, since it was certain that we would not be long in coming upon the dangerous fugitive.

And so it was. Sultan and Litero discovered him hidden in some brush. Their barks, so characteristic of dogs when they come upon the hiding place of the hunted prey, were confirmed by an angry shout. We quickened our pace when we heard painful howls between furious curses. We arrived too late. Sultan was writhing, dying at the feet of the Bull, who crazily brandished an enormous club.

"Ah, cursed dog!" he roared pale from anger. "Because of you I couldn't return!"

He was about to unleash another blow on the animal to finish off his victim, but our presence stopped him. The three rifles were pointing at him. He threw down the club and fell on his knees, imploring cowardly:

"Don't kill me! I surrender! I didn't want to do it! I'm sorry!"

The Matero went at him and dealt him a fierce blow with the rifle butt, which made him fall facedown, stunned.

"This prey is mine!" the Matero shouted excitedly. "Let me have him . . . ! Let me have him . . . !"

Coming closer, I had the impression that I was in the presence of a monster. A hairy beard covered his face. His hair fell over his forehead, covering it completely. From within his tangled hair huge open eyes appeared, surrounded by bloody eyelids. He had a wound on his right side. On his arms and feet, marks could be made out that had been left by the Sultan's fierce teeth and the avenging branches of the jungle. That muscular figure was strange, converted into a brutal mass of bones and tendons, clumsy and overwhelmed. Seeing him in that condition, the Matero imprudently approached him, defying the fierceness that could still be predicted to be hidden in the remnants of the beaten-down colossus. From between his lips, swollen and dry, came his hoarse voice, full of terror. He could not look at us directly, except for brief moments. His eyes looked everywhere for something that they couldn't find, something unknown that was undoubtedly the principal cause of his terror. Soon he stopped lamenting, in order to curse the bewitched jungle.

"Here it is!" he said in a tired and cavernous voice. "Here it is! I feel it taking me prisoner! It's the demon that hides behind every tree!"

The Matero proceeded to tie his ankles tightly, without the Bull making the slightest effort to defend himself, in spite of the roughness with which he was treated. He continued imploring, possessed by a strange madness, and spoke incoherently:

"She was different from all the other women I have taken in the jungle. I did not want to hurt her. It was the demon that got into the Piquicho that caused me to be lost! I fought, but it was in vain! It is the soul of the Governor that is taking vengeance . . . ! All the souls of those that I killed . . . ! Yes, they're all here threatening me . . . ! But I don't want to die . . . ! I don't want to!"

His voice was acquiring a progressive wildness. He offered the final exclamations in a desperate frenzy, as if he were wishing to free himself from something that held him with supernatural force. It was hard to tell whether that condemned man was crying at the same time he was cursing. His words surged forth as noisy snorts, but deep down they were pained and pleading. He fell silent one moment, to start again in a soft tone, almost tender, a prayer that was then transformed, between convulsive laments, into an overflowing cascade of blasphemies and curses.

"Pardon! Pardon, Sangama! I know that I did you a great wrong . . . ! But the Piquicho urged me. The Piquicho, who is hunting me now . . . ! I don't want to hear his laugh . . . ! I didn't know what I was doing. She tried to resist with her weak arms, but it was in vain; she fell like a little dove under the claws of the jaguar. She struggled an instant, like a little deer in the embrace of a strangling anaconda. She was so tender, so delicate, that I thought I had killed her . . . ! Horror . . . ! And I left after removing the bonds from her lifeless body. And there was the Piquicho, eager. But I didn't let him. I was punishing him when he fell dead at my feet. This bullet that has hit me here made me flee into this accursed wilderness."

Then he covered his eyes with one arm, while he gestured with the other to push away a phantom that was approaching him. He wanted to get up and run, but since his feet were tied, he crashed into a tree trunk that was in front of him, almost next to me. As he raised his face, his stunned look crossed mine, uncovering all the hatred that he inspired in me and, with meaning sharp as a stake, his words cut through me:

"Ah, cursed one! You're coming to take my life!"

"Shut up, miserable bastard!" the Matero interrupted him threateningly.

It was unbearable. That beast was going to end up killing us all with his insults and laments. Sangama, staring at the ground, had lost that imperturbable and enigmatic serenity that was characteristic of him in supreme moments. His face had horribly lost its color, and he clung to Litero, who was barking desperately.

"Take me from here! Take me anywhere . . . ! Kill me if you wish . . . but over there! Out of this diabolical jungle!"

"We'll gladly do what you're asking, miserable bastard! We're going to take you—have a little patience!" And the Matero leaned over to tie his arms. It was then that the Bull managed to grab him by his clothes, and pulling him down violently, the Bull rolled him on the ground, where he prepared to strangle him.

"Ah! I caught you, little Matero . . . ! Now you are mine! Before they finish me off with shots, I'll have time to choke you!"

They rolled next to the dog, who, with his backbone broken and his body half inert, was at the feet of Sangama. His head was supported on his front paws, and his gaze of a wild animal was fixed on the monster. Sangama made a leap, but before he could intervene to help the Matero, that head leapt forward, dragging its half-crippled body, and plunged its teeth in. We could hear the crunching of the bones of the Bull's right wrist, and the hand that was squeezing Luna's throat had to release him. Two blows of a rifle butt given to the other arm by Sangama freed our companion from a certain death. The Matero, getting up dazed, rubbed his eyes and did not hesitate in reacting. The Bull fell to his knees, exhaling roars of pain. With his free arm, he seized Sultan in a vain effort to choke him.

For an instant we were frozen, watching with astonishment the tremendous scene of the mute fight between a dog, with half his body lifeless, and a mutilated giant almost paralyzed by pain.

When the jaws finally opened, they were never to close again. Bloodied and with the lips pulled back, they seemed to still hold all their fierceness. The dog was dead.

"I have gotten even with you, cursed dog!" the Bull shouted, trying to contain the blood that spurted from his shattered wrist.

That scene could not continue. Sangama seemed moved by the situation of that bestial creature, driven mad by pain and fear.

Meanwhile, the Matero had prepared a noose and indicated to me to make another. Hanging onto the criminal's back, he managed to slip the noose on, tying his arms. Then he wrapped the vine around the trunk of a tree and pulled it tight. I was then able to get close without risk and attach the other noose in the same manner, in turn pulling it tight to another tree. When we had him secured this way, reduced to helplessness, the Matero ordered him:

"Get up, Bull. We're going to take you where you won't suffer anymore."

"I can't get up," he said, after making several efforts. "Untie my feet. I can't walk this way."

Sangama cut the ties on his ankles, and the Matero hurried to warn him:

"Now, if you even attempt to disobey, we shoot!"

"Take me away! Take me away quickly!" the Bull clamored. "But quickly!"

At that moment, downcast, like an automaton, Sangama picked up the body of his dog and started out in the direction of the shack. Meanwhile, as if leading a real bull, holding him taut with the cords as we moved from tree to tree, we took the Bull to the place that the Matero indicated, without my realizing what he intended to do. The villain did not object to the orders in the shouts that Luna issued.

"Over there . . . ! Closer . . . ! Face forward . . . ! No farther!"

The Bull had stopped under a small thin tree with a brownish stalk that was growing near the shore.

"You're out of the forest!" he said. "Now wait for me to untie you."

The criminal's horrible face took on a tragic expression of happiness. He fell to the ground heavily, next to that light-colored tree trunk upon which he supported his back as he sat on the ground. Luna ran and, with incredible speed, made several turns with the vine, tying the giant against the trunk and saying at the same time:

"Here you're going to rest! Here you're going to pay all your accounts!"

"No, don't leave me!" roared the Bull, trying to break loose.

The little tree shuddered violently, shaken by the Bull as if it were about to be torn out by its roots. As it was being battered, a dull sound, like that of a disturbed beehive, came from its interior, and a dense mass of reddish ants burst forth through thousands of holes that could be seen on the bark, falling on the Bull, covering his half-naked body.

Realizing the deadly situation in which he found himself, tied to a *tangarana,* the Bull launched thunderous shouts between curses:

"Damn you . . . ! You deceived me . . . ! Ahhh! Uhhh!"

"Take that, little Bull! See if the Devil that you have in your body can save you! Take that, little Bull!" repeated the Matero, pale and panting, but sarcastic.

The collective mass formed by the man and the tree took on a strange aspect. It appeared to be a single deformed thing, monstrous, that was devouring itself. Thick drops of blood appeared on the Bull's body. Even then the wild beast continued insulting and cursing.

The Matero seemed to enjoy the scene. I averted my gaze, but a shout made me turn to look. The Bull had managed to pull out the trunk and was advancing with lurches, hitting against the branches. He stopped. Then I saw him struggling in the most horrendous torture. He could no longer see. A thick, boiling blanket of ants was devouring his eyes, and he fell for the last time, clutching the very tree that was taking his life. Little by little the death rattle that poured forth hoarsely from the chest of the dying man was fading away, until silence covered the scene.

Suddenly Sangama appeared and stopped, paralyzed before the gruesome picture of the death of the Bull, devoured by the tree. Then he turned toward me with the saddest look that I had seen in my life, in which there was both reproach and sympathy.

"The justice of the jungle has been carried out, Sangama!" the Matero said in vindication.

I wanted to speak, to say something; but I couldn't.

Chapter 37

Returning to the shack, Sangama entered the narrow, dark bedroom where Chuya was sobbing. I wanted to follow him, but he stopped me at the door with a stern gesture, leaving me paralyzed.

I stayed there, listening to the murmur of the words of consolation, full of philosophical comforting of the grieving father, and the sobs of the overwhelmed creature, until the distraught figure of Sangama came out again.

"Don't leave her for an instant," he ordered the old woman. "Call me immediately."

And turning toward me, he embraced me with deep emotion.

"This is the worst that could happen to me," he lamented.

"It has happened to all of us," I hastened to say, letting him know that my pain was as great as his.

"Yes," he replied. "I understand."

The Matero and Ahuanari had gone to the wilderness to bury Sultan's body. When they arrived at the place where the noble dog was lying, in the spot where Sangama had left him, they found Litero stretched out next to him, howling sadly.

Afterwards they set about repairing the canoe, which had been perforated, as Ahuanari explained, to prevent the Bull from escaping in it. As they carried out this operation, they realized that many of the provisions the bandits had tried to steal were ruined, since they had been inundated by the rising river. This produced an ensuing alarm, since without them our situation was becoming very serious. An attempt to hunt for something was impossible because the jungle was flooding more each minute. And the return route was long. This news didn't affect us right away. Something more serious was worrying us completely.

Sangama again entered the girl's bedroom. As he was spending an extended time there, I resolved to go to the edge of the river, whose waters had risen considerably. Something there made me remember my years as a youth when my soul, full of illusions and hopes, had not yet been battered by misfortunes. Then I had felt myself capable of withstanding the cruelest sufferings, willing to endure all hardships. I turned my gaze toward the forest and looked at the trees on the shore, lined up like sentinels that were also crying for some awful misfortune. That afternoon the leaves were breaking free and falling, yellow, gray and reddish, like tears of the sympathetic jungle.

When I started to walk back to the shack, the sun was already setting. Slipping away through the half-light, the embracing silhouettes of Sangama and Chuya entered the forest, following the edge of the river. I saw them sink into the shadows. Where were they going? A deep uneasiness took possession of me, and I started to follow them, hiding behind one tree and then another. Total darkness was covering the forest. I could hardly make them out. There was a moment when I stopped, disoriented, not knowing which way to go. At that moment the notes of a *quena* cut through the silence. A strong indescribable sensation filled me when I heard those anguished notes, with great quavering, lamenting, melodiously ill.

Music saturated with pain that only the Indian can produce in the desolation of the high Andean plateau; music that was born in the heart of the warrior conquered by adversity in his struggle with the conquistadors, who swept in relentlessly from distant lands and drove the Indian toward the harsh mountaintops, where the birds do not sing and the trees do not give shade. It was the synthesis of the dying of an entire race that loved work and did not rob or lie; the race of an exemplary civilization sustained in Morality and Religion, over whose wreckage the unblemished souls of the virgins violated in the Temple of the Sun still seem to wail, whose hymns to Huiracocha, the supreme god of the Incas, have been converted into weeping.

Sangama's *quena* filled the jungle with sadness. Under its influence I understood that even if it were not for the eloquence of history and for the expressive physical environment in which he lives, that music alone would be enough to characterize the Indian of the high Andean plateau as the outcast of America. History for him has not changed, as the polar landscape has not changed in the high plateau, where that music that poisons the soul of the Indian lives on supreme.

No longer do any of those elite Inca warriors exist who, in their rebellion, scaled the steep mountain ranges. Their descendants live there without hope, filled with loneliness and silence, with the snow-covered peaks and the rocky distant places as narrow horizons. For them no world but theirs exists; they do not conceive of anything that can disturb its stony stillness. They are the proud sons of the unconquerables of yesteryear, and their isolation constitutes the open manifestation of their inherited lack of docility. They appear insensitive to everything except that music lovingly cultivated, which they make ever more sad, perfuming it with intense melancholy, so that it penetrates to the marrow of their bones and tempers their soul, making it indifferent to everything but the pain that puts them to sleep.

Sangama's music continued, continued . . . enervating the muscles with its poisoning sadness and crushing life like the weight of a mountain.

Evoked by those bewitching notes, the Indian of the highlands appears, with his sharp face and half-moon profile, curled up next to the miserable smoky fire fed with the straw that grows in the frozen plains. He has the stillness of the hard rocks, whose edges rise up eternally. His tranquillity is that of time that does not pass, tranquillity that saturates space, tranquillity somber, hollow, and isolating, like a burial urn. When was he born? No one can say. He is born and grows, unsmiling, with that inherited pain that depresses him and makes him old soon after being born. For the Indian of the high plateau, life has the duration of a dream. He knows only what he experiences of it, that which his memory tells him of a succession of days and nights, without any concept of the passage of time. Thus the Indian of the high plateau lives only the moments of pain that open as a detour in the lives of those who live without hope. It is of no matter to him that the torch of day is extinguished, that the sky is enshrouded in black and the earth in white. He continues alone over the desolate crest, mute, introspective, consuming himself with sadness. In his unhurried mind, made lethargic by pain as if from a narcotic, the confused ancestral memory lives on. It is not the memory of his personal experiences; it is the complex memory of that entire race that protests the great historical drama in which his ancestors were protagonists. That protest is expressed in such a propitious landscape, perpetuating across the centuries the sorrowful music that kills vitality and makes the soul bleed. It is the past that emerges in his consciousness, foggy, murky, without form, choking that race that is disintegrating, that is being extinguished, walled in where ice storms and solitude defend it. There he is, in the inaccessible heights, with his copper sunburned face that blends with the surrounding rocks, suspended between the depths and the peaks. He is alone, because the desolation doesn't matter to him. He is sad, because he doesn't know about happiness. A grimace of pain contracts his face because he was born in mourning, amid the weeping of the clouds, the cold and the silence that anesthetize the soul and deepen sorrow. There, where life seems not to exist, where nothing is found but snow, fog, loneliness, mystery—there in those distant places wrenched from space, of sterile ravines and desert pampas—is where the mournful sound of the *quenas* is heard when night arrives and the senses are put to sleep because it awakens the pain. The shattering notes of the enchanted *quena* vibrate, echoing in the hollow places of the rocks, from which it returns ever more charged with sadness, to spread out, scattered through the infinite lightless spaces.

And Sangama was producing it in circumstances in which his soul was lacking all hope, desolate, and sad, like the high plateau, making the heart of the virgin jungle vibrate with the infinite pain of his misfortune.

The notes continued sounding; now soft, cadenced like the wingbeats of the condor, cutting through the rarefied gusts that blow between the crests of the mountain range; now refined, sharpening its tones progressively until it is converted into the frenetic cry of the heartrending spasm; and again diminishing, almost extinguished in sobbing modulations.

The changing scale of the notes seemed to slide away and then rise up, from the river torrent to the lofty cliff, and from the cliff to the high plateau, from there to wander in quick flight through the paths that wind back and forth on the gray slopes and end up lost in the valleys. They evoked the passage of the traveler, when the sunset has died and the hail falls, covering the land with an icy shroud, while the wind whistles and roars, plunging its icy claws into his very core. It is the music of the suicidal Indian who plunges into the abyss to destroy himself, bouncing between cliffs without releasing from his clasped hands the *quena* or *antara,* symbolic companion of his life.

The *quena* fell mute. It final notes were extinguished, fading away in the distance of the fugitive echo, without the sound of the saving refrain. The soul is left in trembling death throes with the coldness of death. Thus ends the music of the Indian who wants to kill himself in the hidden corner of the high plateau. He has not lit any fire that lulls him with its heat, he has not chewed the sacred leaf that comforts him, putting asleep his senses, nor has he played the fugue that, added to the end of the suicide melody, miraculously returns to him the desire to live.

I waited some seconds in which it seemed that life was abandoning me, escaping in pursuit of the notes that were lost, diluted in the distance. I felt myself dissolve into that atmosphere of inextinguishable sadness.

Making a great effort, I advanced quickly, but I stopped when I saw Sangama gazing at the troubled waters of the river. He held his daughter affectionately against his chest, and he seemed to be hesitating. He was not at the high peak, at the edge of the unfathomable depths, nor feeling the attraction of the abyss.

I could not contain myself any longer.

"The refrain! The fugue, Sangama!" I cried.

I saw him draw back, raising the *quena* to his lips . . . and finally the hoped-for notes vibrated, agile like the fluttering of leaves released by the first gusts of fall, or the flutter of a swarm of butterflies over a flowering rose garden. Notes of the accelerated rhythm that returned hope, produced warmth, and impelled to action; transition from weeping to smiles, the rebellion of the life that defeats death; simultaneous expression of the pain that does not cease being felt and the pleasure that is sought. The spell vanishes. It is the moment in which the defeated Indian lifts himself up, exhales a deep sigh as if to finish freeing himself from the evil influence, takes his bottle of *chicha,* lifts a handful of coca leaves to his mouth, and starts the journey. No one would be able to say where he is from, nor where he is going. A bitter expression crosses his unchangeable face, and looking ahead, he seems to challenge the distant places.

The *quena* fell silent again. Followed by his daughter, Sangama headed to a clearing in the forest, formed by the fall of an ancient tree that had left a piece of the sky uncovered. He stopped in the center and, lifting up his face, started to recite a prayer softly. When the moon appeared between the clouds, bathing that scene that seemed unreal with its rays, he raised his arms and with a deep voice exclaimed:

"Mother Moon! Loving Mother of my race and my bloodline! Let me return to the beloved land of the high places, there, where the great rivers are born and the *pisonay* flourishes. I wanted to complete my sacred mission that my elders left me, and for this I misunderstood the course of action that life was pointing out to me . . . ! Today I return, defeated by the jungle, as the shadow of the Past! Mother Moon, have mercy . . . !"

The solemn attitude of Chuya, with her gaze also turned upward and her arms extended toward the heavens, was, without a doubt, that of an Inca princess in prayer. I saw her face contracted by sadness and her lips opened partially to softly speak a prayer that I was unable to hear.

Then her father pulled her to him; they looked at each other face-to-face for a long time. Finally she smiled with that sweet smile that produced so much happiness in me.

Holding myself back among the trees that surrounded the clearing, I watched, entranced by that pair of martyrs. And when they started on the path back, holding hands, I stepped forward with the eager desire that they should see me. But they passed beside me, almost brushing me, like two shadows. I remained completely silent. I started back slowly, a stranger to all that surrounded me.

An awful uncertainty had just entered into my soul . . .

Chapter 38

Hours later the Matero was sleeping like a log. From his tranquil breathing, I could deduce that his spirit was enjoying complete peace, while I stayed awake, consumed by disillusionment and uncertainty. I wanted to awaken him to share the torture that I was suffering, so that his philosophy of disdaining adversity and his healthy acceptance of facts would bring me some relief, but I was afraid of his lack of understanding or his ironic indifference. I spent the night thinking about Sangama and Chuya.

The day before, everything had united us: goals, desires, hopes. Now, while the future might open a new pathway before them, I found myself the hunter lost in the thicket. However, I did not need to accept falling, defeated by misfortune. Surely there were many paths left to try. As before, I resolved to approach the old woman Ana, whom I found in the kitchen, stirring up the cold ashes of the fire, an early and active riser.

"Old woman," I said, approaching affectionately, "since we returned, I have tried in vain to talk with Chuya. I want to see her."

The old woman looked at me with surprise and, lowering her head as if to hide the expression in her face, answered me:

"Yesterday my little girl saw you seated on the dock on the shore of the river. 'He is very sad,' she said to me. And the girl wept. Poor little thing! Poor little thing!"

The words choked in her throat between convulsive sobs. I was not able to comfort her, and her cries became louder and louder, until Sangama's voice came from the adjoining compartment, where he had shut himself in with Chuya. He asked:

"What is happening? Whose voices are those?"

"It's me, *taita*. I'm lighting the candle! It's nothing!" she replied.

I didn't dare continue talking, so I left.

The Matero was sitting upright among the shadows. Noticing my presence, he spoke to me, lazily yawning his words. As best I could, I gave him to understand that we should not speak there, so as not to disturb Chuya's sleep. Almost embracing, we left and walked a distance from the shack. Taking refuge under a thick tree trunk almost at the edge of the river, which was grumbling as if it also wanted to repel us from its banks, we could finally exchange some words.

"This very day we are leaving here," was the first thing he said.

"To where?"

"To the village! To Santa Inés! Where else would you want us to go? Aren't you fed up yet with adventures, or do you want the winter to catch us here?"

I wanted to tell him about the scene with Sangama and Chuya, but I had hardly started the description of the bewitching music when he interrupted me:

"Ah, yes. A little sad, unpleasant."

"A little?"

"I'll tell you. I was so tired that I almost didn't hear it. The old woman and Ahuanari started to cry. Good grief! With all we have gone through, it occurs to him to come out with that little tune! Sangama has some things . . . !"

"It's just that . . ."

"Of course! To forget the Bull's death throes."

"It was not that . . ."

"A farewell to those places perhaps? It will have to be seen!"

"None of that! They wanted to commit suicide!"

"What are you saying? Commit suicide? Who? Sangama? That one will never die!"

"Well, it's like I said," I affirmed, growing angry.

"But he didn't kill himself . . . ! You see that!"

"Because I intervened . . ."

"Ah! You did very well. We need him to get out of here. Because things are going to be very tough. I assure you of that."

I understood that it was useless to try to unburden myself by making the Matero the confidant of my sorrows. I could not understand anyone who looked at the situation from the vulgar point of view of his immediate interests and was so attached to the material aspect of life. I preferred to remain silent.

As if wrapped in pale gauze, the next morning appeared between the high treetops. It had a misty luminosity that evoked the flame of a sickly lamp struggling not to be extinguished.

Ahuanari started the task of loading the canoe. Shortly thereafter Sangama arrived, carrying some rushes with which he made a small platform in the center of the craft to accommodate the women. I observed him in all his activities without being able to discover the slightest hint that anything disturbed the serenity that characterized him.

We loaded as much as we needed to take. When all was ready, Sangama, who was moving about in front of me with apparent naturalness but without giving me the chance to talk to him, headed toward the shack, emerging shortly thereafter with Chuya, who was leaning on him. The little old woman Ana followed them, bent over as if she were burdened with sorrow at the funeral of a loved one.

At the moment when Chuya boarded the canoe, our eyes met. I saw that she was burning, blushing as if she had surprised me looking at her naked. Then she lowered her eyes and turned her face, embarrassed. I, in turn, felt myself turn pale.

From that time forward, I was not able to see her face, since I was in the stern, steering the canoe.

We departed from the improvised port, plunging into the middle of the current. I could not repress a sigh of satisfaction when feeling the canoe slide over the reddish torrential waters, winding through the jungle and taking us to the frontiers of civilization. Behind us, we were leaving a land that I still remember with horror.

The Matero tried to cheer us up, intoning the refrain of a *marinera,* with the joy that flowed from his untamable soul:

My boss
wants me to sing it.
How can I not sing
when he is dancing . . . !

He was not able to avoid a low-hanging branch catching him off guard as it lashed against him. Recovering from the blow, he searched the faces of the women, regretful as he looked at them. And doubtless, with the thought of sweetening the moment for them, he changed his expression and started to sing a jungle song:

The night is approaching,
its flight is swift,
the birds are flying,
in search of their nests;

The jaguar in the thicket
already roars fiercely
and the serpent whistles
over there in the brush.

Turning swiftly around a bend in the river, we unexpectedly encountered a curtain of vines that covered the river across its entire width. It was not possible to stop the canoe, no matter how much Sangama and Ahuanari rowed backwards with all their strength. Facing such imminent danger, the three of them instinctively grabbed their machetes, and rising up in the front of the canoe, each one slashed away, opening a hole in the mass of vines through which the canoe passed like a well-aimed arrow.

"It would be better for you to look ahead and stop singing," I reproached the poor Matero. "If you had been on guard, we would have had enough time to row to shore."

The river we were navigating was a strip of muddy water that snaked through the forest without revealing its course, since the trees of both sides interlaced their branches overhead as if there were no river between them. Branches and every kind of bush that grows within the stream or on the edges, as well as fallen tree trunks, made the passage difficult and dangerous.

Suddenly the forest became dark. It was the time to camp, but driven by anxiety, we continued on without stopping to eat. The sharp lookout by those in front revealed dangerous places ahead, and when the night enveloped us, we were guided only by the peculiar murmur of the current hitting against the branches and submerged trunks.

"On guard!" was the Matero's cry when the canoe was close to passing underneath logs or clumps of branches. At other times he shouted ironically:

"Hitting against something is our warning!"

And many other times, without giving him time to shout, the jolt of hitting something was truly what warned us. The women were safe, huddled together and covered in the bottom of the canoe.

Suddenly we felt a violent tremor. The canoe had hit something, beaching itself on a log that crossed the river like a bridge. The bow rose up, and the stern started to sink. To lighten it of my weight, I had to throw myself in the water. The current pulled me toward the bow, where Sangama, Ahuanari, and the Matero were making an effort to keep the craft from crossing the log, which would have meant a shipwreck. Beaching itself a little more on the log, it remained secured for the moment. Farther down, the river roared angrily because its course had been blocked. It appeared an obstruction had formed, against which the current was rushing. We had to spend that entire night there.

A strong rain unleashed itself on us. Loud cries and whistles of reptiles pierced the thicket. The sounds of the flight of birds in search of their nests could be heard. Within the jungle there was a rare agitation of excited wildlife. The river continued rising.

It was necessary to secure the canoe to the shore before the waters completely covered the log on which it had been stuck. The work was very painful in those circumstances. Plunging into the water and groping in the dark, we finally tied the canoe with a long vine that we had brought on board; but to do that it was necessary to turn the canoe around completely, placing the bow against the current, something that required an incredible effort in the darkness.

After that exhausting task, I sat down on the mud of the riverbank with my legs submerged up to the thighs in the river. Sangama and the Matero took turns bailing water out of the canoe. The rain increased so much that one could have believed that a river current was pouring over our bodies.

That night seemed interminable. From their hiding place, thousands of luminous insects lit up like sequins in the blanket of darkness, forming a strange nocturnal half-light. The wind, conquered by the waters falling from the sky, had calmed, and the noises of the jungle were choked off. Only the distressing voice of the rain striking the foliage and the bellow of the turbulent current flow were sounding incessantly through this pit of impenetrable blackness.

Many miles away from the civilized centers, enclosed in that infernal darkness, suffering the rigors of the rain that was striking my almost naked body, without eating—but who would think of eating in such circumstances?—I felt isolated, alone, with my soul imprisoned by the jungle. The storm depresses; the darkness isolates. There together, perhaps almost brushing against me, were three men as badly dressed in rags as I, but I didn't see or feel them. It was as if they didn't exist. Three men who represented three different epochs. One, Ahuanari, native of the region, without history and without desires, represented the present, resigned, prevented from looking at the past, from which he didn't come, and incapable of looking to the future, where he had no interest in going. He seemed insensitive to the rigors of Nature and ignorant of everything that was not the jungle. Another, the Matero, projected himself toward the future. He was one of the shapers of the epoch of rubber, the raw material that would revolutionize contemporary industry in noteworthy measure. Our journey signified one more of his many explorations in the jungle. Inspired, satisfied, almost happy, and enduring the winter rigors, he was going to the smiling little house that awaited him, full of affection, on the riverbanks. And the last, Sangama, belonged to the past, from which he came through refined generations and splendid centuries, like a shadow, like a dream lived vaguely, to which he had held tight with all the vitality of his spirit. Since to adapt is to live, and the latter was the only of the three not adapted, he struck me as defeated, condemned to perish at the end.

Also coming like a ship, like a cloud, like a shadow across the centuries, was that woman in the canoe, beautiful with that captivating beauty of her race. There she was, freezing, mute, immobile. She had closed her eyes at the start of the rain, at the moment when I went to cover her with my shabby raincoat. An abyss that I was resisting imagining had opened between us. With that deep remorse caused by irreparable losses when it has been within our power to avoid them, I was remembering the light of her eyes, which shined so lovingly when looking at me, and the soft cooing of her voice.

In the jungle, love is simple, like that of birds that meet one day on a branch and thereafter fly together. Two beings meet without prior plan. That same day they understand each other and the following sunrise awake together, to live thereafter inseparable under the shady forests or on the riverbanks, scorched by the sun.

Within this environment, Chuya's attitude had to be inexplicable and irritating for me. I was far from understanding it! I was stopped short of the use of violence only by the constant vigilance of Sangama, who I knew to be capable of anything to care for her. In my desperation I was thinking of what methods would have been employed by those more expert in the matter: "She resists you? Very well. Stalk her on the edge of the river, where you know that she has to go for water. A well-measured blow on the head to knock her out. Carry her to the foot of the nearest tree, and . . . matter concluded!"

That night she was there, curled up on the platform in the canoe, next to the old woman Ana, where I could have stretched my arm out to caress her. However, I felt her very distanced from me by her impenetrable indifference. In truth, I was unable to understand where that situation was going to take us.

The river continued rising rapidly. Several times I tried to climb that unstable and slippery riverbank because the rising waters were threatening to cover me. An unconquerable sleepiness took possession of me, and I was just about to close my eyes, conquered by sleep, when the Matero's voice woke me with a shout:

"The Devil! . . . I had been asleep, and the current almost carried me away."

To go higher on this muddy land was very dangerous. We had heard nearby the unmistakable screech of the *chicharra-machácuy* and the whistle of the *jergón,* the most poisonous snake of the jungle. On the other hand, within that reigning darkness what could we do up there? A greater safety sheltered us here, with half our body in the river, where we were exercising constant vigilance over the canoe, not only because the two women were inside it but also because our lives depended on having it.

There was no alternative. That fearful night advanced lazily, as if time itself were numbed, walking painfully. When at last the outlines of things around us began to suggest themselves, we hurried to reboard to continue the trip. The log that had stopped us had disappeared under the rising water, and downriver the force of the waters had broken through the obstruction. The morning appeared, shivering as if its clothes were also soaked. We four men seemed completely exhausted, given the slowness with which we moved the oars. The rain had become lighter; it no longer fell like a flood on the jungle. Under the ponchos, the two women remained immobile, huddled up as if all life had abandoned them, converting them into a pair of bundles.

It was a great relief when we succeeded in going ashore in a small cleared spot. We lit a fire and rewarded ourselves with a little boiling broth, prepared with the last reserve of meat that we had. We stayed only as long as was necessary to eat this snack. When we next stopped to give ourselves the deserved rest that our bodies were demanding, the sun had already passed its zenith and the jungle crackled under its fiery rays. We climbed onto the land, where we put up a shelter of palm leaves to accommodate the women, while the men stretched out over the fresh leafy floor, which had dried quickly with the strength of the sun. I was asleep in an instant.

When I woke up, I looked toward the shelter and discovered that it was empty. By the remaining light, I deduced that the sun still remained above the horizon. My thoughts again were taken up with the problem that obsessed me, trying to discover what had turned Chuya against me, changing her to the point of falling to pieces from my simple presence. What guilt did I have in what happened for her to show resentment to the extent of turning her back on me? I imagined that upon arriving back at the Ucayali, she was going to go off with some other man, laughing at me. With my hands clenched in indignation, and seized by a fierce, brutal shaking, I got up to go find her so that I could shout at her:

"Enough with this farce and putting on airs! Go on, light the fire and prepare the bed for two, because from today you are my woman!"

Despite my nervousness, I slipped away softly, so as to not make any noise and wake up those who were still sleeping. I covered a short distance along the shore, until the echo of a choked song that came from below stopped me. With great stealth, I slipped between the tree trunks and the undergrowth, successful at last in discovering them. The old woman, seated on the ground and holding Chuya's head tightly on her lap, was singing a sweet, plaintive melody in a language that was unknown to me. Large tears flowed down her wrinkled cheeks, and her voice rose, broken by the weeping that it contained. Perhaps the old woman was evoking the days long past when the small creature was deposited in her arms shortly after being born, whom she would put to sleep by intoning similar lullabies, in the evenings lived in far distant lands.

A pull made me turn my head suddenly. I found myself facing Sangama, who, without saying a word, almost dragged me to the shelter.

"Miserable bastard! What are you trying to do?" he asked, pale and with an upset voice.

And as he saw my confusion and my sadness, he lowered his forehead and went away, mournful and silent.

We spent that night in the same place. With the canoe conveniently secured, we set about eating some pieces of meat collected from a flock of toucans that seemed to migrate through the lower branches of the trees without taking care of the surrounding dangers, apparently more fearful of something else that was pursuing them.

We went to sleep next to the fire, over which, on green and well-prepared branches, some birds were slowly being cooked that had not yet disappeared as prey to our hunger. My sleep was heavy. I woke up when the Matero's loud shouts startled me:

"Hoo! Get up or the Devil will take us! The entire wilderness is flooded! Hooo . . . !"

The Matero jumped from one place to another, shouting with all his strength, while at the same time wringing out his soaked clothing. He had settled in near the shore of the river to sleep, and the rising waters reached him when they overflowed. Possibly he woke up swimming.

I could not repress a deep raucous laugh upon seeing him in such a messy state of affairs. My laugh exasperated the brave Matero, who turned and said angrily:

"You are laughing because the water hasn't caught you, but you won't escape from what is coming. Listen!"

From the headwaters of the river, a loud sound could be heard, whose intensity was growing by seconds. It was a flood of enormous proportions that was advancing, rolling over everything. By its frightful roar it seemed to be trying to bury the jungle, and it instantly took away my good humor. Hastily I picked up my things, and following the Matero, I headed toward the canoe, to which Sangama was already leading the women. We saw the craft in the semiobscurity of the morning, floating proudly, unconquered, swaying to the pulses of the current. We secured it between two trees to load it better, since we were already standing with our legs in the flood. Then aiming toward the center of the troubled waters, we restarted the trip downriver with extraordinary speed. Now all the avalanches could come upon us. This narrow craft with its sharp bow was capable of resisting the battering and of crossing the entire flooded jungle.

"Get down, Matero!" I yelled.

The Matero was working at spreading his shirt over the bags of equipment, and a low-hanging branch almost sliced his head.

"If I don't die on the trip, it's because I have seven lives, like a cat, or because they still haven't sung for me the *paca-paca*."

The lush jungle had slowed the rushing force of the flood, so that by the time it reached us, it was only a heavy wave that increased the current considerably. However, looking to prevent any mishap, we held on to some branches until the leading edge of the flood passed, threatening to throw us against the thick brush. We then continued the trip, riding on the surface of the higher but less turbulent water.

The jungle was completely flooded. All the land had disappeared under the waters.

Chapter 39

It was the month of March. The torrential rains of the season made the water level rise rapidly; the tributaries of the great river were flowing into it from their sources and causing it to overflow. And the jungle below was flooding, turning into a sea. Nature, luxuriant in itself, was losing its dazzling vitality: the leaves were turning gray, the birds were abandoning their branches, and the lively animals were disappearing completely. A silence ruled absolutely, covering the jungle with sadness and desolation. It is a brief period during which everything languishes. Then, little by little, one notices that the jungle is inhabited by creatures that take refuge in the treetops.

The animals of the jungle for the most part seek asylum on the higher mudbanks, where so many gather together that there are those that claim that it is common to kill a dozen birds with a single stone. Then the jungle dweller often finds, when waking up in the morning, some deer sleeping next to him and, on the roof of the shack, grouped together like domestic chickens, a multitude of partridges that are not frightened to see him. As one might suppose, those guests are welcome for the jungle dweller, who only has to keep an eye out for some hungry puma or to take care that some poisonous snake, which usually makes its presence known when the weight of the sleeping couple disturbs it in the night, doesn't slip furtively under the mats of his bed.

During that period of time, all activity diminishes notably among the civilized settlers along the edges of the great river in the lower jungle. Some improvised concerts give out melancholy melodies, inspired by the desolation of the environment.

Many leagues from the Ucayali, almost prisoners of the jungle, we had to navigate with great caution so that the rough currents did not drag us out of the center of the channel, where we had to stay, since going astray at any bend of the river exposed us to a shipwreck.

That evening the sky started to cloud over again. Gusts of strong wind whipped the foliage, making the entwined branches creak and, at times, break off with loud crashes, not being able to resist the force. Frequently the canoe was covered with dry branches, leaves, and insects. Before it got completely dark, we picked a strong tree for tying up the craft, ready to spend the night there. In this place we endured the lashing of a new storm that shook the jungle until early in the morning, when the fury of the wind calmed, but without any halt to the copious rain. It was the great deluge!

Wrapped in darkness, we prepared to eat what was left of the toucans the Matero had succeeded in catching at the campsite the previous evening. Groping in the darkness, I found my portion and that of the dog arriving attached to the tip of an oar.

Water in the sky! Water on the land! Water everywhere! In that region of the jungle there was not an inch of dry surface. It seemed as if the world had been converted into the water over which we floated and which never ceased to fall over our half-naked bodies. Only the women, curled up in the center of the canoe, were protected under my shabby raincoat and a rubberized blanket that we had managed to save. All of us bailed frequently to keep the water from rising in the bottom of the craft and going above the level of the small platform on which Chuya was riding.

"I hope to God that no viper takes a whim to keep us company!" said the Matero.

"If you think that, shut up," I reproached him, since what the Matero had said was quite possible.

Nobody spoke afterwards. Soaked to the bones, all of us were trembling in the cold. "How much must Sangama be suffering," I thought compassionately, "without a bit of tobacco to smoke!" Only the loud laughs of the *musmuque,* that little nocturnal animal that looks like a cross between a monkey and a mouse, disturbed the monotonous sound of the rain.

I stretched out as best I could and, despite the downpour, fell asleep. When I woke up, it was already becoming light. Everything was still within the canoe. The women remained immobile, as if life had escaped from them, and the men were silhouetted, bunched together in the bow, not having slept all night.

Ahuanari released the ties or, better said, cut the vines that held the craft, and we continued ahead. The current had diminished in force, making the task of gliding over it less laborious. At intervals, through the clear spaces left among the treetops, the lead-colored sky could be made out. The rain persisted without a truce all day.

We were navigating past a sharp bend when we noticed that the shore, against which the current was hitting, was split, revealing a sort of water pathway.

"A *sacarita*! A *sacarita*!" shouted the Matero. "To it, quickly!"

Obeying his shouts, the three men rowed forcefully while I steered the canoe from the stern. Our great efforts were sufficient, and we succeeded in entering that passageway that cut across the flooded forest, which had longer curves and where the current was faster than in the river.

That *sacarita* undoubtedly eliminated a considerable part of the trip for us, which raised our spirits, since our lives depended entirely on the speed with which we could arrive at the edges of the Ucayali.

In the last forty-eight hours our food supplies had been reduced to the few mouthfuls of toucan that we had consumed the night before. It was not possible to hunt anything where we were. In vain the Matero traveled with his rifle ready so as to not miss any prey that happened to come within the range of his vision.

At nightfall the rain diminished noticeably. Before the darkness could envelop us again, we managed to secure the canoe, and arranging ourselves as best we could within its space, we settled down with the intention of sleeping, which a thick swarm of mosquitoes fiercely opposed. Defending ourselves from that voracious attack, we spent a great part of the night awake.

In spite of all, my tiredness was so great that sunrise found me asleep, my maltreated body abandoned to the martyrdom of the sharp little spears that easily passed through the rags of cotton with which I struggled to cover myself. When I awoke, called imperiously by Sangama, I felt languid and weak as never before. How much blood had been extracted from us that night! But that's how the jungle is!

We had to stop again when the sun had already turned the leaves golden. A recently fallen palm tree crossed the *sacarita* from side to side. It was necessary to cut the log to allow free passage, and Ahuanari hurried to cut the trunk in two. But as a single cut was not enough, a second was required in order to extract a piece large enough so that the canoe could pass. The Matero took the ax from Ahuanari's hands to replace him in the work, but at the moment of starting the task, he spotted a beautiful cluster of fruit among the leaves of the palm tree.

It was a *shapaja,* whose stony hard fruits contain veins of sweet nutritious nuts. The Matero pointed it out to Ahuanari, who climbed over the floating log toward the attractive cluster.

Without warning, the Indian gave a startled shout. I saw him turn with the machete raised high, give two consecutive blows between the leaves, and retreat precipitously. From one of his thighs two very thin strings of blood oozed. An instantaneous trembling shook his body, and he fell through the Matero's arms into the interior of the canoe. Sangama hurried to help him, while the Matero found amid the green cover, divided into three still-convulsing pieces, a *loro-machacuy* of extraordinary size that, due to having the same green color as the leaves, was not seen by Ahuanari.

The color of these vipers has caused them to be named after the *loro,* or parrot, and they are considered among the most poisonous of the jungle. It would have been infuriated by the chopping and shaking of the log when it was being cut in two, and when Ahuanari came close without seeing its presence, it struck at him, biting him in the thigh.

Sangama made several incisions with the point of the machete in the affected part and he sucked the wound. He then cauterized it, burning a quantity of gunpowder over it. Even though Ahuanari was only half-conscious, the barbaric cure made him writhe in pain.

The Matero fetched the snake's head, saying it was the best antidote against the bite. He collected some dry twigs and made a fire in which he cooked the brains, which he then placed like a poultice over the wound. Sangama made a grimace and, shrugging his shoulders, said:

"Neither that nor the cauterization will do any good, but we tried everything possible."

The narrowness of the canoe did not permit us to bed down the sick man, which meant that the poor Sangama, who could hardly maintain his own position, had to increase his discomfort by holding the man in his arms.

The task of making a second cut in the palm tree being completed, we continued the interrupted navigation. At each stroke of the oars and each bump of the canoe against the logs that blocked our passage, the Indian moaned in pain.

Finally we exited the *sacarita* back into the river. It was much swifter than when we had left it, showing that we had cut off an extensive portion of the river, in which it would have received the flow of several tributaries. With agreeable smoothness we glided to the center of the current, free of the obstacles of vines, branches, and logs that made the previous navigation difficult.

It was then, with a wide strip of interrupted sky over us, that I noticed the disappearance of the poor little dog Litero. We all lamented the misfortune, without anyone being able to establish the moment or cause of his loss.

Chapter 40

Surely everyone, except the poor Ahuanari, who continued struggling with the suffocation of a very high fever, was experiencing the same deep sensation of relief that I felt upon realizing that we were approaching the end of our painful pilgrimage.

The heroic Chuya, whom I had seen suffer with the resignation of a martyr and from whose lips had escaped not a single word during the hazardous journey, quickly insisted to her father that he let her support the sick man. Holding Ahuanari's head in her lap, accommodated in the best manner possible, the figure of that tender woman produced a respectful admiration, as sad as the Madonna, Lady of Sorrows, leaning over the Indian, whose forehead she wiped with pity.

I finally had a chance to look at my chest and arms and was startled to note that my flesh had become emaciated and that my skin was completely covered with scabs and bruises. The Matero, whom I observed carefully, had an even worse appearance. He had lost his distinctive color of a ripe tomato to display a cadaver-like paleness, darkened by a scraggly beard. And Sangama . . . ? Well, Sangama seemed about to die at any moment. He had expended so much energy that his iron-willed nature finally had to surrender.

The spectacle to be seen on both shores of the river was disastrous. The parched tops of gloomy tree trunks bent over as if under the influence of a deadly lethargy. Branches stripped of leaves, vines and roots torn out, and other floating trash could be seen everywhere one looked. The water had invaded everything as far as the horizon.

Suddenly, the *huancahui,* the feared bird that was a prophet of doom, sang from one of the riverbanks:

"Huancahuí . . . huancahuí . . . huancahuí . . ."

We all turned our heads simultaneously. The song came from a tree with rough bark and a deformed trunk, of extraordinary height, whose highest branches seemed to be lost in the sky. I shuddered involuntarily while I sharpened my eye, trying to find the bird.

"Cursed bird!" screamed the Matero. "It seems to me you're a little late! I can't see you, but I send you another message of death!"

And two shots rang out sharply. The Matero, superstitious and irritated to desperation, would have continued firing if he had not been stopped by a cry from Ahuanari, who leaped to his feet in one jump, roaring and squeezing his head with his clenched hands, in a gesture of containing the explosion. From his eyes, staring and dilated, poured two ribbons of blood. Sangama and Chuya seized him, preventing him from throwing himself in the river.

"You weren't very smart," Sangama criticized the Matero, who did not hide his regrets.

The *huancahui* stayed behind the bend in the river, intoning its fateful song with stupid insistence; and when it could no longer be heard because of the distance, a sort of loud laugh burst out from the thicket. It was the *chicua.*

"Over there is another pest that I would like to see completely burned in hot coals," murmured the Matero.

In a few moments, as if to give life to the impression produced by the prophetic songs that we had just passed, the mournful notes of the *huancahui* sounded again from the high branches of an ancient tree in front of us.

"This is enough to finish off all the patience in the world!" protested the Matero, staring resentfully at the heights. Then, lowering his gaze, he added sadly: "It seems that it is for all of us . . ."

"Perhaps you have become a *chicua* or a *huancahui*?" I replied, somewhere between sarcastic and annoyed.

Driven by the current, the canoe suddenly entered an area of still waters. It was a dammed-up area, an indication that ahead we were going to enter another river that had risen to an even higher level. The proximity of the entrance to it was evident.

Motivated by those signs, we started to row again. We calculated that in two or three bends of the river, we would be in the wide tributary of the Ucayali. But the oars, moving by our diminished energy and without coordination, did no more than enter and leave the water, without giving the craft the thrust necessary to advance with the speed we would have wished. However, the canoe did move with the waters, and the trees on the shores paraded past on the sides, drifting behind. But the ill-fated song of the *huancahui* continued resounding insistently, as if the same bird, following us among the branches, was trying to drive us forward with its fateful monotonous song.

In those moments, Ahuanari's moans were more frequent, although less sharp. When the poor Indian definitively stopped complaining, the *huancahui* fell silent.

What relationship could exist between the death of a human being and the song of that bird? There are things that reason resists admitting, but which happen and then repeat in the same situation, leaving us to ponder them all our lives.

We had to redouble our efforts. Before us, a great clearing opened. It was the entrance to the river! There it was, finally, the swift tributary that would take us to the edges of safety. Before entering its waters, we stopped to attach two logs at one side of the canoe, on which we deposited the body of our lost companion, covered with palm leaves, while the women sobbed silently.

A final push placed us in the center of the wide river. We no longer needed to row, because the strong current was carrying us. It was no longer necessary to keep watch that the canoe did not strike something, since there was no longer any danger.

We left that tragic jungle, which we had entered six months earlier, overflowing with energy and enthusiasm, and from which we returned providentially alive, as mere ghosts of those who had entered. And what was most lamentable was that we had buried our illusions and hopes in the thicket. The outcome was devastating; our bodies and souls were in ruins.

We still needed another day of navigation to arrive at the waters of the Ucayali. The sun began to roast us. Abandoning the oars, we used our hands to throw water over our entire bodies, from which spirals of steam immediately rose. For a period of several days we had not eaten anything. We approached the shore at the suggestion of the Matero, who had discovered some branches loaded with *shimbillos* sweeping the passing water. Soon we were able to taste those small packs of tiny grains, as if we were little birds. But no matter how much we filled our mouths with those seeds, covered with thin pulp, we only succeeded in awakening the hunger that had gone to sleep. The Matero, bored, threw his handful of husks into the water and rowed to the center of the river.

Under the intense burning sun of the afternoon, I began to feel feverish. An overwhelming weakness paralyzed my body. The sun became dark before my eyes, and in a reddish half-light a thousand fleeting lightning bugs shone. Soon I fell into a chaos of sensations and thoughts. It seemed to me that an unreal atmosphere enveloped the world, a dense atmosphere in which my body wandered, floating, rocked by soft ethereal undulations. From above I saw the jungle, the river, and the canoe, all wrapped in a veil of murky air. Immediately an impression of bliss made my body throb, at the same time that the edges of things blurred to make room in my vision for a table full of delicacies and delicious wines. I felt the satisfaction of eating and drinking in abundance! But I wanted to know where I was. How could I have been transferred from the miserable canoe in which I was traveling, covered with rags, between squalid companions? Something told me it was a question of a simple hallucination, the hallucination that I had heard precedes death in many cases. I tried to shake myself from the spell and return to reality, without accomplishing more than seeing myself wrapped in a whirlwind in which indescribable figures and outrageous sounds were mixed. Then all became quiet. My mind reasoned, but without a point of reference. I had the sensation that I was never going to wake up. What did it matter if I died on any particular day, if I had to die eventually! But why that sensation of happiness . . . ?

They say those lost in the desert and dying of hunger and thirst in the burning sands suddenly see themselves transported to the saving oasis, and under the fresh shade of the palm trees, they eat the fruit of the date tree and drink from the clear spring . . . and drink, drink . . . until the life goes out like a used-up lamp.

There are those who affirm that the shipwrecked castaway also experiences an equal sensation of well-being: he arrives suddenly at the hospitable shore, where he fills himself with water and fruits and satiates his eagerness for shade and peace.

Why do they assert that the swan sings upon dying? The song expresses satisfaction. Perhaps the swan feels happy as its life ends? An irreverent legend claims that the mule, that hybrid that results from crossing the donkey and the mare, will give birth on the day of Final Judgment. Does that mean it will have the good fortune to be a mother on the day that all the beings of the Creation perish?

But what is it that I see now . . . ? Ah! It's Chuya, who looks at me, smiling. I feel her woman's breath, which intoxicates me. I see her green pupils facing mine, as deep as the abyss and as luminous as the sky. I feel her warm lips join mine in a passionate unending kiss . . . Keep kissing me, Chuya. Don't take from me your lips, which fill me to overflowing with pleasure. Kiss me more . . . much more! Blessed is death when it arrives so, allowing me to drink of the infinite tenderness of which I have dreamed! But stop—all the blood from my veins is flowing, absorbed by your mouth, and a strange and painful coldness is entering me from the tips of my feet! Your teeth torture me as they sink into my flesh! You have turned into a vampire! I feel the flapping of the wings of the vampire when it closes in on its prey. Leave me, for you are sucking out my life!

Vague diaphanous objects lit up before my eyes, and suddenly I could see light.

When I awoke, if you could call it that, Sangama and the Matero were rubbing my body and waving my arms, making an effort to return life to me.

"He is still alive!" I heard them say. "His heart has started to beat!"

Sitting up, I noticed that we were in a shack, over a high

emponado. It was one of the workstations that the *shiringueros* use in the summer. We were surrounded by an abandoned farm in which, hidden among the brush and almost covered by water, some banana and papaya trees showed their yellowish leaves. Looking farther on, I discovered two *shiringa* trees already being worked. Up to the height that could be reached by that little hatchet with which incisions are made in the bark to extract the latex, the trunks were swollen, deformed, scabbed. Poor trees! They gave me the impression of people suffering scabies attacks from the knees to the feet. Chuya and the old woman, who were next to the fire, trying to make use of the pots, looked up at me, startled.

They prepared a bed for me and covered it with the mosquito netting that was in the best condition. Then the Matero and Sangama set out to investigate the flooded farm. They were not long in returning happily, because they had collected a bunch of ripe bananas and an abundant supply of mature papayas that the waters had not been able to destroy.

A hot *mazamorra* of ripe bananas revived my spirits greatly, so that by nightfall I accepted with gusto the ration of papaya that fell to me when it was divided. The inevitable invasion of the mosquitoes found us with the beds prepared. But no one went to bed. Everyone remained seated around the crackling fire. The timid sobs of the "mama" indicated to me that she was mourning our fallen companion.

Little by little, sleep was coming over me, but the Matero took charge of chasing it away, offering me another pot of the agreeable *mazamorra* of bananas.

"Your resurrection was miraculous," he told me. "You were almost dead when we brought you up here . . . This station has saved us all. Tomorrow we'll be able to continue the trip, sure to arrive alive at the Ucayali."

Chapter 41

Some early morning activity woke me up, and I realized that I was well recovered. I accepted immediately the *mazamorra,* which was more nutritious this morning due to the Matero's discovery of two packets of flour and manioc that were hidden under the leaves of the roof.

I watched as they returned to deposit the dead man on the logs on which he had traveled the day before. They then directed me to occupy some logs that they had added to the other side of the craft, since Sangama insisted in that I should travel lying down and there was no way to do it in the canoe. Thus we again undertook our journey. The canoe advanced, carrying me on one side, sick, and Ahuanari on the other, dead . . . It was good that they made room for me on a thick mattress of leaves, placing a blanket over me, as well as some branches that shaded my face.

That afternoon we entered the Ucayali. When they told me, I felt an overwhelming desire to sit up and look at its expansive shores. I could not believe that this fresh breeze was the same as that I had so yearned to feel across my forehead for so many months. I almost believed I could detect, in the gentle sound of the waves hitting the bow of the craft, musical voices giving us a welcome.

When we arrived at Santa Inés, the people broke into an uproar.

"Madre mía!" exclaimed a woman, astounded when she saw us. "How skinny and ragged they are! It doesn't even look like them!"

Each one of us went in his own direction. I went to the house of Señor Rojas, which was my responsibility, but not before determining the direction taken by Sangama. Some pious people took charge of burying Ahuanari's body.

My room was as I had left it. The conviction that I had escaped forever from the dangers, and that from now on I would enjoy my comforts, gave me the energy to start on the duties of my job immediately. I washed and dressed with happiness, but I suffered a great displeasure on finding out that my feet had grown so much that my boots fit too tightly. Too much time walking barefoot through the jungle! I had to wear a pair of old shoes temporarily, cutting the leather so they wouldn't hurt me too much.

My first concern the following day was to search for Sangama. I found the little house completely sealed, and my calls went unanswered, although smoke coming out of the roof indicated that its occupants were inside. In the days that followed, I made an even greater effort, always receiving the same result. One evening, when I had already started to despair, I found Sangama seated on the top step in front of the door of the house, smoking his enormous cigar philosophically. I stopped at the foot of the stairs and spoke from there:

"Hello, Sangama! It has been days since I saw you. Are you well?"

"We're getting by here," he limited himself to telling me, sucking nervously on his cigar, without inviting me to come up.

The attitude and tone that he used left me cold. There was an interval of silence that increased my embarrassment. I judged the time inopportune to ask him about Chuya, notwithstanding that knowing about her was the main reason for my presence in that place. Without stopping to think, I spoke of the first thing that occurred to me:

"They say the river continues rising and that very soon there will not be any land left anywhere. The riverbank is being eaten away and causing fear. Last night it carried away a structure that was in front of my house."

"What the river has placed, it will take away when it wishes," he answered me like an oracle, and after a long silence spent in puffing on his cigar, he added: "We are on a mudbank formed by sedimentation from the floods, against which the force of the waters will attack someday. Nothing is stable here. All is subject to the whim of the powerful river . . . And it is as inescapable as Destiny!"

I wanted to talk to him about many other things, but my lips remained sealed. The tone with which Sangama had spoken was unwelcoming. He had pronounced the last sentences almost as if he were speaking to himself.

"Until another day, Sangama," I said, bidding farewell.

"Until another day," he responded, getting up to enter the house.

I would have preferred that he had said: "Don't ever come back here." At least I would not have remained in doubt. Had the day arrived in which our destinies would separate? If so, why continue holding on to something that was fading away? Why follow after a woman who seemed sealed in a tomb? I quickened my step, becoming angry. "Well!" I said to myself out loud. "They don't want me to return? Then I won't ever come back!" And while I was walking, I kept repeating: "It's over! It's over!"

On the steps on my house, I came upon the Matero, who waited for me happily.

"We're having a party at the Don Puricho's house," he informed me. "You're invited!"

"Wonderful! Let's go! I have this sudden desire to have some fun!" I shouted, and as I noticed a certain surprise in his expression, I added emphatically: "It's over! It's over! Understand? It's over . . . ! But come in, man. I have a bottle of the good stuff, and it's my treat for us to finish it off together."

"It's about time, man! That's the way I like it!" approved the Matero, stretching out his hand to take the glass, filled to the top, that I was offering him. His face, full of enthusiasm, started to take on the reddish color that characterized it.

When we had finished off the bottle, we headed to the party. In Don Puricho's house, a wild party was now in full swing.

"Men, take a partner!" someone shouted, and the Matero hurried to choose his.

The reed of the *quena* vibrated, intoning one of those sad *marineras* from the mountains, accompanied by several *redoblantes* and a drum, which loudly marked the rhythm of the dance. The Matero, passing the handkerchief under his legs, moved his feet tirelessly, as if he wished to pay himself back in that one night for all that he had not danced during the expedition. The people applauded wildly. One of the most enthusiastic of them sang, accompanied by the *quena:*

My heart is happy.
It says that it wants to dance
the marinera, *the* marinera.
It says that it wants to dance
as if tomorrow
it would leave, disappear, or die.

The music and the song made me sad. I went to sit down in a corner, from which I enviously watched the overflowing happiness that surrounded me. Sadly, I was remembering the happy days that would not return.

"Now the women choose!" cried several voices.

"Don Abel!" someone called to me, touching my shoulder. "Señorita Trini wants you as a partner."

I looked in the center of the room where there was a line of women waiting for the partners they had chosen. A gracious, smiling girl with firm breasts was looking at me suggestively.

"I don't feel well, understand? Do me the favor of asking Señorita Trini to excuse me," I begged the intermediary.

Unable to avoid it, I again sank into my meditations. My thoughts were rebelling against me and, like runaway horses, were going exactly where I didn't want them to go. Welling up from the depths of my imagination was the smiling face of that pretty girl with green eyes and musical throat who made me feel the purest emotions of love.

"Young man, what's the matter?" The speaker was Señorita Trini, the prettiest girl in the village, according to the general opinion. I stood up politely. She continued talking: "How can you spurn someone like that? Perhaps they aren't attending to you properly. I'm going to bring you some *chicha.* Which do you want, white or yellow?"

"Whatever you like, Trini. Coming from your hands . . ."

"Go on, I see that I am not talking to a complete loser!"

She disappeared, to return quickly with an overflowing glass of foamy *chicha,* which I drank eagerly. Before consuming the last swallow, I was thinking that Trini was right, and then I felt better. I realized at that moment that my companion was truly beautiful.

"Shall we dance?" she asked, somewhat indecisive.

"I'd be delighted, Trini. Let's go!"

"A *shimayshi*! A *shimayshi*!" several were requesting.

The *quena* poured out its sharp notes again, and the drum and the *redoblantes* thundered. Like the most natural thing in the world, a tenor voice sang this spicy stanza, while the couples moved their feet crazily:

When I went to Yavarí
you cried a lot.
That same night, with Pablo-Chino
you did it to me.

I am not a common rubber worker.
I already have a boat
and some good land that I have acquired,
but without dishonor.

The Matero approached, offering me a glass of brandy.

"Bring it on! And don't let it be the last," I shouted, emptying it in one swallow. "And also bring on that glass of *chicha*." And I was thinking: "Have you seen any foolishness equal to suffering for a woman? But where did I have my head, when the world is full of pretty women?"

The dance over, I took the arm of my partner, telling her with the heat of the drink:

"Listen, Trini . . . tell me: are you a palm tree, a puma, or a woman? You sway like the palm or the bamboo when the wind brushes them; when you walk, your body has the undulations of a cat; and your breasts arouse like two ripe apples . . ."

The girl had a fresh, happy face, like the morning sunrise, and she laughed without answering, looking at me with scarcely veiled wickedness. I also was laughing, joyfully touching the firm flesh of her arms. I was attacked by a bout of nervous laughter. But immediately my blood was boiling.

"Listen, Trini, who is that guy who is looking at you with such insistence and seems like an angry wild animal about to attack us . . . ? Is he, perhaps, the one . . . the one who is waiting for you out there in the banana grove?"

"Don't talk like that!" she answered, pretending anger. "It is Pascual, Pascual López, my boyfriend. He is already thinking like my husband. He says that only he can go with me go to the sugar fields any more, and when the Missionary comes next year, we're going to get married."

"You mean to say that you're going to live with him first and get married afterward. Now I understand!" I answered, furious. "But you're going to learn right now that you can't continue with Pascual López . . . Matero . . . ! Where the hell has the Matero gone? Luna! Bring another glass, man. I'm dying of thirst. There aren't enough bottles in the house! Don Puricho, take this to the storehouse!"

And I immediately wrote on a piece of paper, reading out loud with ill temper while I was writing: "Deliver to the bearer two large bottles of brandy and two cases of beer."

"There it is . . . ! Now the signature . . . the flourish . . . Ready!"

"Don't move from here, Trini . . . !" I said as I grabbed the girl, who was trying to slip away.

The beer and the bottles of brandy were brought with extraordinary speed, and the filled glasses circulated again.

"That *quena* no longer sounds as it should," a drunken voice commented from the corner. "We need to give the player something to drink, man . . . And let the singer also drink a double, to clear his throat. I really like it when the jugs are passed around freely . . . ! Hip . . . ! Hip . . . !"

The party was on fire! The bass drum and the *redoblantes* were being punished violently. The Matero, spilling over with enthusiasm, did not miss a single dance. During the refrains his legs pounded like two pistons. From time to time he stopped to wipe his forehead, and then he danced with more fire. I took advantage of the noise to speak to Trini, whose arm I continued to hold:

"As I was telling you . . . you aren't going with Pascual López to the fields, because you're going with me this very night."

"Don't joke, man! Doesn't everyone know that you're stuck on the sorcerer's girl? Hahayyy! Don't make me laugh, man . . . !"

"Oh . . . ! That's over with . . . ! Now I'm in love with you."

The Matero was at my back, trying to get my attention, pulling on my shirt.

"Matero, another glass! Why are you pulling on me, man? This rascal is tired of dancing like a demon and is entertaining himself by tugging at my shoulders! Hurry, and bring me another glass!"

"Here it is, and this other for the *señorita*! I like things this way! Finally you're acting the way you always should! To forget, there is nothing better than to fall in love. Listen, I have to talk to you urgently . . . !"

The girl picked up on the allusion of the indiscreet Matero:

"So it is to forget the other that you fall in love with me? How about that! And tell me why you want to forget her?"

"I don't want to forget anyone! This is the first time that I have fallen in love, and it is with you, Trini," I lied shamelessly, feeling indignant toward the Matero. And again turning to the girl, I added: "Look, Trini . . . That guy keeps staring at us with bulging eyes. I won't take any more, you know?"

"Don't be quarrelsome," she answered, holding me back. "Be careful in messing with the Lópezes . . . !"

"It's time for us to leave now," the Matero said, intervening. "You're getting a little out of control." And pulling me to one side, he announced in my ear: "This is becoming ugly, because the Lópezes won't hesitate to attack you! And this is the worst that could happen to us! They are furious. They have noticed . . . !"

"Who said I'm afraid of fighting! Listen, Matero . . . it's over, understand . . . ? Don't you leave here, Trini . . . ! Good! Listen, Matero . . . ! There being so many beautiful women in the world, eh . . . ? That wasn't living . . . ! But it's over . . . ! Get yourself another glass, Matero. You, Trini, you come with me . . . !"

What happened next I almost don't remember. Suddenly I felt blows, kicks, attacks of every kind, along with crude threats. I tried to identify the attackers, but the lights went out. A knife cut hurt me in the shoulder. Then I drew my revolver and started to shoot right and left. I remember vaguely that when I got free, I went outside, following the people who were scattering. The shouting was frightful.

In the street someone shouted a rebuke:

"You ruined the party!"

"Party or no party! That's also finished! Understand?"

In search of more bullets, I headed for my house.

***

Some violent hammering on the door woke me the next day, very early in the morning.

"Open up, man. It's me—Luna!"

It was the Matero's voice. I got up, grumbling, with my head numb. It felt as if a headband was tightening around it, causing terrible pain. My eyes refused to open, as if each eyelid weighed a ton.

"What an idiot this Matero has become! Waking the honest people this early!" and I shouted: "Can't you come back later?"

The blows continued, calling with increasing insistence. I opened the door, displeased, and asked, "What's happening?" alarmed by the expression of unusual nervousness that my visitor had.

"You really did it, bringing the girl with you! The Lópezes are preparing to attack the house . . . ! You'll be a sorcerer if you manage to escape!"

"I brought the girl . . . ? Are you crazy, Matero?"

Luna, pushing me aside, entered the room and, stopping short, pointed to a corner:

"And that . . . ? What is it?"

Right there on some mats, pretending to sleep, was Trini. I broke into a cold sweat. I couldn't speak. I couldn't understand how the girl ended up there, since I hadn't even seen her until that moment. And to this day I still can't imagine how it happened. Seeing my sincerity, Luna conjectured:

"Surely she followed you home in the middle of the ruckus, and you didn't realize it because you were so drunk."

"Trini! Trini!" I said to her, shaking her arms. "Get up and go back to your house. I don't want complications! I'll explain it to your father later! Go on!"

She got up remorsefully, and lifting her head, she asked me disdainfully:

"You are afraid of the Lópezes?"

When I didn't answer her, she lay down again, turning her back to me and murmuring:

"Since here I came, here I stay . . . ! I can't go back now . . . !" And she closed her eyes.

We were stunned.

"The important thing right now is to know what the Lópezes are doing," I suggested thoughtfully.

"I saw the old man, very early, egging on his four sons," assured the Matero. And then, looking at the place where Trini was, he asked me: "Is it true that you didn't stay with her?"

"I really don't know what's happened . . . ! I'm still not out of the fog. Go see how you can return her! After all, nothing has happened!"

The Matero left, telling me that in no event was I to take the risk of going outside. But I couldn't hold myself back, and I went after him. I saw that the people were moving away from me, whispering. In the doorway of a nearby house, I saw two old women who were looking at me with pity.

"Poor little thing!" one of them said. "It's been sworn! They're going to kill him! So young and he has to die!"

"The Lópezes don't forgive!" added the other. "He has messed with them, and they have sworn it . . . ! And all for that high-spirited girl . . . ! I was like that in my time . . . !"

"Listen, you!" I interrupted angrily. "It's still to be seen whether they'll kill me! And before I fall . . . !"

Two shots rang out, and the bullets passed, whistling next to my ears. I flung myself to the ground and shot back randomly. The people disappeared, as if by some magic spell. Having emptied my revolver, I crawled back to my house.

When the Matero returned, he had a marked expression of discouragement on his face.

"I went to see Don Juan José, and he treated me badly when I tried to explain about his daughter. Nobody denied to me that he and his sons are in league with the Lópezes. He says he will take Trini back only after he has tasted your blood. In reality," he added, as if talking to himself, "what they all actually want is to burn the books where their accounts are kept and afterwards steal everything they find here. The Lópezes have promised the villagers that after burning the books, they'll deliver all the supplies in the storehouse to them. And there are supplies here to turn those men into wild beasts!"

"Things are ugly!" I said thoughtfully. "What do you suggest, Luna?"

"The ports are being watched, and to flee by the river would be the worst, because they would finish us off with gunfire even more quickly. The new Governor is drunk in a shack down there, and there is no one to send to notify him, which in any event would be useless. The villagers are stirred up, and you know that they don't have the slightest sympathy for the store. The best, you know, is to make a stand here. There's no other choice!"

Without losing any time, we made the necessary preparations. We improvised parapets with sacks of rice, flour, and sugar, placing them the whole length of the exterior wall in such a way that notches were left that would permit us to shoot without risk. We bolted the rear door, to prevent an attack from that direction. We laid out an abundant supply of bullets and rifles. We would sell our lives dearly.

While I was looking over the preparations, a bout of remorse attacked me.

"Look, Matero," I spoke to him in a convincing tone. "It's not right for you to risk your life for me. You have a wife and three young children. I have nothing. Nobody will miss me."

"And you think that I could stand by while they killed a man in cold blood?" he asked, pretending indifference. "And what a death! Maybe they'll tie you to a *tangarana*! Conshe and my children are in the house of Bartolomé, my father-in-law, and nobody messes with him . . . ! We have to make a stand here. There's nothing else to do!"

At that moment we saw two shadows advancing stealthily. The Matero recognized them and hurried to open the door. They were two young men armed with shotguns.

"Brave boys! These are Pedro and Francisco, the sons of my godfather, Esteban," said the Matero by way of introduction. "Now we are four!"

"They're already on the way!" one of them informed us. "There are lots of them! We saw Don Luna come in here, and we came to help . . . !"

Trini turned around and opened her eyes to identify the new arrivals. On her anxious face appeared a slight smile of approval at the attitude of the young men, who looked at her, intrigued. Then she turned to her original position, as if she gave no importance to all that was happening through her fault.

We had Pedro and Francisco exchange their antique shotguns for brand-new "Winchesters" and showed them where the boxes of bullets were, so that they could supply themselves at will.

Already the voices of the attackers could be heard. When they arrived in a mob, shooting randomly and without order, we welcomed them with a tight volley. We clearly heard the curses and complaints of the injured. Without doubt, our welcome caused a surprise because they had believed me alone. After retreating some distance, they stopped to talk in confusion. Some argued for an immediate assault, and others recommended prudence. Finally they retreated, and the place remained submerged in the most complete silence.

Turning my gaze to celebrate our triumph, I was struck with astonishment. Trini, well sheltered, had a smoking rifle in her hands. We had been five!

During the whole rest of the day, they did not return to bother us. Even with our constant vigilance we could not make out any sound that would tell us what was happening outside the house. By evening, one of the young men commented:

"It seems they don't want to return for another."

The Matero, mistrustful, showed his fears:

"That is bad. God only knows what they are plotting."

That night passed without our being able to sleep. With alert eyes we scrutinized the surrounding area, spying through the cracks in the *ponas*. Several times Trini prepared coffee for us so we could resist sleep, and she appeared disconsolate upon finally realizing that she was the cause of the situation we were going through. We moved in complete darkness, speaking in a low voice. We were sure that it was only a matter of a temporary lull that would be interrupted in any moment.

At midnight we had a discussion, analyzing the situation, and arrived at the conclusion that it was necessary to know the plans and activities of the attackers, whose greed and thirst for vengeance could not have disappeared before the discourtesy with which we received their visit. Pedro, the older of the boys, bravely offered to go out and spy on the Lópezes' house, an offer that we rejected as rash. But the young man's insistence ended up overcoming our doubts. Gathered in the back part of the house, we watched in suspense as Pedro slid off, crawling into the brush and pushing apart the spiny branches to proceed in the direction of the residence of our enemies. At that moment I had the impression that the audacious explorer would not return, and I said to myself, regretful that I let him leave: "Poor boy!"

The moon hid its dull disk behind the thick curtain of drizzle that enveloped the sleeping wilderness. Thousands of toads were singing a chorus in the soaked jungle, and amid that monotonous croaking, from time to time, the scraping sound of the snakes that slithered between the mud and the branches could be discerned. The leaves of the banana grove nearby sounded sharply as they scraped against each other, moved by the wind. In that vague light, the trunks of the trees that we could distinguish had a depressing aspect.

Holding our breath, we kept a vigil, watching the brush through which Pedro had disappeared. We numbly endured the attacks of clouds of mosquitoes. In spite of the chill that the rain produced, my forehead oozed with abundant sweat.

Suddenly, like the realization of something already sensed, a sharp shout was heard in the direction that the boy had taken. It was a strange cry, followed by choked moans of death throes. Some bushes were shaken violently, as if a tragic gust of death were convulsing them. Then all remained sunken in a tomblike silence.

Crazed, I seized my rifle and started to go to the aid of Pedro, who had been sacrificed in my defense. But the Matero quickly held me back, murmuring in my ear:

"Don't go. It's death!"

At that moment the sound of a shot rang out, and a bullet lodged in the *ponas* of the door. Francisco, overcome but still brave, suffered the death of his brother with suppressed weeping. Trini sobbed nervously.

The time passed with exasperating slowness. Suddenly we perceived sounds of an ax, whistles, and strange noises in the heavy brush that encircled the back part of the storehouse.

The Matero dragged me through the darkness toward the end of the house and, with a voice that reflected great worry, told me:

"Those damned men are bewitching the jungle behind us."

"Explain yourself!" I demanded, alarmed.

Chapter 42

As part of his explanation, the Matero told me the tale of the extraordinary history of the López family.

From the Peruvian department of San Martín came a rebel *mestizo* named Apolinario López, attracted by the rubber trade. His wife and three young children followed him. The fourth child was born on the Yurúa River, which is why they call him the *yuruino*.

A daring and intelligent man, in one year of work in the jungle he produced an appreciable profit and earned the high opinion of the supply houses of Iquitos, which opened an unlimited credit line for him. Plunging into the jungles of the Alto Ucayali with sufficient workers and abundant supplies, in successive expeditions he extracted great quantities of raw rubber.

Carrying out daring explorations and defeating the savages, whose attacks he thwarted by dint of astuteness and courage, he advanced until he finally arrived at the edges of the Yurúa River with a considerable quantity of goods. From there he went down that river to the city of Manaos, then one of the most important rubber trading centers of the world. There, as was obligatory, he put on shoes and involved himself totally in the frivolities of the extravagant life of the rich rubber barons. His wife became a matron, socializing with rich adventuresses and helping him waste the treasure taken from the jungle. López learned to drink champagne and play *la pinta* with notable mastery until, fed up with such activities, he returned to his domains in the Yurúa in his own launch, lord and master of the surrounding area, where he established great commercial warehouses.

He remembered that he was Peruvian and that he should occupy the territories he possessed in the name of the Fatherland. To stimulate the patriotism of men, nothing is as effective as to take them to a foreign country for a time and return them afterwards to some frontiers being contested. Apolinario López showed himself to be a fervent patriot. He knew he was in Peruvian lands, according to the treaty of San Ildefonso.

"And if they weren't," he said frequently, "I have discovered and conquered those places, and I have taken possession of them in the name of Peru."

Thus it was that he resisted when the Brazilians tried to persuade him with logic that the situation had changed and that he was in the territory of a brother country. They first urged him and finally ordered him, giving him a fixed time to recognize the sovereignty of that country.

The last time extension given to Don Apolinario expired without producing any new development. Even then the Brazilian authorities, gentlemen by tradition, did not decide to resort to arms against that man whom they esteemed and, moreover, whom they knew to be well armed.

But as everything comes to an end, the Brazilian patience ended, and the grace period having expired, organized forces attacked the rubber dealer's station. Taking it, they found only wreckage, since Don Apolinario, seeing it was impossible to resist, burned his house and warehouses before fleeing with his family into the jungle.

But even if he went far in his flight, he did not wish to leave the river. At a distance many leagues away, he cleared the wilderness in an almost inaccessible place and erected his new residence.

"No one will move me from here!" he said.

Unfortunately for him, that was not so. The pack of adventurers who appropriated the extensive area that had been abandoned by López burned with greed and saw the possibility of exploiting the entire Yurúa River, expelling him definitively. To that end, they organized a large well-armed expedition that was supposed to go up the river and attack the new outpost of Don Apolinario by surprise.

Warned in advance of such machinations and knowing that the back end of the house was vulnerable, he resorted to the vast experience that he had in life, and with the customs and ruses of the savages. With diabolical skill he constructed a series of traps and poisoned the paths through which the attackers had to advance. His plan of defense had such success that the entire attack expedition disappeared in one night, swallowed by the jungle. They claim that the sorcery of Don Apolinario still weighs over that area. Since then, no one has dared to pass through that jungle, and the few who do adventure there never return. This even horrified Don Apolinario himself, who, crossing back through the lands over which he had made his way like a conqueror, returned, defeated and poor, to the edges of the Ucayali. He stayed some time in Iquitos, unsuccessfully soliciting the help of the Peruvian authorities to support his return.

It is not possible to say precisely when, but he appeared with his sons in the village of Santa Inés, where at that time he possessed some *estradas* to whose exploitation he dedicated himself.

He had the reputation of a man strong and unyielding in his decisions, for which he was feared; but as he went about peacefully and did not meddle in things that did not concern him, the people treated him with friendship. It was said that he had participated in certain dark events that occurred in the village, a tale that shook the villagers with horror.

Three adventurers had settled there, who with their bullying made life unbearable to the peaceful neighbors. One of them fell in love with the wife of the elder son of Don Apolinario, and on an occasion when the husband was absent, he broke into the house and abused her.

This offense irritated the elder López, who set out to take vengeance. The people who lived in houses contiguous to that of the adventurers heard the same sounds of axes chopping and the same strange noises that the Matero and I had just heard.

When on the following day, before sunrise, the Lópezes set fire to the house and riddled it with heavy volleys, the adventurers had no way to escape except into the thicket. They fled, plunging into the wilderness behind the house. The last that was heard of them was their dying cries. And there they rotted, without anyone daring to recover the bodies in order to bury them. Even the ravens stayed away!

Without doubt it is due to this reputation of Don Apolinario that the celebrated Portunduaga maintained pleasant relations with him and his sons during that ill-fated period of his governing.

As the Matero assured me upon finishing the story of the Lópezes, they had again bewitched the jungle to take vengeance on me. The tragedy was about to repeat itself.

With tense nerves and the consequent anxiety, we awaited the sunrise. We had the advantage that the roof of the warehouse was of zinc, and the strong walls of the building could not be burned easily. The night yielded slowly to the dawn, which brought us, along with the light, a sensation of relief. Nothing occurred during that day. While we three men mounted guard, patrolling through the warehouse and spying outside, Trini prepared food for us from the abundant and varied supplies that we had available. When the shadows of the night ruled again, we heard once more the hair-raising noises, the whistles, and the indefinable blows. And thus passed another day. The tension was draining our energies. Near sunrise of the fourth day of the siege, I was at the point of going to sleep, lulled by the monotonous striking of the rain on the roof, when I was awakened by a nearby shot and the voices of people coming to the attack.

We all ran to our posts. Trini, who had taken a place at my side, fired without rest. In the darkness, which had not yet dissipated, we could only aim, guided by the flashes of the shots they were firing.

In the noise of the battle, shouts could be heard, demanding: "Firewood! Firewood!"

Almost immediately, we sensed under the *emponado,* at our feet, the sound of firewood being piled up. Soon a thick smoke was asphyxiating us. The Matero and Francisco left their rifles and came close to me, desperate.

"Now the hour is sounding for us," said the Matero, anguished. "We'll die here roasted, but don't flee into the wilderness for any reason."

Trini continued firing angrily.

Suddenly we heard frightened shouts.

"The sorcerer! The sorcerer!"

The scene was suddenly illuminated with the light of a torch, which was thrown into the position occupied by the attackers and which sputtered on contact with the water, without going out.

Trini, Francisco, and the Matero took advantage of the opportunity to aim well and wound several of those who were fleeing at that moment. I went to open the door. On one side of the storehouse, standing among the bushes in front of it, Sangama held a lit torch in his raised right hand, like a ghostly apparition.

Slowly he came up the stairs and, with a tired voice, said to me:

"I couldn't come before . . ."

"Sangama!" I exclaimed emotionally. "It could only be you!"

We lit a candle that cast almost no light, being obscured by the dissipating smoke. By plan, the attackers had used green and wet wood in order to make us flee, suffocated by the smoke and abandoning the merchandise to them undamaged, so that they could loot it.

My three companions were very emotional upon seeing the new arrival, to whom, without doubt, we owed our lives.

Sangama fixed a strange look on Trini. Pulling him to one side, we explained to him the truth of what had happened. When I finished, he shrugged his shoulders, murmuring:

"The important thing is to end all of this without losing any time. Tomorrow they will return and completely burn this storehouse."

Chapter 43

Sangama again took the torch, which spread a flickering light, and arming himself with a rifle and ammunition, he headed to the back part of the house.

"Follow me!" he ordered. "We're going to surprise the Lópezes in their own den! It's the only choice we have! Only the woman stays here."

He resolutely descended the staircase, escorted by the three of us, but the Matero, noticing that he was heading toward the thicket, stopped him violently, grabbing him by the arm.

"This wilderness is bewitched . . . ," the Matero warned him with superstitious terror.

Sangama stopped his advance. He remained silent, as if wishing to explain something that seemed extremely complicated. Finally, he admitted:

"Ah, now I get it! Now we're going to see what the Lópezes have done here."

We all retreated to the storehouse. Once there, Sangama's sharp eyes looked over everything. We watched him in silence without guessing his intentions. Discovering a rake, he picked it up saying:

"Wonderful! This is the best thing that we could possibly find."

At the sign from our guide, we finished equipping ourselves with two shovels and a long pole. We headed back to the forest, carrying the tools in our hands and the rifles slung across our backs. I was surprised to see the resolution and confidence with which the Matero walked at Sangama's side. I quickly realized that alongside that man, he was recovering his courage and serenity.

Before entering the jungle, Sangama proceeded to examine in great detail everything that surrounded us. He seemed especially diligent in distinguishing the diverse and confusing sounds.

"The croaking of the toads can be heard everywhere except here. Don Apolinario López is very ingenious," he commented.

Holding the torch high, he lit the greatest possible area. At that moment the Matero leapt backwards and pointed to a spot barely perceptible in the mud.

"Huy . . . ! It was next to my foot . . . ! There!" he shouted, startled, with fire pouring from his eyes.

Following the direction he pointed to, we were able to discover the end of a very strange small branch that scarcely protruded from the puddle. Sangama, getting as close as he could, used the end of the pole to try to touch the point that so intrigued us. In doing so, the small branch acquired unexpected mobility. It could be seen rising repeated times and attacking the pole, hitting it with such force that it made a sound as if hit by a point of steel.

"It is a *naca-naca,*" he announced. "Now I understand . . ."

He exchanged the pole for the rake, using it to dig into the mud, moving it in several directions. Soon, in addition to the one discovered by the Matero, Sangama pulled out two more of those serpents, so greatly feared for their deadly poison as well as for the treacherousness of their attack. The *naca-nacas* pulled from the mud were captives, tied to pieces of wood.

Always cautious, we risked going into the stirred-up mud and again entered the thicket. Sangama took the lead, brandishing the pole as if he feared hitting something invisible, but always raking the ground. We walked after him, stepping exactly in his footprints. The cane hit something, and instantly, from several directions, some darts were launched that whistled past us and lodged in the neighboring trees. One of them lodged in the pole. Examining it in the light of the torch, the Matero assured us with apprehension that each one of them had sufficient poison to kill a man instantly. He said that it was a terrible and little-known poison that certain tribes prepared.

As we started ahead, Sangama again stopped us by signaling with his hand. He brought the torch near an arched reed that he had noticed. He analyzed it in detail, noting finally that a vine extended from the lower end, invisible at first sight, and crossed the path, half sunken in the mud. Following Sangama's gaze, we looked upward and discovered, suspended over our heads, two enormous logs capable of crushing a dozen men. We backtracked the distance necessary to be safe. Sangama cut a piece of a branch and threw it with such accuracy that it hit the reed, and at that instant the logs fell on the pathway, splashing water and mud everywhere.

With that episode over, we calmed down, and our advance continued. I had the impression of being enclosed in some of the tormenting regions of Hell itself. The jungle seemed horrifying, scarcely lit by the crackling torch. Our clothes were soaked with water, and we were sweating profusely. Passing over the fallen logs, we continued the difficult advance with a slowness imposed by Sangama, who stopped to examine each stalk and branch minutely. Again he urgently signaled us to stop. Looking at him, I observed that his face had lost its color.

"Luckily I didn't touch it with the pole," he commented. "It would have been frightful."

He remained indecisive for several minutes.

"This presents something more complicated than I expected," he murmured. "The only way to avoid it is improvise a defensive wall."

Sunk in the mud up to his knees, he set about digging into it, piling it up on one side, while the rest of us peered ahead carefully without noticing anything unusual. He dropped the tool and, aided by the torch, started to scrutinize uneasily the branches that extended over us. The meticulousness of his examination increased our unease.

"It's what I was afraid of," he said thoughtfully. Then, apparently satisfied with his investigation, he added, "Let's go back!"

The Matero and Francisco looked as if their eyes were going to pop out of their sockets. They looked about, anguished, without having any idea of the exact nature of the danger that was threatening us. In our retreat, we arrived again at the fallen logs, and Sangama renewed his meticulous observation of the tangled overhead dome.

"We're safe here!" he told us triumphantly.

He again took the shovel and set about digging feverishly, depositing the mud in front of us.

"But . . . What's this?" the Matero asked impatiently.

"Help me and you'll find out."

Mixing the branches and small logs that we found at hand with the wet earth that he was extracting, we raised a wall, behind which we could shelter ourselves against the invisible enemy ahead of us.

"We must lie flat in the mud and protect our heads," Sangama told us as he stretched out on the marshy terrain behind the wall, which barely sheltered us even while lying flat. Convinced that we had followed his example, he sat up partially and threw a stick forward with all his strength.

Nothing happened. We raised our heads, expecting something terrible.

"Crouch down!" Sangama ordered again, repeating the prior operation.

The thrown stick sank into the tunnel of hazy light that extended before us.

We remained quiet a few seconds, waiting the feared phenomenon. When the second projectile fell among the shadows of the muddy area, the noise, by one of those strange whims of jungle sounds, seemed like a mocking laugh to us.

"I have calculated badly," lamented Sangama. "But there it is, at a distance over the water," and, very annoyed, he took from me the pole that I was holding at that moment and flung it with such skill that it cut through the air at an angle, falling flat somewhat beyond the point from which we had retreated.

Only the speed with which we flung ourselves into the mud, complying with the orders of our guide, saved our lives. Instantly we heard passing over us the whistling of numerous arrows, with the points of some of them lodging in the very mud wall that protected us. Simultaneously, a cloud of small darts made of palm shoots fell from above us and lodged in the soil, protruding from the surface as far as our eyes could see.

In a panic, Francisco jumped up and started to flee. The Matero grabbed him, perhaps by that instinctive impulse that obliges us, when facing danger, to prevent those who accompany us from fleeing. One of the arrows had taken off the boy's hat and his hair was standing on end with fear. Sangama calmed us, shouting:

"It's over! It's over!"

"There were enough arrows to finish off a battalion," the Matero commented, still clinging tightly to Francisco's legs.

Sangama was already standing up on the mud wall, making signs for us to follow him. Carried away by curiosity, I picked up one of those many darts, and the point easily came off. With the greatest care, I extracted another from the mud and discovered that it was designed so that once the point was inserted, the slightest effort to extract it would make it separate from the shaft.

"What a diabolical instrument," observed Sangama, who had stopped to examine the little arrow that I held. "It is the most vicious device that the cunning of the savage has been able to contrive. The point," he said, indicating it, "breaks off upon penetrating something hard, like a man's skull, leaving itself lodged inside."

We found ourselves again in the spot from which we had retreated. Once there, Sangama again took the rake, with which he succeeded in discovering a thin string that crossed the path. Cutting it with his teeth, he explained:

"This insignificant and invisible string has put in motion that most infernal machinery that the jungle cunning has been able to conceive to finish off its enemies."

"What are you looking for?" I asked, intrigued, seeing that he continued raking in every direction the mud in which we found ourselves.

"You'll see. You'll see . . ."

His persistence finally paid off, as he hit upon some small planks of very hard wood with barbs of palm shoots sticking up.

"Careful!" he warned us. "Don't touch them—they are poisoned."

Our progress was very slow. We were leaving the muddy land behind us, and in a few moments we were walking laboriously through the flooded jungle. Sangama was no longer raking the bottom. He seemed to search for something hidden almost at the level of the water.

"This is what I wanted to find!" he told us, lifting up some shafts with sharpened points, hidden in the murky water and placed at an angle like lances that were defending the path we were following.

Only the rake could have prevented them from being driven into Sangama's stomach. Their points were placed in such a way that if anyone were fleeing from the prior traps, he would have fallen hopelessly into this one, pierced through the stomach.

The task of clearing the path of such an obstacle was arduous and dangerous. When he was sure that all the shafts had been pulled out, Sangama so informed us, with a sigh of relief.

"This part is over. Now we have to complete our mission. Follow me!"

We found ourselves in a place where the tangled, lush brush on the sides of the path was growing scarce. Over the stagnant waters the trunks of the trees stood isolated, emerging from the moving surface that the rain was marking with infinite circles.

We left the path we were following, which in summer led to the small farms of the interior, and made a turn to one side, toward the back part of the house of the Lópezes. Then I understood Sangama's intention. To attack them from this side was advantageous since, defended by the poisonous jungle that we had just crossed, they could not imagine that we would attack from this direction.

We put down our packs, leaving among the low branches the tools that had been so useful for us, especially that providential rake. With the water up to our waists and driving ourselves forward by pulling on the branches, we tried to advance with the greatest speed possible. We were going to confront the Lópezes and the people who were with them, and we would do it with the assurance of defeating them under Sangama's direction.

The Matero, knowledgeable about that area, indicated to us that we were going in exactly the right direction. The land was sloping upward gradually, and in a short time we were treading the muddy path that led to the house of our enemies. Amid the forest we made out the lights and, soon afterwards, the sound of the conversation that the conspirators were holding. We stopped a moment to recover our breath and plan the attack.

"There are so many people we are going to kill!" exclaimed the Matero, burning with rage and caressing his rifle.

My attention was drawn to a long stick that he carried across his back. And responding to my questions, he told me:

"It's one of the dart guns with which those demons wanted to kill us. I have three poisoned arrows that I succeeded in taking from the trunks where they lodged."

"We will try not to kill . . . ," sighed Sangama in response to the Matero's comments.

Crawling on all fours, we were able to approach the house in order to take them by surprise. But before we had gotten close enough, the fierce dogs of the elder López discovered us. Charging from the house, they advanced to meet us, barking. The Matero loaded his dart gun with one the darts and waited until the most daring of the dogs came within range. The animal let out a pained howl upon being hit and retreated toward the house, where he remained in silence. He had surely fallen dead at the feet of the plotters, some of whom ventured to come down to the yard with rifles ready. The torch that Sangama was brandishing like a flag made arches of flames, illuminating the forest.

"The sorcerer! The sorcerer!" we heard alarmed voices cry. Some shots could be heard, and the bullets passed by us at a distance.

With the exception of Sangama, all of us had taken cover.

There was complete confusion in the house of the Lópezes. A large number of the conspirators took flight, possessed by a superstitious terror. Then Sangama, slipping through the brush, advanced along one side of the house until he could throw his torch on the straw roof. Quickly the fire took hold, illuminating the flight toward the river, where the fugitives were hastily getting into their canoes and moving to the center of the current in their great effort to gain distance from us.

"Forward! Forward!" Sangama urged us.

Bursting into the yard with rifles at the ready, we found only Don Apolinario López, surrounded by his four sons. They stood very still, their rifles fallen on the ground, showing complete defeat. The scene represented the great loss of hope endured by that group of defeated men, terrified and incapable of even attempting to defend themselves. The old López moved forward to meet with Sangama and spoke to him in an emotional tone:

"Only you could have defeated me! Only you could have crossed the poisoned jungle without perishing in it!" And raising his right hand to the level of his chest, he continued: "Here I have my heart, where all men have it. Pierce it once and for all!"

"We have not come to kill anyone," answered Sangama, lowering his rifle. "I come to bring to you the common sense that has fled from your befuddled mind, and to remind you of something that you seem to have forgotten: the existence of God!"

Those sentences were said with his arms raised toward the sky and in a very grave tone, giving Sangama the appearance of a prophet.

Don Apolinario inclined his head and remained silent.

Seeing Pascual López stunned, along with his father, I approached him and said to him:

"You still have your Trini, there in the storehouse, man! Neither she nor I are to blame. It was the excess of beer and brandy. Nothing happened."

"Yes, nothing happened," the Matero intervened. "I, the Matero Luna, swear it to you by this cross!" And making a cross with his fingers, he kissed it ceremoniously as a solemn oath.

After that scene, all of us stood in silence. The rain had stopped. Only the crackling of the flames could be heard devouring the house of the Lópezes.

From the morning mist that covered the path toward the other houses, a new figure appeared, running and demanding anxiously:

"My sons! Where are my sons?"

"Here I am, *taita*!" shouted Francisco, going to meet his father.

The new arrival embraced the young man, as if finding him anew after having thought him lost.

"And Pedro? Where's Pedro?" he asked the boy, looking uneasy and fearful.

Francisco lowered his head and broke out in sobs.

"They killed him!" he finally answered.

Don Esteban placed himself between the Lópezes and us, full of agitation and anguish. And looking from one group to the other, he inquired desperately:

"Who killed him? Tell me, who killed him? I have just arrived, after traveling down the river all night with the intention of protecting my sons, because I knew they were attacking the warehouse . . . Who killed Pedro? Who?"

"I did," answered the *yuruino,* with a voice barely perceptible.

The old man, Esteban, shaking with indignation, stood paralyzed. But suddenly, without giving us time to stop him, he seized Sangama's rifle and dropped the *yuruino* with a single shot.

Illuminated by the flames of the gigantic bonfire into which the house had been converted, the expression of the elder López contracted in a strange grimace of contained rage and pain, as if the bullet that had killed his son had also wounded his heart.

The other three young men ground their teeth grimly, squirming with impotence. Pascual tried to lift up his dying brother, but realizing that, with the last moan, life had left him, he lowered him to the ground.

"Let's go, Pascual. Let's take him to the warehouse for a vigil," the Matero proposed. "Let's go—Trini is there waiting for you."

The three brothers and the Matero picked up the dead man and left. Francisco and I stood there, contemplating the portrait that the three old men formed. Only Sangama revealed serenity. Don Esteban and Don Apolinario looked at each other without rancor, since the identical affliction weighed down on each of them.

When the funereal group sank into the night en route to the storehouse, we set out to follow them, but a sudden shot made us turn to look at the place where it originated. We could see the elder López falling, struck down by his own bullet. We all rushed back to the place. To help their father, the young men left the corpse of the *yuruino* nearby. And it was then that the scene occurred that I will never be able to erase from my memory.

Struggling in the tortures of his death throes, Don Apolinario, with an energy unusual for his years and his condition, staggered to the inanimate body of his son and spoke in his ear very quietly, as if he was attempting to say something that only his son would hear:

"My son! My *yuruino* . . . ! I couldn't stay here without you! I'm going with you along the great *trocha,* from which there is no return. Maybe at the end of it we will find the immense *cauchal,* like the one that we had, in a land were frontiers don't exist and where we can live in peace without forgetting God."

Chapter 44

After arranging everything necessary for the wake, we sat near the store counter, commenting on the tragic events just described. In the course of the conversation, I felt a gradual weakness invading me, as if a hypnotic sleep were slowly taking possession of me.

"How pale you are!" Luna said to me.

"You're hurt," noted Trini, who had taken a place at my back. "There in the shoulder!"

I remembered the knife stab received in the uproar that had put an end to the party, as well as the strange twinge that I had experienced in the right shoulder when we heard the sounds of the shots with which the men at the López house had greeted us. It was the same place where I had received the treacherous cut. For that reason I believed it was a consequence of the original superficial wound, and I didn't give it greater importance. At that moment I realized that my clothes were soaked in blood.

Everyone came closer to examine me. Sangama's expression revealed a deep concern, which impressed me, since it was evident that he was giving considerable importance to the wound. He proceeded to tear off my clothes to uncover the affected part, which he examined carefully, and then told me with relief:

"It's good that it is a bullet wound! I was afraid that some arrow or poisoned palm dart might have hit you. You've lost a lot of blood because it hit you in the prior wound."

After tolerating one of the drastic cures that Sangama employed with proverbial efficiency, I had to go to bed because my strength was failing me. And so I spent the night, unable to sleep because of the fever that overcame me. From my bed I heard sounds of the people holding the wake for the dead men in the next room. Laments, sobs, and protests went on without interruption. Some strange sounds worried me exceedingly. I almost ventured to leave the bed and crawl to the door to learn the cause. Instead, I called out in the loudest voice that I could manage. The Matero came in and informed me that they had taken Pedro's body away because it was disfigured by the bites of the dogs, and that had been the cause of many protests. After that, I either slept or passed out, since I was unaware of anything that happened from that time.

When I awoke the next day, I noted that everyone had just returned from the burial and continued commenting on the events. The Matero's wife was seated next to my bed. From her, I learned that Sangama had departed, advising her that she should not leave me and that she should give me a potion he had prepared.

I asked her to open the window, since I wished to see the natural world outside: the river, the sky, the trees . . . and to feel, looking at them, the satisfaction of being alive. The day was clear. A piece of blue sky made me sigh for better days in the future.

Sitting up in bed, I was able to see more of the countryside, where the shades of green are so varied that, despite being so universal, they are quite interesting. If the jungle were not so capricious and changing, if it did not contain in some areas a hotbed of lurking dangers, nowhere else could one live so placidly as under the shelter of its luxuriant and constant flowering. In the yard, next to the banana grove that bordered the river, several exotic rose patches flourished, brought there, no doubt, from some remote garden cultivated by exquisite hands. The multitude of buds opening up filled the ambience with penetrating fragrances. The wind was bringing to my ears the song of the jungle when it is happy, when one finds blended together the caresses of the sun and the sounds of the rustling foliage, the sudden squall, the breeze, and the chirping of the birds.

Thus I found myself that afternoon watching everything that fit within the frame of the window, an open entrance to hope. I refused to continue thinking. I felt true delight. Nature presented itself to me as more beautiful than ever, and the sky was so clear that it seemed to me a profanation to blemish it even with the cloud of a thought.

From time to time, like the evocation of something very far away, of something that surged suddenly from among forgotten things, a clear image passed fleetingly through my inner world, darkening it, like the condor casting its shadow over the crystal of the lakes when it crosses over them, flying under the sun.

Chuya! Chuya! The evocation of her image enveloped my soul in the sensation of beautiful faraway things and of infinite pains, which live paradoxically associated in a single memory. Chuya, a portrait of an innocent childhood. Chuya, a lullaby soft and soothing. Chuya, an evening prayer of enchanting melancholy. Chuya, an early country morning . . . and, Chuya! Sphinx, enigma, question . . . ! How could I tear this memory out my soul, enclose it in an urn, bury it in the catacombs of forgetfulness!

Night had fallen, and everyone had already left me alone. The memory became an obsession for me. Tired of thinking, I was dozing when timid knocks sounded at the door. At first I though it was a dream. But the insistence woke me up, and I realized that in reality someone was calling me.

"Come in!" I said and waited.

The door half opened softly and, before my eyes, bulging from the shock, appeared the image of which I had been dreaming so much. The old woman Ana followed her. The unexpected appearance energized me. Like a runaway stampede, all my thoughts surged out mixed together and confused, without any one thought able to define itself with clarity. I only managed to say to her dryly:

"Come in! Finally you have remembered that I am alive!"

Disturbed, trembling, fighting not to cry, she stood in silence next to my bed.

I wanted to give free reign to my repressed reproaches. To make her see my immense suffering caused by her inexplicable attitude. To demand that she define our situation. But her pained expression held me back.

"Thanks for coming, Chuya," I said in a soft tone, while my eyes searched in vain for hers. She was very pale. The black shawl with which she covered her adorable head increased the pained appearance. As our eyes met, I noticed that she was blushing, as if she were about to explode. She was making an effort to tell me something, but the words died on her pale lips. Finally she managed to regain herself and said:

"They told me you had been hurt you, and I was alarmed. I hurried to come, thinking that you would be in grave condition . . . I have come without my father's permission . . . Now I will return and tell him . . . Well, I have seen you . . ."

And she left without my being able to stop her. Such a meeting, offering the chance to speak with her I had so desired, and my being unable to take advantage of it, left me disheartened. I accused myself of timidity, of discourtesy, of indifference. But . . . she had changed so! She was no longer the same Chuya, smiling, graceful, with two pieces of the jungle for eyes and with the throat of singing larks. What I had just seen was the picture of martyrdom.

What a great sadness took possession of me! I felt downcast. How did I let her leave without a single word of consolation? Perhaps she was full of hopes to hear from my lips the tonic that she needed to continue living, to recover her youthful vigor, to be again the Chuya of before. And, poor me, I had lost the opportunity. Ah, if she had only been able to read my heart and my mind!

Chapter 45

The steamboat arrived in which Señor Rojas was sending a large shipment of merchandise for the store, together with the order to make ready the inventory of raw rubber that the same craft would take to Iquitos on its return trip downriver. I was deep into the task of verifying the accuracy of the inventory when the Matero burst into my office to tell me that Sangama and his daughter had boarded the steamboat. The news left me perplexed. I wanted to go to the port to find out the purpose of the trip and try to talk to Chuya, but almost instinctively I resolved to follow them.

From the time that I had left my sickbed, cured of the wound that had afflicted me, I had made a great effort to meet with Chuya, but I had not been able to accomplish it. Without a doubt she had kept her distance since that night, determined not to see me again nor to let herself be seen by me. In vain I called time and again at the door of that little house where she was cloistered, sealed under lock and key. Silence invariably welcomed me. Sangama avoided meeting with me, at times almost to the point of rudeness. Passing long hours near their house, I saw the dawns and evenings pass in continuous succession.

Having decided to depart immediately, I charged the Matero and Francisco with the care of the store and instructed them on how to handle the next shipment of products for the departure of the riverboat. I then wrote a letter to Señor Rojas, stating that personal matters compelled a brief absence. I prepared my bag and went aboard.

I found Chuya and Sangama leaning on the railing of the deck designated for first-class passengers. They could not hide a certain annoyance on learning that I would be their traveling companion, a circumstance that I pretended was due to chance.

"What! Leaving without saying good-bye?" I hurried to say with feigned surprise.

"I won't say that it displeases me to see you, but the truth is that we wanted to save ourselves the sadness of the farewell," Sangama answered me.

Chuya limited herself to smiling slightly and lowering her gaze.

We then spoke of trivial things that I can't remember precisely, since my mind was completely occupied in searching for a way to be alone with Chuya for even a minute, but apparently Sangama had resolved to prevent it, for he did not leave his daughter alone for even an instant. In his zeal he even went to the extreme of responding hurriedly for her each time that I tried to bring her into the conversation.

Soon we had to separate because they had to arrange their things. It was already nighttime when I again found Sangama, walking on the deck.

"The girl is a little indisposed," he told me as soon as I approached him.

In response to my inquiry, he told me he did not know the destination of their trip, that it depended on the circumstances. He added that, for the time being, they were going to the Huallaga.

"We get off in Tierrablanca," he said, letting a sigh escape, and continued: "It saddens me enormously to leave forever the places where I have lived so many years. But this has to happen. Life has become impossible for me in Santa Inés."

"But where are you taking Chuya?"

"She doesn't want to separate from me. She insists in following my fate and joining my destiny."

"So you intend to sacrifice your daughter, sacrificing me along the way," I said bitterly.

"Do you believe that?" he asked me.

"I cannot judge it any other way. You know that we love each other!"

"It's not enough to love each other."

"You are speaking in a way that I don't understand."

"One day you will understand. Now it would be impossible. Pardon me, I have to go see her."

And he left, disappearing into the first opening on the deck. I did not succeed in seeing him the next day.

The evening of our entry into the lake on whose shores stood Tierrablanca, I spent almost the entire night watching the wide river, which appeared dappled in the light of the moon. At dawn I turned my gaze to the left, attracted by an inexplicable force. Also standing at the rail was Chuya, unrestrained, with her hair ruffled by the breeze and staring at me. Upon being noticed, she turned her gaze away instantly. I wanted to run toward her, but a vacillation held me back. Sangama's words—"She insists in following my fate"—resounded with insistence in my ears and made me hesitate. She quickly left.

The small village of Tierrablanca was located on a piece of land that rose up a little more than the height of a man from the level of the water, a considerable elevation in that past winter, which, like all winters, had flooded the region almost completely.

It was growing dark when we disembarked. And while they isolated themselves in their lodging, I dedicated myself to hiring porters to carry the baggage to the Catalina River, three hours away by foot, so that when Sangama appeared later with the same objective, he found the porters already at the doors of their bedrooms.

Very early the next morning, we departed. During the trip I managed to be useful to them. Only once or twice did I succeed in crossing fleeting glances with Chuya. I could scarcely see even part of her face, since she covered herself in a way that made it almost impossible to discern her expression. In spite of that, I noted that she was extremely pale. She was walking slowly, tired and supporting herself constantly on her father's arm. I was able to follow them, as silent as a shadow. One time they stopped, an opportunity that gave me the hope of talking with them, but Sangama begged me to get them some water from a little waterfall nearby. Drinking a few swallows, they restarted the journey. It seemed to me that a very deep pain was quavering in Sangama's voice, and I almost believed that I saw him wipe away a tear.

Like a desperate irony, the name of the place where we ended that painful day was Providence. There they rented a small canoe to continue up the narrow river. When I asked Sangama to let me go in the stern to the next village, he said to me in a very sad tone:

"Why do you keep following us?"

"I am searching for salt. There isn't any in Santa Inés."

"That statement sounds like a pretext. Well, come on!"

The Catalina was low because, as they informed us, the heat was severe and it was not raining. For that reason the canoe, impelled by poles rather than oars, went upriver rapidly. At sunset the next day, we arrived at the little village of Catalina.

Located on the left bank of a river of the same name, a tributary of the Ucayali, the village of Catalina stood almost in the center of the great flatland that separated the Ucayali and Huallaga Rivers. From there a trail departed that led to the Quillucaca hacienda, the oldest route connecting those two watercourses and used very much in that period, especially by the shippers of salt from the flats of Callana-yacu, who provided this product to those who lived along the Ucayali.

The lack of salt in the village obliged me to continue to the Huallaga, fulfilling my desire to remain the greatest amount of time possible near Chuya. Our caravan took two long days to arrive at the Huallaga, the swift-flowing lord of the expanded basin. When we arrived at the hacienda, I noted that the vegetation, different from that which we had left, continued to be very lush. The refreshing breeze, almost cold, permitted my body to feel the closeness of the mountain range.

As soon as we arrived at the Huallaga, I went to the red shore that the river washes. At my feet ran torrents of reddish water. Toward the south an enormous blue strip protruded upward, with a capriciously jagged edge. It was the Cordillera Oriental, which, as it merges into the Hoya Amazónica, is crossed by the Huallaga River, forming the Pongo de Aguirre. It was the first mountain range that I had ever laid eyes on.

We lodged in the house of the honorable innkeeper. Sangama, planning to depart at sunrise the following day, asked for a craft with space for only three passengers. By making that condition clear, he was telling me that the moment of definitive separation had arrived. I felt the entire weight of the mountain range that was in view fall upon my soul. I no longer had a pretext to follow them. I consequently decided to let them leave. But I resolved to stay awake all that night, if necessary, to see them depart that one last time.

But tiredness and sleep overcame me. Waking up, I was startled to see the bedroom flooded with light. I leaped from the bed and ran to the river's edge. I desperately searched over the waters of the river and was able to discover a canoe in the distance that was moving toward the Pongo. I analyzed the moving silhouette and could distinguish the two women and Sangama in the center of the craft.

The canoe cut through the current, propelled by three rowers. It looked like an arrow shot at water level that appeared and disappeared over the irregular line of the riverbank. As they continued their flight toward that forgetfulness that they would never reach, just as I would never reach it, I watched as the craft's silhouette faded away, until my eyes could no longer make it out. Just when I was about to turn around to begin my return, it seemed to me that the canoe reappeared on the horizon, crossing the river toward the opposite shore. But that was impossible! Such a maneuver had no explicable objective. To cross a swift river meant a loss of time and energy. The truth was that the rushing waters at the center of the river were bringing them back down swiftly. In a short time they were in front of me. I saw them again! Sangama and Chuya raised their hands. He waved his large hat and she a white handkerchief. The old woman Ana covered her face as if she were crying. Sangama's voice resounded loudly:

"Farewell, young friend! Farewell forever! Don't ever forget us, who truly love you!"

I waved my arms excitedly. With that I wanted to show them how much I loved them. I wanted to speak, but the words did not come to my aid.

Sangama and Chuya, embracing, continued making signs of farewell. I believe that I even saw them smile. How close they were, and yet I was forever separated from them! In that moment, the enormous mass of water that was flowing between them and me seemed like the abyss that separated life from death.

They finished crossing the river, and the canoe turned to go upriver swiftly along the opposite side while I, seated on the shore with my head supported in my hands, watched it disappear into the distance.

As if I were awakening from a dream, my bewildered eyes passed over the strange landscape that surrounded me. Everything had a hostile look about it. All of nature seemed obstinate in separating me from the past. But that very contrast provoked a sensation of intense nostalgia, awakening, with all the greatness of nature, the good fortunes and misadventures that formed links of the chain that tied me to the past.

Sangama's last words resounded in my ears, overwhelming me: "Farewell forever! Don't ever forget us, who truly love you!" A fine way to love someone! They condemned me to lose them forever.

And my imagination suddenly produced the image of Chuya, waving the handkerchief in an emotional farewell. How beautiful she seemed in that moment! From the depths of my stunned consciousness a voice suddenly emerged that shouted at me: "Coward!"

I sat up, measuring by sight the height of the riverbank, which plunged down abruptly, in a vertical drop, to sink into the restless waters of the imposing river. At that moment I had the intention of throwing myself into the abyss, but when I already felt the fatal vertigo, the same voice resounded again: "Coward!"

A sudden reaction took control of my mind, and I moved away from the riverbank. Actually, I thought, that would really be the greatest cowardice. I directed my gaze toward the sky and seemed to see in the clarity of its crystalline blue that there was something better for my pains than to plunge myself into the torrential waters that were flowing at my feet.

The immaculate sky, devoid of clouds and birds, and the wide river, full of water but empty of boats, had the anguished loneliness of those roads that lead to abandoned cemeteries, which one cannot look at for long without being attacked by a strong desire to weep.

I returned to the main house of the hacienda. During the short walk, I made a rapid inventory of all that I had experienced in those short hours. And again the accusing word could be heard: "Coward!"

The innkeeper was waiting for me, to ask me what he should do with the small box that his guests had forgotten. Offhandedly, I answered:

"Keep it until they reclaim it."

"Aren't you a friend of theirs?" he asked.

"Yes . . . somewhat," I answered in pain.

"Who are they?" he insisted. "The girl is very beautiful . . . They seem to be distinguished people, given their manner of conducting and expressing themselves."

"Yes, they are," I limited myself to saying to him, withdrawing quickly.

Alone in my room, obsessed with the memory of the happy days that I had spent feeling myself loved by that creature, whom I had allowed to leave without a fight to keep her, I felt indignant with myself. I left in a hurry, since the room was choking me. I wandered, disoriented, through the nearby area, absorbed in my thoughts, a stranger to all that surrounded me. When I realized that I had unconsciously wandered a long distance from the house, I returned to it, finding it already wrapped in the shadows of the night. The evening meal was waiting for me. The innkeeper again referred to the two travelers:

"There's no doubt, I can assure you that they are distinguished people . . ."

"Yes," I confirmed laconically.

"Where are they going? I'm afraid that I won't be able to return the little box to them."

"I don't know."

"But aren't they your friends? You have more chance of seeing them again . . . ," he insisted.

"They are my friends . . . but I don't know where they are headed." And to avoid more questions, I said good night.

I was already in my room when the memory of the little box came to my mind. Surely it was in there that Chuya kept that series of mementos that every young woman collects and that form the history of her youth. There might also be something that would relate to our love. Perhaps that box would contain the key to the enigma that I so much desired to decipher. From that moment, I counted the minutes that remained for the return of the new day.

Before sunrise, I was up. I approached the innkeeper, who was busy preparing for the day's work, and, not without a certain hesitation, I asked him to show me the little box.

Quickly he placed it in my hands, saying to me:

"You'll be able to keep it better than I . . . Take it!"

In possession of the relic box, I went almost all the day without deciding to open it, although to do so, I had only to press a spring. I contemplated it, vacillating, thinking that Chuya would have had it in her hands. The voice shouted again in my consciousness: "Coward!"

And wavering between the fear of someone committing a crime and the eagerness of someone fighting to save himself from a danger, I opened the box and set myself to examining its contents.

A book of verses, the photograph of a very beautiful woman—her mother—ribbons, engravings, locks of hair, a succession of small things without meaning for one who does not know how to read them. And at the bottom was a notebook full of observations. It was a kind of diary, where, with delicate and small handwriting, she had left her impressions. After kissing it effusively, as if I were kissing her in person, I began to read it. Certainly I had the right to fathom the heart of someone I loved so! The contents, which I was reading with growing eagerness, left me bewildered. I had just realized the true greatness of that soul that I had judged with a mean-spirited criterion. What a wretch I was! And I had let her depart . . . ? "Coward! Coward!" This time it was my very own lips that hurled the accusation.

Chapter 46

The revelation contained in Chuya's diary seemed to me a dream. How could I have remained so ignorant of her spiritual purity? How could I have attributed to her qualities so different, to the extent of offending her with the thought? But there was no room for doubt. The open pages were there, containing the suffering of a martyr and her resignation to self-sacrifice.

A terrible remorse was destroying my soul, while I went over the pages of that notebook again. The diary spoke:

"Day . . .

"In the blue transparent sky of my simple life shines the magic splendor of the star of good fortune. I believed myself the happiest, the most fortunate of women for being the possessor of your love. I almost felt jealous of the breeze that was caressing you, of the singing birds that pleased your ears, of the delicate orchids that you stopped to contemplate on the pathways. I wanted to be everything for you: the breeze, the bird, the flower . . . But suddenly the darkness stretched out its mantle of mourning before my eyes. No more will the light of good fortune return to lend its brilliance to my path! I will no longer be able to watch over you, swelling with joy and offering you my pure soul. A frightful monster has made me the toy of his depravity. My little star, where have you gone?

"Day . . .

"Yesterday I saw you seated next to the river. I understood your sadness that has not found consolation, not in the current that flows away before you, nor in the sky to which you lift your eyes, nor in the jungle where you immerse your gaze. You are searching, without doubt, the explanation of the inexplicable. I guessed your thoughts, plunged into the same depths in which my own are lost. How I wish I could have read them and known whether you disdained me or still loved me; whether your understanding reached me in the abyss of my fate! I felt a great desire to fly to your side to mitigate your sadness with my kisses, which will never be for another; to sing to you the songs that pleased you so much, and offer you my lap until you fall asleep on it. I wanted to run, to throw myself at your feet and beg your pardon . . . ! But pardon for what? What fault could I have, my love . . . ? But I lacked the courage and stayed hidden, weeping for my immense misfortune.

"Day . . .

"I feel your gaze sink into my heart like a dagger. Life weighs on me like an enormous burden, and I can't endure it any longer! I look at the restless waters over which we navigate, and it seems to me that the river is saying to me compassionately: 'Come, let me give you the rest that you seek; my breast will welcome you softly and sweetly. Here the martyrdom ends. Come . . . !' But very close by is my father, whose life is in defeat. I can hardly find in him the strong man of the past. He is no longer the refuge where I could seek shelter, secure against all dangers. What would be his fate if I were to abandon him, selfishly, to end my own suffering? Several times I seemed to feel that while I slept, his trembling lips were poised over my forehead to tell me softly: 'Courage!' I should have the courage to follow him until together we arrive defeated in some far corner of the Earth.

"Day . . .

"I was dreaming . . . ! Perhaps I dream too much. I dreamt that I was going to be the inseparable companion of your life, that I would follow you on every path, not asking you where you were taking me nor for how long we would travel. And if your will would have been to leave me somewhere, as those who go in search of the *cauchales* leave their women and return after many long years of absence, I would have been waiting for you, counting the years, the months, the days . . . anxiously watching the bend of the river from which you would return and the entrance of the *trocha* through which you left. There you would have found me bedecked with the flowers of the jungle, certain that you would return, because nested in my heart, as great as love, was faith.

"Day . . .

"I have seen you pass the area around my house many times, as if you were searching for me. I have also seen you look down the river, as if you were thinking of leaving me on it . . . This is horrible: the consolation of seeing you close, followed by the enormous pain of imagining your departure . . . ! Don't go to the beautiful city downriver yet! Let the last illusion embrace me a few hours more!

"Day . . .

"I am consumed with waiting for you, as the earth awaits the kiss of the rain to again become green and adorn itself, as the bud awaits the caresses of the sun and the moon to color itself with many hues and cover itself with fragrances. All my being vibrates in this interminable wait. The evil fairy of the jungle, envious of my happiness, threw her curses at me. Here I am transformed into the bird that does not even have the consolation of flying away in pursuit of the good fortune that it will never find.

"Day . . .

"Do you remember? It was a muggy summer day. The jungle groaned, burning under the sun. The tree at whose feet we were resting, stretched out on the dried leaves, covered us with the canopy of its thick branches, swaying softly from the caressing breezes from the east. You poured faltering words into my ears, full of passion, which shook me and made me throb with anxiety and fear. Your breath of fire burned my soul. With a background of reddish lights, you appeared, gallant, incarnating the prince of childhood tales that the maiden awaits in a girlish dream, as for the lord and master who will knock on the doors of the cloister to take her and carry her happily through the World. When you sat up ablaze, sinking your gaze into my eyes, I saw that your lips were as dry as the dry leaves and that your eyes were burning with a strange fire. The beating of my fainting heart accelerated, and I felt that something indefinable was enveloping me and announcing the great events of life. I would not have had the strength to reject you. It was then that you returned my gaze, telling me with a soft voice that still resounds in my ears: 'Let's go—it's already late.'

"Day . . .

"Life becomes more unbearable when one returns from the artificial paradise that memories weave. Today I woke from a delicious dream, and I feel desolate.

"Day . . .

"Hiding the pain that is tearing my soul, I went to see you because I knew you were sick, and I believed I could bring you some consolation and that when I placed my hands on your forehead, they would be able to alleviate your illness. But I found you almost happy. And you wounded me with your indifference.

"Day . . .

"My eyes have dried. I can no longer cry. I have wept so much since that day when I knew you were lost forever . . . !

"Day . . .

"My good father consented that we could go visit our old dwelling. The day broke, smiling. I believed that I would find you on the trail, trying to recognize the places where we lived such happy hours. But all had changed, and even the paths fought to erase themselves under the invading brush. For as much as I tried, I could not recognize a single one of the branches on which we had left our memories hanging.

"The house that sheltered us so many years, linked so closely to all my past, where my young soul opened like a white rose to the kiss of love, was empty and desolate. Deep silence ruled in the spacious interior, over which a vengeful spirit seemed to float, reproaching our absence. Through the open cracks of the back walls, impudent creeping plants penetrated, advance attacks of the absorbing jungle. My favorite rosebush, crushed by the surrounding wild plants, doubtless sensed my approaching visit since its branch, reaching out to me like the arm of a drowning person, offered me its final, most exquisite flower.

"My father shut himself behind the creaking door in what had been his favorite room. Perhaps he wanted to leave me alone so that I could release my pain, which in vain I wished to repress, or perhaps he wanted to hide so as not to increase my sadness by letting me see his eyes full of tears. One by one I passed through all the places in which our dreams and hopes were born. I arrived at the staircase when the shadows were already driving away the half-light. I felt something strange in my soul. In my hallucination I saw you as on that night when our lips joined and we gave each other the first and only kiss that blessed our love. All my being was moved by that memory. 'Kiss me again!' I asked, believing that you heard me. And I felt myself yours, as if the dream that is all that I live for were coming true. I looked intensely at all the things that surrounded me in order to engrave them in my mind and to be able to reproduce them on the day in which my eyes close, never to open again. And I wanted to die thus, intoxicated by happiness, looking for your image in the uncertain brightness of the fireflies that were fluttering about. 'Kiss me!' I implored again, and fell into a faint . . .

"I regained consciousness in the arms of my father. And with our eyes full of tears, we fled from the house, the symbol of our souls, over which a curse seemed to have fallen.

"Day . . .

"The decision is made. 'Daughter,' my father said to me last night, 'nothing is holding us here anymore in this land that we love so. Emptiness surrounds us. Emptiness of ideas, emptiness of affection. Everything rejects us. We must leave. I failed to hear the voice of life, and in pursuit of a sacred mission I left you without my protecting shadow. And the lightning, let loose from the most abject darkness, cut you down, my tender sprout, as the monster from the past has cut off my life. You have wanted to leave me alone several times. I understand the torments of your soul. You no longer enjoy the things that before you saw with delight: the pool, the dawn, the flowering of the jungle under the moon, the lake hidden among the foliage, the singing birds . . . you no longer enjoy life! One time I asked you to have courage. The hour of decision has arrived. Very well, we will depart together, but we'll depart from another place, from that high peak that I know, so that our souls, freed of all their chains, will float among the clouds close to Heaven. There we will bid farewell to the Earth, looking at its infinite horizons, beseeching the mercy of God . . .'

"Day . . .

"Good-bye, my love! These lines, destined to follow me to the end, will never reach your hands; but someday your soul will read them and you will know then that Chuya renounced her life because love, instead of extending its hand to her, left her sunken in the torment of her cruel fate. Farewell! My last thought will be for you, my delicious dream, the only dream of my existence!

"Day . . .

"Why are you following us? Perhaps you are unaware that you are disturbing the serenity of those who are going to the sacrifice? I don't know how to explain your conduct. Is it that you still love me? But why do I try to deceive myself? One day I went to see you, and you let me leave your house without making the slightest gesture to hold me back. You see me leaving now, and you don't say: 'Stop!'

"Day . . .

"Don't abandon me! I beseech you for the last time, before it's too late! I hope to God that you are hearing the voice of my soul! I'm frightened of this departure to the unknown. I have an immense fear that my soul will remain a vagabond, eternally wandering, as they say the souls of the suicides and the unrepentant wander.

"Day . . .

"If I had not found you in my path, if you had not inflamed every fiber of my heart, if I had not idealized you to delirium, perhaps I would shelter the hope of finding the balm that would cure my great misfortune: blessed forgetfulness. Perhaps life would have supplied to my youth a shelter full of consolation, where an understanding love would have erased the ghost of the past, giving my life a goal and an end.

"Day . . .

"The morning has already become light. From the window where I look out with the hope of seeing you once again, I contemplate a mother who feeds her offspring with the sap of her very life, feeling next to her heart its warm palpitations. She feels the satisfaction of not being alone, the joy of having flowered.

"Beyond, there are people leaving the nocturnal embrace, giving each other the last kiss of the hour. He departs toward the forest, rifle in hand; she stays waiting for him, so that she can pluck the feathers of the birds that he catches on the hunt and happily prepare lunch.

"A girl lights the fire while she sings with a joyful soul. The farmer, full of happiness, sharpens his machete. And the hunter departs along the shore, whistling a jungle tune.

"And those of us who suffer? We look upon this new day with the obsessive torture of knowing that all happiness is forbidden to us. How I envy the existence of those beings, humble but fortunate, because they feel the happiness of living.

"Day . . .

"No feeling for anything! The radiant dawn that blooms through the color-filled sky of clouds and the chatter of the animals; the evening that is dying among ribbons stained as if with blood. Roses of light in the sky: the stars; those resplendent meteors in the blackness of the jungle: the fireflies. A parade of new faces, and the finger of Fate, sternly pointing out the mysterious route by which all go and none return.

"Day . . .

"Now it does not matter to me what is before my eyes. I want to relive the hours of the past. Do you remember your words of ominous prophecy? 'Your eyes, Chuya,' you told me one day, 'while I look into them today, wrapped in your breath, are not the simple green that they seem. They have all the indefinable nuances of the virgin jungle. Gazing into them deeply, one observes the depths of the heart of the jungle. There is my imprisoned image, like a lost hunter.'

"Day . . .

"To suffer enclosed within four walls of reeds . . . ! This is worse than receiving a stab in the heart and being left with the dagger plunged in. I once read that it is easy for a woman to cross the skies of the World, when beauty lends her its wings. Why can I not extend my wings and free myself? What poisoned voice is it that speaks to me of the pleasures that life holds, of the exciting music that invites one to dance, of the intoxicating nectars, of the words of love poured into the ears, of the passionate kisses that anesthetize the will, of bewitching incenses, of the softness of velvet, of the bright gleam of silk . . . ? Forgiveness, Lord! I felt the attraction of the abyss in which sin rules. I lived with the thought of its milieu of madness, between the wild laughs, the brilliantly shining jewels, bluish mists, golden wings . . . I want to live as a martyr—it doesn't matter!—so that at the end I can climb to the sky, white as a cloud touched by the rays of the sun.

"Day . . .

"It is useless to continue clinging to this valley of bitterness. What does it matter that life is extinguishing itself like an exhausted lamp if tomorrow, an instant after darkness falls on my eyes, I will attend the funeral of Sorrow, tasting the headiness of infinite liberty, and if I am going to wake up in a place without horizons, between a mistiness softer than the flower of the *huimba* and with wings of feathers whiter than those of the stork!

"Day . . .

"The sorrow bites when the rain falls, covering all with its lead-colored mantle. The cold drills into the soul and makes it shiver. And you follow us like an accusation. Have pity on me! My God, how heavy is the cross that you have placed on my shoulders!

"Day . . .

"Again the torture of remembering! My childish hands planted a rosebush next to my house, before leaving to attend school. Returning, I found it transformed into a bush in whose thick foliage the roses half-opened in an eternal spring. Their scents penetrated the house, giving it the aromas of Christmas, which make one happy, and others, aromas of the Dead, which make one sad.

"Searching among the branches, one day I discovered a small nest with featherless baby doves, which I dedicated myself to care for lovingly. I did not know that I betrayed one of the strictest laws of the jungle, which prohibits human contact with young birds. The serpents know when this law has been mocked. One evening when I went to search for them, they were no longer there. We cried together for them: the parent birds, fluttering in the branches, and I, repentant, next to the rosebush.

"That scene sticks out in my memory with the clarity of recent events. I feel again the anguish of that afternoon, today when roses of blood cover the foliage of my soul and when my hopes have disappeared, devoured by the serpent of evil.

"Day . . .

"How sadly the afternoon passes after the rain! The sky is opaque, the jungle is silent, the breeze does not move the leaves, and the birds, numb with cold, have folded their wings. The gloomy night is already arriving slowly, very slowly, carrying on its black wings the insatiable monster of the past to torment me, punishing my nerves, my blood, my flesh of martyrdom.

"Day . . .

"Another river, more reddish waters . . . The horizon is limited by a chain of enormous mountains. Looking at the bluish peaks, my father exclaimed: 'There!' And an icy shiver shook me. The hour of the definitive separation is now sounding. My last hope is dying. My love, the only beautiful dream of my life, farewell!"

I was overwhelmed. My hands frantically pressed that notebook, where Chuya's dying soul seemed to throb. I felt the deadly oppression of the irreparable. From the foggy depths of the jungle, now fading into the arms of the twilight, the same accusing voice arose that so many times had said to me: "Coward!" My heartbeat quickened. A wave of shame colored my cheeks purple, burning them like hot coals. The voice was no longer coming from the distance. It was vibrating with growing intensity within my very being, repeating: "Coward! Coward!"

Almost crazy, I went to knock on the door of the innkeeper, despite the late hour. I begged him to supply me immediately with a light craft and skilled crewmen.

"It is urgent that I overtake them with the box!" I concluded, pleading.

"I will help you," he responded in a compassionate tone, after a short silence. "Unfortunately, the only thing that I can do now is to notify the people to be ready early in the morning."

"Coward?" I asked myself, as I paced the yard of the hacienda. "Me, a coward? I will move the world to be with her!"

Chapter 47

My feverish agitation diminished only a little when I found myself in one the swiftest canoes, accompanied by five strong crew members, speeding upriver through the turbulent waters of the Huallaga. However, it seemed to me that the speed was not sufficient, since I would have wished to fly across the distance.

I kept urging the rowers on, repeating tirelessly:

“Row! Row faster! Two lives depend on our efforts . . . !”

The sun was fierce. Under its merciless rays, the rowers were melting, sweat pouring off them. The blue line of the mountain range rose up, growing larger as we advanced. And the oars cut through the water in a rhythmic beat, making the craft glide over the surface, slicing through the blanket of foam that the bow was forming.

The red disk of the fiery sun was cutting across the sky, and toward the last hour of the afternoon, my monotonous pleas followed the rhythm of the oar strokes.

“Row! Row faster!”

“We have already rowed too much!” came the exhausted voices of the crew.

“Don’t stop! I’ll be forever grateful! If we lose heart for one instant, we’ll arrive too late,” I moaned, pleading.

They must have seen something in my expression, because they continued rowing, making supreme efforts. We soon entered into the labyrinth of rocks of the Pongo, defying its dangers. The night grew dark.

“The river is very high. It is impossible to navigate by night through the Pongo!” exclaimed one of the rowers.

"Forward! Forward! If we delay, we'll arrive too late . . . !"

The navigator in the rear showed prodigious acts of skill, dodging the cliffs and whirlpools that came one after another. The constantly shifting bow of the craft stayed clear of dangers, orienting itself by the bends of the current. The waters seemed to boil, crashing against the rocks. The canoe shook as it passed miraculously from one maelstrom to another.

Tirelessly, I continued cheering on the intrepid crew members, who were risking their lives, infected by the anxiety that had possession of me. Exhausted by the nervous tension, I fell half asleep to the lulling of my own voice, which was repeating:

"Row! Row . . . ! Row faster!"

I woke up to a tremor produced by the crashing of the canoe against a rock. We almost capsized. Then I asked for an oar so that one of the men could rest. The others, redoubling their enthusiasm, rowed feverishly. The vague lights of the dawn began to spread across the length of the Pongo.

The lead rower suddenly shouted:

"A woman . . . !"

I looked at the point he indicated, and there, seated on a rock on the opposite shore like an Inca mummy, was the old servant woman. My eyes eagerly searched the area around her. But she was alone. A bad sign! I thought.

"Finally we're there!" I said, possessed by a great anxiety. "Forward, toward her!"

We crossed the river. I was the first to leap from the canoe. The old woman was muttering to herself, waving a purse in which some gold coins were clinking. Her faded eyes were fixed on some indefinable distant place.

"Where are they? Where are they?" I asked insistently.

The "mama" looked at me with a vague expression, as if she were facing someone unknown to her. I drew close and embraced her affectionately, and I again asked her, devoured by anxiety:

"Where is Chuya? Where is Sangama?"

The poor woman continued to talk to herself:

"They have left me because this old woman is of no more use to them . . . They have left me! They wanted me to go in search of my village with this." And she shook the bagful of coins.

Desperate, I shook her. She remained mute. A grimace of pain contracted her cracked face, and thick teardrops rolled down her wrinkled cheeks. Almost enraged, I shook her again:

"Answer me! Where are they? Where have they gone?"

She spoke again, amid sobs:

"In the village no one will know me anymore . . . No one . . . ! Those who waited for me have died long ago . . . long ago . . . They will give me a corner near the fire so that I can live with no one caring for me, so that I can die with no one weeping."

"For the love of God, old woman, tell me where they went!" I shouted in anguish, shaking her strongly.

The "mama" wiped her tears and continued talking: "Yes, they left me alone because they no longer need me . . . Alone . . . ! As if I could live without them . . . ! They went up there . . . They left me . . . !"

And with her trembling right hand, she pointed to a type of goat path that zigzagged up the imposing slope of a mountain.

I did not wait any longer, and after asking the stunned rowers to take care of the old woman until my return, I started the ascent.

The path I was scaling, using in some places both hands and feet to avoid falling, divided frequently but there was no risk of going astray since the tracks of recent footsteps and the damages caused by those who had preceded me were well marked. I passed from one mountain to another, even higher one.

The sun now being at its zenith, I stopped to calculate the path I had already covered. It was so small, compared with what still remained for me to climb, that I renewed the climb, calling to my aid all the strength that I still had. It was a frantic struggle to reach the cloudless blue sky that extended over the high summits. I violently grabbed the bushes, the roots, and the rocks, to propel myself forward. In making such a determined effort I slipped and fell, exhausted, and barely caught myself hanging over an abyss, holding on to branches of a small tree. My chest seemed as if it were going to explode. But I didn't stop. The minutes were precious. I started the ascent again.

Thus I arrived at a promontory on which I observed the ground flattened, as if two bodies had stayed on it a long time. I supposed that they had spent the night in that place. That hope renewed my depleted energies. The night was still at a distance, and as long as the shadows did not arrive, the danger was kept away. I calculated the height: the crest stretched forth endlessly. I turned to look back: the jungle was spread out like a blue-green sea that stretched beyond the horizon.

That mountain was a daring leap of the earth, reaching up toward the infinite. When I looked upward, it seemed like a whirlwind of cataclysmic forms that rose up in a suicidal expanse of blue; below, it could be described as a cascade of piled-up rocks, which went sinking into an abyss of half-darkness and muffled echoes.

I breathed deeply and kept climbing. On the path that wound like a capricious spiral, the tracks appeared more recent. The frozen wind of the heights lashed my burning back, and my face was bathed in sweat. The declining of the sun filled me with fear. It would not be long in setting beyond the summit.

Suddenly the countryside became gray. Was it the fatal hour in which the day dies? At my back, the distant fields were still golden; above me the last sparks of a burning arc tinted the mountain crests with red. No! I said to myself. The sun must still pass a stretch of the sky on the other side.

In the leaden gauze of the hour, the gray path could hardly be detected with that sadness that all things collect at nightfall. The branches of the trees trembled, stirred by the cold gusts. And there, in the dark depths, the ill-omened *chicua* emitted its evil laugh.

I continued climbing. Each step upward required an enormous effort. My arms and legs suddenly became paralyzed, and I stopped all movement, embracing a tree and looking upward with indescribable pain, toward the nearby summit outlined against the sky, which was starting to display its weeping stars. A deadly anguish came over me. All had been useless! Powerless, as if bound by heavy chains, I was thinking desperately, looking at the heights:

when I arrive there today, tomorrow, whatever day . . . it will already be too late! My eyes will find the emptiness, and my soul will find the eternal misfortune of irreparable things.

Suddenly the notes of a *quena* cut through the air. It was the melody of the High Plateau. The song of the Indian suicide! How close to them I found myself! But that short distance represented Eternity! I tried to shout, but my throat, painfully squeezed and dry, could only emit a groan.

The heartrending notes of the *quena* numbed my brain, producing in me the same effect as if I were attending my own funeral to the slow beat of a march. I closed my eyes in despair. In an excess of frenzy, beyond all common sense, I started to climb again. I almost didn't touch the ground. Loose rocks tumbled downward at my passage. I climbed. I climbed, staggered by the gentle breeze of death that was already reaching my senses, without anything being able to stop me. Suddenly I found myself on the flat top of the summit at the exact moment when the *quena* ended its fatal melody. I flung myself at the two silhouettes outlined at the edge of the abyss and grabbed Chuya, as I was shouting:

"The refrain, Sangama! The fugue!"

I rolled on the ground with Chuya's body, passed out in my arms, feeling the trembling beats of her heart on my panting chest. Sangama looked at me with surprise, as if he doubted the reality of what was happening, and then he carried the *quena* to his lips and released into the wind the desired notes.

Chapter 48

Having recovered consciousness, Chuya sat up, looking about like a startled dove. She appeared to be trying to figure out what had happened. Staring at me, as if she were doubting my presence, she asked:

"Is it you . . . ? Tell me it's not a dream, that I'm awake!"

"Thanks to God, you are very much awake, Chuya," I answered emotionally, squeezing her hand in mine with delight. "I also have awoken from a dream. I have been able to see you as you really are, and I have come in search of you, to offer you my life."

"Let me understand your words! Let me understand you! Only an instant ago you found me leaning toward the abyss, reciting my last prayer. I had already lost all hope, and, of course, I was pronouncing your name. It was then that I felt myself swept away . . . I succeeded in recognizing you, and the shadow fell over my eyes . . . Speak to me. I see in your eyes the tenderness I dreamed of. Is this redemption? Don't be silent . . . Speak to me . . . !"

The *quena* continued emitting is artful notes. It was the triumphal march of the condors on high. Chuya, alarmed and hurt, fell to her knees and exclaimed:

"Your hands are bloodied, your forehead sweaty and injured, your clothing torn . . . !"

"Don't get up . . . Be calm . . . I beg you," I pleaded, pulling her to me affectionately. "Come here, next to me."

Sangama, having ended the refrain, looked at us intently.

"You come rest too, father, next to your children," I said to him affectionately. "It is the hour of forgetfulness . . ."

He did not give signs of having heard me. He remained

completely still, contemplating us in silence. Suddenly he gathered a rare energy and with an emotional voice murmured:

"I had the deep sorrow of carrying away to the region of the mysteries my poor daughter, whose youth offered to life the gift offered by good people. How grateful I am for your arrival! I also loved a companion. That love was born in a distant city . . . and there it left me as soon as I, being happy, had started to forget the mandate of my elders. I believed I saw in it the design of Heaven that was pointing out to me the path that I should follow across the jungle to the mystery . . . And with you, my daughter, carrying you in my arms, I took the path, determined to complete my destiny . . ."

I had never heard Sangama speak with such deep emotion. He did so with a tender voice, emotional, soft as if he were carefully carrying a sleeping child whom he feared awakening in his passage under the imposing foliage of the jungle.

"Until today I was the guide . . . ! A bad leader, I have been defeated by the jungle, as all who live for their dreams are conquered. I lived in the past and for the past . . . and the marvelous jungle, which fed my obsession, had as its destiny to sacrifice me . . . ! I love the jungle because I learned to understand and interpret it as no one else. It is the book of Nature open before my eager eyes. An immense book written by the very hand of God. In it I discovered the secrets that gave me passion. I held in awe its incomparable power and trembled, knowing it invincible.

"Who said the jungle has no history?" he asked, looking into the immenseness of the sky. America was still wrapped in darkness, and the confused tribes wandered through the fields of old Europe, when the awesome struggle of the jungle with civilization had already started on the Asian continent. In those times the peoples who inhabited the jungle, after erecting their marvelous monuments and marking their history in imperishable stone, gave themselves over confidently to indolence and immorality. Symptoms of old age and decadence! It was then that the jungle started its transcendental, never-ending work. It expanded over the vital arteries: the roads. The roots advanced, lifting the paving stones, and the dry leaves started to cover them; the creeping plants grew on the surfaces, where long caravans had passed for many centuries, and above them the branches and stalks wove together, sprouting forth again and again to consummate their destructive work. Spiny creeping vines caught their hooks in the cracks of the stone walls. The snakes nested in the caves and wrapped around the altars. The insects invaded everywhere. And the streets of the ancient cities remained silent and deserted. The wild beasts grazed freely, mating among the foliage under the star-filled awning of the nights and afterward, with progressive audacity, entered the few houses that were still inhabited and sunk their claws and fangs into the palpitating flesh of the men who remained there, sunk in the lethargy of their memories, chained to ancestral superstitions . . ."

I listened to him, captivated, as if he were a mystic whose voice was trying to rouse the World. In my arms, Chuya remained asleep in a consuming lethargy, like a captive turtledove. Sangama continued:

"And the men perished. The jungle strangled the civilizations to which they belonged. The cities and villages were buried under its relentless blanket. And they say it has no history . . . ! The jungle gave life to two human beings, who, conquering the adverse conditions of that remote period, managed to survive. It was the miracle of the Ages that those beings, bereft of sharp fangs and sharpened claws, covered with soft skin unsuitable for resisting harsh blows, not only could defend themselves from their powerful enemies but could even attack and defeat them. And when the time was right and the life of man could extend itself beyond the jungle's borders, the two brothers parted ways. One remained among the forests. The other advanced over the meadows, plowed and cultivated the fields, domesticated animals, and founded the cities, thus originating the awesome civilization . . . of which we are a part. The misfortune was that with the passage of time the latter no longer recognized his brother and became a fratricide, fighting to subjugate him and conquer the jungle . . ."

Sangama ceased talking. Standing upright next to the trees, which were shaking from the beating of all the winds, he seemed the very image of a biblical prophet. Raising his hands to his forehead as if trying to concentrate again upon the historic events, he proceeded once more:

"I see great conflagrations that will occur in all the dominions of the civilized brother! Social upheavals will convulse the times! Civilization will be concentrated in the great cities, and the roads will again be erased from the surface of the Earth. The machine, perfected to an extent inconceivable, will replace human energy and will give origin to the All-Powerful Monster. One day the war of the supermen will start! The collapse of civilization . . . ! The jungle dweller will listen, aghast, to the horrible sound of the struggle and the devastation on the surface of the earth, in the ocean depths, and in the ethereal heights. And when the deep silence finally covers the fields of destruction, a bewildering sound will come forth, followed by defiant shouts arising from the jungle that will penetrate the gloomy city. The jungle dweller will appear in the historic scene in the fullness of his vigor."

"That upsets me papa," said Chuya softly. "It seems as if you are placing an anathema on civilization."

"Thus the two brothers will find themselves together again after the passage of centuries," continued Sangama. "There will be a struggle, but a brief one. The jungle brother, transformed according to the evolution of his environment, vibrant with pain and pleasure, open to suffering and laughter, will flex his powerful muscles, and the superman will fall defeated at his conquering feet. The balance will come afterwards. The fusion of the dehumanized man with the man of the jungle, leaving behind all that the former has lost—his enormous effectiveness—will produce a new civilization based on Religion and Morality, solid foundations of the Universal Empire, under the aegis of God . . ."

He stopped and directed his gaze toward the jungle. With an emotional and hesitating tone, he continued:

"I loved the jungle, I repeat it! For long years it welcomed me in its bosom. My youth and all the rest of my life passed in a perennial curiosity to penetrate its indecipherable secrets. And I was happy because I lived conforming myself to its laws. Thus I would have been able to end my days in it, without more worries than studying it and contributing to science the heritage of unsuspected knowledge. But . . . I had my soul saturated with the Past. My blood, the marrow of my bones, all my being was nourished by that great dream that consumed my ancestors and was the only reason for which they lived and perished! Such a man should have been buried centuries ago! It was already too late when I woke up! I am defeated, incapable of undertaking a new life . . . !"

The changing silhouette was outlined against the star-filled sky. Our breathing had stopped. Sangama proceeded, lowering his voice:

"The warrior who lost the imperial favor was ejected from the bosom of the Court, from which he vanished in order to enter the land of the Antis. No one knew how his life ended. Well then, he came here. He climbed this mountain, and looking at the World at his feet and after saying farewell with the fatal melody, he threw himself into the abyss . . ."

And with those last words Sangama disappeared, swallowed by the darkness. We felt a violent shudder. The abyss, which opened like an enormous yawn, now held in its depths the body of the dreaming martyr.

"My father! What have you done?" shouted Chuya with a heartrending cry, struggling to sit up. "My father, you have abandoned me . . . !"

***

When the sun of the next day evicted the cold from the peak and sealed it into our souls, Chuya wanted to look into the abyss. I couldn't stop her, so I accompanied her, never letting go of her. For a long time she peered over the precipice, her eyes filled with sadness. The light of the day filled the unfathomable chasm with a living mist, as if the blood of Sangama had mixed into it and was ascending from the depths, converted into a reddish sunrise.

Then, holding each other tightly, forming a group sculpted by Sorrow in the days of its most mournful inspiration, we started to descend slowly from the high kingdom of the clouds toward the fertile and marvelous lap of Mother Earth: the Jungle.

Glossary

achiote A cultivated tree whose fruit is used as a coloring in food and as a face paint. Also has medicinal value.

achuni Coati. An animal related to the raccoon and about the size of a housecat.

afaninga A large nonpoisonous snake similar to the boa. It has the trait of striking with its tail when approached.

alto High, upper. Alto Ucayali is the Upper Ucayali.

Amaru Tupac Amaru. The last of the Inca rulers. *See* Vilcabamba.

amauta A class of wise men who kept alive the traditions of the Incas by teaching the culture, history, and customs to the young men.

antara A native musical instrument of the Andes region in the form of a panpipe. See *quena*.

Antis Indians native to the Amazon jungle, as opposed to the Andes region.

Atahualpa The Inca ruler who was captured and killed by Pizarro.

ayahuasca Also *ayac-huasca*. "Vine of the soul." A jungle plant whose consumption causes visions or hallucinations.

bajo Low, lower. Bajo Ucayali is the Lower Ucayali.

Bravos Indians hostile to outsiders.

bufeo Freshwater dolphin. According to local superstition, it has supernatural powers, including the ability to transform itself into a man and seduce or kidnap women.

cacique A local leader or chief.

camunguy A large bird similar to a turkey and native to the Amazon area. It lives near ponds and swamps and is edible. Its call resembles its name.

catahua A tree with greenish bark covered with small spines. Its resin is caustic and poisonous and is used in making the curare that some Amazon tribes use to poison darts and arrows. Contact of the resin with the eyes can cause blindness.

cauchal A group of rubber trees. From the Spanish *caucho:* rubber.

cauchero A worker or harvester of rubber.

cético A tree whose wood is soft and light. It is very common along rivers in the lower jungle. Its bark can be used as a lubricant.

Chamas An Indian tribe of the Amazon.

chambira A palm tree whose fruit is an edible nut similar to a small coconut. A strong fiber of the same name is extracted from the core of the tree and is used to make hammocks, bags, and rope.

champi A cutting tool that is used like a machete.

chicha A type of beer made from corn and native to South America.

chicharra-machácuy A nocturnal moth that is blind and has a head with the appearance of a snake's. It has a sting that is painful but not poisonous.

chicua A bird whose laughlike call is considered to be an ill omen and is often thought to predict rain.

chilcano A fish soup.

chonta A very hard wood from the *pona* palm. Also the edible core of some palm trees that is considered a great delicacy.

chuchuhuasha Also *chuchuhuahsi*. A tree whose bark is considered a medicine and a stimulant. Its juice forms a popular drink when mixed with brandy. The juice is considered a cure for rheumatism and colds and an aphrodisiac when mixed with honey.

chulla-chaqui A jungle demon with unequal feet of different size. According to legend it can convert itself into the form a person in order to deceive that person's friends or relatives and get them lost in the jungle.

collpa A muddy area where the *huangana* herd rests and sleeps.

cordillera A mountain range.

correría An expedition (for hunting slaves).

cotomono Also *coto mono*. Red howler monkey. Largest of the apes of the Ucayali region.

cuadras A losing roll in a dice game.

cupiso A large river turtle smaller than the *taricaya.*

curandero A native healer.

cushma A type of garment woven from cotton and worn by the local tribes.

emponado A platform built with boards from a local palm tree called *pona.*

estrada A group of about one hundred rubber trees *(shiringas).*

gamitana Tambaqui. A fish of moderate size with large scales that is native to the Amazon area. It is highly prized for its meat.

hoya A wide valley or river basin.

huacapú A tree known for its hard wood, which is resistant to weather. The wood is highly prized.

huaico A flood of water, mud, and rocks brought on by torrential rains that cause the rivers to overflow.

huancahui A bird whose call is thought to be an ill omen. Its call resembles its name.

huangana A type of javelina or peccary noted for its herding instincts.

Huillac Umu The Inca high priest.

huimba A very large tree whose buds form a vegetable silk of very fine fiber, which it releases to float in the air.

Huiracocha Also **Viracocha**. The Inca sun god and chief of the Inca gods.

Huitotos A tribe of the Amazon.

inciral A local tree whose resin is used to remove the roots of teeth.

Iquitos The principal Peruvian city in the Amazon.

javelina Also peccary. An animal that looks like a small wild pig and is native to North and South America.

jergón Common lance-head viper. A snake known for its deadly poison. Commonly found in ponds and other water.

Jibaros A tribe of the Amazon noted for the process of shrinking the heads of enemies, which are then kept as trophies.

la pinta A game of chance and gambling.

lisa A fish native to the Amazon area.

loro parrot.

loro-machacuy Green tree viper. A poisonous snake that gets its name from its green color, similar to that of a parrot *(loro).*

lupuna White floss silk tree. One of the largest trees of the jungle, with a top in the shape of a mushroom.

manchari Illness caused by fear, fright, or panic.

manzanillo Manchineel. A poisonous tree with a milky juice that causes blisters. It has an apple-shaped fruit.

marinera A dance native to Peru. Originally favored by sailors *(marineros).*

masato A type of beer made from corn, yucca or rice and native to South America.

matero An expert in jungle exploration and the opening of *estradas.*

mazamorra A dish made with ground corn, sweetener, and sometimes fruits.

mestizo A person of mixed Indian and European ancestry.

mijanada A migration of fish during the spawning season in such large numbers that they fill the river from bank to bank.

mocahua A terra-cotta container that has a wide mouth and is used to store and pour *chicha.*

musmuque Also *musmuqui.* Night monkey or owl monkey. A very small monkey with nocturnal habits that looks like a cross between a monkey and a mouse.

naca-naca Coral snake. A small poisonous snake.

ojé Fig tree. A tree with a medicinal resin effective in curing anemia and intestinal parasites.

paca-paca Also *pacapaca.* A bad result or bad ending.

patacón An old coin no longer in circulation at the time of the story.

piquicho One who limps because of foot problems. Also, a useless person.

pisonay Large tree that grows up to seventy-five feet in height and thrives in the Andes region from sea level up to 10,000 feet in altitude.

pona An Amazon palm tree. Also, boards from the same tree.

pongo A ravine.

puca-curo Also *pucacuro*. A small reddish ant that upon contact with the skin gives off an acid that causes sharp pain. Contact with the eyes can cause blindness, a frequent problem with hunting dogs.

Puricho A nickname or short form for the given name Purificación.

pusanga A love potion.

quena A native reed flute of the Andes region. See *antara.*

quipu Also *khipu*. A device used by the Incas and other Andean Indians for keeping records by means of tying knots along a string or ribbon.

quipucamayo Also *khipucamayuq*. A person skilled in the use of *quipus*.

rabia Rage; anger.

redoblante A double-headed drum.

renacal A group or grove of *renacos*.

renaco Strangler fig. A type of tree that grows in the Amazon in low and wet places. It grows in compact groups and strangles any other tree within reach of its branches. It is used in medicine to cure wounds.

sacarita Also *zacarita*. A narrow channel that connects rivers and lakes or cuts through the base of a peninsula formed by an oxbow in a river, thus forming a shortcut.

sachamaman Also *sacha mama*. The mother of the jungle. A legendary serpent that is the subject of many jungle stories and myths.

sachavaca Also *sacha vaca.* Tapir. The name means "wild cow" or "jungle cow."

shapaja A type of palm tree common to lowland tropical forests in Peru.

shihuahuaco A tree that is found in the upper Amazon of Peru and is noted for its size and strength and the hardness of its wood.

shimayshi A dance.

shimbillo A tree that is similar to the guava tree but grows wild. Its fruits have a small casing and are called by the same name.

shiringa A tree that is the source of the natural rubber.

shiringal A group of *shiringas*.

shiringuero The owner of one or more *shiringales*.

shirue Also *shirui*. A small fish native to the Amazon area and living in ponds and swamps. It has very little flesh and is eaten only in soups.

shitari A very small, long fish native to the Amazon area and living in ponds and swamps. It has very little flesh and is eaten only in soups.

shuyo A fish without scales that is native to the Amazon area and lives in ponds and swamps. It is known for ability to migrate over land during dry the dry season.

supay The Devil or an evil spirit.

Tahuantinsuyo The Inca Empire. The four *Suyos* or regions.

taita Father.

tampu Also *tambo.* A structure for shelter and food storage built by the Incas along the frontier and along roads.

tangarana A tree with a hollow trunk and soft wood. Also, the name of dangerous ants that live inside the tree's trunk.

tangrilla A small bird native to the Amazon area and known for its beautiful plumage.

taricaya A large river turtle bigger than the *cupiso*.

topa Balsa tree or wood.

trocha A path cut by men through the jungle.

tuqui-tuqui Also *tuquituqui*. A small bird native to the Amazon area and known for its pretty colors. It lives in swamps and flooded areas.

unchala A small bird native to the Amazon area and known for its pretty colors and its loud, sharp call.

ushate A short, curved knife, sharpened on the interior edge of the curve.

Vilcabamba The last stronghold of the Incas, held by the ruler Tupac Amaru until his final defeat.

virote A small dart used in a dart gun.

yacaruna A demon that lives in cities under the water. It looks like a human except that its head is facing backwards. It is said to kidnap young women to live with it in the river depths.

yacumama A large legendary snake said to be the mother or creator of the waters.

yungururo A bird native to the Amazon area, similar in appearance to a partridge, and often called a partridge.

CPSIA information can be obtained
at www.ICGtesting.com
Printed in the USA
LVOW08s1752161216
517618LV00002B/143/P

9 780978 691400